WUTHERING HEIGHTS

IN MODERN ENGLISH

THE READABLE CLASSICS
BOOK 1

EMILY BRONTË

Translated by
AVERY FROST

Original work: *Wuthering Heights* by Emily Brontë (1847)

eBook ISBN: 978-1-944912-49-9
Print ISBN: 978-1-944912-53-6

First Edition

For Heathcliff and Catherine—
still toxic after all these years.

CONTENT WARNING

First, everyone in *Wuthering Heights* is an asshole.

Second, this book doesn't pull punches.

This story includes domestic violence, child abuse, animal cruelty, death (including of children), racist language and attitudes, suicide ideation, psychological abuse, and manipulation. Brontë wrote unflinchingly about a brutal world, about toxic obsession, cruelty, and the cycle of violence. This story reflects the harsh realities of its time and setting, and this translation preserves that darkness.

TRANSLATOR'S NOTE

This may be surprising, but I love *Wuthering Heights*. I've read it multiple times. And every single time, even knowing what's coming, I've had to push through pages where the prose felt like wading through mud.

That shouldn't be the case. This is one of the greatest novels ever written. A dark, twisted, unforgettable story about obsession, revenge, and the kind of love that destroys everything it touches. But for too many readers, the 1847 language creates a barrier between them and the experience Emily Brontë intended.

I decided to do something about it.

This edition exists because I believe stories, especially great ones, deserve to be enjoyed, not endured. And I approached this project not as a simplification, but as a translation.

What I Changed (And Why)

I used a principle called dynamic equivalence: preserving the meaning, emotional impact, and authorial intent while updating the delivery system. If Brontë were writing today, she wouldn't use Victorian syntax and vocabulary. She'd use the clearest, most powerful language available to tell her story.

So I updated:

- Archaic vocabulary that creates unnecessary barriers ("ere," "hither," "thither")
- Tangled Victorian syntax that buries the meaning in clauses
- Lengthy descriptive passages that lose modern readers (streamlined for clarity while preserving atmosphere)
- Yorkshire dialect (modernized so it reads naturally without a glossary)

What I Didn't Change (And Why)

Everything else. Seriously.

- Every scene. Not one cut.
- Every character. Exactly as Brontë wrote them.
- The plot. Unchanged.
- The setting. Still the Yorkshire moors in the early 1800s.
- The themes. Obsession, class, revenge, the cycle of violence are left all intact.
- The darkness. Brontë didn't pull punches, and neither do I.
- The emotional weight. If a passage is devastating in the original, it's devastating here.

This isn't a sanitized version. This isn't a study guide. This is *Wuthering Heights,* the full story, the way Brontë meant it to hit you.

On Author Intent and "Accessibility"

Here's the thing some people won't like hearing: Emily Brontë didn't write this book to be difficult. She wrote it to be read. By regular people. In 1847, this novel was published for a general audience, not for scholars, not for academics, but for anyone who could get their hands on it.

The language has become difficult because language changes. What was clear in 1847 requires effort today. My job as a translator was to restore that clarity without losing what makes the story powerful.

Some people will hate this edition. That's okay. This edition isn't for purists who believe difficulty equals literary value. It's for readers who want to experience one of the greatest novels ever written without needing a dictionary, a glossary, or three degrees in Victorian literature.

It's for you.

How to Read This Edition

However you want. Curl up with it like you would any other book. Race through the dramatic parts. Sit with the devastating moments. Get angry at the characters (you will). Feel the wind on those moors.

You can legitimately say you've read *Wuthering Heights*, because you will have. This is the full story, exactly as Brontë structured it, with all its gothic intensity and psychological complexity intact.

The only thing that's different is that you won't need to fight the language to get to the experience.

Welcome to the moors.

Avery Frost

1

1801 — I'VE JUST COME BACK FROM VISITING MY LANDLORD— the only neighbor I'll have to deal with out here.

This place is stunning, honestly. I doubt there's anywhere in England more perfectly cut off from civilization. It's a hermit's paradise, and Mr. Heathcliff and I make the perfect pair to share all this isolation. What a character! He had no idea how much I liked him immediately when I saw those black eyes pull back suspiciously under his brows as I rode up—or when his hands dug deeper into his waistcoat pockets as I announced myself.

"Mr. Heathcliff?" I said.

He nodded.

"Mr. Lockwood, your new tenant. I wanted to stop by as soon as I arrived, to make sure I haven't caused you any trouble by renting Thrushcross Grange. I heard yesterday you'd had second thoughts—"

"Thrushcross Grange is mine," he cut me off, flinching. "I wouldn't let anyone inconvenience me if I could help it— come in!"

He said "come in" through clenched teeth, like he was

really saying "go to hell." Everything about the place felt just as unwelcoming—even the gate seemed to resist my entering. That's probably why I was so determined to go in. I was fascinated by someone who seemed even more antisocial than me.

When my horse pushed against the gate, Heathcliff finally reached out to unlatch it, then led me up the path without a word. As we entered the courtyard, he called out: "Joseph, take Mr. Lockwood's horse and bring up some wine."

So this is the entire staff, I thought at his oddly bundled command. *No wonder grass grows between the stones and the cattle do all the hedge trimming.*

Joseph was elderly—ancient, really, though still tough and wiry. "Lord help us!" he muttered under his breath, sounding thoroughly irritated as he took my horse. The look he gave me was so sour, I decided he must have indigestion and his prayer had nothing to do with my arrival.

Wuthering Heights is what Mr. Heathcliff calls his house. "Wuthering" is the local word for the wild winds that batter this place during storms. They must get plenty of fresh air up here—you can tell how hard the north wind blows by the way those stunted firs at the end of the house lean sideways, and how all the thorns stretch their branches in one direction, like they're begging the sun for mercy. Good thing the builder knew what they were doing: the windows are set deep in thick walls, and huge corner stones jut out for protection.

Before going in, I stopped to look at all the bizarre carvings covering the front of the house, especially around the main door. Through a mess of crumbling griffins and cherubs, I could make out "1500" and the name "Hareton Earnshaw." I wanted to ask about it, maybe get some history of the place from my *charming* host, but his stance at the door made it clear I should either get inside or get lost. I didn't feel like testing his patience before seeing what lay beyond that threshold.

One step took us straight into the family living room—no hallway or entrance, just right into what they call "the house" around here. Usually that means kitchen and parlor combined, but at Wuthering Heights the kitchen seems to be somewhere else. I could hear voices and clattering pots from deep inside the building, but there was nothing cooking at the massive fireplace, no copper pots or pans hanging on the walls.

One end of the room blazed with light reflecting off rows of huge pewter plates, mixed with silver jugs and tankards, stacked on an enormous oak dresser that reached the ceiling. The roof beams were completely exposed overhead, except where a wooden frame hung with oatcakes and legs of beef, mutton, and ham. Above the fireplace hung some nasty-looking old guns and a pair of horse pistols, plus three garishly painted canisters for decoration. The floor was smooth white stone, the chairs were high-backed primitive things painted green, with a couple of heavy black ones lurking in the shadows. In an alcove under the dresser, a huge liver-colored pointer was nursing a swarm of squealing puppies, while other dogs haunted the dark corners.

The room and furniture would've been perfectly normal for a rough Northern farmer—the type with a stubborn face and thick legs shown off in knee breeches and gaiters. You can find that man in his armchair with a foaming mug of ale any day after dinner within five or six miles of here. But Mr. Heathcliff is completely at odds with his house and lifestyle. He's dark-skinned, looks Romani, but dresses and acts like a gentleman—well, as much of a gentleman as any country squire. Maybe a bit careless with his appearance, but it suits him because he's tall and handsome, though gloomy. Some might think he's got a chip on his shoulder about his background, but I sense it's something else. His coldness isn't about insecurity—it's about hating any show of emotion. He'll love and hate quietly, keeping everything buried, and probably thinks it's presumptuous for anyone to expect feelings from him in return.

But wait—I'm projecting. I'm giving him all my own traits. Mr. Heathcliff might avoid human contact for completely different reasons. God, I hope my particular brand of dysfunction is unique. My dear mother used to say I'd never find domestic happiness, and just last summer I proved her exactly right.

While spending a month at the seaside, I met the most fascinating woman. She was a goddess to me, as long as she paid me no attention. I never spoke my feelings aloud, but if looks could talk, any idiot would've known I was completely smitten. She finally noticed and returned my interest with the sweetest glance imaginable.

And what did I do? I'm ashamed to admit I withdrew like a snail into its shell. The more she showed interest, the colder and more distant I became. Eventually the poor woman convinced herself she'd misread everything. Mortified by what she thought was her own mistake, she persuaded her mother to leave.

Thanks to this twisted personality quirk, I've earned a reputation as a deliberate heartbreaker. Only I know how undeserved that label is.

I sat down at one end of the hearth while my landlord took the other. To fill the silence, I tried to pet the mother dog, who'd left her puppies and was creeping behind my legs like a wolf, lips curled back, white teeth ready to bite. My attempt at friendliness got me a long, guttural growl.

"You'd better leave the dog alone," Heathcliff growled in harmony with her, stopping worse with a kick. "She's not used to being petted—she's not a pet." Then, heading to a side door, he shouted, "Joseph!"

Joseph mumbled something from deep in the cellar but didn't come up, so his master went down after him, leaving me face-to-face with the vicious bitch and a pair of grim shaggy sheepdogs who watched my every move with hostile suspicion. Not wanting to test their teeth, I sat still. But stupidly thinking they wouldn't understand silent insults, I started winking and making faces at them. Something about my expression enraged the mother dog—she flew into a fury and jumped at my knees. I shoved her back and grabbed the table as a shield.

That set off the whole pack. Half a dozen four-legged demons of various sizes burst from hidden corners and converged on me. They went for my heels and coattails while I fought off the bigger ones with the poker, forced to yell for help to restore some kind of order.

Mr. Heathcliff and his man climbed the cellar steps with infuriating calm—I don't think they moved any faster than normal, even though the hearth was complete chaos of snarling and yelping. Luckily, someone from the kitchen moved faster. A sturdy woman with her sleeves rolled up, bare arms, and flushed cheeks charged in swinging a frying pan. She used that weapon and her tongue so effectively that the storm died instantly, leaving her standing there heaving like the ocean after a gale when her master walked in.

"What the devil is going on?" he asked, looking at me in a way I could barely stand after this hostile reception.

"What the devil, indeed!" I muttered. "The possessed pigs in the Bible had better spirits than your animals. You might as well leave a stranger with a pack of tigers!"

"They won't bother people who don't touch anything," he said, setting the wine bottle in front of me and fixing the table. "The dogs are right to be watchful. Have some wine?"

"No, thank you."

"Not bitten, are you?"

"If I had been, I would've left my mark on the biter."

Heathcliff's face relaxed into a grin. "Come now," he said, "you're rattled, Mr. Lockwood. Here, have some wine. Guests are so incredibly rare here that my dogs and I, I'll admit, barely know how to receive them. Your health?"

I raised my glass and returned the toast, realizing it would be stupid to sulk over a pack of dogs. Besides, I didn't want to give him more entertainment at my expense, since he seemed to find this funny. He—probably realizing it was stupid to offend a good tenant—loosened up his clipped way of talking and brought up what he thought would interest me: the pros and cons of my new isolated home. I found him very intelligent on every topic we discussed, and before I left, I felt bold enough to say I'd visit again tomorrow. He obviously didn't want me to.

I'm going anyway. It's amazing how sociable I feel compared to him.

2

Yesterday afternoon turned misty and cold. I was tempted to stay by my study fire instead of trekking through heath and mud to Wuthering Heights. But after lunch—side note: I eat between noon and one, and the housekeeper, who came with the house, either can't or won't understand that I want dinner at five—I headed upstairs planning to be lazy. Then I walked into my room to find a servant girl on her knees surrounded by brushes and coal buckets, raising clouds of dust as she smothered the fire with ashes.

That sight drove me right back out. I grabbed my hat and after a four-mile walk, reached Heathcliff's garden gate just as the first snowflakes started falling.

On that bleak hilltop, the ground was frozen black and the wind cut through me. I couldn't get the chain off the gate, so I jumped over and ran up the flagstone path lined with scraggly gooseberry bushes. I knocked until my knuckles burned and the dogs started howling.

"Miserable people!" I muttered. "You deserve to be cut off from civilization with hospitality like this. At least I wouldn't lock my doors during the day. To hell with it—I'm getting in!"

I grabbed the latch and rattled it hard. Joseph's sour face appeared at a round barn window.

"What d'you want?" he shouted. "Master's down in the field. Go round by the barn end if you want him."

"Isn't anyone inside to open the door?" I yelled back.

"Only the missus, and she won't open it no matter how much racket you make."

"Why? Can't you tell her who I am, Joseph?"

"Not my business," he grumbled, disappearing.

The snow started coming down hard. I was about to try the handle again when a young man without a coat appeared in the yard, carrying a pitchfork. He waved me to follow him through a wash-house and a paved area with a coal shed, water pump, and pigeon coop, until we finally reached the huge, warm main room where I'd been received before.

A massive fire of coal, peat, and wood blazed in the hearth. Near the table set for dinner, I was surprised to see "the missus"—someone whose existence I hadn't known about. I bowed and waited for her to invite me to sit. She just leaned back in her chair, staring at me without moving or speaking.

"Rough weather!" I said. "I'm afraid, Mrs. Heathcliff, your door is suffering from your servants' laziness. I had to work hard to make them hear me."

She didn't open her mouth. We stared at each other—she kept her eyes on me with a cool indifference that was incredibly uncomfortable.

"Sit down," the young man said gruffly. "He'll be in soon."

I sat and cleared my throat, then called to the dog Juno, who barely moved the tip of her tail to acknowledge me this time.

"Beautiful animal!" I tried again. "Are you planning to sell the puppies, madam?"

"They're not mine," she said, even more coldly than Heathcliff would have.

"Oh, so your favorites are among these?" I continued, turning to a dark cushion that looked full of cats.

"Strange choice of favorites," she said with contempt.

Unfortunately, it was a pile of dead rabbits. I cleared my throat again and moved closer to the fire, commenting once more on the wild evening.

"You shouldn't have come out," she said, standing to reach for two of the painted canisters on the mantelpiece.

Now that she'd moved into the light, I could see her clearly. She was slender, barely past girlhood, with a beautiful figure and the most exquisite face I'd ever seen—delicate features, very fair skin, golden curls hanging loose on her neck. Her eyes would have been irresistible if they'd had any warmth, but they showed only scorn mixed with a strange desperation that seemed completely unnatural for someone so young.

The canisters were almost out of reach. When I moved to help, she turned on me like a miser caught counting gold.

"I don't want your help," she snapped. "I can get them myself."

"I beg your pardon!"

"Were you asked to tea?" she demanded, tying an apron over her neat black dress and holding a spoonful of tea leaves over the pot.

"I'd be glad to have a cup," I answered.

"Were you asked?" she repeated.

"No," I said, half-smiling. "You're the proper person to ask me."

She threw the tea back, spoon and all, and dropped into her chair sulking, her forehead creased and her bottom lip pushed out like a child about to cry.

Meanwhile, the young man had put on a shabby coat and stood by the fire, looking at me sideways as if we had some blood feud between us. I couldn't tell if he was a servant or not. His clothes and speech were rough, without any of the Heathcliffs' refinement. His thick brown curls were wild, his whiskers grew thick over his cheeks, and his hands were brown like a laborer's. But he carried himself almost arrogantly and showed none of a servant's attention to the lady of the house. Without clear proof of his position, I decided to ignore his strange behavior.

Five minutes later, Heathcliff's arrival somewhat relieved my discomfort.

"You see, sir, I came as promised!" I said cheerfully. "Though I'm afraid I'll be stuck here for half an hour if you can shelter me that long."

"Half an hour?" he said, shaking snow from his clothes. "Why would you choose the middle of a snowstorm to wander around? Don't you know you could get lost in the marshes? People who know these moors well lose their way on nights like this, and I can tell you the weather's not changing anytime soon."

"Maybe I could get one of your men as a guide, and he could stay at the Grange till morning—could you spare someone?"

"No, I couldn't."

"Oh, really! Well then, I'll have to trust my own judgment."

"Hmph!"

"Are you going to make the tea?" the young man in the shabby coat demanded, shifting his fierce look from me to the young lady.

"Is HE having any?" she asked, appealing to Heathcliff.

"Get it ready, will you?" he answered so savagely that I flinched. The tone revealed genuine nastiness. I no longer thought of Heathcliff as a decent fellow.

When tea was ready, he said, "Now, sir, bring your chair over." We all gathered around the table, including the rough young man, eating in grim silence.

I figured if I'd caused this cloud, I should try to lift it. They couldn't possibly sit around this grim and silent every day. No matter how bad-tempered they were, those permanent scowls couldn't be their normal expressions.

"It's strange," I began, between cups of tea, "how differently we can imagine happiness. Many people couldn't imagine being happy living so cut off from the world as you do, Mr. Heathcliff. Yet I'm sure, surrounded by your family, with your lovely wife presiding over your home and heart—"

"My lovely wife!" he interrupted with an almost demonic sneer. "Where is she—my lovely wife?"

"Mrs. Heathcliff, your wife, I mean."

"Well, yes—oh, you think her spirit watches over Wuthering Heights as a guardian angel, even though her body's gone. Is that it?"

Realizing my mistake, I tried to fix it. I should have noticed the age difference made them unlikely as husband and wife. He was about forty—old enough to know girls don't marry men his age for love. That delusion is saved for old age. She didn't look seventeen.

Then it hit me—the rough man at my elbow drinking

tea from a basin and eating with unwashed hands must be her husband. Heathcliff Junior, obviously. This is what happens when you're buried alive in the country: she'd thrown herself away on this oaf, not knowing better men existed. What a pity—I'd better not make her regret her choice. That last thought wasn't conceited. My neighbor struck me as borderline repulsive, and I knew from experience that I was reasonably attractive.

"Mrs. Heathcliff is my daughter-in-law," Heathcliff said, confirming my guess. He gave her a peculiar look as he spoke—a look of hatred, unless his facial muscles work backwards from everyone else's and don't show what's in his soul.

"Ah, of course—I see now. You're the lucky husband of this enchanting fairy," I said, turning to my neighbor.

This was worse than before. The young man turned crimson and clenched his fist, looking ready to attack. But he caught himself and smothered his rage in a brutal curse muttered on my behalf, which I pretended not to notice.

"Wrong again, sir," my host observed. "Neither of us has that privilege. Her husband is dead. I said she was my daughter-in-law, so she must have married my son."

"And this young man is—"

"Not my son, definitely not."

Heathcliff smiled again, as if the idea of fathering that bear was too ridiculous.

"My name is Hareton Earnshaw," the other growled, "and you'd better respect it!"

"I've shown no disrespect," I replied, internally laughing at his self-important announcement.

He stared at me longer than I wanted to stare back, afraid I might be tempted to either hit him or laugh out loud. I felt completely out of place in this pleasant family circle. The oppressive atmosphere overwhelmed even the warm fire and comfort around me. I decided to be very careful about visiting here a third time.

When we finished eating, with no one attempting conversation, I went to the window to check the weather. What I saw was dismal—night falling early, sky and hills lost in one bitter whirl of wind and blinding snow.

"I don't think I can get home without a guide," I couldn't help saying. "The roads will be buried already, and even if they weren't, I can barely see a foot ahead."

"Hareton, drive those dozen sheep into the barn porch. They'll be buried if left out all night. Put a plank in front of them," said Heathcliff.

"What am I supposed to do?" I asked, getting irritated.

No one answered. Looking around, I saw only Joseph bringing in porridge for the dogs, and Mrs. Heathcliff leaning over the fire, amusing herself by burning a bundle of matches that had fallen from the mantelpiece when she'd put the tea canister back. Joseph set down his bucket, looked around critically, and croaked, "I wonder how you can stand there doing nothing when everyone's gone out! But you're worthless, and there's no use talking—you'll never change your wicked ways, but go straight to the devil like your mother before you!"

For a moment I thought this speech was aimed at me. Furious, I stepped toward the old bastard to kick him out the door. But Mrs. Heathcliff stopped me with her response.

"You scandalous old hypocrite!" she replied. "Aren't you afraid of being carried off when you mention the devil's name? I'm warning you to stop provoking me, or I'll arrange for your abduction as a special favor! Wait—look here,

Joseph," she continued, taking a long, dark book from a shelf. "I'll show you how far I've come with the Black Arts. Soon I'll be able to clear this whole house. The red cow didn't die by accident, and your rheumatism is hardly a divine punishment!"

"Oh, wicked, wicked!" the old man gasped. "May the Lord deliver us from evil!"

"No, you old sinner! You're a lost soul—get out, or I'll hurt you seriously! I'll make wax and clay figures of you all! And the first one who crosses the line I draw—I won't say what I'll do, but you'll see! Go, I'm watching you!"

The little witch put mock evil in her beautiful eyes, and Joseph hurried out trembling with genuine horror, praying and muttering "wicked" as he went. I thought she must be having some kind of grim fun with him. Now that we were alone, I tried to get her sympathy for my situation.

"Mrs. Heathcliff," I said earnestly, "forgive me for troubling you. But with a face like yours, I'm sure you can't help being good-hearted. Please just tell me some landmarks so I can find my way home. I have no more idea how to get there than you'd know how to get to London!"

"Take the road you came," she answered, settling into a chair with a candle and the long book open before her. "Brief advice, but the best I can give."

"So if you hear I've been found dead in a bog or pit full of snow, your conscience won't whisper it's partly your fault?"

"How would it be? I can't escort you. They won't let me go past the garden wall."

"You! I wouldn't ask you to step outside for my sake on a night like this," I said. "I want you to tell me the way, not show it—or else convince Mr. Heathcliff to give me a guide."

"Who? There's himself, Earnshaw, Zillah, Joseph, and me. Which would you like?"

"Aren't there any boys at the farm?"

"No, that's everyone."

"Then I'm forced to stay."

"That's between you and your host. Nothing to do with me."

"I hope this teaches you not to make any more rash journeys on these hills," Heathcliff's harsh voice called from the kitchen entrance. "As for staying here, I don't keep accommodations for visitors. You'll have to share a bed with Hareton or Joseph, if you stay."

"I can sleep on a chair in this room," I replied.

"No, no! A stranger is a stranger, rich or poor. I won't have anyone wandering the place while I'm off guard!" said the rude bastard.

That insult ended my patience. I swore in disgust and pushed past him into the yard, running into Earnshaw in my rush. It was so dark I couldn't see the way out. As I stumbled around, I heard another example of their charming behavior. At first the young man seemed about to help me.

"I'll go with him as far as the park," he said.

"You'll go with him to hell!" exclaimed his master, or whatever he was to him. "And who's going to look after the horses?"

"A man's life is worth more than one evening's neglect of the horses. Someone should go," Mrs. Heathcliff murmured, more kindly than I expected.

"Not at your command!" Hareton shot back. "If you care about him, you'd better keep quiet."

"Then I hope his ghost will haunt you, and I hope Mr. Heathcliff never gets another tenant until the Grange is a ruin," she answered sharply.

"Listen, listen, she's cursing them!" muttered Joseph, who I'd been heading toward.

He sat within earshot, milking cows by lantern light. I grabbed the lantern without ceremony and called out that I'd return it tomorrow as I rushed to the nearest door.

"Master, master, he's stealing the lantern!" the old man shouted, chasing after me. "Hey, Gnasher! Hey, dog! Hey Wolf, hold him, hold him!"

When I opened the little door, two hairy monsters flew at my throat, knocking me down and putting out the light. Heathcliff and Hareton's laughter topped off my rage and humiliation. Fortunately, the beasts seemed more interested in stretching their paws and yawning than eating me alive, but they wouldn't let me up. I was forced to lie there until their malicious masters decided to free me. Then, hatless and shaking with fury, I ordered the villains to let me out—threatening to make them pay if they kept me one minute longer—with several incoherent threats that probably sounded like King Lear in their vague but violent fury.

My agitation gave me a massive nosebleed, and still Heathcliff laughed, and still I raged. I don't know how it would have ended if someone more rational and kind than my host hadn't appeared. This was Zillah, the stout housewife, who finally came out to investigate the commotion. She thought they'd been attacking me, and not daring to confront her master, she turned on the younger scoundrel.

"Well, Mr. Earnshaw," she cried, "what will you do next? Are we murdering people on our doorstep now? I see this house will never do for me—look at the poor lad, he's choking! Hush, hush, you mustn't go on so. Come in, and I'll fix that. There now, hold still."

With that, she suddenly threw a pint of ice water down my neck and pulled me into the kitchen. Mr. Heathcliff followed, his amusement quickly fading back to his usual gloom.

I was violently sick, dizzy, and faint—forced to accept lodging under his roof. He told Zillah to give me brandy, then went to the inner room while she sympathized with my sorry state. After following his orders and somewhat reviving me, she showed me to bed.

3

As she led me upstairs, Zillah whispered that I should hide my candle and stay quiet—her master had strange ideas about the room she was putting me in and never willingly let anyone sleep there. When I asked why, she said she didn't know. She'd only worked there a year or two, and with all the weird things that went on in this house, she'd learned not to ask questions.

Too exhausted to care, I locked my door and looked around for the bed. The room had almost no furniture—just a chair, a wardrobe, and a massive oak cabinet with openings cut near the top like coach windows. When I looked inside, I realized it was actually an old-fashioned box bed, cleverly designed so not everyone in the family needed their own room. It formed a small enclosed space, with a window ledge inside that served as a table. I slid open the paneled doors, climbed in with my candle, pulled them shut behind me, and finally felt safe from Heathcliff and everyone else.

The ledge where I set my candle had a few moldy books stacked in one corner, and the paint was covered with scratched writing. But this writing was just one name repeated over and over in different handwriting styles, large and small—CATHERINE EARNSHAW, sometimes changed to CATHERINE HEATHCLIFF, and then to CATHERINE LINTON.

Half-asleep, I leaned my head against the window and kept reading those names—Catherine Earnshaw—Heathcliff—Linton—until my eyes closed. But I'd barely dozed five minutes when white letters blazed out of the darkness like ghosts—the air swarmed with Catherines. Jerking awake to escape that haunting name, I saw my candle had tipped onto one of the old books, filling the space with the smell of burning leather. I snuffed it out and, still queasy and cold, sat up and opened the damaged book on my knee.

It was a Bible, printed in tiny type and reeking of mold. On the flyleaf was written "Catherine Earnshaw, her book," with a date from twenty-five years ago. I shut it and picked up another, then another, examining them all. Catherine's library was small but well-used—though not for reading. Nearly every page was covered with pen-and-ink notes crammed into every blank space the printer had left. Some were random thoughts; others formed diary entries written in messy, childish handwriting. At the top of one blank page (probably exciting to find back then), I was amused to discover a crude but vivid sketch of Joseph. Right then, I felt strangely drawn to this unknown Catherine and started decoding her faded writing.

"Awful Sunday," the entry began. "I wish Father was still alive. Hindley is a horrible replacement—he's brutal to Heathcliff—H. and I are going to rebel—we started tonight.

"It rained all day so we couldn't go to church. Joseph insisted on holding his own service in the attic while Hindley and his wife stayed warm by the fire downstairs—

doing anything but reading their Bibles, I'm sure. Heathcliff, the farmhand, and I were ordered to bring our prayer books upstairs. We sat in a row on grain sacks, freezing and miserable, hoping Joseph would get cold enough to keep it short. Not a chance! The service went on for exactly three hours, and when we finally came down, my brother had the nerve to say, 'Done already?' We used to be allowed to play on Sunday evenings if we were quiet. Now even laughing gets us sent to our rooms.

"'You forget I'm master here,' the tyrant says. 'I'll thrash anyone who annoys me! I demand complete silence. Boy! Was that you? Frances darling, pull his hair as you pass.' Frances yanked his hair hard, then sat on her husband's lap, and they spent hours kissing and babbling like idiots—embarrassing nonsense. We made ourselves comfortable under the dresser. I'd just pinned our aprons together as a curtain when Joseph came in from the stable. He ripped down our little shelter, boxed my ears, and growled:

"'Master barely buried, Sabbath not over, gospel still ringing in your ears, and you dare play games! Shame on you! Sit down, wicked children! There's good books if you'll read them—sit down and think of your souls!'

"Then he forced us to arrange ourselves so the distant firelight would barely let us see the religious garbage he shoved at us. I couldn't stand it. I grabbed my grimy book and hurled it into the dog kennel, declaring I hated good books. Heathcliff kicked his after mine. Then all hell broke loose!

"'Master Hindley!' our chaplain shouted. 'Master, come here! Miss Cathy's torn the back off "The Helmet of Salvation," and Heathcliff's kicked in the first part of "The Broad Way to Destruction!" It's terrible you let them act this way.

The old man would've whipped them proper—but he's gone!'

"Hindley rushed from his cozy spot by the fire, grabbed us each by the collar, and threw us into the back kitchen. Joseph swore the devil would come for us, and with that comfort, we each found a corner to wait for Satan. I grabbed this book and some ink from a shelf, cracked the door for light, and I've been writing for twenty minutes. But my companion's getting restless and suggests we steal the dairy maid's cloak and run out on the moors. Good idea—if that miserable old man comes in, he can think his prophecy came true. We can't get any wetter or colder out there than we are in here."

I GUESS Catherine did steal that cloak and run off, because her next entry changed the subject—now she was crying.

"I never dreamed Hindley could make me cry like this!" she wrote. "My head pounds so badly I can't keep it on the pillow, but I can't stop crying either. Poor Heathcliff! Hindley calls him a vagabond and won't let him eat with us or sit with us anymore. He says we can't play together and threatens to throw him out if we disobey. He blames our father (how dare he!) for treating H. too well, and swears he'll put him back in his place—"

I STARTED NODDING off over the faded page, my eyes drifting from the handwriting to the printed text. I saw an ornate red title: "Seventy Times Seven, and the First of the Seventy-First. A Pious Discourse delivered by the Reverend Jabez

Branderham, in the Chapel of Gimmerden Sough." While I was half-consciously trying to figure out what Jabez Branderham could possibly do with that subject, I sank back into bed and fell asleep.

God, the things bad food and bad temper will do to you! What else could have given me such a horrific night? I can't remember another nightmare that even comes close.

I started dreaming almost before I fully fell asleep. I thought it was morning and I was heading home with Joseph as my guide. The snow was yards deep on our road, and as we struggled through it, he kept harassing me about not bringing a pilgrim's staff. He said I'd never get into the house without one, waving around a heavy club that apparently counted as one. For a moment I thought it was ridiculous that I'd need a weapon to get into my own home. Then it hit me—I wasn't going home. We were traveling to hear the famous Jabez Branderham preach on "Seventy Times Seven," and either Joseph, the preacher, or I had committed the "First of the Seventy-First" and would be publicly exposed and excommunicated.

We reached the chapel. I've actually passed it on my walks a few times—it sits in a hollow between two hills, near a swamp whose bog water supposedly preserves the few corpses buried there. The roof is still intact, but since the minister's salary is only twenty pounds a year and a two-room house that's falling apart, no one will take the job. Especially since everyone knows the congregation would rather let their pastor starve than contribute a penny more. But in my dream, Jabez had a packed, attentive congregation, and he preached—good God, what a sermon! It was divided into FOUR HUNDRED AND NINETY parts, each as long as a normal sermon, each covering a different sin! Where he found them all, I have no idea. He had his own bizarre interpretation of the phrase, apparently requiring that the brother sin differently each time. They were the strangest sins—weird transgressions I'd never even imagined.

God, I was exhausted. I writhed, yawned, nodded off, jerked awake! I pinched myself, rubbed my eyes, stood up, sat down, and kept nudging Joseph to ask if this would EVER end. I was condemned to hear it all. Finally, he reached the "FIRST OF THE SEVENTY-FIRST." At that moment, sudden inspiration struck. I had to stand up and denounce Jabez Branderham as guilty of the one sin no Christian should forgive.

"Sir!" I shouted. "Sitting here within these four walls, I have endured and forgiven four hundred and ninety parts of your sermon. Seventy times seven times I've grabbed my hat to leave—seventy times seven times you've forced me back to my seat. The four hundred and ninety-first is too much! Fellow martyrs, get him! Drag him down and tear him apart so this place will never know him again!"

"YOU ARE THE MAN!" Jabez cried after a dramatic pause, leaning over his pulpit. "Seventy times seven times you yawned in my face—seventy times seven times I consulted my soul—This is human weakness and can be forgiven! But the First of the Seventy-First has come. Brothers, execute the judgment written. Such honor have all His saints!"

With that, the whole congregation raised their pilgrim's staffs and rushed at me. Having no weapon to defend myself, I grappled with Joseph, my nearest and fiercest attacker, trying to get his. In the chaos, clubs meant for me hit other people instead. Soon the whole chapel erupted with the sound of blows and counter-blows—everyone fighting everyone else. Branderham, not wanting to be left out, pounded his pulpit so hard that—thank God—the noise woke me up.

What had caused all that racket? What had played Jabez's part in the riot? Just a fir branch hitting my window as the wind howled by, rattling its dry cones against the glass. I listened for a moment to be sure, identified the real culprit, then rolled over and fell asleep again—into an even worse dream, if that was possible.

This time I remembered I was in the oak closet, and I could hear the wind howling and the snow driving against the window. I heard that fir branch scratching again and knew what it was, but it irritated me so much I decided to stop it if I could. I thought I got up and tried to open the window. The latch was rusted shut—something I'd noticed earlier but forgotten.

"I have to stop it anyway!" I muttered, punching my knuckles through the glass and reaching out to grab the annoying branch. But instead, my fingers closed on the fingers of a small, ice-cold hand!

The pure horror of nightmare washed over me. I tried to pull my arm back, but the hand clung to it, and a heart-broken voice sobbed, "Let me in—let me in!"

"Who are you?" I asked, struggling to get free.

"Catherine Linton," it replied, shivering. (Why did I think LINTON? I'd read EARNSHAW twenty times for every Linton.) "I'm come home—I lost my way on the moor!"

As it spoke, I could barely make out a child's face looking through the window. Terror made me cruel. When I couldn't shake the creature off, I pulled its wrist onto the broken glass and rubbed it back and forth until blood ran down and soaked the bedsheets. Still it wailed, "Let me in!" and kept its grip, nearly driving me insane with fear.

"How can I?" I finally said. "Let ME go if you want me to let you in!"

The fingers loosened. I yanked my hand back through the hole, frantically piled the books against it, and covered my ears to block out that pitiful begging. I kept them covered for what felt like fifteen minutes, but when I listened again, that mournful cry was still going.

"Get away!" I shouted. "I'll never let you in, not if you beg for twenty years!"

"It is twenty years," the voice mourned. "Twenty years. I've been a waif for twenty years!"

Then came a weak scratching outside, and the pile of books shifted as if being pushed. I tried to jump up but couldn't move a muscle, so I screamed in absolute terror. To my shock, I realized my scream was real—footsteps rushed toward my door. Someone shoved it open, and candlelight flickered through the openings at the top of the bed. I sat there shaking, wiping sweat from my forehead. The intruder seemed to hesitate, muttering to himself. Finally, in a half-whisper, clearly not expecting an answer, he said, "Is anyone here?"

I figured I'd better speak up—I recognized Heathcliff's voice and was afraid he'd investigate further if I stayed quiet. So I pushed open the panels. I'll never forget what happened next.

Heathcliff stood near the door in just his shirt and trousers, candle wax dripping over his fingers, his face as white as the wall behind him. The first creak of the oak hit him like an electric shock—the candle flew from his hand, and he was shaking so badly he could barely pick it up.

"It's only your guest, sir," I called out, wanting to spare him further embarrassment about his obvious fear. "I had a terrible nightmare and screamed in my sleep. Sorry I disturbed you."

"God damn you, Mr. Lockwood! I wish you were at the —" my host started, setting the candle on a chair because his hands were shaking too much to hold it. "Who showed you to this room?" he continued, digging his nails into his palms and grinding his teeth to control the spasms in his jaw. "Who was it? I should throw them out right now!"

"Your servant Zillah," I replied, jumping out of bed and quickly getting dressed. "I wouldn't blame you if you did, Mr. Heathcliff. She deserves it. I suppose she wanted to prove the place was haunted at my expense. Well, it is—swarming with ghosts and goblins! You're right to keep it locked. No one would thank you for a night in this hellhole!"

"What do you mean?" Heathcliff asked. "And what are you doing? Lie down and finish the night since you're here. But for God's sake, don't make that horrible noise again—nothing could excuse it unless someone was cutting your throat!"

"If that little demon had gotten through the window, she probably would have strangled me!" I shot back. "I'm not enduring any more persecution from your hospitable ancestors. Was the Reverend Jabez Branderham related to you on your mother's side? And that brat, Catherine Linton, or Earnshaw, or whatever her name was—she must have been a changeling—wicked little soul! She told me she's been walking the earth for twenty years—just punishment for her mortal sins, no doubt!"

The second those words left my mouth, I remembered seeing Heathcliff's name linked with Catherine's in the book —something I'd completely forgotten until now. I flushed at my thoughtlessness but hurried to add without acknowledging my mistake, "The truth is, sir, I spent the first part of the night—" I stopped again. I'd been about to say "reading those old books," which would reveal I'd seen the private writing as well as the printed pages. So I corrected myself: "—spelling out the name scratched on that window ledge. Boring work, meant to put me to sleep, like counting sheep, or—"

"How DARE you talk to me like this!" Heathcliff thundered with savage fury. "How—how DARE you, under my roof? God, he's insane!" And he struck his forehead in rage.

I didn't know whether to be offended or keep explaining, but he seemed so violently affected that I took pity on him and continued with my dream story. I swore I'd never heard the name "Catherine Linton" before, but reading it over and over had made such an impression that it came alive in my dreams when I lost control of my imagination.

As I spoke, Heathcliff gradually retreated to the bed, finally sitting down almost hidden behind it. But I could tell from his ragged, broken breathing that he was fighting to control some violent emotion. Not wanting him to know I'd noticed his struggle, I made extra noise getting dressed, checked my watch, and talked to myself about how long the night was: "Not even three o'clock! I would've sworn it was six. Time crawls here—we must have gone to bed at eight!"

"Always at nine in winter, and up at four," said my host, suppressing a groan and—I think—wiping a tear from his eyes with the shadow of his arm. "Mr. Lockwood," he added, "you can use my room. You'll only be in the way coming downstairs so early, and your childish screaming has ruined any chance of sleep for me."

"For me too," I replied. "I'll walk in the yard until daylight, then leave. You don't have to worry about me coming back. I'm completely cured of seeking company, whether in the country or town. A sensible man should find sufficient company in himself."

"Delightful company!" Heathcliff muttered. "Take the candle and go where you want. I'll join you shortly. But stay out of the yard—the dogs are loose, and Juno guards the house. Just stay on the steps and passages. Now go! I'll come in two minutes."

I left the room but, not knowing where the narrow hallways led, I stopped and accidentally witnessed something that completely contradicted my host's apparent rationality. He climbed onto the bed and wrenched open the window, bursting into uncontrollable sobs as he pulled at it.

"Come in! Come in!" he sobbed. "Cathy, do come. Oh, do —ONCE more! Oh! My heart's darling! Hear me THIS time, Catherine, at last!"

The ghost showed a ghost's typical indifference—no sign of appearing. But snow and wind whirled violently through the window, reaching where I stood and blowing out my candle.

The anguish in his grief was so raw that my pity overcame my judgment. I backed away, half-angry at myself for listening, and upset that my stupid nightmare had triggered such agony—though I couldn't understand why. I carefully made my way downstairs to the back kitchen, where glowing coals let me relight my candle. Nothing stirred except a gray tabby cat that crept from the ashes and greeted me with a cranky meow.

Two curved benches nearly circled the hearth. I stretched out on one while the cat claimed the other. We were both dozing when Joseph shuffled down a wooden ladder from a trapdoor in the ceiling—his attic room, I assumed. He gave me a nasty look for daring to kindle the fire, swept the cat off its bench, took its place, and started packing a pipe with tobacco. He clearly considered my presence too insulting to acknowledge—just silently lit his pipe, folded his arms, and puffed away. I let him smoke in peace. After exhaling his last cloud and heaving a deep sigh, he got up and left as grimly as he'd come.

Next came quicker footsteps. I opened my mouth to say "good morning" but stopped when I saw Hareton Earnshaw muttering a stream of curses at everything he touched while digging through a corner for a shovel to clear the snow. He glanced at me over the bench, nostrils flaring, with no more interest in greeting me than the cat. Seeing his preparations, I figured it was safe to leave and started to follow him. He noticed and jabbed his shovel at an inner door, grunting to show that's where I should go.

It opened into the main house, where the women were already up. Zillah was pumping a huge bellows at the chimney while Mrs. Heathcliff knelt by the fire reading, one hand shielding her eyes from the heat. She seemed completely absorbed, only pausing to scold Zillah for showering her with sparks or to push away dogs that stuck their noses in her face. I was surprised to see Heathcliff there too. He stood with his back to me, finishing a tirade at poor Zillah, who kept stopping her work to clutch her apron and groan indignantly.

"And you, you worthless—" he spun toward his daughter-in-law as I entered, using some word I'll leave to your imagination. "There you are with your lazy tricks again! Everyone else earns their keep—you live on my charity! Put that trash away and find something useful to do. You'll pay for plaguing me with your constant presence—do you hear me, you damned—"

"I'll put my trash away because you can make me," the young woman answered, closing her book and tossing it on a chair. "But I won't do anything else, no matter how much you rant—only what I choose!"

Heathcliff raised his hand, and she quickly backed away, clearly familiar with its force. Not wanting to watch a fight, I stepped forward briskly, pretending to warm myself at the fire and acting oblivious to their conflict. They both had enough manners to stop—Heathcliff shoved his fists in his pockets, and Mrs. Heathcliff sneered and moved to a distant seat where she sat like a statue for the rest of my stay.

Which wasn't long. I declined breakfast, and at first light escaped into the fresh air, now clear and still and cold as ice.

My landlord called after me before I reached the garden gate, offering to guide me across the moor. Good thing, too—the entire hillside was a rolling white ocean, with nothing to show where the ground rose or fell. Pits were filled level with the surface, and the quarry mounds I'd mentally mapped yesterday had vanished. I'd noticed yesterday a line of white-painted stones every six or seven yards along the path, meant as guides in the dark or when snow obscured the solid path from the swamps on either side. But except for a dirty spot here and there, they'd disappeared. My companion had to constantly warn me to veer right or left when I thought I was following the road perfectly.

We barely spoke, and he stopped at the entrance to Thrushcross Park, saying I couldn't miss it from there. We exchanged quick bows, and I pushed on alone—the gatekeeper's lodge was still empty. It's two miles from the gate to the Grange, but I must have made it four, getting lost among trees and sinking neck-deep in snow—something you can't appreciate unless you've experienced it. However long I wandered, the clock struck noon as I entered the house—exactly an hour for each mile of the normal route from Wuthering Heights.

My housekeeper and her helpers rushed to greet me, exclaiming they'd given me up for dead. Everyone assumed I'd died in the storm, and they were discussing how to search for my body. I told them to calm down now that I was back, then dragged myself upstairs, frozen to the bone. After changing into dry clothes and pacing for thirty or forty minutes to warm up, I retreated to my study, weak as a kitten —almost too weak to enjoy the cheerful fire and hot coffee the servant had ready for me.

4

God, what hypocrites we are! Here I was, congratulating myself on finding the perfect isolated spot where I'd never have to deal with people—and after one day of fighting off depression and loneliness, I completely caved. When Mrs. Dean brought my dinner, I practically begged her to sit and talk while I ate, using the excuse that I needed information about running the household. Honestly, I was desperate for her to either cheer me up or bore me to sleep with gossip.

"You've been here quite a while, haven't you?" I started. "Sixteen years, you said?"

"Eighteen, sir. I came when the mistress married, as her personal maid. After she died, the master kept me on as housekeeper."

"I see."

Silence. Damn—maybe she wasn't the chatty type after all. She sat there with her hands on her knees, clearly thinking something over, her weathered face clouded with memories. Then suddenly she burst out, "God, things have changed since then!"

"Yes," I encouraged her, "you must have seen quite a bit happen?"

"Changes and troubles both," she said.

Perfect opening to ask about my landlord's family, I thought. And especially that beautiful young widow—I wanted to know her story. Was she local, or some exotic outsider these harsh Yorkshire people would never accept as their own?

"Why does Heathcliff rent out Thrushcross Grange?" I asked. "Why live in that inferior house when he could be here? Can't he afford to maintain the estate properly?"

"Can't afford it?" She almost laughed. "Nobody knows how much money that man has, and it grows every year. He could live in a palace if he wanted. But he's tight-fisted—couldn't stand to miss the chance of getting a few hundred more in rent from you. Strange how greedy people get when they have no one to share it with."

"He had a son, didn't he?"

"Had one. He's dead."

"So young Mrs. Heathcliff is his widow?"

"Yes."

"Where's she from originally?"

"Why, sir, she's my late master's daughter—Catherine Linton before she married. I raised that poor girl! I keep hoping Mr. Heathcliff will move here so we can be together again."

"Catherine Linton?" I nearly jumped out of my chair. But wait—it couldn't be my ghostly Catherine from last night. "So my predecessor here was named Linton?"

"That's right."

"And what about that Earnshaw—Hareton Earnshaw, who lives with Heathcliff? How are they related?"

"They're not. He's the late Mrs. Linton's nephew."

"So he's the young lady's cousin?"

"Yes, and her husband was also her cousin—one on her mother's side, the other on her father's. Heathcliff married Mr. Linton's sister."

"I noticed 'Earnshaw' carved above the door at Wuthering Heights. Old family?"

"Very old, sir. Hareton's the last of them, just as Miss Cathy is the last of the Lintons. Have you been to Wuthering Heights? Sorry for asking, but I'd love to know how she's doing."

"Mrs. Heathcliff looked well—very beautiful, actually. But not happy, I think."

"Oh dear, I'm not surprised! And what did you think of the master?"

"Rather rough, Mrs. Dean. That's his reputation, isn't it?"

"Rough as sandpaper and hard as granite. The less you have to do with him, the better."

"He must have been through hell to become such a bastard. Do you know his history?"

"It's a strange one, sir—I know everything except where he was born, who his parents were, and how he first got his money. And poor Hareton's been thrown out like a baby bird pushed from the nest. The unfortunate boy is the only person around here who doesn't realize how badly he's been cheated."

"Well, Mrs. Dean, you'd be doing me a kindness by telling me about my neighbors. I'm too wound up to sleep, so please, sit and talk for an hour."

"Of course, sir! Let me just get my sewing, then I'll sit as long as you like. But you've caught cold—I saw you shivering. You need something hot to chase it out."

She hustled off and I huddled closer to the fire. My head burned while the rest of me was freezing. I was also ridiculously keyed up, my nerves completely shot. The last two days had rattled me more than I wanted to admit—I couldn't shake the feeling that something worse was coming.

She returned with a steaming bowl of soup and her sewing basket. After setting the soup near the fire to keep warm, she pulled up her chair, clearly pleased to have someone to talk to.

"Before I came to work here," she began without waiting for encouragement, "I was almost always at Wuthering Heights. My mother had been wet nurse to Mr. Hindley Earnshaw—that's Hareton's father—and I grew up playing with the children. I ran errands, helped with the hay, did whatever needed doing around the farm.

"One beautiful summer morning—it was the start of harvest season, I remember—Mr. Earnshaw, the old master, came downstairs dressed for traveling. After giving Joseph instructions for the day, he turned to Hindley, Cathy, and me—I was eating breakfast with them—and said to his son, 'Now, my boy, I'm going to Liverpool today. What should I bring you back? Pick something small, though—I'm walking both ways, sixty miles each direction.'

"Hindley asked for a fiddle. Then he asked little Miss Cathy—she was barely six, but could already ride any horse in the stable. She wanted a whip. He didn't forget me either—he had a kind heart, even if he was strict sometimes. He promised to bring me a pocketful of apples and pears. Then he kissed his children goodbye and set off.

"Those three days felt endless. Little Cathy kept asking when he'd be home. Mrs. Earnshaw expected him by dinnertime on the third evening, but hour after hour passed with no sign of him. The children wore themselves out running to the gate to look for him. When it got dark, she tried to send them to bed, but they begged to stay up. Finally, around eleven o'clock, we heard the door latch lift quietly, and the master stumbled in.

"He collapsed into a chair, laughing and groaning at the same time, waving us all back. 'Nearly killed myself,' he gasped. 'I wouldn't make that walk again for all the money in England.'

"'And at the end of it, I get scared to death!' he said, opening his coat, which he'd bundled up around something in his arms. 'Look here, wife! I've never been so beaten down by anything in my life. But you'll have to take it as a gift from God—though it looks dark enough to have come from the devil.'

"We all crowded around. Over Miss Cathy's head, I caught sight of a dirty, ragged child with black hair—old enough to walk and talk, with a face that somehow looked older than Catherine's. But when Mr. Earnshaw set it on its feet, it just stared around, repeating some gibberish nobody could understand.

"I was scared, and Mrs. Earnshaw was ready to throw it right back out. She exploded—how could he bring some foreign brat into their house when they had their own children to feed and care for? What was he thinking? Had he lost his mind?

"The master tried to explain, but he was half-dead from exhaustion. Through all her yelling, apparently he'd found the child starving and homeless on the streets of Liverpool. He'd looked for its family, asked around, but nobody knew where it belonged. With limited time and money, he figured it was better to bring it home than waste resources there. He was determined not to leave it to die.

"Well, eventually my mistress wore herself out

complaining. Mr. Earnshaw told me to wash the child, give it clean clothes, and put it to bed with the children.

"Hindley and Cathy had stayed quiet during the argument, but once things calmed down, they started digging through their father's pockets for their presents. Hindley, who was fourteen, pulled out what had been a fiddle—now crushed to pieces in the coat—and burst into tears. When Cathy learned her father had lost her whip while dealing with the stranger, she showed her anger by making faces and spitting at the poor creature. That earned her a hard slap from her father to teach her better manners.

"Both children absolutely refused to have it in their bed or even their room. I wasn't any kinder—I left it on the stair landing, hoping it would be gone by morning. But somehow, maybe hearing Mr. Earnshaw's voice, it crept to his bedroom door. That's where he found it when he came out in the morning. When he found out what I'd done, I was thrown out of the house for my cruelty.

"That was Heathcliff's first introduction to the family.

"When I came back a few days later—my banishment wasn't permanent—I found they'd named him 'Heathcliff' after a son who'd died young. It's been both his first and last name ever since. Miss Cathy had already taken to him, but Hindley hated him. To be honest, so did I. We tormented him terribly—I wasn't mature enough to see how wrong it was, and Mrs. Earnshaw never defended him when she saw him being mistreated.

"He was a strange child—sullen and patient, probably hardened by whoever had abused him before. He'd take Hindley's beatings without flinching or crying. When I pinched him, he'd just draw in a breath and open his eyes, as if he'd accidentally hurt himself and no one was to blame. This endurance infuriated old Mr. Earnshaw when he caught his son persecuting 'the poor fatherless child,' as he called him. He became strangely attached to Heathcliff—maybe he saw something of himself in that abandoned child, or maybe it was just pity. Either way, he believed everything the boy said—not that he said much, and what he did say was usually true. He even favored him over Cathy, who was too wild and mischievous to be the favorite.

"So from the very start, Heathcliff caused division in the house. When Mrs. Earnshaw died less than two years later, young Hindley had learned to see his father as an enemy and Heathcliff as a thief who'd stolen his father's love and his rightful place. He grew more bitter by the day, brooding over these injustices.

"I sympathized with Hindley at first. But then the children got measles, and I had to nurse them all—suddenly taking on a woman's responsibilities. That's when my feelings changed. Heathcliff was dangerously ill and insisted I stay by his bed constantly. I suppose he felt grateful for my care, though he didn't realize I had no choice. But I will say this—he was the easiest patient I ever nursed. The difference between him and the others made me less biased against him. While Cathy and her brother drove me crazy with their complaints, he was quiet as a lamb—though it was from toughness, not gentleness.

"He recovered, and the doctor said it was largely thanks to my care. I was proud of his praise, and I softened toward the boy who'd earned it for me. So Hindley lost his last ally. Still, I couldn't bring myself to love Heathcliff. I never understood what Mr. Earnshaw saw in that sullen boy who never showed any gratitude for the favoritism. He wasn't openly disrespectful—he was just indifferent, though he knew perfectly well the power he had over the old man's heart. He knew he only had to speak and the whole household would bend to his will.

"Here's an example: Mr. Earnshaw once bought two colts at the fair and gave one to each boy. Heathcliff picked the prettier one, but it soon went lame. When he discovered this, he told Hindley, 'You're going to trade horses with me. I don't like mine. And if you won't, I'll tell your father about the three beatings you gave me this week and show him my arm—it's bruised black to the shoulder.'

"Hindley stuck out his tongue and hit him.

"'You'd better do it now,' Heathcliff continued, backing toward the porch—they were in the stable. 'You'll have to eventually. And if I tell about these beatings, you'll get them back with interest.'

"'Get lost, dog!' Hindley shouted, grabbing an iron weight used for weighing hay and potatoes.

"'Throw it,' Heathcliff said calmly, standing still. 'Then I'll tell him how you bragged you'd throw me out the minute he dies. We'll see who gets thrown out first.'

"Hindley threw it, hitting him square in the chest. Heathcliff went down but got right back up, gasping and pale. If I hadn't stopped him, he would've gone straight to Mr. Earnshaw like that, letting his injuries speak for themselves.

"'Take the damn horse then, foreign devil!' young Earnshaw spat. 'I hope it breaks your neck! Take it and be damned, you worthless parasite! Manipulate my father out of everything he has—but someday he'll see what you really are, you devil! And take this too—I hope it kicks your brains out!'

"Heathcliff had gone to move the horse to his stall and was walking behind it when Hindley finished his rant by shoving him under its hooves. Without checking if he'd actually hurt him, Hindley ran off.

"I was amazed at how calmly the child picked himself up and continued switching the horses, saddles and all. Then he sat on a hay bale until the dizziness from the blow passed before going inside. I easily convinced him to let me blame his bruises on the horse—he didn't care what story we told as long as he got what he wanted. He complained so rarely about these attacks that I thought he wasn't vengeful. I was dead wrong. That boy was keeping score, as you'll soon hear."

5

Mr. Earnshaw began dying the way he'd lived—suddenly and stubbornly. He'd been strong and healthy, but his strength left him overnight. Once he was confined to his chair by the fire, he became unbearably irritable. The smallest thing set him off, and any hint of disrespect sent him into a rage.

This was especially true if anyone tried to cross or dominate his favorite. He was paranoid about anyone speaking harshly to Heathcliff—convinced that because he loved the boy, everyone else hated him and wanted to hurt him. This actually worked against Heathcliff. We servants didn't want to upset the master, so we went along with his favoritism. But that just fed the child's pride and dark moods.

Still, we had no choice. Two or three times when Hindley showed his contempt while his father was nearby, the old man flew into such a fury that he grabbed his walking stick to beat him, shaking with rage that his body was too weak to do it.

Finally, our curate—who made ends meet by tutoring the Linton and Earnshaw children and farming his own small plot—suggested sending Hindley to college. Mr. Earnshaw agreed, though it broke his heart. He said Hindley was worthless and would never amount to anything no matter where he went.

I hoped we'd have some peace after that. It was hard watching the master made miserable by his own good intentions. I thought all the family fighting was making him sicker—that's what he believed, anyway. But really, sir, it was just his body giving out.

We might have managed well enough if not for two people: Miss Cathy and Joseph, that servant you met. He was—and probably still is—the most self-righteous, scripture-spouting hypocrite who ever twisted scripture to bless himself and curse everyone else. With his constant preaching and religious talk, he got his hooks into Mr. Earnshaw. The weaker the master got, the more power Joseph gained.

He was relentless, constantly harassing him about his soul and about controlling his children with an iron fist. He encouraged him to see Hindley as damned, and night after night, he'd drone on with complaints about Heathcliff and Catherine—always making sure to blame Catherine more, knowing that was Earnshaw's weakness.

She certainly had ways I'd never seen in a child before. She drove us all past our breaking point fifty times a day. From the moment she came downstairs until she went to bed, we never had a minute's peace—never knew when she'd cause chaos. Her energy was always at full throttle, her mouth always running—singing, laughing, tormenting anyone who wouldn't join in. I'd never seen a child that wild—but she had the brightest eyes, the sweetest smile, and the lightest step in the whole parish. Deep down, I don't think she meant any harm. When she made you cry for real, she'd usually stay to keep you company and make you feel better.

She adored Heathcliff too much. The worst punishment we could give her was keeping them apart, and she got in more trouble on his account than for anything else. When they played, she loved acting like a little tyrant—slapping and ordering everyone around. She tried it with me once, but I wouldn't stand for it and let her know. Of course, I couldn't say much—I was just the help—but I made my limits clear.

Now, Mr. Earnshaw never understood playfulness from his children. He'd always been strict and serious with them, and Catherine couldn't grasp why her father was even more impatient and harsh when he was sick than when he'd been healthy. His constant scolding sparked something defiant in her—she was never happier than when we were all yelling at her at once while she stared us down with that bold, sassy look, always ready with a smart answer. She'd mock Joseph's religious curses, bait me, and do exactly what her father hated most: showing that her fake defiance (which he thought was real) had more power over Heathcliff than all his kindness. The boy would do anything she asked, but only followed Earnshaw's orders when he felt like it.

After being horrible all day, she'd sometimes come cuddle up at night to make amends. "No, Cathy," the old man would say. "I can't love you—you're worse than your brother. Go say your prayers, child, and ask God's forgiveness. I think your mother and I will regret the day we raised you!"

That made her cry at first. But being pushed away over and over hardened her. Eventually she'd laugh if I told her to apologize and ask forgiveness.

But the hour finally came that ended Mr. Earnshaw's troubles on earth.

He died quietly in his chair one October evening, sitting by the fire. A fierce wind battered the house and roared in the chimney—it sounded wild and stormy, but it wasn't cold, and we were all together. I sat a little away from the hearth with my knitting. Joseph was reading his Bible near the table—servants usually sat in the main room then, after work was done. Miss Cathy had been sick, which kept her calm. She leaned against her father's knee while Heathcliff lay on the floor with his head in her lap.

I remember the master, just before he dozed off, stroking her pretty hair—he loved these rare moments when she was gentle—and saying, "Why can't you always be a good girl, Cathy?"

She turned her face up to his, laughed, and answered, "Why can't you always be a good man, Father?"

But when she saw she'd upset him, she kissed his hand and said she'd sing him to sleep. She began singing very softly until his fingers slipped from hers and his head dropped to his chest. I told her to hush and stay still so she wouldn't wake him. We all stayed silent as mice for half an hour, and would have continued, but Joseph finished his chapter, stood up, and said he needed to wake the master for prayers and bed.

He stepped forward, called his name, and touched his shoulder. When he wouldn't move, Joseph took the candle and looked at him. I knew something was wrong when he set down the light. He grabbed both children by the arm and whispered for them to go upstairs quietly—they could pray alone tonight, he had something to do.

"I want to say goodnight to Father first," Catherine said,

throwing her arms around his neck before we could stop her.

The poor child realized immediately. She screamed, "Oh, he's dead, Heathcliff! He's dead!"

They clung to each other, sobbing desperately.

I joined them, crying loud and bitter. But Joseph asked what we thought we were doing, carrying on like that when he's already with the angels. He told me to put on my cloak and run to Gimmerton for the doctor and minister. I couldn't see what good either would do then, but I went anyway, through wind and rain, and brought the doctor back with me. The minister said he'd come in the morning.

Leaving Joseph to handle things, I ran to the children's room. Their door was cracked open—I saw they'd never gone to bed, though it was past midnight. But they were calmer and didn't need my comfort. The little souls were consoling each other with better thoughts than I could have offered. No minister in the world ever described heaven as beautifully as they did in their innocent talk. As I stood there sobbing and listening, I couldn't help wishing we were all there safe together.

6

HINDLEY CAME HOME FOR THE FUNERAL—AND SHOCKED everyone by bringing a wife with him. The whole neighborhood was gossiping about it. He never told us who she was or where she came from. She probably had no money or respectable family, or he wouldn't have hidden the marriage from his father.

She wouldn't have caused much trouble on her own. Everything delighted her the moment she walked through the door—every little detail of the house fascinated her. Except for the funeral preparations and the mourners themselves. Her behavior struck me as odd. She'd run to her room and drag me with her when I should have been dressing the children. She'd sit there shaking, wringing her hands, constantly asking, "Are they gone yet?"

Then she'd get hysterical describing how the sight of black clothing affected her. She'd jump at nothing, tremble, and finally break down crying. When I asked what was wrong, she said she didn't know—she was just terrified of dying! Which seemed ridiculous to me at the time. She was thin but young, with fresh skin and eyes that sparkled like diamonds. Sure, I noticed climbing stairs left her breathless, that sudden noises made her jump, and she had a troublesome cough that wouldn't go away. But I had no idea what these symptoms meant—tuberculosis wasn't something we talked about then. We don't usually warm up to outsiders here, Mr. Lockwood, unless they make the first move.

Young Earnshaw had changed dramatically during his three years away. He was thinner, paler, and everything about him was different—how he spoke, how he dressed. The very day he returned, he told Joseph and me we'd have to move to the back kitchen and leave the main house to him. He'd actually planned to carpet and wallpaper a small room as a proper parlor, but his wife went on about how much she loved the white stone floor, the massive fireplace, the pewter dishes, the china cabinet, even the dog kennel. She loved having so much space to move around in the main room that he dropped the whole idea.

She also seemed thrilled to have found a "sister" in Catherine. At first, she chattered away with her, kissed her, followed her around, and showered her with presents. But her affection wore off quickly. When she got moody, Hindley turned tyrannical. All it took was a few words from her showing she disliked Heathcliff, and all his old hatred for the boy came roaring back. He banished Heathcliff from their company to live with the servants, stopped his lessons with the curate, and sent him to work in the fields like any other farmhand.

Heathcliff handled his demotion pretty well at first, because Cathy taught him everything she learned and they worked and played together in the fields. They were both growing up wild as savages. The young master didn't care what they did as long as they stayed out of his way. He wouldn't even have noticed them skipping church if Joseph and the curate hadn't complained about it—which only reminded him to order Heathcliff a beating and Catherine to miss meals.

But one of their favorite games was escaping to the moors in the morning and staying out all day. The punishments afterward became something to laugh about. The curate could assign Catherine as many Bible verses to memorize as he wanted, and Joseph could beat Heathcliff until his arm ached—they forgot everything the moment they were together again. Or at least, the moment they'd cooked up some new scheme for revenge. I often cried watching them grow more reckless by the day, but I didn't dare say anything for fear of losing what little influence I still had over those friendless children.

One Sunday evening, they got thrown out of the sitting room for being too noisy or some other minor offense. When I went to call them for supper, they were nowhere to be found. We searched the entire house, top to bottom, the yard, the stables—nothing. Finally, Hindley lost his temper, ordered us to bolt the doors, and swore nobody would let them in that night.

The household went to bed, but I was too anxious to sleep. I opened my window and stuck my head out to listen, even though it was raining. I was determined to let them in despite Hindley's orders if they came back. After a while, I heard footsteps on the road and saw a lantern bobbing through the gate. I threw a shawl over my head and ran out to stop them from waking Mr. Earnshaw by knocking.

There was Heathcliff, alone. My heart jumped seeing him by himself.

"Where's Miss Catherine?" I asked frantically. "Nothing's happened to her, has it?"

"She's at Thrushcross Grange," he answered. "I would've

been there too, but they didn't have the manners to invite me to stay."

"You're going to catch hell for this!" I said. "You won't be satisfied until you're thrown out for good. What on earth made you wander all the way to Thrushcross Grange?"

"Let me get out of these wet clothes and I'll tell you everything, Nelly," he replied.

I warned him not to wake the master, and while he changed and I waited to put out the candle, he continued: "Cathy and I snuck out through the washhouse to explore. When we saw the lights at the Grange, we decided to go see if the Lintons spend their Sunday evenings shivering in corners while their parents feast and laugh by the fire. Do you think they do? Or maybe getting lectured by servants and memorizing Bible verses?"

"Probably not," I said. "They're good children and don't deserve the treatment you get for your bad behavior."

"Don't preach at me, Nelly," he said. "We ran all the way from the Heights to their park without stopping—Catherine lost because she was barefoot. You'll have to look for her shoes in the bog tomorrow. We squeezed through a broken hedge, felt our way up the path, and positioned ourselves in a flower bed under the drawing-room window.

"The shutters were open and the curtains only half-drawn. We could both see in by standing on the basement wall and gripping the ledge. And we saw—God, it was beautiful! A magnificent room with crimson carpets, crimson chairs and tables, a pure white ceiling trimmed in gold, and a crystal chandelier hanging from silver chains, glittering with candles.

"Old Mr. and Mrs. Linton weren't there—Edgar and Isabella had the place to themselves. You'd think they'd be happy, right? We would've thought we were in heaven! But guess what your 'good children' were doing?"

He paused for effect.

"Isabella—she's eleven, I think, a year younger than Cathy—was screaming at one end of the room like someone was stabbing her with hot needles. Edgar stood by the fireplace crying silently. And in the middle of the table sat a little dog, shaking its paw and yelping. From what they were yelling at each other, we figured out they'd nearly torn it in half fighting over it.

"The idiots! That was their idea of fun—fighting over who got to hold a ball of fur, then both crying because neither would take it after they'd hurt it. We burst out laughing at those spoiled brats. When would you ever catch me wanting something just because Catherine wanted it? Or find us entertaining ourselves by screaming and rolling on the ground? I wouldn't trade my life here for Edgar Linton's at Thrushcross Grange—not even if it meant I could throw Joseph off the roof and paint the house with Hindley's blood!"

"Quiet!" I interrupted. "You still haven't told me how Catherine got left behind."

"I told you we laughed," he answered. "The Lintons heard us and rushed to the door like a pack of arrows. Everything went quiet, then they started wailing, 'Oh, Mama! Papa! Come here!' They really did howl like that. We made horrible noises to scare them even more, then jumped down because someone was unlatching the door and we figured we'd better run. I had Cathy by the hand, pulling her along, when she suddenly fell down. 'Run, Heathcliff, run!' she whispered. 'They've let the bulldog loose and he's got me!'

"The devil of a dog had her ankle, Nelly. I could hear his

disgusting snorting. But she didn't scream—no! She wouldn't have made a sound if she'd been gored by a mad bull. I did though—I cursed enough to send any demon back to hell. I grabbed a stone and jammed it between the dog's jaws, trying to shove it down his throat. Finally this brute of a servant came with a lantern, shouting, 'Hold him, Skulker, hold him!' But his tone changed when he saw what Skulker had caught. They pulled the dog off—his huge purple tongue hanging out half a foot, drooling bloody spit. The man picked up Cathy. She was sick, not from fear but from pain. He carried her inside while I followed, swearing revenge.

"'What did you catch, Robert?' Mr. Linton called from the doorway.

"'Skulker's caught a little girl, sir,' he replied, 'and there's a boy here'—he grabbed at me—'who looks like a real criminal! Probably thieves trying to get the children to open the windows so their gang could murder us in our beds. Shut your filthy mouth, you thief! You'll hang for this! Mr. Linton, sir, keep your gun ready!'

"'No, no, Robert,' the old fool said. 'These rascals knew yesterday was rent day—they thought they'd catch me with money. Come in, I'll give them a reception they won't forget. John, lock the chain. Get Skulker some water, Jenny. Attacking a magistrate in his own home, and on Sunday! Where will their nerve end? Oh, Mary dear, look at this! Don't be frightened, it's just a boy—but look how the evil shows in his face. Wouldn't we be doing the country a favor to hang him now, before he acts on his nature?'

"He dragged me under the chandelier while Mrs. Linton put on her glasses and threw up her hands in horror. The cowardly children crept closer, Isabella lisping, 'Horrible thing! Put him in the cellar, Papa. He looks just like that fortune-teller's son who stole my pet pheasant. Doesn't he, Edgar?'

"While they examined me, Cathy came around. She heard that last comment and laughed. Edgar Linton stared at her, then finally recognized her. They see us at church, though we rarely meet otherwise. 'That's Miss Earnshaw?' he whispered to his mother. 'Look how Skulker bit her—her foot's bleeding!'

"'Miss Earnshaw? Impossible!' the lady cried. 'Miss Earnshaw roaming the countryside with a Romani! But wait, dear, the child is in mourning—yes, she is—and she might be crippled for life!'

"'How careless of her brother!' Mr. Linton exclaimed, turning from me to Catherine. 'I've heard from Shielders'—that's the curate, sir—'that he lets her grow up like a complete heathen. But who is this? Where did she find this companion? Ah! I know—he's that strange creature my late neighbor brought back from Liverpool. A little sailor from the East Indies, or maybe an American or Spanish castaway.'

"'A wicked boy, regardless,' the old lady remarked. 'Completely unfit for a decent house! Did you hear his language, Linton? I'm appalled our children had to hear it.'

"I started cursing again—don't be mad, Nelly—and Robert was ordered to throw me out. I refused to leave without Cathy. He dragged me to the garden, shoved the lantern in my hand, promised Mr. Earnshaw would hear about my behavior, and locked the door behind me. The curtains were still pulled back at one corner, so I went back to spying. If Catherine had wanted to leave, I was ready to smash their windows into a million pieces if they didn't let her go.

"But she sat quietly on the sofa. Mrs. Linton took off the

dairymaid's gray cloak we'd borrowed for our adventure, shaking her head and scolding her—probably reminding her she was a young lady, which is why they treated her differently than me. A servant brought warm water to wash her feet. Mr. Linton mixed her a hot toddy, Isabella piled cakes in her lap, and Edgar stood gaping from across the room.

"Then they dried and combed her beautiful hair, gave her huge slippers, and wheeled her to the fire. I left when she was happily sharing her food between the little dog and Skulker, tweaking his nose as he ate, bringing life to those vacant blue Linton eyes—a dim reflection of her own enchanting face. I saw they were completely dazzled by her. She's so far above them—above everyone on earth. God, Nelly, isn't she everything?"

"This is going to cause more trouble than you think," I answered, covering him up and putting out the light. "You're hopeless, Heathcliff. Mr. Hindley's going to take drastic measures, mark my words."

My prediction came true sooner than I wanted. The disastrous adventure made Earnshaw furious. Then Mr. Linton himself visited the next day and gave the young master such a lecture about how he was raising his family that it finally made him take notice. Heathcliff wasn't beaten, but he was warned that if he spoke even one word to Miss Catherine, he'd be thrown out immediately. And Mrs. Earnshaw promised to keep her sister-in-law under control when she came home—using persuasion, not force. Force would have been impossible anyway.

I should have known then what was coming. That night at Thrushcross Grange changed everything—though we wouldn't see the full damage for years to come.

7

CATHY STAYED AT THRUSHCROSS GRANGE FOR FIVE WEEKS—until Christmas. By then her ankle had completely healed, and her manners had undergone a dramatic transformation. Mrs. Linton visited often during her recovery, working to reform her with beautiful clothes and constant flattery, which Cathy eagerly absorbed.

So instead of a wild, barefoot little savage bursting through the door to smother us with hugs, a very different creature arrived. She dismounted from a handsome black pony like a proper lady, brown curls tumbling from beneath a feathered hat, wearing a long riding habit she had to hold up with both hands just to walk.

Hindley lifted her down, exclaiming with delight, "My God, Cathy, you're absolutely beautiful! I barely recognize you—you look like a real lady now. Isabella Linton can't hold a candle to you, can she, Frances?"

"Isabella doesn't have Catherine's natural advantages," his wife replied. "But she needs to be careful not to go wild again here. Ellen, help Miss Catherine with her things—wait, dear, you'll mess up your curls. Let me get your hat."

I removed the riding habit to reveal a gorgeous plaid silk dress underneath, white trousers, and polished shoes. Though her eyes lit up when the dogs bounded over to greet her, she barely dared touch them, afraid they'd dirty her fine clothes. She kissed me gently—I was covered in flour from making Christmas cake, so a real hug was out of the question—then looked around for Heathcliff.

Mr. and Mrs. Earnshaw watched anxiously, hoping this reunion would show them whether they had any chance of separating the two friends.

Heathcliff was hard to spot at first. If he'd been neglected before Catherine left, it had gotten ten times worse since. I was the only one who even bothered to call him a dirty boy and tell him to wash once a week—and boys his age rarely enjoy soap and water anyway. His clothes had seen three months of mud and dust, his thick hair was matted and uncombed, and his face and hands were covered in grime. No wonder he hid behind the bench when this bright, elegant young lady walked in instead of the rough-haired companion he expected.

"Where's Heathcliff?" she asked, pulling off her gloves to reveal fingers pale from five weeks of doing nothing indoors.

"Heathcliff, you may come forward," Hindley called out, enjoying his humiliation and eager to see what a disgusting sight the boy would make. "Come wish Miss Catherine welcome, like the other servants."

Cathy spotted her friend in his hiding place and flew to embrace him. She kissed his cheek seven or eight times in a second, then stopped, pulled back, and burst out laughing. "God, you look so dirty and angry! And how—how funny and grim! But that's just because I'm used to Edgar and Isabella Linton now. Well, Heathcliff, have you forgotten me?"

She had good reason to ask—shame and pride darkened his face and kept him frozen in place.

"Shake hands, Heathcliff," Mr. Earnshaw said condescendingly. "Just this once, I'll allow it."

"I won't," the boy finally found his voice. "I won't stand here to be laughed at. I won't take it!" He tried to break away, but Cathy grabbed him again.

"I didn't mean to laugh at you," she said. "I couldn't help it. Heathcliff, at least shake hands! Why are you being so sulky? You just looked strange. If you wash your face and brush your hair, you'll be fine—but you're so dirty!"

She stared at his grimy fingers in her clean ones, then at her dress, worried it might be stained from touching him.

"You didn't have to touch me!" he snapped, following her gaze and jerking his hand away. "I'll be as dirty as I want. I like being dirty, and I'm going to stay dirty."

With that, he bolted from the room while the master and mistress laughed, leaving Catherine genuinely confused about why her comments had upset him so badly.

After helping the "new" Catherine and getting my cakes in the oven, I'd made the house and kitchen cheerful with roaring fires for Christmas Eve. I was ready to sit down alone and sing carols—ignoring Joseph's complaints that my cheerful songs were practically sinful. He'd retreated to his room for private prayer, while Mr. and Mrs. Earnshaw were showing Cathy the pretty gifts they'd bought for her to give the little Lintons tomorrow as thank-you presents. The Lintons had invited everyone to spend Christmas Day at Thrushcross Grange, and they'd accepted—with one condition: Mrs. Linton insisted her precious children be kept well away from "that foul-mouthed boy."

So I sat alone in the kitchen, breathing in the rich smell of baking spices, admiring the gleaming utensils, the polished clock decorated with holly, the silver mugs waiting to be filled with mulled ale for supper, and especially my spotless, well-scrubbed floor.

As I admired my work, I remembered how old Mr. Earnshaw used to come in when everything was tidy, call me a good girl, and slip a shilling into my hand as a Christmas present. That led me to think about how much he'd loved Heathcliff and how terrified he'd been that the boy would be mistreated after he died. Thinking about the poor boy's situation now, my singing turned to crying.

But then I realized I'd do more good trying to fix some of his problems than crying over them. I got up and went out to find him. He wasn't far—I found him in the stable, brushing the new pony's coat and feeding the other animals as usual.

"Hurry up, Heathcliff!" I said. "The kitchen's so warm and cozy, and Joseph's upstairs. Come on, let me clean you up before Miss Cathy comes back out. Then you two can have the whole fireplace to yourselves and talk until bedtime."

He kept working without even looking at me.

"Come on—are you coming?" I pressed. "There's a little cake for each of you, and you'll need half an hour to get ready."

I waited five minutes, but when he didn't answer, I left.

Catherine ate dinner with her brother and sister-in-law. Joseph and I had our own miserable meal, with him preaching and me talking back. Heathcliff's cake and cheese sat on the table all night, untouched. He worked until nine o'clock, then marched silently to his room. Cathy stayed up late, preparing for her new friends' visit. She came to the kitchen once to look for him, but he was already gone. She only asked what was wrong with him before going back.

In the morning, he got up early and, since it was a holiday, took his bad mood out to the moors. He didn't come back until the family had left for church. The fasting and solitude seemed to have improved his spirits. He hung around me for a while, then suddenly worked up the courage to say, "Nelly, make me look decent. I'm going to be good."

"About time, Heathcliff," I said. "You've hurt Catherine—she probably wishes she'd never come home! It looks like you're jealous because everyone's paying more attention to her than you."

The idea of envying Catherine made no sense to him, but the idea of hurting her—that he understood perfectly.

"Did she say she was hurt?" he asked, looking deadly serious.

"She cried when I told her you were off again this morning."

"Well, I cried last night," he shot back, "and I had more reason to cry than she did."

"Yes—you had the reason of going to bed with wounded pride and an empty stomach," I said. "Proud people create their own misery. But if you're sorry for being so sensitive, you need to apologize when she comes in. Go up to her, offer to kiss her, and say—well, you know what to say. Just mean it. Don't act like her fancy dress has turned her into a stranger. Now, I've got dinner to prepare, but I'll make time to fix you up so Edgar Linton looks like a doll next to you—and he already does. You're younger but I'd bet you're taller and twice as broad across the shoulders. You could knock him flat in a second—you know you could, right?"

Heathcliff's face brightened for a moment, then darkened again as he sighed.

"But Nelly, if I knocked him down twenty times, that

wouldn't make him less handsome or me more so. I wish I had light hair and pale skin, and could dress and act like him, and had a chance of being as rich as he'll be!"

"And cried for mama at every little thing," I added, "and shook if a farm boy raised a fist at you, and stayed inside all day because of a little rain. Oh, Heathcliff, you're being pathetic! Come to the mirror and I'll show you what you should want. See those two lines between your eyes? And those thick brows that sink in the middle instead of arching up? And those black eyes buried so deep, never looking at anyone directly, just glinting from underneath like devil's spies? You need to smooth away those angry wrinkles, look people in the eye, and turn those demons into confident, innocent angels who trust people and see friends instead of enemies everywhere. Don't look like a beaten dog that knows it deserves its kicks but still hates the whole world for it."

"In other words, I should wish for Edgar Linton's big blue eyes and smooth forehead," he replied. "I do—and that won't help me get them."

"A good heart will give you a beautiful face, my boy," I continued, "even if you were completely black. And a bad heart will turn the prettiest face into something worse than ugly. Now that we've washed and combed you and you've stopped sulking—don't you think you look rather handsome? I do. You look like a prince in disguise. Who knows? Maybe your father was Emperor of China and your mother an Indian queen, each rich enough to buy Wuthering Heights and Thrushcross Grange with a week's income. Maybe wicked sailors kidnapped you and brought you to England. If I were you, I'd imagine I had noble blood—it would give me the courage and dignity to stand up to a petty farmer!"

I kept chattering away, and Heathcliff gradually stopped frowning and started to look almost happy—when suddenly we heard carriages rumbling up the road into the courtyard. He ran to the window while I rushed to the door, just in time to see the two Lintons climb out of their carriage, bundled in cloaks and furs, while the Earnshaws dismounted from their horses—they often rode to church in winter. Catherine took each child by the hand and brought them inside to the fire, which quickly brought color back to their pale faces.

I urged my companion to hurry and show his good mood now, and he was ready to—but as luck would have it, just as he opened the door from the kitchen, Hindley opened it from the other side. They met face to face, and the master—either irritated at seeing him clean and cheerful, or remembering his promise to Mrs. Linton—shoved him back hard and angrily ordered Joseph to "keep that fellow out of the room—send him to the attic until dinner's over. He'll be sticking his fingers in the pies and stealing fruit if we leave him alone with them for a minute."

"No, sir," I couldn't help saying, "he won't touch anything, and he should have his share of treats like the rest of us."

"He'll have his share of my hand if I catch him downstairs before dark," Hindley snarled. "Get out, you vagrant! What, trying to play the gentleman now? Wait till I get hold of that fancy hair—I'll make it even longer!"

"It's long enough already," Master Linton observed from the doorway. "I'm surprised it doesn't give him headaches. It's like a horse's mane hanging over his eyes!"

He meant no insult, but Heathcliff's violent temper couldn't handle even the appearance of mockery from someone he already saw as a rival. He grabbed a bowl of hot apple sauce—the first thing within reach—and threw it right in Edgar's face and neck. Edgar immediately started wailing, bringing Isabella and Catherine running. Mr. Earnshaw grabbed Heathcliff and dragged him to his room, where he obviously gave him a beating to cool his temper—he came back red-faced and breathless.

I got a dishcloth and rather roughly scrubbed Edgar's nose and mouth, saying it served him right for interfering. His sister started crying to go home, and Cathy stood there shocked, blushing for everyone.

"You shouldn't have spoken to him!" she scolded Master Linton. "He was already angry, and now you've ruined your visit, and he'll be whipped—I hate when he's whipped! I can't eat my dinner. Why did you speak to him, Edgar?"

"I didn't," the boy sobbed, pulling away from me to finish cleaning himself with his fancy handkerchief. "I promised Mama I wouldn't say one word to him, and I didn't."

"Well, don't cry," Catherine replied with contempt. "You're not dead. Don't make more trouble—my brother's coming. Be quiet! Hush, Isabella! Is anyone hurt?"

"There, there, children—to your seats!" Hindley called, bustling in. "That brute warmed me up nicely. Next time, Master Edgar, defend yourself—it'll give you an appetite!"

The little party calmed down at the sight of the feast. They were hungry after their ride and easily comforted since no real harm had been done. Mr. Earnshaw carved generous portions while his wife kept them entertained with lively conversation. I stood behind her chair and was hurt to see Catherine, dry-eyed and seemingly indifferent, start cutting into the goose wing on her plate.

An unfeeling child, I thought. *How easily she forgets her old playmate's troubles. I never thought she could be so selfish.*

She lifted a bite to her lips, then set it down. Her cheeks flushed and tears spilled over. She dropped her fork and quickly ducked under the tablecloth to hide her emotions. I didn't think her unfeeling for long—I could see she was in torment all day, desperately looking for a chance to be alone or to visit Heathcliff, who'd been locked up by the master. I discovered this when I tried to sneak him some food.

That evening we had a dance. Cathy begged for Heathcliff to be let out since Isabella Linton had no partner, but her pleas were ignored, and I had to fill in. The excitement of dancing lifted everyone's spirits, especially when the Gimmerton band arrived—fifteen musicians with trumpet, trombone, clarinets, bassoons, French horns, cello, plus singers. They made rounds to all the respectable houses every Christmas for donations, and we always loved hearing them. After the usual carols, we had them play songs and choruses. Mrs. Earnshaw loved music, so they gave us plenty.

Catherine loved the music too, but she said it sounded sweetest from the top of the stairs, so she went up in the dark. I followed. They shut the door below, not even noticing we'd left—the house was so packed with people. She didn't stop at the landing but climbed higher, all the way to the attic where Heathcliff was locked up, and called to him. He stubbornly refused to answer at first, but she kept at it until he finally agreed to talk to her through the boards.

I let the poor things talk undisturbed until I thought the music was ending and the singers would want refreshments. When I climbed up to warn her, instead of finding her in the hallway, I heard her voice coming from inside. The little monkey had crawled through the skylight of one attic, across the roof, and into his skylight. It took forever to coax her back out. When she finally emerged, Heathcliff came with her, and she insisted I take him to the kitchen since my fellow servant had gone to a neighbor's house to escape what he called our "devil's music."

I told them I wasn't about to encourage their tricks, but since the prisoner hadn't eaten since yesterday's dinner, I'd turn a blind eye to deceiving Mr. Hindley just this once. He came down. I set him a stool by the fire and offered him plenty of good food, but he was sick and could barely eat. My attempts to cheer him up were useless. He sat with his elbows on his knees, chin in his hands, lost in dark thoughts.

When I asked what he was thinking about, he answered grimly, "I'm trying to settle how I'll pay Hindley back. I don't care how long I wait, if I can only do it at last. I hope he won't die before I do!"

"For shame, Heathcliff!" I said. "It's God's job to punish wicked people. We should learn to forgive."

"No, God won't get the satisfaction that I will," he replied. "I just wish I knew the best way! Leave me alone, and I'll figure it out. While I'm planning that, I don't feel any pain."

"BUT MR. LOCKWOOD, I'm forgetting these tales can't be entertaining to you. I'm annoyed with myself for chattering on like this while your soup's gone cold and you're nodding off! I could have told you Heathcliff's history—everything you need to know—in half a dozen words."

With that, the housekeeper stood up and started putting away her sewing. But I wasn't ready to move from the fire-place, and I was far from falling asleep.

"Sit down, Mrs. Dean," I insisted. "Please, sit for another

half hour. You're telling the story exactly right—taking your time with it. That's how I like it, and you must finish the same way. I'm interested in every character you've mentioned."

"It's striking eleven, sir."

"No matter—I'm not used to going to bed early. One or two o'clock is early enough for someone who sleeps until ten."

"You shouldn't sleep until ten. The best part of the morning's long gone by then. Anyone who hasn't done half their day's work by ten o'clock risks leaving the other half undone."

"Nevertheless, Mrs. Dean, sit back down. Tomorrow I plan to extend the night into the afternoon. I can feel a stubborn cold coming on."

"I hope not, sir. Well, you must let me skip ahead about three years. During that time, Mrs. Earnshaw—"

"No, no, I won't allow any skipping! You know that mood when you're watching a cat groom its kitten so intently that if it misses one spot, it genuinely irritates you?"

"That sounds terribly lazy."

"On the contrary—it's exhaustingly active. That's my mood right now, so please continue with all the details. I've realized that people in these remote places mean more to each other than city people do—like a spider in a dungeon versus a spider in a cottage means more to their respective watchers. But it's not just about isolation. They live more genuinely here, more in themselves, less concerned with surface things and trivial matters. I could almost imagine falling in love here permanently—and I never believed in love lasting more than a year. It's like giving a hungry man one dish to focus all his appetite on versus presenting him with a French feast—he might enjoy the variety, but each individual dish barely registers."

"Oh, we're the same as anywhere else once you get to know us," Mrs. Dean said, looking puzzled by my philosophy.

"Excuse me," I responded, "but you, my good friend, are proof against that. Except for a few minor local phrases, you show none of the manners I'd expect from someone of your class. I'm sure you've thought more deeply than most servants. You've had to develop your mind since you haven't had opportunities to waste your life on silly distractions."

Mrs. Dean laughed. "I do consider myself a steady, reasonable person," she said. "Not just from living among the hills and seeing the same faces and routines year after year, but I've been through hard times that taught me wisdom. And I've read more than you'd think, Mr. Lockwood. There's not a book in this library I haven't looked at and learned something from—except the Greek and Latin ones, and the French, though I can tell them apart. That's as much as you can expect from a poor man's daughter. But if I'm going to tell this story properly, like a real gossip, I'd better continue. Instead of jumping three years, I'll move to the next summer—the summer of 1778, nearly twenty-three years ago."

8

On a beautiful June morning, my first precious charge—and the last of the ancient Earnshaw line—was born. We were working in the hayfields far from the house when the girl who usually brought our breakfast came running across the meadow an hour early, calling my name breathlessly.

"Such a gorgeous baby!" she gasped. "The most perfect boy you've ever seen! But the doctor says the mistress won't make it. He told Mr. Hindley she's had tuberculosis for months. Now that the baby's here, she has nothing left to keep her going—she'll be dead before winter. You need to come home right away, Nelly. You're to nurse the baby—feed him sugar and milk, take care of him day and night. I wish I were you, because he'll be all yours when there's no mistress!"

"But is she really that sick?" I asked, dropping my rake and tying on my bonnet.

"I suppose so, though she looks strong enough," the girl replied. "And she talks like she expects to watch him grow into a man. She's out of her mind with joy—he's that beautiful! If I were her, I know I wouldn't die. I'd get better just looking at him, no matter what Kenneth says. I was furious with that old fool. Dame Archer brought the angel down to show the master, and his face was just starting to light up when that miserable doctor steps forward and says, 'Earnshaw, it's a blessing your wife lived long enough to give you this son. When she arrived here, I knew we wouldn't have her long. Now I must tell you—the winter will probably kill her. Don't take it too hard; it can't be helped. Besides, you should've known better than to marry such a fragile girl.'"

"What did the master say to that?" I asked.

"I think he swore, but I wasn't listening—I was trying to see the baby," and she launched into another rapturous description. Just as excited as she was, I hurried home to see for myself, though my heart ached for Hindley. He only had room in his heart for two things—his wife and himself. He worshipped them both, adored one, and I couldn't imagine how he'd survive losing her.

When we reached Wuthering Heights, he was standing at the front door. As I passed him, I asked, "How's the baby?"

"Almost ready to run around, Nell!" he answered with a forced smile.

"And the mistress?" I ventured. "The doctor says she's—"

"Damn the doctor!" he interrupted, his face flushing. "Frances is perfectly fine. She'll be completely well by next week. Are you going upstairs? Tell her I'll come if she promises not to talk. I left because she wouldn't stop chattering, and Mr. Kenneth says she needs to rest."

I delivered his message to Mrs. Earnshaw. She seemed giddy and replied cheerfully, "I barely said a word, Ellen, and he's already stormed out twice, crying. Well, tell him I promise not to speak—but that doesn't mean I can't laugh at him!"

Poor soul. That bright spirit never failed her until a week

before she died. Her husband kept insisting—desperately, furiously—that she was getting better every day. When Kenneth warned him that medicine was useless at this stage and he was wasting money on visits, Hindley snapped back, "I know that—she's well—she doesn't need you anymore! She never had tuberculosis. It was just a fever and it's gone. Her pulse is as steady as mine, her cheek as cool."

He told his wife the same lie, and she seemed to believe him. But one night, as she leaned on his shoulder saying she thought she'd be able to get up tomorrow, a coughing fit seized her—just a small one. He lifted her in his arms; she wrapped her hands around his neck, her face changed, and she was dead.

As the girl had predicted, baby Hareton became entirely my responsibility. Mr. Earnshaw was satisfied as long as the child looked healthy and didn't cry in his presence. As for himself, he fell into desperate despair. His grief was the kind that won't cry out—he neither wept nor prayed. Instead, he cursed and raged against God and man, drowning himself in reckless drinking.

The servants couldn't stand his tyranny and cruelty for long. Only Joseph and I stayed. I couldn't abandon my little charge, and besides, I'd been Hindley's foster sister—I could forgive his behavior more easily than a stranger would. Joseph stayed to boss around the tenants and workers, and because condemning wickedness was his calling, and there was plenty to condemn.

The master's debauchery and terrible friends set a pretty example for Catherine and Heathcliff. His treatment of Heathcliff was enough to turn a saint into a demon. And truly, it seemed like the boy was possessed during that time. He took pleasure in watching Hindley destroy himself and grew more savage and sullen by the day. I can't even describe what a hellish house we lived in. The curate stopped visiting, and no respectable people came near us—except for Edgar Linton's visits to Miss Cathy.

At fifteen, she was the undisputed queen of the countryside—beautiful, proud, and headstrong. I'll admit I didn't like her much after she outgrew childhood, and I often tried to humble her arrogance, though she never held it against me. She had remarkable loyalty to old attachments—even Heathcliff kept his grip on her heart, and young Linton, for all his superiority, struggled to make as deep an impression.

Edgar was my late master—that's his portrait above the fireplace. His wife's used to hang beside it, but it's been removed, or you'd see something of what she was like. Can you make it out?

Mrs. Dean raised the candle, and I saw a gentle face that strongly resembled the young lady at the Heights, but with a more thoughtful, kinder expression. It made a lovely picture—light hair curling softly at the temples, large serious eyes, an almost too-graceful figure. I couldn't understand how Catherine Earnshaw could forget her first friend for such a person. I was even more puzzled how he, with a mind to match his refined appearance, could love my idea of Catherine Earnshaw.

"A very nice portrait," I said to the housekeeper. "Is it a good likeness?"

"Yes," she answered, "but he looked better when he was animated. That's his everyday expression—he generally lacked spirit."

Catherine had stayed friends with the Lintons since her five-week recovery at their house. Since she had no reason to show her rough side around them, and was smart enough to be ashamed of rudeness when they were so unfailingly polite, she unconsciously charmed the old couple with her sweet manners. She won Isabella's admiration and Edgar's complete devotion—achievements that flattered her ambition and led her to develop a double personality without exactly meaning to deceive anyone.

At the Grange, where she heard Heathcliff called a "vulgar young thug" and "worse than an animal," she was careful not to act like him. But at home, she saw no point in practicing manners that would only be mocked, or controlling her wild nature when it wouldn't earn her any credit or praise.

EDGAR RARELY WORKED up the courage to visit Wuthering Heights openly. He was terrified of Earnshaw's reputation and avoided running into him whenever possible. Still, we always tried to receive him politely. The master himself avoided offending Edgar, knowing why he came, and if he couldn't be pleasant, he simply stayed out of the way.

I think Catherine actually hated having Edgar visit the Heights. She wasn't manipulative, never played games with men's feelings, and clearly didn't want her two friends to meet. When Heathcliff insulted Linton to his face, she couldn't agree the way she did behind his back. And when Linton showed his disgust for Heathcliff, she couldn't brush off his comments as if they didn't matter.

I laughed plenty at her struggles and the endless problems she tried desperately to hide from my teasing. That sounds mean, but she was so proud it was impossible to feel sorry for her until life humbled her a bit. Eventually, she did break down and confide in me—there was literally no one else she could talk to.

One afternoon when Mr. Hindley was away, Heathcliff

decided to give himself the day off. He was about sixteen then, and though his features weren't ugly and he wasn't stupid, he'd developed this air of inner and outer repulsiveness that you'd never guess from looking at him now.

First off, he'd lost all benefit from his early education. Years of hard labor from dawn to dusk had killed any curiosity he'd once had for knowledge, any love of books or learning. That sense of superiority old Mr. Earnshaw had given him as a child had completely faded. He'd struggled for a long time to keep up with Catherine in her studies, giving up with silent but obvious heartbreak. Once he realized he'd inevitably fall below his former level, he gave up completely—nothing could convince him to try improving himself.

His appearance matched his mental decline. He developed a slouching walk and sullen look. His naturally quiet personality twisted into an almost idiotic level of antisocial bitterness. He seemed to take grim pleasure in making people hate rather than respect him—the few people he knew, anyway.

Catherine and he still spent all his free time together, but he'd stopped expressing his feelings for her in words. He pulled away from her affectionate gestures with angry suspicion, as if he knew there was no point in her wasting such affection on him.

On this particular day, he came into the house announcing he wasn't going to work, while I was helping Miss Cathy get dressed. She hadn't expected him to take the day off. Thinking she'd have the house to herself, she'd sent word to Edgar that her brother was gone and was getting ready to see him.

"Cathy, are you busy this afternoon?" Heathcliff asked. "Going anywhere?"

"No, it's raining," she answered.

"Then why are you wearing that silk dress? Nobody's coming here, I hope?"

"Not that I know of," she stammered. "But you should be in the field, Heathcliff. It's an hour past lunch—I thought you'd left."

"Hindley doesn't often free us from his damned presence," the boy observed. "I'm not working anymore today. I'll stay with you."

"Oh, but Joseph will tell," she suggested. "You'd better go!"

"Joseph's loading limestone on the far side of Penistone Crags. It'll take him till dark—he'll never know."

With that, he strolled to the fire and sat down. Catherine frowned, thinking for a moment—she needed to figure out how to handle this problem. "Isabella and Edgar Linton mentioned they might visit this afternoon," she said after a minute's silence. "Since it's raining, I doubt they'll come, but if they do, you'll get in trouble for nothing."

"Tell Ellen to say you're busy, Cathy," he persisted. "Don't throw me out for those pathetic, silly friends of yours! Sometimes I'm about to complain that they—but I won't—"

"That they what?" Catherine cried, looking at him with concern. "Oh, Nelly!" she added irritably, jerking her head away from my hands. "You've combed all the curl out of my hair! That's enough, leave me alone. What were you about to complain about, Heathcliff?"

"Nothing—just look at the calendar on that wall." He pointed to a framed sheet near the window. "The crosses mark the evenings you've spent with the Lintons, the dots are for those spent with me. See? I've marked every day."

"Yes—very childish, as if I'd notice!" Catherine replied peevishly. "What's the point of that?"

"To show that I DO notice," said Heathcliff.

"And should I always be sitting with you?" she demanded, growing more irritated. "What good does it do me? What do you talk about? You might as well be mute—or dead—for all you say or do to interest me!"

"You never told me before that I talked too little, or that you disliked my company, Cathy!" Heathcliff exclaimed, clearly upset.

"It's not company at all when people know nothing and say nothing," she muttered.

Her companion stood up, but before he could express his feelings further, they heard horse hooves on the flagstones. After a gentle knock, young Linton entered, his face glowing with delight at the unexpected invitation he'd received. Catherine couldn't help but notice the difference as one friend came in and the other went out. The contrast was like exchanging a bleak, hilly coal country for a beautiful fertile valley. His voice and greeting were as different as his appearance—he had a sweet, gentle way of speaking, pronouncing his words properly, not rough like we talked, but softer.

"I'm not too early, am I?" he said, glancing at me. I'd started wiping plates and organizing drawers at the far end of the dresser.

"No," Catherine answered. "What are you doing there, Nelly?"

"My work, Miss," I replied. (Mr. Hindley had ordered me to stay as a third party whenever Linton visited.)

She stepped behind me and whispered angrily, "Take yourself and your dusters and get out! When we have company, servants don't start scrubbing and cleaning in the same room!"

"It's a good opportunity while the master's away," I

answered loudly. "He hates when I clean these things while he's around. I'm sure Mr. Edgar will excuse me."

"I hate you cleaning while I'M around," the young lady said imperiously, not giving her guest time to speak. She still hadn't recovered from her argument with Heathcliff.

"I'm sorry, Miss Catherine," I responded, and kept working diligently.

Thinking Edgar couldn't see her, she snatched the cloth from my hand and pinched me hard on the arm, twisting the skin viciously. I've mentioned I didn't love her and occasionally enjoyed taking her down a peg. Besides, she'd hurt me badly. So I jumped up from my knees and cried out, "Oh, Miss, that's a nasty trick! You have no right to pinch me, and I won't stand for it!"

"I didn't touch you, you lying creature!" she cried, her fingers twitching to do it again, her ears red with rage. She never could hide her temper—it always set her whole face blazing.

"What's this, then?" I shot back, showing the purple bruise already forming.

She stamped her foot, hesitated for a moment, then—driven by the demon inside her—slapped me across the face. The stinging blow brought tears to my eyes.

"Catherine, love! Catherine!" Linton interrupted, shocked by this double offense of lying and violence from his idol.

"Get out, Ellen!" she repeated, trembling all over.

Little Hareton, who followed me everywhere, was sitting on the floor near me. Seeing my tears, he started crying too, sobbing complaints against "wicked Aunt Cathy." This turned her fury on the unlucky child. She grabbed his shoulders and shook him until the poor boy turned pale. Edgar instinctively grabbed her hands to free him.

In an instant, she wrenched one hand free and slapped Edgar across the ear—hard enough that he couldn't mistake it for playfulness. He stepped back in shock. I scooped up Hareton and carried him to the kitchen, leaving the door open because I was curious how they'd resolve this disaster. The insulted visitor moved toward his hat, pale, his lip trembling.

That's right, I thought. *Take the warning and leave! It's a kindness to see her true nature.*

"Where are you going?" Catherine demanded, moving toward the door.

He turned aside and tried to pass her.

"You can't go!" she exclaimed forcefully.

"I have to—and I will!" he replied quietly.

"No," she persisted, grabbing the door handle. "Not yet, Edgar Linton. Sit down. You can't leave me like this. I'll be miserable all night, and I won't be miserable for you!"

"Can I stay after you've struck me?" Linton asked.

Catherine was silent.

"You've made me afraid and ashamed of you," he continued. "I won't come here again!"

Her eyes began to glisten, her eyelids fluttering.

"And you told a deliberate lie!" he said.

"I didn't!" she cried, finding her voice. "I did nothing deliberately. Well, go then—get away! And now I'll cry—I'll cry myself sick!"

She dropped to her knees by a chair and began weeping in earnest. Edgar stuck to his decision as far as the courtyard, where he lingered. I decided to encourage him.

"She's a spoiled brat, sir," I called out. "As bad as any ruined child. You'd better ride home, or she'll make herself sick just to upset us."

The soft-hearted fool looked back through the window.

He had about as much power to leave as a cat has to abandon a half-killed mouse or a half-eaten bird. *Ah,* I thought, *there's no saving him. He's doomed and rushing toward his fate!*

And so it was. He turned abruptly, hurried back into the house, and shut the door behind him. When I went in later to warn them that Earnshaw had come home raging drunk, ready to tear the place apart (his usual state when drinking), I saw the quarrel had actually brought them closer together. It had broken through their youthful shyness and forced them to drop the pretense of friendship and admit they were in love.

News of Hindley's arrival sent Linton rushing to his horse and Catherine to her room. I went to hide little Hareton and remove the shot from the master's hunting rifle —he liked playing with it when drunk and insane, endangering anyone who provoked or even caught his attention. I'd developed this plan of unloading it so he'd do less damage if he actually pulled the trigger.

9

HE BURST IN, SWEARING HORRIBLY, AND CAUGHT ME IN THE act of hiding his son in the kitchen cupboard. Hareton lived in constant terror of his father—when Hindley was affectionate, he might squeeze and kiss the boy to death; when enraged, he might throw him into the fire or against the wall. The poor child stayed perfectly still wherever I put him.

"There! I've finally figured it out!" Hindley shouted, dragging me back by the neck like a dog. "By heaven and hell, you've both conspired to murder that child! Now I know why he's always hidden from me. But with Satan's help, I'll make you swallow this carving knife, Nelly! Don't laugh—I've just shoved Kenneth headfirst into the Blackhorse marsh, and two is the same as one. I need to kill some of you—I'll have no peace until I do!"

"But I don't like the carving knife, Mr. Hindley," I answered. "It's been cutting fish. I'd rather be shot, if you please."

"You'd rather be damned!" he said. "And so you shall. No

law in England can stop a man from keeping his house decent, and mine's disgusting! Open your mouth."

He held the knife in his hand and pushed its point between my teeth. But I was never really afraid of his crazy episodes. I spat it out and told him it tasted awful—I wouldn't take it for anything.

"Oh!" he said, releasing me. "I see that hideous little villain isn't Hareton. I beg your pardon, Nelly. If it was him, he deserves to be skinned alive for not running to welcome me, and for screaming like I'm some kind of monster. Unnatural brat, come here! I'll teach you to trick a good-hearted, deluded father. Now, don't you think the boy would look better with his hair cut? It makes dogs fiercer, and I love something fierce—get me scissors—something fierce and trim! Besides, it's ridiculous vanity to cherish our ears—we're stupid enough without them. Hush, child, hush! Well then, my darling! Shh, dry your eyes—there's a good boy. Kiss me. What! You won't? Kiss me, Hareton! Damn you, kiss me! By God, as if I would raise such a monster! I swear I'll break the brat's neck."

Poor Hareton was screaming and kicking in his father's arms with all his might, and his shrieks doubled when Hindley carried him upstairs and dangled him over the banister. I cried out that he'd terrify the child into fits and ran to rescue him. As I reached them, Hindley leaned forward on the rails to listen to a noise below, almost forgetting what he held in his hands.

"Who is that?" he asked, hearing someone approaching the stairs.

I leaned forward too, trying to signal Heathcliff—whose footsteps I recognized—not to come any closer. But the instant I looked away from Hareton, he gave a sudden twist, slipped from his father's careless grip, and fell.

There was barely time to feel the shock of horror before we saw the child was safe. Heathcliff had arrived underneath at exactly the right moment. By pure instinct, he caught the falling boy and set him on his feet, then looked up to see who'd dropped him.

A miser who'd sold a winning lottery ticket for five dollars, only to discover he'd lost five thousand, couldn't have looked more devastated than Heathcliff did when he saw Mr. Earnshaw above. His face showed, clearer than words, the most intense agony at having accidentally saved the life of his enemy's son—ruining his own revenge. If it had been dark, I believe he might have tried to correct his mistake by smashing Hareton's skull on the steps. But we'd all witnessed the rescue, and I quickly gathered my precious charge to my heart. Hindley came down more slowly, sobered and ashamed.

"It's your fault, Ellen," he said. "You should have kept him out of sight—you should have taken him from me! Is he hurt anywhere?"

"Hurt!" I cried angrily. "If he's not killed, he'll be traumatized! I wonder his mother doesn't rise from her grave to see how you treat him. You're worse than a savage—treating your own flesh and blood like that!"

He tried to touch the child, who'd stopped crying once he was safe with me. But the moment his father's finger touched him, he shrieked even louder and thrashed as if he'd have a seizure.

"Don't you touch him!" I continued. "He hates you—they all hate you—that's the truth! What a happy family you have, and what a mess you've become!"

"I'll become an even prettier mess, Nelly," laughed the deluded man, recovering his hardness. "For now, get yourself and him away. And listen, Heathcliff! Stay completely out of my reach and hearing. I wouldn't murder you tonight —unless, maybe, I set the house on fire. But that depends on my mood."

While saying this, he took a bottle of brandy from the dresser and poured some into a glass.

"No, don't!" I begged. "Mr. Hindley, please listen to reason. Have mercy on this poor boy, if you care nothing for yourself!"

"Anyone will do better for him than I will," he answered.

"Have mercy on your own soul!" I said, trying to snatch the glass from his hand.

"Not I! On the contrary, I'll take great pleasure in sending it to hell to punish its Maker," the blasphemer exclaimed. "Here's to its hearty damnation!"

He drank the liquor and impatiently ordered us out, following his command with a string of horrible curses too vile to repeat or remember.

"It's a pity he can't kill himself with drink," Heathcliff observed, muttering curses back when the door was shut. "He's trying his hardest, but his constitution won't let him. Dr. Kenneth says he'd bet his horse that Hindley will outlive any man around here and go to his grave an ancient sinner —unless some unusual accident happens."

I went into the kitchen and sat down to rock my little lamb to sleep. Heathcliff, I thought, had walked through to the barn. But it turned out he'd only gone to the other side of the settle, where he'd thrown himself on a bench by the wall, away from the fire, and stayed silent.

I was rocking Hareton on my knee, humming a song that began:

It was far in the night, and the children cried,
The mother beneath the earth heard that...

when Miss Cathy, who'd been listening to the chaos

from her room, put her head in and whispered, "Are you alone, Nelly?"

"Yes, Miss," I replied.

She entered and approached the fireplace. I looked up, expecting her to say something. Her face seemed troubled and anxious. Her lips were slightly parted as if she meant to speak, and she drew a breath—but it escaped as a sigh instead of words. I resumed my song, not having forgotten her recent behavior.

"Where's Heathcliff?" she said, interrupting me.

"Working in the stable," I answered.

He didn't contradict me—perhaps he'd fallen asleep. Another long pause followed, during which I noticed a tear or two roll down Catherine's cheek to the floor. *Is she actually sorry for her shameful behavior?* I wondered. *That would be a first. But even if she comes to the point—which she will—I won't help her!* No, she rarely felt troubled about anything except her own concerns.

"Oh, God!" she finally cried. "I'm so unhappy!"

"What a pity," I observed. "You're hard to please—so many friends, so few cares, and still you can't be content!"

"Nelly, will you keep a secret for me?" she asked, kneeling beside me and lifting her beautiful eyes to my face with that look that melts away anger, even when you have every right to be furious.

"Is it worth keeping?" I asked, less coldly.

"Yes, and it's driving me crazy, and I have to tell someone! I need to know what to do. Today, Edgar Linton asked me to marry him, and I've given him an answer. Now, before I tell you whether I said yes or no, you tell me which it should have been."

"Really, Miss Catherine, how would I know?" I replied. "Considering the performance you gave in front of him this afternoon, I'd say it would be wise to refuse him. If he asked you after that, he's either hopelessly stupid or recklessly brave."

"If you're going to talk like that, I won't tell you anything," she said peevishly, rising to her feet. "I accepted him, Nelly. Be quick and tell me if I was wrong!"

"You accepted him! Then what's the point of discussing it? You've given your word—you can't take it back."

"But tell me if I should have—please!" she exclaimed irritably, wringing her hands and frowning.

"There's a lot to consider before that question can be answered properly," I said seriously. "First and foremost, do you love Mr. Edgar?"

"Who could help it? Of course I do," she answered.

Then I put her through the following interrogation—not inappropriate for a twenty-two-year-old:

"Why do you love him, Miss Cathy?"

"That's nonsense—I just do. That's enough."

"Not at all. You must say why."

"Well, because he's handsome and pleasant to be with."

"Bad reason!" I commented.

"And because he's young and cheerful."

"Still bad."

"And because he loves me."

"Mediocre at best."

"And he'll be rich, and I'll be the most important woman in the neighborhood, and I'll be proud to have such a husband."

"Worst reason of all. Now, tell me how you love him?"

"The way everyone loves—you're being silly, Nelly."

"Not at all. Answer me."

"I love the ground under his feet, and the air over his head, and everything he touches, and every word he says. I love all his looks, all his actions, him entirely and completely. There!"

"And why?"

"Stop it—you're making fun of me! This is cruel! It's not a joke to me!" said the young lady, scowling and turning her face to the fire.

"I'm not joking at all, Miss Catherine," I replied. "You love Mr. Edgar because he's handsome, young, cheerful, rich, and loves you. The last one doesn't count for much—you'd probably love him without it, and with it you wouldn't, unless he had the other four qualities."

"No, definitely not. I'd only pity him—hate him, maybe, if he were ugly and crude."

"But there are other handsome, rich young men in the world—possibly more handsome and richer than he is. What's stopping you from loving them?"

"If there are any, I haven't met them. I've seen no one like Edgar."

"You might meet some. And he won't always be handsome and young, and may not always be rich."

"He is now, and I only care about the present. I wish you'd be reasonable."

"Well, that settles it. If you only care about the present, marry Mr. Linton."

"I don't need your permission—I SHALL marry him. But you still haven't told me if I'm right."

"Perfectly right, if people should marry only for the present. Now, let's hear what you're unhappy about. Your brother will be pleased. The old Lintons won't object, I think. You'll escape from a chaotic, miserable home to a wealthy, respectable one. You love Edgar, and Edgar loves you. Everything seems smooth and easy—where's the problem?"

"HERE! and HERE!" Catherine replied, striking one hand on her forehead and the other on her chest. "In whichever place the soul lives. In my soul and in my heart, I'm convinced I'm wrong!"

"That's very strange! I don't understand."

"It's my secret. But if you won't mock me, I'll explain it. I can't do it clearly, but I'll give you a sense of how I feel."

She sat beside me again, her face growing sadder and more serious, her clasped hands trembling.

"Nelly, do you ever have strange dreams?" she asked suddenly, after a few minutes of reflection.

"Yes, now and then," I answered.

"So do I. I've had dreams that have stayed with me forever and changed my ideas. They've gone through me like wine through water, and altered the color of my mind. And this is one of them. I'm going to tell you—but don't you dare smile at any part of it."

"Oh, don't, Miss Catherine!" I cried. "We're miserable enough without conjuring up ghosts and visions to confuse us. Come on, be happy and be yourself! Look at little Hareton! He's not dreaming anything terrible. How sweetly he smiles in his sleep!"

"Yes, and how sweetly his father curses alone in his room! You remember him, I'm sure, when he was just like that chubby baby—nearly as young and innocent. But Nelly, you have to listen. It's not long, and I can't pretend to be happy tonight."

"I won't hear it, I won't!" I repeated quickly.

I was superstitious about dreams then, and still am. Catherine had such an unusual darkness in her expression that I dreaded hearing something that might become a prophecy, foreseeing some terrible catastrophe. She was annoyed but didn't continue. Apparently changing the subject, she started again after a moment.

"If I were in heaven, Nelly, I'd be extremely miserable."

"Because you're not fit to go there," I answered. "All sinners would be miserable in heaven."

"But that's not why. I dreamt once that I was there."

"I told you I won't listen to your dreams, Miss Catherine! I'm going to bed," I interrupted again.

She laughed and held me down as I tried to leave my chair.

"This is nothing," she cried. "I was only going to say that heaven didn't seem to be my home. I broke my heart crying to come back to earth, and the angels were so angry that they threw me out into the middle of the moor on top of Wuthering Heights, where I woke up sobbing for joy. That explains my secret as well as anything. I have no more business marrying Edgar Linton than I have being in heaven. And if that wicked man in there hadn't brought Heathcliff so low, I wouldn't have thought of it. It would degrade me to marry Heathcliff now, so he'll never know how I love him. And that's not because he's handsome, Nelly, but because he's more myself than I am. Whatever our souls are made of, his and mine are the same, and Linton's is as different as a moonbeam from lightning, or frost from fire."

Before she finished speaking, I became aware of Heathcliff's presence. I noticed a slight movement, turned my head, and saw him rise from the bench and slip out silently. He'd listened until he heard Catherine say it would degrade her to marry him, and then he stayed to hear no more. My companion, sitting on the ground with her back to the settle, hadn't noticed him come or go. But I jumped up and told her to hush!

"Why?" she asked, looking nervously around.

"Joseph is here," I answered, catching the sound of his cart wheels on the road just in time. "And Heathcliff will come in with him. I'm not sure he wasn't at the door just now."

"Oh, he couldn't have heard me from the door!" she said. "Give me Hareton while you get supper ready, and when it's done, ask me to eat with you. I want to trick my guilty conscience and convince myself that Heathcliff has no idea about any of this. He doesn't, does he? He doesn't know what being in love means!"

"I see no reason why he shouldn't know as well as you," I replied. "And if you're his choice, he'll be the most unfortunate creature ever born! As soon as you become Mrs. Linton, he loses friend, love, everything! Have you considered how you'll bear the separation, and how he'll bear being completely abandoned in the world? Because, Miss Catherine—"

"Him abandoned! Us separated!" she exclaimed indignantly. "Who's going to separate us? They'll meet the fate of Milo—torn apart! Not as long as I live, Ellen—not for any mortal creature. Every Linton on earth could disappear before I'd consent to abandon Heathcliff. Oh, that's not what I intend—that's not what I mean! I wouldn't be Mrs. Linton if that was the price! He'll be as much to me as he's always been. Edgar must get over his hatred and tolerate him, at least. He will, when he learns my true feelings. Nelly, I see now you think I'm a selfish wretch. But didn't it ever occur to you that if Heathcliff and I married, we'd be beggars? But if I marry Linton, I can help Heathcliff rise and get him out of my brother's power."

"With your husband's money, Miss Catherine?" I asked. "You'll find him not as agreeable as you think. And though

I'm hardly one to judge, I think that's the worst motive you've given yet for marrying young Linton."

"It's not," she retorted. "It's the best! The others were just to satisfy my whims—and Edgar's feelings too, to make him happy. This is for someone who embodies my feelings for both Edgar and myself. I can't explain it properly, but surely you and everyone else sense that there is, or should be, an existence beyond yourself. What would be the point of my creation if I were entirely contained here? My greatest miseries in this world have been Heathcliff's miseries—I've watched and felt each one from the beginning. My greatest thought in living is him. If everything else perished and HE remained, I would still continue to exist. But if everything else remained and he were destroyed, the universe would become a complete stranger to me—I wouldn't seem part of it. My love for Linton is like the leaves in the woods—time will change it, I know, as winter changes the trees. My love for Heathcliff is like the eternal rocks beneath—a source of little visible delight, but necessary. Nelly, I AM Heathcliff! He's always, always in my mind—not as a pleasure, any more than I'm always a pleasure to myself, but as my own being. So don't talk about our separation again—it's impossible, and—"

She stopped and hid her face in my apron, but I yanked it away forcefully. I was completely out of patience with her foolishness!

"If I can make any sense of your nonsense, Miss," I said, "it only convinces me that you're either ignorant of the duties you take on in marriage, or you're a wicked, unprincipled girl. But don't trouble me with more secrets—I won't promise to keep them."

"You'll keep this one?" she asked eagerly.

"No, I won't promise," I repeated.

She was about to insist when Joseph came in, ending our conversation. Catherine moved to a corner and took care of Hareton while I finished making supper. After it was ready, my fellow servant and I argued about who should take some to Mr. Hindley, until everything was nearly cold. Finally we agreed we'd let him ask if he wanted any—we were especially afraid to go near him when he'd been alone for a while.

"Where's that boy from the field?" the old man demanded, looking around for Heathcliff. "What's he doing? Lazy good-for-nothing!"

"I'll call him," I replied. "He's in the barn, I'm sure."

I went and called, but got no answer. When I came back, I whispered to Catherine that he'd definitely heard a good part of what she'd said. I told her how I'd seen him leave the kitchen just as she was complaining about her brother's treatment of him. She jumped up in panic, dumped Hareton on the settle, and ran to find her friend herself—not stopping to think about why she was so flustered or how her words might have affected him.

She was gone so long that Joseph suggested we shouldn't wait any longer. He cleverly guessed they were staying away to avoid hearing his lengthy blessing. "They're ill-mannered enough for any foul behavior," he declared. And on their behalf, he added a special prayer to his usual fifteen-minute grace before meals, and would have added another at the end if his young mistress hadn't burst in with a frantic command that he must run down the road and find Heathcliff wherever he'd wandered off to, and bring him back immediately!

"I need to speak to him—I MUST, before I go upstairs," she said. "And the gate is open. He's somewhere out of earshot, because he won't answer even though I shouted as loud as I could from the top of the field."

Joseph objected at first, but she was too desperate to accept any argument. Finally he put on his hat and walked out grumbling. Meanwhile, Catherine paced the floor, exclaiming, "I wonder where he is—where can he be? What did I say, Nelly? I've forgotten. Was he upset by my bad mood this afternoon? God! Tell me what I said to hurt him? I wish he'd come. I really wish he would!"

"What a fuss over nothing!" I cried, though I was getting uneasy myself. "What a tiny thing frightens you! It's surely no great cause for alarm that Heathcliff would take a moonlight walk on the moors, or even be too sulky to talk to us from the hayloft. I bet he's hiding there. Watch me flush him out!"

I left to search again, but came back disappointed, and Joseph's search ended the same way.

"That boy gets worse and worse!" he observed, coming back in. "He's left the gate wide open, and Miss's pony has trampled two rows of corn and wandered right through to the meadow! The master will raise hell tomorrow, and rightly so. He's patience itself with such careless, worthless creatures—patience itself! But he won't be forever—you'll see, all of you! You mustn't drive him out of his mind for nothing!"

"Have you found Heathcliff, you idiot?" Catherine interrupted. "Have you been looking for him like I told you?"

"I'd rather look for the horse," he replied. "It would make more sense. But I can't look for horse or man on a night like this—black as a chimney! And Heathcliff won't come to MY whistle—maybe he'll hear YOU better!"

It WAS a very dark evening for summer. The clouds looked

ready to thunder, and I said we should all sit down—the coming rain would certainly bring him home without more trouble. But Catherine couldn't be calmed. She kept wandering from the gate to the door, too agitated to rest. Finally she took up a permanent position by the wall near the road, where—ignoring my protests, the rumbling thunder, and the large drops beginning to fall around her—she remained, calling at intervals, then listening, then crying openly.

She could outcry Hareton, or any child, when she really got going.

Around midnight, while we still sat up, the storm hit the Heights with full fury. There was violent wind along with thunder, and one or the other split a tree at the corner of the building. A huge branch fell across the roof and knocked down part of the east chimney, sending stones and soot crashing into the kitchen fire. We thought lightning had struck right in the middle of us. Joseph dropped to his knees, begging the Lord to remember the patriarchs Noah and Lot, and spare the righteous while punishing the ungodly, as in biblical times. I felt we were being judged too. The Jonah in my mind was Mr. Earnshaw, and I shook his door handle to make sure he was still alive. He answered loudly enough, which made Joseph pray even more dramatically about the difference between saints like himself and sinners like his master. But the storm passed in twenty minutes, leaving us all unharmed—except Cathy, who'd gotten completely soaked from her stubborn refusal to take shelter, standing without bonnet or shawl to catch as much rain as possible in her hair and clothes. She came in and collapsed on the settle, drenched, turning her face to the back and covering it with her hands.

"Well, Miss!" I exclaimed, touching her shoulder. "Are you trying to catch your death? Do you know what time it is? Half past twelve. Come to bed! There's no use waiting for that foolish boy anymore. He's gone to Gimmerton and he'll stay there now. He knows we wouldn't wait this late—or at least, he knows only Mr. Hindley would be up, and he'd rather avoid having the master open the door."

"No, no, he's not at Gimmerton," Joseph said. "I wouldn't be surprised if he's at the bottom of a bog. This storm wasn't for nothing, and you'd better watch out, Miss—you might be next. Thank Heaven for everything! All works together for good for the chosen ones, picked out from the rubbish! You know what Scripture says." And he began quoting several texts, giving us chapter and verse references.

After begging the stubborn girl to get up and change out of her wet things with no success, I left him preaching and her shivering, and went to bed with little Hareton, who slept soundly as if nothing was happening. I heard Joseph reading for a while longer, then his slow steps on the ladder, and then I fell asleep.

Coming down later than usual the next morning, I saw by the sunbeams coming through the shutters that Miss Catherine was still sitting by the fireplace. The house door was open too, light streaming through the unclosed windows. Hindley had come out and stood by the kitchen hearth, looking haggard and drowsy.

"What's wrong, Cathy?" he was saying when I entered. "You look like a drowned puppy. Why are you so damp and pale, child?"

"I got wet," she answered reluctantly, "and I'm cold, that's all."

"Oh, she's been naughty!" I cried, seeing the master was reasonably sober. "She got soaked in yesterday evening's storm, and she's sat there all night. I couldn't get her to move."

Mr. Earnshaw stared at us in surprise. "All night?" he repeated. "What kept her up? Not fear of thunder, surely? That ended hours ago."

Neither of us wanted to mention Heathcliff's absence as long as we could hide it, so I said I didn't know why she'd stayed up, and she said nothing. The morning was fresh and cool. I opened the window, and the room filled with sweet scents from the garden, but Catherine called irritably, "Ellen, shut the window. I'm freezing!" Her teeth chattered as she huddled closer to the dying embers.

"She's ill," said Hindley, taking her wrist. "I suppose that's why she wouldn't go to bed. Damn it! I don't want more sickness here. What made you go out in the rain?"

"Running after the boys, as usual!" Joseph croaked, seizing the opportunity our hesitation gave him to thrust in his poisonous opinion. "If I were you, master, I'd slam the doors in all their faces! Every day you're gone, that Linton boy comes sneaking here. And Miss Nelly, fine woman she is, sits watching for you in the kitchen—as soon as you come in one door, he goes out the other. Then our grand lady goes courting on her own! Fine behavior, lurking in the fields after midnight with that foul, frightening heathen devil, Heathcliff! They think I'm blind, but I'm not! I saw young Linton coming and going, and I saw YOU"—directing this at me—"you good-for-nothing, sloppy witch! Run up and lock yourself in the house the minute you heard the master's horse on the road."

"Silence, eavesdropper!" cried Catherine. "None of your insolence! Edgar Linton came yesterday by chance, Hindley, and I told him to leave because I knew you wouldn't want to meet him in your condition."

"You're lying, Cathy, obviously," her brother answered, "and you're an idiot! But never mind Linton now—tell me, were you with Heathcliff last night? Tell the truth. You don't need to worry about harming him—though I hate him as much as ever, he did me a favor recently that makes my conscience tender about breaking his neck. To prevent that, I'll send him away this very morning. And after he's gone, I advise you all to watch out—I'll only be harder on the rest of you."

"I never saw Heathcliff last night," Catherine answered, beginning to sob desperately. "And if you throw him out, I'll go with him. But maybe you'll never get the chance—maybe he's already gone." Here she burst into uncontrollable grief, and the rest of her words were incomprehensible.

Hindley unleashed a torrent of scornful abuse and ordered her to her room immediately, or she'd really have something to cry about. I helped her obey, and I'll never forget the scene she made when we reached her bedroom—it terrified me. I thought she was going mad and begged Joseph to run for the doctor.

It turned out to be the beginning of delirium. Mr. Kenneth, as soon as he saw her, pronounced her dangerously ill with fever. He bled her and told me to feed her only whey and water-gruel, and make sure she didn't throw herself down the stairs or out the window. Then he left—he had plenty to do in the parish, where cottages were two or three miles apart.

Though I wasn't the gentlest nurse, and Joseph and the master were no better, and though our patient was as difficult and stubborn as any patient could be, she pulled through. Old Mrs. Linton visited several times, putting things right, scolding and ordering us all around. When Catherine was recovering, she insisted on taking her to Thrushcross Grange, for which we were very grateful. But the poor woman had reason to regret her kindness—she and her husband both caught the fever and died within days of each other.

Our young lady returned to us more spoiled, passionate, and haughty than ever. Heathcliff hadn't been heard from since the night of the thunderstorm. One day, when she'd provoked me terribly, I had the misfortune to blame his disappearance on her—where the blame truly belonged, as she well knew. After that, for several months, she wouldn't speak to me except as a servant. Joseph was also banned—he'd speak his mind and lecture her like she was a little girl, while she considered herself a woman, our mistress, and thought her recent illness entitled her to special treatment. The doctor had said she shouldn't be crossed much, that she should have her way, and in her eyes it was practically murder for anyone to contradict her. She kept away from Mr. Earnshaw and his friends. Warned by Kenneth about the fits that often came with her rages, her brother let her do whatever she wanted and generally avoided triggering her temper. He was far too indulgent with her whims—not from affection, but from pride. He desperately wanted her to bring honor to the family by marrying into the Lintons, and as long as she left him alone, she could treat us like slaves for all he cared!

Edgar Linton, like countless men before and after him, was infatuated. He believed himself the happiest man alive the day he led her to Gimmerton Chapel, three years after his father's death.

I really didn't want to leave Wuthering Heights, but I was persuaded to accompany her here. Little Hareton was nearly five years old, and I'd just begun teaching him his letters. We had a sad parting, but Catherine's tears were more powerful than ours. When I refused to go, and when my refusal didn't move her, she went crying to her husband and brother. Edgar offered me generous wages; Hindley ordered me to pack—he wanted no women in the house now that there was no mistress, and as for Hareton, the curate would take care of him eventually. So I had only one choice—to do as I was told. I told the master he was getting rid of all decent people just to ruin himself faster. I kissed Hareton goodbye, and since then he's been a stranger. It's strange to think, but I'm sure he's completely forgotten Ellen Dean, and that he was once everything to her, and she to him!

At this point in the housekeeper's story, she happened to glance at the clock over the fireplace and was amazed to see it was half past one. She wouldn't hear of staying a second longer. In truth, I was rather inclined to postpone the rest of her story myself. And now that she's gone to rest, and I've thought for another hour or two, I'll summon the courage to go to bed too, despite my aching head and limbs.

10

A CHARMING INTRODUCTION TO THE HERMIT LIFE! FOUR weeks of torture—tossing, turning, and sickness. These bitter northern winds, impassable roads, and country doctors who take forever to arrive! Worst of all, the complete absence of human faces. And now Dr. Kenneth tells me I won't be able to leave the house until spring.

Mr. Heathcliff honored me with a visit about seven days ago. He'd sent me a pair of grouse—the last of the hunting season. The bastard! He's not entirely innocent in my getting sick, and I almost told him so. But how could I be angry with a man charitable enough to sit by my bedside for an hour, talking about something other than medicine and treatments?

This is a decent break from the misery. I'm too weak to read, but I could enjoy something interesting. Why not have Mrs. Dean come up and finish her story? I remember where she left off—her hero had vanished for three years and never been heard from, and the heroine had gotten married. I'll ring for her. She'll be thrilled to find me well enough for conversation.

Mrs. Dean arrived.

"Twenty minutes until your medicine, sir," she began.

"Forget the medicine!" I replied. "I want to hear—"

"The doctor says you must take the powders."

"Fine, fine! But don't interrupt me. Come sit here. Keep your hands away from those awful bottles. Get your knitting—that's good. Now continue Mr. Heathcliff's story from where you left off. What happened to him? Did he finish his education abroad and come back a gentleman? Did he go to university on scholarship? Escape to America and make his fortune? Or make money faster on the English highways as a thief?"

"He might have done all of those things, Mr. Lockwood, but I couldn't swear to any of them. As I said before, I don't know how he got his money or how he transformed himself from savage ignorance into what he became. But if you'll let me, I'll tell it my own way—if you think it will entertain rather than tire you. Are you feeling better this morning?"

"Much better."

"Good to hear."

I TOOK Miss Catherine with me to Thrushcross Grange, and to my pleasant surprise, she behaved infinitely better than I'd dared hope. She seemed almost too fond of Mr. Linton, and even showed real affection to his sister. They were both very attentive to her comfort, certainly. But it wasn't the thorn bending to the honeysuckles—it was the honeysuckles embracing the thorn. There was no compromise: Catherine stood firm while the others yielded. And who can be bad-tempered when they meet neither opposition nor indifference?

I noticed Mr. Edgar had a deep fear of upsetting her. He hid it from her, but if he ever heard me answer sharply, or saw another servant look annoyed at one of her imperious commands, he'd frown with displeasure—though he never frowned on his own behalf. He often scolded me about my attitude, insisting that a knife wound would hurt less than seeing his wife upset. Not wanting to distress such a kind master, I learned to hold my tongue. For six months, the gunpowder lay harmless as sand because no spark came near it.

Catherine had periods of gloom and silence. Her husband respected these with sympathetic quiet, blaming them on her constitution being weakened by her dangerous illness—she'd never been prone to depression before. When her sunshine returned, he answered with his own. I believe they were truly happy, and that happiness was growing.

Then it ended.

Well, we all must look out for ourselves in the long run. The mild and generous are just more subtly selfish than the domineering. It ended when circumstances made each realize they weren't the most important thing in the other's thoughts.

On a mellow September evening, I was coming from the garden with a heavy basket of apples I'd been gathering. Dusk had fallen, and the moon hung over the high courtyard wall, casting strange shadows in the corners of the building. I set my basket on the kitchen doorstep and paused to rest, breathing in the soft, sweet air. My eyes were on the moon, my back to the entrance, when I heard a voice behind me:

"Nelly, is that you?"

It was a deep voice with a foreign tone, yet something in

how it pronounced my name sounded familiar. I turned around fearfully to see who spoke—the doors were shut, and I'd seen no one approaching. Something stirred in the porch. Moving closer, I made out a tall man in dark clothes, with dark face and hair. He leaned against the side, his fingers on the latch as if about to let himself in.

Who can it be? I thought. *Mr. Earnshaw? No, the voice sounds nothing like his.*

"I've been waiting here an hour," he said while I stared. "Everything's been dead silent the whole time. I didn't dare go in. You don't recognize me? Look—I'm not a stranger!"

A ray of moonlight fell on his face. His cheeks were sallow, half-covered with black whiskers, his brows heavy, his eyes deep-set and strange. But I remembered those eyes.

"What!" I cried, raising my hands in amazement, uncertain if I was seeing a ghost. "You've come back? Is it really you?"

"Yes, Heathcliff," he replied, glancing from me up to the windows, which reflected dozens of moons but showed no lights from inside. "Are they home? Where is she? Nelly, you're not glad to see me! Don't look so disturbed. Is she here? Speak! I need one word with her—your mistress. Go tell her someone from Gimmerton wants to see her."

"How will she take it?" I exclaimed. "What will she do? The shock—it'll drive her out of her mind! And you ARE Heathcliff! But so changed! I can't comprehend it. Have you been a soldier?"

"Go deliver my message," he interrupted impatiently. "I'm in hell until you do!"

He lifted the latch and I went inside, but when I reached the parlor where Mr. and Mrs. Linton were sitting, I couldn't bring myself to proceed. Finally I made an excuse to ask if they wanted the candles lit, and opened the door.

They sat together at a window that looked out beyond the garden trees and wild green park to the valley of Gimmerton. A long line of mist wound nearly to its top—just after you pass the chapel, the stream from the marshes joins a brook that follows the glen's curve. Wuthering Heights rose above this silver vapor, though our old house was invisible, dipping down on the far side. Both the room and its occupants, and the scene they gazed on, looked wonderfully peaceful.

I shrank from my errand and was actually leaving without speaking when common sense forced me to return and mutter, "A person from Gimmerton wishes to see you, ma'am."

"What does he want?" Mrs. Linton asked.

"I didn't ask," I answered.

"Well, close the curtains, Nelly," she said, "and bring up tea. I'll be back directly."

She left the room. Mr. Edgar asked casually, "Who was it?"

"Someone mistress doesn't expect," I replied. "That Heathcliff—you remember him, sir—who used to live at Mr. Earnshaw's."

"What! The stray—the farmhand?" he cried. "Why didn't you say so to Catherine?"

"Hush! You mustn't call him those names, master," I said. "She'd be heartbroken to hear you. She was nearly destroyed when he ran off. I imagine his return will be like Christmas to her."

Mr. Linton walked to a window overlooking the courtyard. He opened it and leaned out. They must have been below, because he called quickly, "Don't stand there, love! Bring the person in, if it's anyone special."

Soon I heard the latch click, and Catherine flew upstairs,

breathless and wild—too excited to show simple gladness. Indeed, by her face, you'd have thought something terrible had happened.

"Oh, Edgar, Edgar!" she panted, flinging her arms around his neck. "Oh, Edgar darling! Heathcliff's come back —he has!" And she squeezed him even tighter.

"Well, well," her husband said irritably, "don't strangle me for that! He never struck me as such a wonderful treasure. There's no need to be hysterical!"

"I know you didn't like him," she answered, trying to contain her delight. "But for my sake, you must be friends now. Should I tell him to come up?"

"Here?" he said. "Into the parlor?"

"Where else?" she asked.

He looked annoyed and suggested the kitchen as more suitable. Mrs. Linton eyed him with a mocking expression—half angry, half laughing at his snobbery.

"No," she added after a moment. "I can't sit in the kitchen. Set two tables here, Ellen—one for your master and Miss Isabella, being gentry; the other for Heathcliff and myself, being of the lower orders. Will that please you, dear? Or should I have a fire lit elsewhere? If so, give directions. I'll run down and secure my guest. I'm afraid the joy is too great to be real!"

She was about to dash off again, but Edgar stopped her.

"YOU invite him up," he said to me. "And Catherine, try to be glad without being absurd. The whole household doesn't need to witness you welcoming a runaway servant like a brother."

I went down and found Heathcliff waiting under the porch, clearly expecting an invitation. He followed me without a word, and I brought him to the master and mistress, whose flushed cheeks showed they'd been arguing.

But Catherine's face glowed with different emotion when her friend appeared. She sprang forward, took both his hands, and led him to Linton. Then she seized Linton's reluctant fingers and crushed them into Heathcliff's.

Now, fully revealed by fire and candlelight, I was more amazed than ever at Heathcliff's transformation. He'd become a tall, athletic, well-built man who made my master look slender and boyish by comparison. His upright posture suggested military training. His face looked much older and more decisive than Mr. Linton's—intelligent, with no trace of his former degradation. A half-civilized ferocity still lurked in his dark brows and black-fire eyes, but it was controlled. His manner was dignified, free of roughness, though stern rather than graceful.

My master's surprise equaled or exceeded mine. He stood for a minute at a loss, unsure how to address the "farmhand," as he'd called him. Heathcliff dropped Edgar's hand and stood looking at him coolly, waiting for him to speak.

"Sit down, sir," Edgar said at last. "Mrs. Linton, remembering old times, would have me give you a warm reception. And of course, I'm gratified when anything pleases her."

"And I also," Heathcliff answered, "especially if it's something I'm part of. I'll stay an hour or two willingly."

He took a seat opposite Catherine, who kept her eyes fixed on him as if she feared he'd vanish if she looked away. He didn't often raise his eyes to hers—a quick glance now and then was enough—but each time it reflected back more confidently the undisguised delight he saw in her face. They were too absorbed in their mutual joy to feel embarrassed.

Not so Mr. Edgar. He grew pale with pure annoyance, a feeling that peaked when his wife rose, stepped across the rug, seized Heathcliff's hands again, and laughed like someone possessed.

"I'll think it's a dream tomorrow!" she cried. "I won't be able to believe I've seen, and touched, and spoken to you again. And yet, cruel Heathcliff! You don't deserve this welcome. To be absent and silent for three years, and never think of me!"

"More than you thought of me," he murmured. "I heard about your marriage, Cathy, not long ago. While I waited in the yard below, I made a plan—get one glimpse of your face, see your surprise, maybe catch some hint of pleasure at seeing me. Then I'd settle my score with Hindley and cheat the hangman by killing myself afterward. But your welcome has changed everything. You drove those dark thoughts away. Just beware. If you're cold to me next time we meet, they'll come back. You won't push me away again so easily. You really were sorry for me, weren't you? Well, you had reason to be. I've fought through a bitter life since I last heard your voice. You must forgive me—I struggled only for you!"

"Catherine, unless we're having cold tea, please come to the table," Linton interrupted, trying to maintain his normal tone and proper politeness. "Mr. Heathcliff will have a long walk, wherever he's staying tonight, and I'm thirsty."

She took her place at the tea table, and Miss Isabella came when summoned by the bell. After pulling their chairs forward, I left the room. The meal barely lasted ten minutes. Catherine's cup was never filled—she could neither eat nor drink. Edgar spilled tea in his saucer and hardly swallowed a bite. Their guest didn't stay more than an hour longer. As he left, I asked if he was going to Gimmerton.

"No, to Wuthering Heights," he answered. "Mr. Earnshaw invited me when I called this morning."

Mr. Earnshaw invited HIM! And HE called on Mr. Earnshaw! I puzzled over this painfully after he left. Was he becoming a hypocrite, coming to the country to cause trouble under cover? I had a deep feeling he should have stayed away.

Around midnight, I was woken from my first sleep by Mrs. Linton gliding into my room, sitting on my bedside, and pulling my hair to wake me.

"I can't rest, Ellen," she said by way of apology. "And I want some living creature to share my happiness! Edgar is sulking because I'm glad about something that doesn't interest him. He refuses to speak except to make petty, silly comments. He said I was cruel and selfish for wanting to talk when he was so sick and sleepy. He always manages to be sick at the slightest upset! I said a few nice things about Heathcliff, and he—either from a headache or jealousy—started to cry. So I got up and left him."

"What use is it praising Heathcliff to him?" I answered. "As boys they hated each other, and Heathcliff would hate hearing Edgar praised just as much. It's human nature. Leave Mr. Linton alone about him, unless you want an open fight between them."

"But doesn't it show great weakness?" she persisted. "I'm not jealous. I never feel hurt by Isabella's golden hair and pale skin, her dainty elegance, and how the whole family adores her. Even you, Nelly—if we argue sometimes, you always take Isabella's side, and I give in like a foolish mother. I call her darling and flatter her into a good mood. It pleases her brother to see us getting along, and that pleases me. But they're very much alike—they're spoiled children who think the world was made for them. And though I humor both, I think a sharp lesson might improve them."

"You're mistaken, Mrs. Linton," I said. "They humor YOU. I know what would happen if they didn't. You can afford to indulge their little whims as long as their business is anticipating all your desires. But you might eventually fight over something that matters equally to both sides—and then those you call weak are very capable of being as stubborn as you."

"And then we'll fight to the death, won't we, Nelly?" she laughed. "No! I tell you, I have such faith in Linton's love, I believe I could kill him and he wouldn't want revenge."

I advised her to value him more for his affection.

"I do," she answered, "but he doesn't need to whine over trifles. It's childish. Instead of crying because I said Heathcliff was now worthy of anyone's respect, and it would honor the finest gentleman in the country to be his friend, Edgar should have said it for me and been delighted out of sympathy. He must get used to him, and he might as well like him—considering how Heathcliff has reason to hate him, I'm sure he behaved excellently!"

"What do you think of him going to Wuthering Heights?" I asked. "He seems reformed in every way—quite a Christian, offering friendship to all his enemies!"

"He explained it," she replied. "I wondered as much as you. He said he called to get information about me from you, thinking you still lived there. Joseph told Hindley, who came out and started questioning him about what he'd been doing and how he'd been living, then finally invited him in. There were people playing cards. Heathcliff joined them and my brother lost money to him. Finding him well-supplied with cash, Hindley asked him to come again in the evening, which he agreed to. Hindley is too reckless to choose his company wisely—he doesn't bother thinking about why he should mistrust someone he's terribly wronged. But Heathcliff says his main reason for reconnecting with his old tormentor is wanting to stay within walking distance of the Grange, his attachment to the house where we lived together, and hope that he'll see me more often there than if he settled in Gimmerton. He plans to offer good money for permission to lodge at the Heights, and my brother's greed will definitely make him accept. He was always greedy—though what he grabs with one hand he throws away with the other."

"What a nice place for a young man to live!" I said. "Aren't you afraid of the consequences, Mrs. Linton?"

"Not for my friend," she replied. "Heathcliff's strong mind will keep him from danger. I'm a little worried for Hindley—but he can't become morally worse than he already is, and I'll stand between him and physical harm. Tonight's events have reconciled me to God and humanity! I'd been rebelling so angrily against Providence. Oh, Nelly, I've endured very, very bitter misery! If Heathcliff knew how bitter, he'd be ashamed to cloud my happiness now with petty complaints. It was kindness to him that made me bear my suffering alone—if I'd shown him the agony I felt, he would've wanted it to end it as desperately as I did. But that's over now, and I won't punish him for his foolishness. I can bear anything now! If the lowest creature alive slapped me, I'd not only turn the other cheek, I'd apologize for provoking it. And to prove it, I'll go make peace with Edgar right now. Good night! I'm an angel!"

With this self-satisfied conviction she left, and her success was obvious the next day. Mr. Linton had not only given up his sulking (though his spirits still seemed dampened by Catherine's excessive energy), but he didn't object when she took Isabella to Wuthering Heights that afternoon. She rewarded him with such sweetness and affection that the house became paradise for several days, both master and servants basking in the perpetual sunshine.

Heathcliff—Mr. Heathcliff, I should say now—was cautious about visiting Thrushcross Grange at first, seeming to gauge how far its owner would tolerate his presence. Catherine also thought it wise to moderate her joy at seeing him, and he gradually established his right to be expected. He kept much of the reserve that marked his boyhood, which helped prevent any dramatic displays of feeling. My master's uneasiness quieted down, and other circumstances soon diverted his worry elsewhere.

His new source of trouble came from an unexpected misfortune—Isabella Linton developing a sudden, irresistible attraction to the tolerated guest. She was then a charming eighteen-year-old, childlike in manner but with sharp wit, keen feelings, and a sharp temper when irritated. Her brother, who loved her dearly, was appalled by this bizarre preference. Setting aside the disgrace of an alliance with a nameless man, and the possibility that his property might pass to such a person if he had no male heirs, he understood Heathcliff's nature. He knew that though Heathcliff's exterior had changed, his mind was unchangeable and unchanged. He dreaded that mind—it revolted him—he shrank from the idea of putting Isabella in its keeping. He would have been even more horrified if he'd known her attachment was unrequested and given where it awakened no return of feeling. The minute he discovered it existed, he blamed Heathcliff's deliberate scheming.

We'd all noticed for some time that Miss Linton was fretting and pining over something. She grew irritable and tiresome, constantly snapping at and teasing Catherine, risking exhausting her limited patience. We excused her somewhat, thinking she was ill—she was wasting away before our eyes. But one day, when she'd been particularly difficult—refusing breakfast, complaining the servants didn't obey her, that the mistress ignored her and Edgar neglected her, that she'd caught cold from open doors, that we let the parlor fire die just to spite her, plus a hundred more trivial complaints—Mrs. Linton firmly insisted she go to bed and, after scolding her thoroughly, threatened to send for the doctor. Mention of Dr. Kenneth made her instantly claim her health was perfect, and only Catherine's harshness made her unhappy.

"How can you say I'm harsh, you naughty pet?" cried the mistress, amazed at the unreasonable accusation. "You're surely losing your mind. When have I been harsh? Tell me!"

"Yesterday," Isabella sobbed, "and now!"

"Yesterday!" said her sister-in-law. "On what occasion?"

"On our walk along the moor. You told me to wander where I pleased while you strolled with Mr. Heathcliff!"

"And that's your idea of harshness?" Catherine laughed. "Wasn't it obvious your company was unwanted? We didn't care whether you stayed with us or not. I just thought Heathcliff's conversation wouldn't interest you."

"Oh no," the young lady wept, "you wished me away because you knew I wanted to be there!"

"Is she sane?" Mrs. Linton asked, turning to me. "I'll repeat our conversation word for word, Isabella, and you tell me what charm it could have had for you."

"I don't care about the conversation," she answered. "I wanted to be with—"

"Well?" said Catherine, noticing her hesitation.

"With him! And I won't always be sent away!" she

continued, firing up. "You're a dog in the manger, Cathy—you don't want anyone to be loved but yourself!"

"You're an impertinent little monkey!" exclaimed Mrs. Linton in surprise. "But I won't believe this idiocy! It's impossible you could want Heathcliff's admiration—that you think him agreeable! I hope I've misunderstood you, Isabella?"

"No, you haven't," said the infatuated girl. "I love him more than you ever loved Edgar, and he might love me if you'd let him!"

"I wouldn't be you for a kingdom!" Catherine declared emphatically, and she seemed to mean it. "Nelly, help me convince her she's mad. Tell her what Heathcliff is—an untamed creature, without refinement or cultivation, a barren wilderness of thorns and stone. I'd as soon put that little canary outside on a winter's day as recommend you give your heart to him! It's deplorable ignorance of his character, child, nothing else, that makes you dream this way. Don't imagine he conceals depths of kindness and affection beneath a stern exterior! He's not a rough diamond or a pearl-containing oyster of a rustic—he's a fierce, pitiless, wolfish man. I never say to him, 'Leave this or that enemy alone because it would be ungenerous or cruel to harm them.' I say, 'Leave them alone because I'd hate them to be wronged.' And he'd crush you like a sparrow's egg, Isabella, if he found you troublesome. I know he couldn't love a Linton. Yet he'd be quite capable of marrying your fortune and expectations—greed is becoming his besetting sin. There's my picture of him, and I'm his friend—so much so that if he'd seriously tried to catch you, I might have kept quiet and let you fall into his trap."

Miss Linton looked at her sister-in-law with indignation.

"For shame! For shame!" she repeated angrily. "You're worse than twenty enemies, you poisonous friend!"

"Ah! You won't believe me?" said Catherine. "You think I speak from wicked selfishness?"

"I'm certain you do," Isabella retorted, "and I shudder at you!"

"Good!" cried Catherine. "Try pursuing him yourself if that's how you feel. I'm done arguing. Your stubborn insolence wins."

"And I must suffer because of her selfishness!" Isabella sobbed as Mrs. Linton left the room. "All she wants is to keep him for herself—she's ruined my only comfort. But she's lying, isn't she? Mr. Heathcliff isn't a devil. He has an honorable soul, a true one—otherwise how could he remember her so devotedly all these years?"

"Banish him from your thoughts, Miss," I said. "He's a bird of bad omen—no match for you. Mrs. Linton spoke strongly, but I can't contradict her. She knows his heart better than I or anyone else, and she'd never make him seem worse than he is. Honest people don't hide their deeds. How has he been living? How did he get rich? Why is he staying at Wuthering Heights with a man he hates? They say Mr. Earnshaw has gotten worse since he came. They stay up all night together, and Hindley's been borrowing money on his land, doing nothing but gambling and drinking. I heard just last week—Joseph told me when I met him at Gimmerton."

Joseph had painted an ugly picture: violence at the Heights, someone nearly losing a finger in a fight, Hindley so drunk he challenged God himself, while Heathcliff laughed and counted his winnings. He'd said Catherine's father's gold was flowing into Heathcliff's pocket while her brother galloped down the road to ruin.

"Now, Miss Linton," I concluded, "Joseph's an old rascal but no liar. If his account of Heathcliff's conduct is true, you'd never want such a husband, would you?"

"You're just like the others, Ellen!" she replied. "I won't listen to your slander. What malice you must have, trying to convince me there's no happiness in the world!"

Whether she would have gotten over this fancy on her own or nursed it forever, I can't say—she had little time to reflect. The next day there was a justice meeting in town that my master had to attend. Mr. Heathcliff, knowing he'd be absent, called earlier than usual. Catherine and Isabella were sitting in the library on hostile terms but silent. Isabella was alarmed by her recent indiscretion, having revealed her secret feelings in a passionate outburst. Catherine, after thinking it over, was truly offended with her companion and inclined to make her regret her boldness.

She laughed when she saw Heathcliff pass the window. I was sweeping the hearth and noticed a mischievous smile on her lips. Isabella, absorbed in her thoughts or a book, didn't move until the door opened—too late to escape, which she would gladly have done if possible.

"Come in, perfect timing!" exclaimed the mistress cheerfully, pulling a chair to the fire. "Here are two people badly needing a third to thaw the ice between them, and you're exactly who we'd both choose. Heathcliff, I'm proud to show you someone who adores you more than I do. You should feel flattered. No, it's not Nelly—don't look at her! My poor little sister-in-law is breaking her heart just contemplating your physical and moral beauty. You have the power to become Edgar's brother! No, no, Isabella, you can't run away," she continued, playfully restraining the mortified girl who had risen indignantly. "We were quarreling like cats about you, Heathcliff. She swore she loves you far more than

I ever could. And she informed me that if I'd just get out of the way, she'd win your heart so completely that you'd forget I ever existed."

"Catherine!" said Isabella, trying to keep her dignity and not struggling against the tight grip holding her. "I'd thank you to stick to the truth and not slander me, even as a joke! Mr. Heathcliff, please tell your friend to release me. She forgets we're not close friends, and what amuses her is deeply painful to me."

The guest said nothing, just took his seat and looked thoroughly indifferent to what she thought of him. Isabella turned and whispered an earnest plea to Catherine to let her go.

"Absolutely not!" Mrs. Linton answered. "I won't be called a dog in the manger again. You SHALL stay! Now then, Heathcliff, why don't you show satisfaction at my pleasant news? Isabella swears the love Edgar has for me is nothing compared to what she feels for you. I'm sure she said something like that—didn't she, Ellen? And she's been fasting since our walk two days ago, from sorrow and rage that I sent her away from you, thinking your company was unsuitable."

"I think you're lying about her," Heathcliff said, turning his chair to face them. "She wishes to be away from me now, at any rate!"

He stared hard at the object of discussion like someone examining a strange, repulsive animal—a centipede from the Indies, for instance—which curiosity compels you to study despite your disgust. The poor thing couldn't bear it. She turned white and red in rapid succession, and while tears beaded her lashes, she used all her strength to loosen Catherine's firm grip. When she realized that as soon as she pried one finger off her arm another clamped down, and she couldn't remove them all at once, she began using her nails. She dug them in, leaving bloody half-moons across Catherine's hand.

"There's a tigress!" exclaimed Mrs. Linton, releasing her and shaking her wounded hand. "Get out, for God's sake, and hide that wild face of yours! How foolish to show him your claws like that. Can't you imagine what he'll think of you now? Look, Heathcliff! Those nails are weapons—you'd better watch out for your eyes."

"I'd wrench them off her fingers if they ever threatened me," he answered brutally when the door had closed behind her. "But what did you mean by teasing the creature like that, Cathy? You weren't telling the truth, were you?"

"I assure you I was," she returned. "She's been pining for you for weeks, and raving about you this morning. She let loose a flood of abuse at me because I described your failings plainly, trying to cool her infatuation. But don't worry about it—I just wanted to punish her impudence. I like her too well, my dear Heathcliff, to let you completely devour her."

"And I dislike her too much to even try," he said, "except in the most sadistic way. You'd hear of strange things if I lived alone with that simpering, doll-like face. The very least would be painting bruises on that white skin and blackening those blue eyes every day or two—they look detestably like Linton's."

"Delightfully!" Catherine observed. "They're dove's eyes—angel's eyes!"

"She's her brother's heir, isn't she?" he asked after a brief silence.

"I should hope not," his companion returned. "Half a dozen nephews will erase her claim to the estate, God willing! Stop thinking about it—you're too prone to wanting what belongs to your neighbors. Remember, THIS neighbor's possessions are mine."

"If they were mine, they'd be yours," said Heathcliff. "But though Isabella Linton may be silly, she's hardly mad enough to marry me. In short, we'll drop the matter, as you suggest."

They did drop it from their conversation, and Catherine probably from her thoughts. But I felt certain Heathcliff recalled it often during the evening. I saw him smile to himself—grin rather—and lapse into ominous brooding whenever Mrs. Linton left the room.

I decided to watch his movements. My heart always sided with the master over Catherine—with good reason, I thought, for he was kind, trustworthy, and honorable. She—well, she couldn't exactly be called the virtuous either, but she gave herself such freedom that I had little faith in her principles and even less sympathy for her feelings. I wanted something to happen that would quietly rid both Wuthering Heights and the Grange of Mr. Heathcliff, restoring things to how they'd been before his arrival. His visits were a continual nightmare to me and, I suspected, to my master as well. His living at the Heights was an oppression I can't fully explain. I felt that God had abandoned Hindley to his own wicked ways, and an evil beast—Heathcliff—prowled between him and salvation, waiting to pounce and destroy him.

11

Sometimes, when I was alone with my thoughts, I'd get this sudden dread that made me throw on my coat and rush toward the farm. I'd convince myself it was my duty to warn Hindley about what people were saying. But then I'd remember his drinking, his hopeless state, and I'd stop before reaching that miserable house, wondering if I could even bear to go through with it.

Once, on my way to Gimmerton, I took a detour past the old gate. It was right around this time in my story—a bright, frosty afternoon with bare ground and a hard, dry road. I came to the stone marker where the highway splits off toward the moor on your left. It's a rough sandstone pillar with "W.H." carved on the north side, "G." on the east, and "T.G." on the southwest—a signpost pointing to the Grange, the Heights, and the village.

The sun lit up its gray surface, reminding me of summer, and suddenly I was flooded with childhood memories. Hindley and I had loved this spot twenty years ago. I stared at the weathered stone for a long time, then bent down and found a hole near the bottom, still filled with snail shells and pebbles we used to hide there along with our other treasures. And as vivid as if it were happening right now, I could see my childhood playmate sitting on the dead grass, his dark head bent forward, his little hand digging in the earth with a piece of slate.

"Poor Hindley!" I said without thinking.

I jumped—for a moment I could have sworn the child looked up and stared straight into my eyes. The vision disappeared instantly, but I felt an overwhelming need to go to the Heights. Superstition took hold of me: What if he was dead? Or dying? What if this was a sign?

The closer I got to the house, the more anxious I became. By the time I saw it, I was shaking. Then I noticed someone had beaten me there—a figure looking through the gate. At first I thought it was my vision again, but then I saw it was a real boy with tangled hair and brown eyes, pressing his rosy face against the bars. After a moment, I realized this had to be Hareton—MY Hareton, not much changed in the ten months since I'd left him.

"God bless you, darling!" I cried, instantly forgetting my silly fears. "Hareton, it's Nelly! Nelly, your nurse."

He backed out of reach and picked up a large rock.

"I've come to see your father, Hareton," I added, realizing he didn't recognize me—if he remembered Nelly at all.

He raised the rock to throw it. I started talking soothingly, but couldn't stop him—the stone hit my bonnet. Then this little boy let loose a string of curses, delivered with practiced skill whether he understood them or not, his baby face twisted into a shocking expression of rage.

This hurt more than it angered me. Nearly in tears, I pulled an orange from my pocket to calm him down. He hesitated, then snatched it from me as if I might take it back. I showed him another, keeping it just out of reach.

"Who taught you those nasty words, sweetheart?" I asked. "The teacher?"

"Screw the teacher, and you! Give it here," he replied.

"Tell me where you learned to talk like that and you can have it," I said. "Who's your master?"

"Devil daddy," he answered.

"And what does daddy teach you?" I continued.

He jumped for the fruit; I raised it higher. "What does he teach you?"

"Nothing," he said, "just to stay out of his way. Daddy hates me 'cause I swear at him."

"Oh! And the devil teaches you to swear at daddy?" I observed.

"Yeah—no," he drawled.

"Who then?"

"Heathcliff."

I asked if he liked Mr. Heathcliff.

"Yeah!" he answered again.

When I asked why, all I could get was: "He gets dad back for hitting me—he curses daddy for cursing me. He says I can do whatever I want."

"And doesn't anyone teach you to read and write?" I asked.

"No, Heathcliff said he'd knock the teacher's teeth out if he came near the house—he promised!"

I gave him the orange and told him to tell his father that a woman named Nelly Dean was waiting to speak with him by the garden gate. He went up the path and into the house. But instead of Hindley, Heathcliff appeared in the doorway. I turned and ran down the road as fast as I could, not stopping until I reached the signpost, feeling like I'd summoned a demon.

This doesn't have much to do with Isabella's situation,

except that it strengthened my resolve to stay vigilant and do everything I could to stop Heathcliff's poisonous influence from spreading at the Grange—even if it meant causing trouble by going against Mrs. Linton's wishes.

THE NEXT TIME HEATHCLIFF CAME, my young lady happened to be feeding pigeons in the courtyard. She hadn't spoken to Catherine for three days, but she'd also stopped her constant complaining, which was a relief to everyone. I knew Heathcliff never wasted politeness on Miss Linton.

Now, as soon as he saw her, his first move was to check if anyone was watching from the house. I was standing by the kitchen window but ducked out of sight. He walked over to her and said something. She looked embarrassed and tried to leave, but he grabbed her arm to stop her. She turned her face away. He seemed to ask her something she didn't want to answer. He took another quick look at the house, and thinking no one could see him, the bastard had the nerve to embrace her.

"Judas! Traitor!" I exclaimed. "You're a hypocrite too? A deliberate liar."

"Who is, Nelly?" Catherine's voice said at my elbow. I'd been so focused on watching the pair outside that I hadn't heard her come in.

"Your worthless friend!" I answered hotly. "That sneaking scoundrel out there. Oh, he's seen us—he's coming in! I wonder if he'll have the guts to make up some excuse for romancing Miss Isabella when he told you he hated her?"

Mrs. Linton saw Isabella pull herself free and run into the garden. A minute later, Heathcliff opened the door. I couldn't help showing my disgust, but Catherine angrily demanded silence and threatened to throw me out of the kitchen if I dared say another word.

"To hear you talk, people would think YOU were the mistress!" she cried. "You need to remember your place! Heathcliff, what the hell are you doing, causing this scene? I told you to leave Isabella alone! I'm warning you—unless you want to be banned from this house and have Linton lock you out!"

"God forbid he should try!" answered the black-hearted villain. I hated him in that moment. "God keep him meek and patient! Every day I get angrier thinking about sending him to heaven!"

"Shut up!" said Catherine, closing the inner door. "Don't provoke me. Why did you ignore what I asked? Did she run into you on purpose?"

"What's it to you?" he growled. "I have a right to kiss her if she wants me to, and you have no right to object. I'm not YOUR husband—you don't need to be jealous of me!"

"I'm not jealous of you," she replied. "I'm jealous FOR you. Wipe that scowl off your face! If you like Isabella, you can marry her. But do you actually like her? Tell the truth, Heathcliff! There—you won't answer. I'm certain you don't."

"And would Mr. Linton approve of his sister marrying that man?" I asked.

"Mr. Linton will approve," my lady said decisively.

"He can save himself the trouble," said Heathcliff. "I don't need his approval. And as for you, Catherine, I've got a few things to say while we're at it. I want you to know that I KNOW you've treated me terribly—absolutely terribly! Do you hear me? And if you think I don't see it, you're a fool. If you think sweet words will make it better, you're an idiot. And if you think I won't get revenge, I'll prove you wrong very soon! Meanwhile, thanks for telling me your sister-in-law's secret. I swear I'll make the most of it. Now get out of my way!"

"What the hell is this?" exclaimed Mrs. Linton, shocked. "I've treated you horribly and you'll take revenge? How exactly will you do that, you ungrateful bastard? How have I treated you horribly?"

"I'm not seeking revenge on you," Heathcliff replied, calmer now. "That's not the plan. When a tyrant crushes his slaves, they don't turn on him—they take it out on those weaker than themselves. You're welcome to torture me to death for your entertainment, just let me entertain myself the same way, and try not to insult me more than necessary. You destroyed my palace—don't build me a shack and then pat yourself on the back for your charity. If I thought you really wanted me to marry Isabella, I'd cut my throat!"

"Oh, so the problem is that I'm NOT jealous?" cried Catherine. "Well, I won't offer you a wife again. It would be like offering Satan a lost soul. Your happiness, like his, comes from making others miserable. You prove it. Edgar's recovered from his bad mood about your visit, I'm starting to feel secure and peaceful, and you—unable to stand seeing us happy—are determined to start a fight. Fight with Edgar if you want, Heathcliff, and seduce his sister. You'll hit on exactly the most effective way to get revenge on me."

The conversation stopped. Mrs. Linton sat by the fire, flushed and brooding. The demon inside her was growing impossible to control—she could neither suppress it nor command it. He stood by the hearth with his arms folded, dwelling on his dark thoughts. I left them like that to find the master, who was wondering what was keeping Catherine downstairs so long.

"Ellen," he said when I entered, "have you seen your mistress?"

"Yes, she's in the kitchen, sir," I answered. "She's very upset by Mr. Heathcliff's behavior. And honestly, I think it's time to change how we handle his visits. Being too soft causes problems, and now look what's happened."

I told him about the scene in the courtyard and, as carefully as I could, the whole argument that followed. I thought it couldn't hurt Mrs. Linton much—unless she made it worse by defending her guest. Edgar could barely stand to hear me finish. His first words showed he didn't absolve his wife of blame.

"This is unbearable!" he exclaimed. "It's disgraceful that she calls him a friend and forces me to tolerate him! Ellen, call two men from the hall. Catherine won't waste any more time arguing with that lowlife—I've indulged her enough."

He went downstairs, telling the servants to wait in the hallway, and I followed him to the kitchen. The occupants had started arguing again. Mrs. Linton, at least, was scolding with renewed energy. Heathcliff had moved to the window and hung his head, apparently subdued by her fierce criticism. He saw the master first and quickly signaled for her to be quiet, which she did when she realized why.

"What's going on here?" Linton said to her. "What kind of propriety allows you to stay here after the things that scoundrel has said to you? I suppose because it's his normal way of talking, you think nothing of it. You're used to his vulgarity, and maybe you think I can get used to it too!"

"Have you been eavesdropping, Edgar?" the mistress asked in a tone perfectly designed to provoke her husband, showing both indifference and contempt for his anger.

Heathcliff, who had looked up at Edgar's speech, gave a mocking laugh at Catherine's response—clearly trying to get Mr. Linton's attention. He succeeded, but Edgar wasn't going to give him the satisfaction of losing his temper.

"I've been remarkably patient with you, sir," he said quietly. "Not because I didn't know what a miserable, degraded character you are, but because I felt you were only partly to blame for it. And since Catherine wanted to maintain your friendship, I went along with it—foolishly. Your presence is a poisonous influence that would corrupt the most virtuous person. For that reason, and to prevent worse consequences, I'm banning you from this house. I'm giving you notice right now that you need to leave immediately. If you're still here in three minutes, I'll have you thrown out."

Heathcliff looked Edgar up and down with complete contempt.

"Cathy, this lamb of yours is trying to roar like a lion!" he said. "He's going to crack his skull against my knuckles. By God, Mr. Linton, I'm genuinely sorry you're not worth knocking down!"

My master glanced toward the hallway and signaled me to get the men—he had no intention of fighting Heathcliff himself. I moved to obey, but Mrs. Linton, guessing what was happening, followed me. When I tried to call them, she pulled me back, slammed the door, and locked it.

"Fair fight!" she said, answering her husband's angry surprise. "If you don't have the courage to attack him, apologize or let yourself get beaten. It'll teach you not to pretend you're braver than you are. No, I'll swallow the key before you get it! This is what I get for being kind to both of you! After constantly indulging one's weakness and the other's wickedness, I get two perfect examples of blind ingratitude, stupid beyond belief! Edgar, I was defending you and yours, and I hope Heathcliff beats you senseless for daring to think badly of me!"

The master didn't need a beating to be affected. He tried to grab the key from Catherine's hand, and for safety she threw it into the hottest part of the fire. Mr. Edgar started trembling uncontrollably, his face going deathly pale. He couldn't control the overwhelming emotion—the mix of anguish and humiliation completely undid him. He leaned on the back of a chair and covered his face.

"Oh, for God's sake! In the old days, this would earn you a knighthood!" exclaimed Mrs. Linton. "We're defeated! We're defeated! Heathcliff would no more raise a finger against you than the king would march his army against a bunch of mice. Cheer up! You won't be hurt! You're not a lamb—you're a scared little rabbit."

"I wish you joy with your spineless coward, Cathy!" said her friend. "I congratulate you on your taste. And this is the sniveling, shaking thing you chose over me! I wouldn't waste my fist on him, but I'd kick him and enjoy it immensely. Is he crying, or is he going to faint from fear?"

Heathcliff stepped forward and shoved the chair Linton was leaning on. That was a mistake—my master sprang up instantly and drove his fist hard into Heathcliff's throat, a blow that would have knocked down a smaller man. It knocked the wind out of Heathcliff for a moment. While he gasped for air, Mr. Linton walked out the back door into the yard, then around to the front entrance.

"There! You're done coming here," cried Catherine. "Get out, now! He'll come back with pistols and half a dozen men. If he heard what we were saying, he'll never forgive you. You've destroyed me, Heathcliff! But go—hurry! I'd rather see Edgar cornered than you."

"You think I'm leaving with that punch burning in my throat?" he thundered. "By hell, no! I'll crush his ribs like a rotten nut before I leave this house! If I don't floor him now, I'll murder him later. So if you value his life, let me at him!"

"He's not coming back," I said, making up a quick lie. "The coachman and two gardeners are out there. You don't want to be thrown into the road by them! They all have clubs, and the master is probably watching from the parlor windows to make sure they follow his orders."

The gardeners and coachman were there—but Linton was with them. They'd already entered the courtyard. Heathcliff reconsidered fighting three servants. He grabbed the poker, smashed the lock on the inner door, and escaped as they came in.

Mrs. Linton, who was extremely agitated, told me to come upstairs with her. She didn't know I'd helped cause the trouble, and I wanted to keep it that way.

"I'm going out of my mind, Nelly!" she exclaimed, throwing herself on the sofa. "My head feels like a thousand hammers pounding! Tell Isabella to stay away from me. This mess is her fault, and if she or anyone else annoys me right now, I'll lose it completely."

She shifted dramatically on the cushions. "And Nelly, if you see Edgar tonight, tell him I might be seriously ill. I hope it's true. He's shocked and upset me horribly! I want to scare him."

She sat up slightly, eyes glittering. "Besides, he might come up here and start lecturing or complaining. I know I'd fight back, and God knows where that would end! Will you do that for me, Nelly? You know I'm not to blame here. What possessed him to eavesdrop?"

She pressed her hand to her forehead. "Heathcliff said terrible things after you left, but I could have easily distracted him from Isabella. Now everything's ruined because that fool had to listen in! If Edgar hadn't overheard us, none of this would have happened."

Her voice rose with irritation. "Really, when he attacked me with that unreasonable anger after I'd yelled at Heathcliff until I was hoarse defending him, I didn't care what they did to each other. Especially since I felt that however this ended, we'd all be torn apart for who knows how long!"

She clutched at the sofa arm. "Well, if I can't keep Heathcliff as my friend—if Edgar's going to be petty and jealous—I'll break both their hearts by breaking my own. That would end everything quickly when I'm pushed to the limit! But that's a last resort." She paused, calculating. "I wouldn't spring it on Linton without warning. So far he's been careful not to provoke me. You need to warn him how dangerous it is to change that approach, and remind him about my passionate temper—how it borders on madness when I'm pushed."

She looked at me sharply. "I wish you'd stop looking so blank and show more concern about me!"

The calm way I received these instructions obviously annoyed her—she was completely serious. But I figured someone who could plan her fits of passion in advance could probably control herself if she tried, even during them. I didn't want to "frighten" her husband as she asked, or add to his troubles just to serve her selfishness. So I said nothing when I saw the master heading toward the parlor, though I did turn back to listen if they'd start arguing again. He spoke first.

"Stay where you are, Catherine," he said without anger, but with deep sadness. "I won't stay long. I'm not here to fight or make up. I just need to know if, after tonight's events, you plan to continue your friendship with—"

"Oh, for mercy's sake," the mistress interrupted,

stamping her foot, "for mercy's sake, no more of this now! Your cold blood can't work up a fever—your veins are full of ice water. But mine are boiling, and seeing you so cold makes them rage!"

"Answer my question and I'll leave," Mr. Linton persisted. "You have to answer, and your violence doesn't scare me. I know you can control yourself when you want to. Will you give up Heathcliff, or will you give up me? You can't be my friend and his at the same time. I absolutely need to know which you choose."

"I need to be left alone!" exclaimed Catherine furiously. "I demand it! Can't you see I can barely stand? Edgar, you—you leave me!"

She rang the bell so hard it broke. I entered slowly. These senseless, wicked tantrums would try the patience of a saint! There she was, banging her head against the arm of the sofa, grinding her teeth like she might shatter them to pieces. Mr. Linton stood watching her in sudden remorse and fear. He told me to get water. She couldn't speak. I brought a full glass, and when she wouldn't drink, I splashed it on her face. In seconds she went rigid, her eyes rolled back, and her face turned both white and blue, looking like death. Linton was terrified.

"There's nothing wrong with her," I whispered. I didn't want him to give in, though I was scared myself.

"She has blood on her lips!" he said, shuddering.

"Never mind!" I answered sharply. And I told him how she'd decided before he came to fake a fit. I carelessly said this out loud, and she heard me. She jumped up—hair flying, eyes blazing, the muscles in her neck and arms standing out unnaturally. I braced for broken bones at least, but she just glared around wildly for a moment, then ran from the room. The master told me to follow. I went to her bedroom door, but she'd locked me out.

When she didn't come down for breakfast the next morning, I went to ask if she wanted something brought up. "No!" she replied firmly. I asked the same question at dinner and tea, and again the next day, getting the same answer. Mr. Linton, for his part, spent his time in the library and didn't ask about his wife's activities. He'd had an hour-long conversation with Isabella, trying to get her to show proper horror at Heathcliff's advances. But he couldn't get anything clear from her vague responses and had to end the discussion unsatisfied. He did, however, give her a serious warning: if she was insane enough to encourage that worthless man, it would destroy their relationship as brother and sister completely.

12

While Isabella moped around the park and garden, always silent and usually crying, and her brother buried himself in books he never actually read—waiting, I assumed, for Catherine to apologize and beg for forgiveness—Catherine herself stayed locked in her room, refusing food. She probably thought Edgar was dying to see her and only his pride kept him from rushing to her feet. Meanwhile, I went about my work, convinced I was the only sane person left in the Grange.

I didn't waste sympathy on Isabella or lectures on my mistress. I paid little attention to my master's sighs either, though he clearly ached to hear Catherine's name since he couldn't hear her voice. I decided to let them sort themselves out. It was painfully slow, but I started to see signs of progress—or so I thought.

On the third day, Mrs. Linton unlocked her door. She'd finished all the water in her room and demanded more, plus some gruel, claiming she was dying. I knew this was meant for Edgar's ears—I didn't believe it for a second. So I kept quiet and brought her tea and dry toast instead.

She ate and drank eagerly, then collapsed back on her pillow, clenching her fists and groaning. "Oh, I'm going to die," she moaned, "since nobody cares about me. I wish I hadn't eaten that." Then after a while, I heard her mutter, "No, I won't die—he'd be glad. He doesn't love me at all—he'd never miss me!"

"Did you need something, ma'am?" I asked, keeping my composure despite her ghostly appearance and dramatic behavior.

"What's that cold-hearted creature doing?" she demanded, pushing tangled hair from her thin face. "Has he fallen into a coma, or is he dead?"

"Neither," I replied. "If you mean Mr. Linton, he's doing fine. Though he's spending too much time with his books since he has no other company."

I shouldn't have said it so bluntly if I'd known how sick she really was. But I still thought she was acting.

"His books!" she cried, shocked. "While I'm dying! I'm at death's door! My God, does he know how I've changed?" She stared at herself in the mirror on the opposite wall. "Is that Catherine Linton? He thinks I'm throwing a tantrum—playing games. Can't you tell him this is deadly serious? Nelly, if it's not too late, once I know how he feels, I'll choose: either starve to death—though that's no punishment if he has no heart—or recover and leave the country. Are you telling me the truth about him? Be careful. Is he really so completely indifferent to whether I live or die?"

"Ma'am," I answered, "the master has no idea you're this ill. He certainly doesn't think you'll starve yourself to death."

"You don't think so? Can't you tell him I will?" she shot back. "Convince him! Tell him you're certain I'll do it!"

"No, Mrs. Linton," I reminded her. "You forget you just

ate with appetite this evening. Tomorrow you'll feel better for it."

"If I knew for sure it would kill him," she interrupted, "I'd kill myself right now! These three horrible nights I haven't slept at all—I've been tormented! Haunted, Nelly! But I'm starting to think you don't like me either. How strange! I thought even if everyone hated each other, they couldn't help but love me. And they've all turned into enemies in just a few hours—everyone here. How awful to die surrounded by cold faces! Isabella, terrified and disgusted, afraid to even enter the room because watching me die would be too terrible. And Edgar standing solemnly by, waiting for it to be over so he can thank God for restoring peace to his house before returning to his BOOKS! What the hell do books matter when I'm dying?"

She couldn't bear the idea I'd planted about Mr. Linton's philosophical acceptance. Thrashing around, she worked herself into a feverish frenzy and bit into the pillow. Then, burning with fever, she sat up and demanded I open the window. We were in the middle of winter with a harsh northeast wind blowing, so I refused. Her changing expressions and wild mood swings terrified me, reminding me of her previous illness and the doctor's warning not to upset her.

One moment she was violent; the next, propped on one arm and ignoring my refusal, she seemed childishly fascinated with pulling feathers from the tears she'd made in the pillow, sorting them on the sheet by type. Her mind had drifted somewhere else entirely.

"That's a turkey's," she murmured to herself. "And this is a wild duck's, and this is a pigeon's. Oh, they put pigeon feathers in pillows—no wonder I can't die! Let me take care

—I'll throw it on the floor when I lie down. And here's a moorhen's, and this—I'd know it among a thousand—it's a lapwing's. Beautiful bird, wheeling over our heads in the middle of the moor. It was trying to reach its nest because the clouds had touched the hills and it felt rain coming. This feather was picked up from the heath—the bird wasn't shot. We saw its nest in winter, full of tiny skeletons. Heathcliff set a trap over it, and the parent birds wouldn't dare come back. I made him promise he'd never shoot a lapwing after that, and he didn't. Yes, here are more! Did he shoot my lapwings, Nelly? Are any of them red with blood? Let me look."

"Stop this childish nonsense!" I interrupted, pulling the pillow away and turning the torn side toward the mattress as she was pulling out feathers by the handful. "Lie down and close your eyes—you're delirious. Look at this mess! The down is flying around like snow."

I went around collecting the feathers.

"I see you, Nelly," she continued dreamily, "as an old woman with gray hair and hunched shoulders. This bed is the fairy cave under Penistone Crags, and you're gathering elf-arrows to hurt our cattle, pretending they're just bits of wool while I'm watching. That's what you'll become in fifty years—I know you're not like that now. I'm not delirious. You're wrong, or I'd really believe you were that withered hag, and I'd think I was under Penistone Crags. But I know it's night, and there are two candles on the table making the black cabinet shine like polished stone."

"The black cabinet? Where?" I asked. "You're talking in your sleep!"

"It's against the wall, where it always is," she replied. "It looks strange—I see a face in it!"

"There's no cabinet in this room and never has been," I

said, sitting back down and pulling back the curtain to watch her.

"Don't you see that face?" she asked, staring intently at the mirror.

No matter what I said, I couldn't make her understand it was her own reflection. Finally, I got up and covered the mirror with a shawl.

"It's still behind there!" she said anxiously. "And it moved. Who is it? I hope it won't come out when you leave! Oh, Nelly, this room is haunted! I'm afraid to be alone!"

I took her hand, trying to calm her as shudders ran through her body. She kept staring at the mirror.

"There's nobody here!" I insisted. "It was YOU, Mrs. Linton. You knew that a moment ago."

"Myself!" she gasped. "And the clock is striking twelve! It's true then! That's dreadful!"

Her fingers clutched the sheets and pulled them over her eyes. I tried to slip out to call her husband, but a piercing shriek brought me back—the shawl had fallen from the mirror.

"What's wrong?" I cried. "Who's the coward now? Wake up! That's the mirror, Mrs. Linton. You see yourself in it, and I'm right there beside you."

Trembling and confused, she gripped me tight. Gradually the horror faded from her face, and her pale skin flushed with shame.

"Oh Lord, I thought I was at home," she sighed. "I thought I was lying in my bed at Wuthering Heights. I'm weak and my mind got confused—I screamed without meaning to. Don't say anything, just stay with me. I'm terrified to sleep. My dreams are horrible."

"A good sleep would help you, ma'am," I answered. "And

I hope this suffering will stop you from starving yourself again."

"Oh, if only I were in my own bed in the old house!" She twisted her hands in anguish. "With that wind rushing through the firs outside the window. Let me feel it—it comes straight off the moor. Please, just one breath!"

To calm her, I opened the window a crack. Cold air rushed in. I quickly closed it and returned to her side. She lay still now, tears streaming down her face. Physical exhaustion had broken her spirit completely—our fierce Catherine was nothing but a sobbing child.

"How long have I been locked in here?" she asked, suddenly alert.

"Since Monday evening," I replied. "It's Thursday night now—actually, Friday morning."

"What! The same week?" she exclaimed. "Only that short?"

"Long enough to live on nothing but cold water and bad temper," I observed.

"It feels like forever," she said doubtfully. "It must be longer. I remember being in the parlor after they fought, and Edgar was being so cruel, provoking me. I ran in here desperate. As soon as I locked the door, everything went black and I collapsed. I couldn't explain to Edgar that I knew I'd have a fit—go completely mad—if he kept tormenting me! I couldn't speak or think straight. Maybe he didn't realize how much I was suffering. I barely had enough sense to escape from him and his voice. When I came to, it was dawn. Nelly, I have to tell you what I thought—what keeps coming back until I'm afraid I'm losing my mind."

She paused, then continued: "I thought, as I lay there with my head against the table leg, barely able to see the gray square of the window, that I was in the oak-paneled bed at home. My heart ached with some terrible grief that I couldn't remember. I struggled to figure out what it was, and strangest of all, the last seven years of my life just... vanished. Like they'd never happened. I was a child again. My father had just been buried, and my misery came from Hindley separating me from Heathcliff. It was my first time sleeping alone. When I woke from that awful half-sleep after crying all night, I reached out to push the bed panels aside—but my hand hit the table! I swept it along the carpet, and then memory crashed back. My recent pain was swallowed by complete despair."

Her voice rose with anguish: "I can't explain why I felt so utterly wretched—it must have been temporary madness. There's hardly a real reason. But imagine if at twelve years old I'd been torn from the Heights, from everything I knew, from Heathcliff who was everything to me then, and suddenly transformed into Mrs. Linton, lady of Thrushcross Grange, wife of a stranger—exiled and cast out from what had been my world. Can you imagine that abyss? Shake your head all you want, Nelly, but you helped cause this! You should have talked to Edgar, made him leave me alone! Oh, I'm burning up! I wish I were outside! I wish I were a girl again—half wild and tough and free, laughing at pain instead of going mad from it! Why am I so changed? Why does my blood boil at a few words? I know I'd be myself again if I were on those hills among the heather. Open the window wide—fasten it open! Quick, why aren't you moving?"

"Because I won't let you catch your death," I answered.

"You won't give me a chance at life, you mean," she said bitterly. "Fine, I'm not helpless yet. I'll do it myself."

Before I could stop her, she slid from the bed and crossed the room unsteadily. She threw the window wide open and leaned out, ignoring the freezing air that cut at her bare shoulders like knives. I begged her to come back, then tried to force her away, but her delirious strength was far greater than mine.

There was no moon, and everything below lay in misty darkness. No lights shone from any house—all had been put out hours ago. Even Wuthering Heights was invisible, yet she insisted she could see lights there.

"Look!" she cried eagerly. "That's my room with the candle in it, and the trees swaying in front! The other candle is in Joseph's attic. Joseph stays up late, doesn't he? He's waiting for me to come home so he can lock the gate. Well, he'll wait a while yet. It's a hard journey with a sad heart, and we have to pass Gimmerton Church to get there! We've walked through that graveyard together so many times, Heathcliff, daring each other to stand among the graves and call to the ghosts. But if I dare you now, will you come? If you do, I'll keep you. I won't lie there alone—they can bury me twelve feet deep and knock the church down on top of me, but I won't rest until you're with me. I never will!"

She paused, then smiled strangely. "He's thinking about it—he'd rather I came to him! Find a way then! Not through the churchyard. You're so slow! Never mind, you always followed me!"

Realizing it was pointless to argue with her delusions, I was trying to figure out how to get something to wrap around her without letting go—I couldn't trust her alone by the open window—when I heard the door handle rattle. Mr. Linton entered. He'd just come from the library and heard us talking in the hallway. Curious or worried about the late-night commotion, he'd come to investigate.

"Oh, sir!" I cried, stopping the exclamation on his lips when he saw the scene and felt the freezing air. "My poor mistress is ill, and I can't control her at all. Please, come persuade her to go to bed. Forget your anger—she won't listen to anyone but herself."

"Catherine ill?" he said, rushing to us. "Shut the window, Ellen! Catherine, why—"

He stopped mid-sentence. The sight of Mrs. Linton's haggard appearance left him speechless. He could only look from her to me in horrified shock.

"She's been up here brooding," I continued, "barely eating anything and never complaining. She wouldn't let any of us in until tonight, so we couldn't tell you how bad she was—we didn't know ourselves. But it's nothing serious."

I knew I was explaining badly. The master scowled. "Nothing, Ellen Dean?" he said harshly. "You'll explain why you kept me ignorant of this!" He took his wife in his arms and looked at her with anguish.

At first she didn't recognize him—he was invisible to her vacant stare. But the delirium wasn't constant. Slowly, she pulled her attention from the darkness outside and focused on him, realizing who held her.

"Ah! You've come, have you, Edgar Linton?" she said with angry energy. "You're one of those things that shows up when nobody wants you, and when you're needed, you're never there! I suppose we'll have plenty of tears now—I can see it coming. But they won't keep me from my narrow home out there—my resting place, where I'll be before spring ends! And it won't be among the Lintons, mind you, under the chapel roof. It'll be in the open air with a headstone. You can decide whether you'll join them or me!"

"Catherine, what have you done?" the master began. "Am I nothing to you anymore? Do you love that wretch Heath—"

"Quiet!" Mrs. Linton cried. "Quiet this instant! Say that name and I'll end this by jumping out the window! You can have what you're touching now, but my soul will be on that hilltop before you lay hands on me again. I don't want you, Edgar. I'm past wanting you. Go back to your books. I'm glad you have that comfort, because everything you had in me is gone."

"She's delirious, sir," I interrupted. "She's been talking nonsense all evening. But with rest and proper care, she'll recover. From now on, we need to be careful not to upset her."

"I don't want any more advice from you," Mr. Linton snapped. "You knew your mistress's temperament, and you encouraged me to provoke her. And not one word about her condition these three days! It was heartless! Months of illness couldn't cause such a change!"

I started defending myself, refusing to take blame for someone else's behavior. "I knew Mrs. Linton was stubborn and domineering," I said, "but I didn't know you wanted me to encourage her wild temper! I didn't know I should ignore Mr. Heathcliff's visits to humor her. I did my duty as a faithful servant by telling you the truth, and this is my reward! Well, it's taught me a lesson. Next time you can find things out for yourself!"

"The next time you bring me tales, you'll lose your job, Ellen Dean," he replied.

"So you'd rather know nothing about it, Mr. Linton?" I asked. "Heathcliff has your permission to court Miss Isabella and visit whenever you're gone, deliberately turning your wife against you?"

Even confused as she was, Catherine caught our meaning instantly.

"Ah! Nelly's betrayed me!" she cried passionately. "Nelly

is my secret enemy. You witch! So you do gather elf-arrows to hurt us! Let me go—I'll make her pay! I'll make her take it all back!"

A maniac's fury blazed in her eyes as she fought desperately to break free from Linton's arms. I didn't wait to see what happened next. Deciding to get medical help on my own, I left the room.

Crossing the garden to reach the road, I saw something white moving strangely by the wall where a bridle hook was mounted—clearly not just the wind. Despite my hurry, I stopped to investigate, not wanting to be haunted later by thoughts of ghosts. To my shock, I discovered Isabella's spaniel, Fanny, hanging by a handkerchief, nearly dead. I quickly freed the poor animal and carried it into the garden. I'd seen it follow Isabella to bed earlier and couldn't imagine how it got outside or who would do such a cruel thing. While untying the knot, I thought I heard horses galloping in the distance, but with so much on my mind, I barely registered it—though it was strange to hear at two in the morning.

Luckily, Dr. Kenneth was just leaving his house to see a patient when I reached the village. My account of Catherine's condition made him return with me immediately. He was a blunt, plain-spoken man, and he didn't hide his doubts about her surviving this second attack unless she followed his orders better than before.

"Nelly Dean," he said, "I suspect there's more to this. What's been happening at the Grange? We've heard odd reports up here. A stout, hearty lass like Catherine doesn't fall ill for a trifle. And that sort of people don't either. It's hard work bringing them through fevers and such things. How did it begin?"

"The master will tell you," I answered, "but you know

the Earnshaws' violent tempers, and Mrs. Linton tops them all. I'll say this much—it started with a fight. She had some kind of fit during a rage. That's what she says, anyway. She stormed off and locked herself in. After that, she refused to eat. Now she goes between raving and half-sleeping, recognizing people but full of strange ideas and delusions."

"Mr. Linton will be upset?" Kenneth asked pointedly.

"Upset? He'll be destroyed if anything happens!" I replied. "Don't alarm him more than necessary."

"Well, I warned him," said my companion, "and he'll face the consequences of ignoring me! Hasn't he been friendly with Mr. Heathcliff lately?"

"Heathcliff visits often," I answered, "though more because the mistress knew him as a boy than because the master likes him. He's banned now, though—he showed romantic interest in Miss Linton. I doubt he'll be allowed back."

"And does Miss Linton reject him?" the doctor asked next.

"She doesn't confide in me," I said, reluctant to continue.

"No, she's clever," he remarked, shaking his head. "Keeps her secrets! But she's a fool. I have it on good authority that last night—and what a night it was!—she and Heathcliff spent over two hours walking in the plantation behind your house. He begged her to mount his horse and run away with him! My source said she only got rid of him by promising to be ready the next time they meet—though when that would be, I don't know. You'd better warn Mr. Linton!"

This news terrified me. I outran Kenneth most of the way back. The little dog was still yelping in the garden. I took a moment to let it in, but instead of going to the house, it ran around sniffing the grass and would have escaped to the road if I hadn't grabbed it. When I went to Isabella's room, my fears were confirmed—empty. If I'd been a few hours earlier, Mrs. Linton's illness might have stopped Isabella's reckless action. But what could I do now? There was a slim chance of catching them if we pursued immediately. But I couldn't chase them myself, and I didn't dare wake the household and cause chaos—especially not tell my master, absorbed as he was with his wife's crisis. He couldn't handle a second disaster. I saw no choice but to stay quiet and let things unfold. When Kenneth arrived, I went to announce him with a forced calm.

Catherine lay in troubled sleep. Her husband had managed to calm her frenzy and now hovered over her pillow, watching every flicker of emotion cross her pained face.

After examining her, the doctor spoke hopefully to Edgar about a good outcome if we could keep her perfectly calm and quiet. To me privately, he indicated the real danger wasn't death but permanent madness.

I didn't close my eyes that night, and neither did Mr. Linton. We never went to bed. The servants were up hours before usual, moving through the house with quiet steps, whispering when they passed each other. Everyone was awake except Isabella, and they began commenting on how soundly she slept. Her brother asked if she'd gotten up yet, seeming impatient for her presence and hurt that she showed so little concern for her sister-in-law. I dreaded that he'd send me to wake her, but I was spared from being the one to reveal her escape.

One of the maids, a thoughtless girl who'd been on an early errand to Gimmerton, came rushing upstairs and burst into the room, crying, "Oh God, what next? Master, master, our young lady—"

"Be quiet!" I snapped, furious at her dramatic entrance.

"Speak softly, Mary—what's wrong?" Mr. Linton asked. "What about Isabella?"

"She's gone! Run off with that Heathcliff!" the girl gasped.

"That's not true!" Linton exclaimed, jumping up in alarm. "It can't be. Where did you get such an idea? Ellen Dean, go find her. It's impossible."

He pulled the servant to the door and demanded to know why she'd say such a thing.

"Well, I met the milk delivery lad on the road," she stammered, "and he asked if we weren't in trouble at the Grange. I thought he meant the mistress being sick, so I said yes. Then he says, 'Someone's gone after them, I guess?' I just stared. He saw I knew nothing about it, so he told me how a gentleman and lady had stopped at a blacksmith's shop two miles out of Gimmerton, just after midnight, to fix a horseshoe. The blacksmith's lass got up to spy who they were—she knew them both directly. She was certain the man was Heathcliff—nobody could mistake him—and she saw him put a sovereign in her father's hand for payment. The lady had a cloak about her face, but when she asked for water and drank, it fell back and the lass saw her plain. Heathcliff held both horses' reins as they rode away, heading from the village as fast as the rough roads would let them. The lass said nothing to her father, but she's told it all over Gimmerton this morning."

I ran to check Isabella's room for appearance's sake. When I returned and confirmed the servant's story, Mr. Linton had returned to his seat by the bed. He looked up, read the truth in my expression, and looked down without saying a word.

"Should we try to catch them and bring her back?" I asked. "What should we do?"

"She left of her own free will," the master answered. "She had the right to go if she wanted. Don't bother me about her anymore. From now on, she's my sister in name only—not because I'm disowning her, but because she's disowned me."

That was all he said about it. He never asked another question or mentioned her again, except to tell me to send her belongings to her new home, wherever that was, once I knew.

13

For two months, the fugitives stayed away. During that time, Mrs. Linton battled through what the doctor called brain fever and survived. No mother could have cared for her child more devotedly than Edgar cared for his wife. Day and night he watched over her, patiently enduring everything her damaged nerves and confused mind threw at him. Dr. Kenneth warned that even if Catherine recovered, she'd only be a shadow of herself—that Edgar was sacrificing his own health to save "a ruin of humanity." But when Catherine was finally declared out of danger, Edgar's gratitude and joy knew no bounds. Hour after hour, he sat beside her, watching her body slowly heal, desperately hoping her mind would heal too—that she'd become herself again.

She first left her room in early March. That morning, Mr. Linton had placed a handful of golden crocuses on her pillow. Her eyes, which hadn't shown pleasure in so long, lit up when she saw them. She gathered them eagerly.

"These are the first flowers at the Heights," she said.

"They remind me of warm winds and melting snow. Edgar, is there a south wind today? Is the snow almost gone?"

"The snow's completely gone down here, darling," her husband replied. "I only see two white patches on all the moors. The sky is blue, the larks are singing, and the streams are overflowing. Catherine, last spring I was desperate to have you under this roof. Now I wish you were up on those hills—the air is so sweet there, I think it would cure you."

"I'll only visit once more," she said quietly. "Then you'll leave me behind, and I'll remain here forever. Next spring, you'll long to have me with you again, and you'll look back on today as a happy time."

Linton showered her with kisses and tried to cheer her with loving words. But she just stared vaguely at the flowers, letting tears stream down her face. We knew she was getting better physically, so we decided her depression came partly from being stuck in one place too long. A change of scene might help.

The master had me light a fire in the parlor that hadn't been used in weeks and set up a comfortable chair by the sunny window. Then he brought her down. She sat for a long time enjoying the warmth, and as we'd hoped, seemed revived by the familiar objects around her—they didn't carry the awful associations of her sickroom.

By evening she was exhausted, but nothing could convince her to go back upstairs. I had to make up the parlor sofa as her bed until we could prepare another room. To avoid the strain of stairs, we set up the room where you're lying now, Mr. Lockwood—on the same floor as the parlor. Soon she was strong enough to move between rooms, leaning on Edgar's arm.

I thought to myself that she might actually recover with

such devoted care. And we had double reason to hope—she was pregnant. We cherished the dream that soon Mr. Linton's heart would be filled with joy, and his property secured from strangers, by the birth of an heir.

I SHOULD MENTION that Isabella sent her brother a brief note about six weeks after she left, announcing her marriage to Heathcliff. The letter seemed cold and formal, but at the bottom she'd penciled a vague apology, begging for forgiveness if she'd hurt him. She said she couldn't help what she'd done, and now it was too late to undo it.

Linton didn't reply, I believe. Two weeks later, I received a long letter from her—strange thing to get from a bride on her honeymoon. I'll read it to you—I've kept it all these years. Any memento of the dead is precious if you loved them when they lived.

Isabella's Letter

Dear Ellen,

I arrived at Wuthering Heights last night and learned for the first time that Catherine has been, and still is, very ill. I suppose I shouldn't write to her, and my brother is either too angry or too upset to answer my letter. But I have to write to someone, and you're my only choice.

Tell Edgar I'd give the world to see his face again—that my heart returned to Thrushcross Grange twenty-four hours after I left and remains there, full of warm feelings for him and Catherine! I CAN'T FOLLOW IT THOUGH—they shouldn't expect me back. They can draw whatever conclusions they want, but don't blame my weak will or lack of love.

The rest of this letter is just for you. I need to ask you two questions:

First—How did you keep your humanity living in that place? I can't find any normal human feeling in anyone here.

Second—and this matters most—Is Mr. Heathcliff even human? If he is, is he insane? And if he's not, is he a devil? I won't explain why I'm asking, but please, Ellen, help me understand what I've married. Come visit me—you must come soon. Don't write, just come, and bring something from Edgar.

Now let me tell you about my reception at my new home. I'm writing about trivial discomforts to amuse myself—they only bother me when I notice them missing. I'd laugh and dance for joy if lack of comfort was my only problem and the rest was just a nightmare!

The sun was setting behind the Grange as we turned onto the moors. I figured it was about six o'clock. My companion stopped for half an hour to examine the park and gardens, probably studying the Grange itself as much as he could see. So it was dark when we arrived in the farmhouse courtyard, where your old colleague Joseph came out to meet us, carrying a single candle.

His greeting was memorable. First, he lifted his torch level with my face, squinted at me maliciously, stuck out his lower lip, and turned away. Then he took our horses to the stable. When he came back, he locked the outer gate like we lived in some ancient castle.

Heathcliff stayed to talk with him while I entered the kitchen—a filthy, chaotic mess. You wouldn't recognize it from when you ran it. By the fire stood a rough-looking child, strong but dirty, with Catherine's eyes and mouth.

"This is Edgar's legal nephew," I thought. "Mine too, in a way. I should shake hands and—yes—kiss him. Best to start on good terms."

I approached and tried to take his chubby hand. "How do you do, my dear?"

He answered in gibberish I couldn't understand.

"Shall we be friends, Hareton?" I tried again.

He swore at me and threatened to set Throttler on me if I didn't "frame off."

"Hey, Throttler, lad!" the little monster whispered, waking a half-bred bulldog from the corner. "Will you be going now?" he demanded.

Fear for my safety made me obey. I stepped outside to wait for the others. Heathcliff had disappeared. When I found Joseph in the stables and asked him to come with me, he stared and muttered, then screwed up his nose and said:

"Listen to her!" he mocked. "Talking all proper and prissy! Can't understand a word of that fancy talk!"

"I said I want you to come with me into the house!" I cried, thinking he was deaf but disgusted by his rudeness.

"Not my job! I've got real work to do," he answered, continuing his tasks while sneering at my dress and face with complete contempt—my dress too fine, my face probably as miserable as he could wish.

I walked around the yard and through a gate to another door. I knocked, hoping to find a more civilized servant. After a moment, a tall, thin man opened it. He had no neckerchief and looked completely unkempt, his features lost in masses of tangled hair hanging to his shoulders. His eyes looked like Catherine's with all their beauty destroyed.

"What do you want?" he demanded grimly. "Who are you?"

"I was Isabella Linton," I replied. "You've seen me before, sir. I just married Mr. Heathcliff, and he brought me here—with your permission, I assume."

"Has he come back then?" asked this wild man, glaring like a starving wolf.

"Yes, we just arrived," I said. "But he left me at the kitchen door, and your little boy scared me off with his bulldog."

"Good thing that hellish villain kept his word!" growled my

future host, peering into the darkness behind me, looking for Heathcliff. Then he launched into a string of curses and threats about what he would have done if the "fiend" had deceived him.

I regretted trying this door and almost ran before he finished cursing, but he ordered me inside and locked the door behind us. A huge fire provided the only light in the enormous room. The floor had turned uniformly gray with dirt, and the once-brilliant pewter dishes I remembered from childhood were now tarnished and dusty.

I asked if I could call for a maid and be shown to a bedroom.

Mr. Earnshaw didn't answer. He just paced back and forth with his hands in his pockets, apparently forgetting I existed. He seemed so deeply lost in thought, so utterly hostile to the world, that I was afraid to speak again.

You won't be surprised, Ellen, that I felt completely miserable, sitting in that unwelcoming place in worse than solitude. Four miles away was my beautiful home with the only people I loved on earth—but those four miles might as well have been an ocean. I couldn't cross them!

I asked myself: where can I turn for comfort? And—don't tell Edgar or Catherine this—above all my other sorrows, this was the worst: realizing that nobody here could or would protect me from Heathcliff. I'd actually been glad to come to Wuthering Heights, thinking I'd be safe from being alone with him. But he knew these people. He knew they wouldn't interfere.

I sat there in misery as the clock struck eight, then nine. My companion kept pacing, head down, completely silent except for occasional groans or bitter curses. I listened for any woman's voice in the house while my mind filled with desperate regrets and dark fears. Finally, I couldn't hold back my tears and sobs anymore.

I didn't realize how openly I was crying until Earnshaw stopped mid-stride and stared at me in surprise. Taking advan-

tage of his attention, I said, "I'm exhausted from traveling and need to go to bed! Where's the maid? Tell me where to find her since she won't come to me!"

"We don't have one," he answered. "You'll have to take care of yourself."

"Where am I supposed to sleep then?" I sobbed, beyond caring about dignity, crushed by exhaustion and misery.

"Joseph will show you to Heathcliff's room," he said. "Open that door—he's in there."

I was about to obey when he suddenly stopped me and added in the strangest tone: "Do me a favor—lock your door and bolt it. Don't forget."

"Why, Mr. Earnshaw?" I asked. The idea of deliberately locking myself in with Heathcliff terrified me.

"Look at this!" He pulled out a strange-looking pistol with a double-edged knife attached to the barrel. "This is quite a temptation for a desperate man, isn't it? Every night I can't help going upstairs with this and trying his door. If I ever find it unlocked, he's dead. I do it every single night, even though just before, I've thought of a hundred reasons not to. Some devil drives me to destroy my own plans by killing him. You can fight that devil with love as long as you can—but when the time comes, not all the angels in heaven will save him!"

I stared at the weapon. A horrible thought struck me: how powerful I'd be with such a thing! I took it from his hand and touched the blade. He was shocked by my expression—it wasn't horror on my face, but desire. He snatched it back jealously and hid it away.

"I don't care if you warn him," he said. "Put him on his guard. Watch out for him. I can see you understand our situation—his danger doesn't shock you."

"What has Heathcliff done to you?" I asked. "How has he

wronged you to deserve such hatred? Why not just tell him to leave?"

"No!" Earnshaw roared. "If he tries to leave, he's dead. Convince him to try it and you're a murderer! Am I supposed to lose EVERYTHING with no chance of getting it back? Should Hareton become a beggar? Damn it! I WILL get it back—and his gold too—and then his blood—and hell can have his soul! It'll be ten times darker with him there!"

You've told me about your old master's behavior, Ellen. He's clearly going insane—he was last night at least. I was terrified being near him and actually found Joseph's rudeness pleasant by comparison.

Earnshaw went back to his pacing, so I lifted the latch and escaped to the kitchen. Joseph was bent over the fire, watching a large pot that hung above it. A wooden bowl of oatmeal sat nearby. When the pot started boiling and he reached for the bowl, I realized this was probably our dinner. Being hungry, I decided to make it edible.

"I'll make the porridge!" I announced, grabbing the pot away from him. I took off my hat and riding coat. "Mr. Earnshaw says I have to take care of myself, so I will. I'm not going to act like a lady and starve."

"Good Lord!" he muttered, sitting down and pulling at his stockings. "Fresh orders now—just when I got used to two masters, now there's a mistress over my head. Time to leave, I think. Never thought I'd see the day I'd have to leave the old place —but it's coming!"

I ignored his complaining and got to work, trying not to remember when cooking would have been fun. Those memories hurt too much. The faster I stirred, the quicker I could forget. Joseph watched my cooking with growing outrage.

"There!" he shouted. "Hareton, you won't eat your porridge tonight—it'll be nothing but lumps the size of my fist! You're

ruining it! Bang, bang—it's a miracle the bottom hasn't fallen out!"

It was pretty awful when I poured it into bowls, I admit. Four bowls had been set out, along with a pitcher of fresh milk that Hareton grabbed and started drinking from directly, spilling it everywhere. I protested and said he should use a mug—I couldn't drink from something he'd slobbered all over. The old man was deeply offended by my "fussiness," repeatedly telling me the "barn" was as good as me and wondering why I was so conceited. Meanwhile, the savage child kept sucking at the jug, glaring at me defiantly as he drooled into it.

"I'll eat in another room," I said. "Don't you have a parlor?"

"PARLOR!" he mocked. "PARLOR! We don't have parlors, your ladyship. If you don't like our company, go find master. If you don't like him either, tough luck."

"Then I'll go upstairs. Show me a bedroom."

I took my bowl and went for more milk. Grumbling constantly, Joseph led me upstairs to the attic, occasionally opening doors to peer into rooms.

"Here's a room," he finally said, shoving open a creaky door. "Good enough for eating. There's grain in the corner—spread your fancy handkerchief if you're worried about your silk getting dirty."

The "room" was a storage area that reeked of malt and grain.

"This isn't a bedroom!" I said angrily. "I need somewhere to sleep!"

"BEDROOM!" he repeated mockingly. "You've seen all there is—that one's mine." He pointed to another bare attic room.

"Doesn't Mr. Heathcliff have a proper room?"

"Oh! You want Master Heathcliff's room?" he cried, pretending sudden understanding. "Should've said so! That's the one room you can't have—he keeps it locked, nobody goes in but him."

"You have a lovely house, Joseph," I couldn't help saying, "and charming residents. I must have been insane the day I tied my life to theirs! But that's not the point—there must be other rooms. For God's sake, hurry up and show me somewhere I can settle!"

He didn't answer, just trudged down the wooden stairs and stopped at a door. From the way he paused and the nicer furniture I glimpsed, I guessed this was the best room. There was a carpet, though covered in dust. Paper decorations hung in tatters from the fireplace. A handsome oak bed had expensive crimson curtains, but they'd been roughly used—the fabric hung in shreds, torn from their rings, and the iron rod was bent, making the curtains drag on the floor. The chairs were damaged, and deep gouges marked the wall panels.

I was gathering courage to go in when my idiot guide announced, "This here is master's room."

By now my dinner was cold and my patience gone. I demanded to be shown somewhere—anywhere—I could rest.

"Where the hell would that be?" the old man snarled. "Lord help us! You've seen everything except Hareton's closet. There's nowhere else!"

I was so frustrated I threw my tray on the floor, then sat on the stairs and cried.

"Well done, Miss High-and-Mighty!" Joseph exclaimed. "Master will stumble over those broken dishes! You deserve to starve for throwing away God's gifts in your tantrums! But Heathcliff won't tolerate this behavior long—just wait till he catches you!"

He continued scolding as he went downstairs, taking the candle and leaving me in darkness. After my childish outburst, I realized I had to swallow my pride and clean up the mess. Help came unexpectedly from Throttler—I recognized him as our old Skulker's son from the Grange. He seemed to know me, touching his nose to mine before eagerly eating the spilled porridge. I felt my way down the stairs, gathering broken pottery and wiping up milk with my handkerchief.

We'd barely finished when I heard Earnshaw coming. The dog tried to hide against the wall while I ducked into the nearest doorway. The dog wasn't lucky—I heard him yelp as he ran downstairs after being kicked. I had better luck—Earnshaw went past me into his room and shut the door.

Then Joseph came up with Hareton to put him to bed. I'd hidden in Hareton's room, and the old man said, "Room enough for you and your pride now. Have it all to yourself—you and the Devil, who always joins bad company!"

Gladly I took his hint. The moment I sat by the fire, I fell into deep sleep—though it ended too soon. Heathcliff woke me, demanding to know what I was doing there. When I explained he had our room key, the word "our" enraged him. He swore the room wasn't mine and never would be—but I won't repeat his vicious language. He works constantly to make me hate him, and he's succeeding. Sometimes I stare at him with such intensity it drowns out my fear—but truly, a poisonous snake couldn't terrify me as much as he does.

He told me about Catherine's illness and blamed Edgar for it. He promised I'd suffer in Edgar's place until he could get his hands on him. He makes my skin crawl, Ellen. Last night he stood over my bed in the dark just breathing for an hour, knowing I was awake, knowing I was terrified. This morning he said Catherine's name while looking at me, then laughed when I flinched.

I hate him—I'm miserable—I've been such a fool! Don't breathe a word of this to anyone at the Grange. But please, come visit every day—don't disappoint me!

ISABELLA

14

As soon as I finished reading Isabella's letter, I went to find the master and told him his sister had arrived at the Heights. She'd sent word about how sorry she was for Mrs. Linton's condition and desperately wanted to see him. She hoped he'd send some sign of forgiveness back with me.

"Forgiveness!" Linton said. "I have nothing to forgive her for, Ellen. You can go to Wuthering Heights this afternoon if you want, and tell her I'm not angry. I'm just sorry to have lost her—especially since I know she'll never be happy. But me going to see her? That's out of the question. We're done forever. If she really wants to do something for me, she can convince that villain she married to leave the country."

"Won't you at least write her a short note, sir?" I asked, practically begging.

"No," he answered. "There's no point. I'll have as little contact with Heathcliff's family as he has with mine. Which means none at all."

Mr. Edgar's coldness depressed me. The whole walk from the Grange, I tried to figure out how to soften his message when I delivered it, and how to make his refusal to write even a few comforting lines seem less harsh. Isabella must have been watching for me all morning—I saw her looking through the window as I walked up the garden path. I nodded, but she pulled back, afraid someone might see her.

I walked in without knocking. The once-cheerful house looked absolutely miserable. I have to admit, if I'd been in her position, I would have at least swept the floor and dusted the tables. But she'd already absorbed the atmosphere of neglect that surrounded her. Her pretty face looked pale and exhausted, her hair hung limp and tangled—some strands hanging down, others twisted carelessly around her head. She probably hadn't changed her dress since yesterday.

Hindley wasn't there. Mr. Heathcliff sat at a table looking through some papers from his pocketbook. When I came in, he stood up, asked how I was doing in a friendly enough way, and offered me a chair. He was the only thing in that place that looked respectable—honestly, I'd never seen him look better. Their circumstances had reversed so completely that any stranger would have thought he was a born gentleman and his wife was a complete slob.

She rushed forward eagerly to greet me, holding out her hand for the letter she expected. I shook my head. She didn't get the hint and followed me to the sideboard where I was setting down my bonnet, whispering urgently for me to give her what I'd brought.

Heathcliff figured out what she was doing. "If you've brought something for Isabella—which I'm sure you have, Nelly—just give it to her. No need to keep secrets. We don't have any between us."

"Actually, I don't have anything," I said, deciding it was best to tell the truth right away. "My master told me to tell his sister not to expect any letters or visits from him. He sends his love, ma'am, and wishes you happiness, and he forgives you for the pain you've caused. But he thinks our two households should stop all contact from now on—nothing good can come from continuing."

Mrs. Heathcliff's lip trembled slightly before she returned to her seat by the window. Her husband stood by the fireplace near me and started asking questions about Catherine. I told him what I thought was appropriate about her illness, but he kept pressing until he'd gotten most of the details about how it started. I made it clear she'd brought it on herself, and finished by hoping he'd follow Mr. Linton's example and stay away from the family from now on.

"Mrs. Linton is recovering," I said, "though she'll never be the same. Her life has been spared, and if you really care about her, you'll stay out of her way. Better yet, leave this part of the country entirely. And so you don't regret it, let me tell you—Catherine Linton is as different from your old friend Catherine Earnshaw as that young lady there is from me. She looks completely different, and her personality has changed even more. The person who has to be her companion now will only be able to love her by remembering what she used to be, out of basic decency and duty."

"That's entirely possible," Heathcliff said, forcing himself to appear calm. "Entirely possible that your master has nothing but basic decency and duty to fall back on. But do you really think I'll leave Catherine to his DUTY and DECENCY? Can you seriously compare my feelings for Catherine to his? Before you leave this house, you're going to promise to arrange a meeting between us. Whether you agree or not, I WILL see her. What do you say?"

"I say absolutely not, Mr. Heathcliff," I replied. "Never—

not through me. Another meeting between you and the master would kill her."

"You could help prevent that," he continued. "And if there's any danger of it—if he causes her even one more moment of pain—I think I'd be justified in taking extreme measures. I wish you were honest enough to tell me whether Catherine would really suffer if she lost him. That fear is the only thing holding me back. See, that's the difference between us—if I were in his place and he in mine, even if I hated him so much it poisoned my entire life, I'd never lay a hand on him. You can look skeptical if you want! I'd never have sent him away as long as she wanted him around. The second she stopped caring about him, I'd have torn his heart out and drunk his blood. But until then—if you don't believe me, you don't know me—until then, I'd have died slowly rather than touch a hair on his head."

"And yet," I interrupted, "you have no problem ruining any chance of her complete recovery by forcing yourself back into her life now, when she's nearly forgotten you. You're just going to cause more chaos and pain."

"You think she's nearly forgotten me?" he said. "Oh, Nelly! You know she hasn't. You know that for every thought she gives Linton, she thinks of me a thousand times. At the worst point in my life, I wondered about that. It haunted me when I came back last summer. But only hearing it from her could make me face that horrible possibility again. And then Linton would be nothing—Hindley would be nothing—all my nightmares would be nothing. Two words would describe my future without her: DEATH and HELL. Losing her would be hell itself. But I was an idiot to think even for a second that she valued Edgar Linton's attachment more than mine. He couldn't love as much in eighty years as I could in a single day. Catherine's heart is as deep as mine—

you could as easily fit the ocean in a horse trough as fit all her love into what she feels for him. He doesn't have what it takes to be loved like I am—how can she love in him what doesn't exist?"

"Catherine and Edgar love each other as much as any two people can," Isabella suddenly burst out with unexpected energy. "Nobody has the right to talk like that, and I won't sit here while you insult my brother!"

"Your brother loves you so much too, doesn't he?" Heathcliff observed sarcastically. "Look how quickly he threw you out into the world."

"He doesn't know what I'm going through," she replied. "I didn't tell him."

"But you've told him something—you've written to him?"

"I wrote to say I was married. You saw the note."

"And nothing since?"

"No."

"Your young lady is looking pretty rough after her change in circumstances," I observed. "Obviously someone's love is falling short here—I could guess whose, but maybe I shouldn't say."

"I'd guess it's her own," said Heathcliff. "She's turning into a complete slob! She got tired of trying to please me remarkably fast. You wouldn't believe it, but the day after our wedding she was crying to go home. Well, she'll fit in better here for not being so picky, and I'll make sure she doesn't embarrass me by wandering off."

"Well, sir," I said, "I hope you'll remember that Mrs. Heathcliff is used to being looked after and waited on. She was raised as an only daughter with everyone ready to serve her. You should get her a maid to keep things tidy, and you need to treat her kindly. Whatever you think of Mr. Edgar, you can't deny she's capable of deep love—otherwise she wouldn't have left behind all the luxury, comfort, and friends of her old life to live contentedly in this wasteland with you."

"She left because she was delusional," he answered. "She imagined I was some romantic hero and expected me to worship her endlessly. I can barely think of her as rational —she's so stubbornly clung to this fantasy version of me and acted on completely false ideas. But I think she's finally starting to see the real me. At least she's stopped with those idiotic smiles and faces that annoyed me at first, and she's stopped being too stupid to realize I was serious when I told her exactly what I thought of her ridiculous infatuation. It took remarkable insight for her to figure out I don't love her. For a while, I thought nothing could teach her that! But she's a slow learner—this morning she announced, like it was shocking news, that she'd finally realized she hates me! What an accomplishment! If it's true, I should celebrate. Can I believe you, Isabella? Are you sure you hate me? If I leave you alone for half a day, won't you come crawling back, whining and begging again?"

He turned to me. "I'm sure she'd prefer I acted all loving in front of you—it hurts her pride to have the truth exposed. But I don't care who knows the passion was completely one-sided. I never lied to her about it. She can't accuse me of showing even a moment of fake tenderness. The first thing she saw me do after leaving the Grange was hang her little dog. And when she begged for its life, the first words I said were that I wished I could hang everyone connected to her —except one. Maybe she thought that exception was her. But no amount of cruelty disgusted her. I guess she actually admires it, as long as she's safe from harm herself. How absolutely absurd—how genuinely idiotic—for that pathetic, groveling, worthless creature to think I could love her? Tell your master, Nelly, that I've never met anyone as pitiful as she is. She's a disgrace to the Linton name. Sometimes I've actually gotten bored testing what she'll put up with, and she still comes crawling back. But tell him not to worry—I'm staying within the law. I haven't given her any legal grounds for separation. And anyway, she'd never thank anyone for splitting us up. If she wanted to leave, she could. Honestly, having her around is more annoying than the pleasure I get from tormenting her."

"Mr. Heathcliff," I said, "you sound insane. Your wife probably thinks you're mad—that's the only reason she's put up with you. But now that you say she can go, she'll surely take you up on it. You're not so deluded, ma'am, that you'd stay with him by choice?"

"Be careful, Ellen!" Isabella answered, her eyes blazing with fury. There was no mistaking that expression—he'd succeeded completely in making her hate him. "Don't believe a single word he says. He's a lying demon! A monster, not a human being! He's told me I could leave before, and I've tried, but I don't dare try again! Just promise me, Ellen—don't tell my brother or Catherine anything about this horrible conversation. Whatever he pretends, he's trying to drive Edgar to desperation. He says he married me specifically to get power over him. But he won't succeed—I'll die first! I just hope—I pray—that he'll lose control and kill me! The only pleasure I can imagine is dying, or seeing him dead!"

"There—that's enough for now!" said Heathcliff. "If you're ever called to testify in court, remember what she said, Nelly! And look at her face—she's almost where I want her. No, you're not fit to look after yourself anymore, Isabella. As your legal husband, I have to keep you in my custody—the law gives me complete control over you, no matter how much I hate it. Go upstairs. I need to talk to Ellen Dean privately. That's not the way—upstairs, I said! This is the way upstairs, child!"

He grabbed her and shoved her from the room, then came back muttering, "I have no pity! None! The more they squirm, the more I want to crush them. It's like moral teething—the more it hurts, the harder I grind."

"Do you even know what pity means?" I asked, reaching for my bonnet to leave. "Have you ever felt it once in your life?"

"Put that down!" he interrupted, seeing I was about to go. "You're not leaving yet. Come here, Nelly. I need to either persuade or force you to help me see Catherine, and it has to be soon. I swear I don't mean any harm. I don't want to cause trouble or upset Mr. Linton. I just want to hear from her how she is, why she's been sick, and if there's anything I can do to help. Last night I spent six hours in the Grange garden, and I'll go back tonight. I'll haunt that place every night and every day until I find a way in. If Edgar Linton confronts me, I'll knock him down and make sure he stays down while I'm there. If the servants try to stop me, I'll threaten them with these pistols. But wouldn't it be better to avoid all that? You could do it so easily. I'd warn you when I was coming, then you could let me in secretly when she's alone and watch until I leave. Your conscience would be clear—you'd be preventing violence."

I refused to play such a treacherous role in my employer's house. Besides, I argued, it was cruel and selfish to destroy Mrs. Linton's peace just for his satisfaction. "The smallest thing upsets her terribly," I said. "She's all nerves—she couldn't handle the shock, I'm certain. Don't do this, sir, or I'll have to tell my master about your plans. He'll make sure to protect his house and family from your intrusions!"

"In that case, I'll make sure YOU'RE secure, woman!" Heathcliff exclaimed. "You won't leave Wuthering Heights until tomorrow morning. It's ridiculous to claim Catherine couldn't bear to see me. And I don't want to surprise her—you'll prepare her, ask if I can come. You say she never mentions me and I'm never mentioned to her. Who would she talk to about me if I'm forbidden in that house? She thinks you're all spies for her husband. Oh, I'm sure she's in hell living with you people! Her silence tells me everything about what she's feeling. You say she's restless and anxious—is that peaceful? You talk about her unsettled mind. How could it be anything else in that horrible isolation? And that weak, pathetic creature taking care of her out of DUTY and HUMANITY! Out of PITY and CHARITY! He might as well plant an oak tree in a flowerpot and expect it to grow as think he can restore her health with his shallow concern. Let's settle this now—will you stay here while I fight my way to Catherine past Linton and his servants? Or will you be my friend, like you've been before, and do what I ask? Decide! There's no reason for me to stay another minute if you're going to be stubborn!"

WELL, Mr. Lockwood, I argued and complained and refused him fifty times. But eventually he forced me to agree. I promised to carry a letter to my mistress, and if she agreed, I'd tell him when Linton would be away so he could come. I wouldn't be there, and I'd make sure the other servants were gone too.

Was it right or wrong? I'm afraid it was wrong, though

practical. I thought I was preventing another explosion by agreeing. I also thought it might help Catherine's mental state. And I remembered Mr. Edgar's harsh warning about carrying tales. I tried to ease my conscience by telling myself repeatedly that this betrayal—if it deserved such a harsh name—would be the last.

Still, my journey home was sadder than my journey there. I had many doubts before I could bring myself to give that letter to Mrs. Linton.

But here's Kenneth now. I'll go tell him how much better you are. My story is dreary, as we say, but it'll help pass another morning.

Dreary indeed! I thought as the good woman went down to meet the doctor. *Not exactly the entertainment I would have chosen.* But never mind! I'll find something useful in Mrs. Dean's bitter tales. And first, let me beware of the fascination in Catherine Heathcliff's brilliant eyes. I'd be in trouble if I fell for that young woman, especially if the daughter turned out to be a second version of the mother.

15

Another week has passed, and I'm that much closer to health and spring. I've heard my neighbor's entire story now, told across several sessions whenever the housekeeper could spare time from her duties. I'll continue in her own words, just a bit condensed. She's an excellent narrator, and I couldn't improve on her style.

That evening—the evening you visited the Heights—I knew Heathcliff was lurking around, even without seeing him. I stayed inside, still carrying his letter in my pocket, not wanting to face more threats or manipulation. I'd decided to wait until my master left before giving it to Catherine, unsure how she'd react.

Three days passed. On the fourth day, Sunday, I brought it to her room after everyone had gone to church. Only a manservant stayed behind with me, and we usually locked up during services. But that day was so warm and pleasant that I left the doors wide open. Knowing who would come, I sent my colleague to the village for oranges—claiming the mistress wanted them—to be paid for tomorrow.

Once he left, I went upstairs.

Mrs. Linton sat by the open window in a loose white dress with a light shawl over her shoulders. They'd cut her thick hair short during her illness, and now she wore it simply combed, falling naturally over her temples and neck. She looked different, as I'd told Heathcliff, but when calm, there was an otherworldly beauty in the change. The fire in her eyes had given way to a dreamy, melancholy softness. She no longer seemed to see what was around her—always gazing beyond, as if looking into another world. Her pale face, though she'd regained some weight, held an expression that came from her mental state. It made her heartbreakingly beautiful, but also marked her as someone not meant for this world much longer.

A book lay open on the windowsill, its pages stirring in the barely-there breeze. Edgar must have left it—she never tried to read or occupy herself anymore, though he spent hours trying to interest her in things she'd once loved. In her better moments, she tolerated his efforts patiently, showing their futility only through occasional weary sighs or the saddest smiles and kisses. Other times, she'd turn away irritably, hide her face, or even push him away angrily. Then he'd leave her alone, knowing it was useless.

The chapel bells were still ringing, and the stream's gentle flow through the valley was soothing. It replaced the summer leaves that usually drowned out such sounds when the trees were full. At Wuthering Heights, you could always hear the water on quiet days after a thaw or heavy rain. And Catherine was thinking of Wuthering Heights as she listened—if she was thinking or listening at all. She had that vague, distant look that showed she wasn't really present.

"There's a letter for you, Mrs. Linton," I said, gently placing it in her hand. "You need to read it now—it needs an answer. Should I open it?"

"Yes," she answered without looking away from the window.

I opened it—very short. "Now, read it."

She let her hand drop. I put the letter back in her lap and waited. When she still didn't look down, I finally asked, "Should I read it to you? It's from Mr. Heathcliff."

She startled, a troubled recognition flickering across her face as she struggled to focus. She lifted the letter and seemed to read it. When she reached the signature, she sighed, but I could tell she hadn't understood it. When I asked for her answer, she just pointed to his name and looked at me with desperate, questioning eyes.

"He wants to see you," I explained, understanding she needed help. "He's in the garden right now, waiting for my answer."

As I spoke, I saw the dog lying in the sunny grass perk up its ears, then relax and wag its tail—recognizing someone familiar. Mrs. Linton leaned forward, listening intently. A moment later, footsteps crossed the hall. The open house was too tempting for Heathcliff to resist. He probably thought I was avoiding my promise and decided to take matters into his own hands.

Catherine stared eagerly toward her door. He didn't find the right room immediately—she motioned for me to let him in, but he found it himself before I could reach the door. In two strides he was beside her, pulling her into his arms.

He didn't speak or let go for five minutes, kissing her more in those moments than he probably had in his entire life. But she had kissed him first, and I saw clearly that looking at her face was agony for him. The same realization that had struck me hit him the instant he saw her—there would be no recovery. She was dying.

"Oh, Cathy! Oh, my life! How can I bear it?" His first words didn't try to hide his despair. He stared at her so intensely I thought his anguish would bring tears, but his eyes only burned with pain—they wouldn't cry.

"What now?" Catherine said, leaning back and looking at him with suddenly angry eyes—her moods changed like weather. "You and Edgar have broken my heart, Heathcliff! And you both come crying to me like you're the victims! I won't pity you—not at all. You've killed me, and you've thrived on it. Look how strong you are! How many years will you live after I'm gone?"

Heathcliff had dropped to one knee to embrace her. He tried to stand, but she grabbed his hair and held him down.

"I wish I could hold you here until we were both dead! I don't care what you suffer. Why shouldn't you suffer? I do! Will you forget me? Will you be happy when I'm in the ground? Will you say twenty years from now, 'That's Catherine Earnshaw's grave. I loved her once and it hurt to lose her, but that's over. I've loved others since—my children mean more to me than she did. When I die, I won't be glad to go to her. I'll be sorry to leave them.' Will you say that, Heathcliff?"

"Don't torture me until I'm as insane as you," he cried, wrenching his head free, grinding his teeth.

To an outside observer, they made a terrifying picture. No wonder Catherine thought heaven would feel like exile unless she could shed her human soul along with her body. Her face was wild with vindictiveness—white cheeks, bloodless lips, glittering eyes. She still clutched strands of his hair in her fist. As for him, while pulling himself up with one hand, he'd grabbed her arm with the other. He had so little gentleness left for her fragile state that when he let go, I saw four distinct bruises already forming on her pale skin.

"Are you possessed by a devil," he snarled, "to talk like that when you're dying? Do you realize those words will be burned into my memory, eating at me forever after you're gone? You know you're lying when you say I killed you. Catherine, you know I could no more forget you than forget I exist! Isn't it enough for your hellish selfishness that while you're at peace, I'll be writhing in torment?"

"I won't be at peace," Catherine moaned, suddenly aware of her physical weakness as her heart pounded violently, visibly beating beneath her skin. She said nothing until the attack passed, then continued more gently.

"I don't wish you any more torment than I have, Heathcliff. I only wish we'd never be separated. If my words hurt you after I'm gone, remember I feel that same pain underground, and forgive me for my own sake! Come here and kneel down again! You never hurt me in your life. No—if you hold onto anger, that will be worse to remember than my harsh words. Won't you come here? Please!"

Heathcliff went behind her chair and leaned over, but not far enough for her to see his face, which was pale with emotion. She twisted around to look at him, but he wouldn't let her. Turning abruptly, he walked to the fireplace and stood with his back to us. Mrs. Linton watched him suspiciously—every movement stirred new feelings in her. After staring at him for a long moment, she turned to me with bitter disappointment.

"You see, Nelly, he won't relent for even a moment to keep me out of the grave. THAT'S how I'm loved! Well, never mind. That's not MY Heathcliff. I'll love mine yet, and take him with me—he's in my soul." She added thoughtfully, "What bothers me most is this broken prison of a body. I'm tired of being trapped here. I'm desperate to escape into that glorious world beyond death and be there always—not glimpsing it through tears, yearning for it through the walls of an aching heart, but really there, really in it. Nelly, you think you're better off than me, healthy and strong. You pity me—but soon that will reverse. I'll pity YOU. I'll be incomparably beyond and above you all. I wonder why he won't come near me!" She murmured to herself, "I thought he wanted it. Heathcliff, dear! Don't be sullen now. Come to me, Heathcliff."

In her eagerness, she rose, supporting herself on the chair's arm. At her desperate appeal, he turned to her, looking absolutely broken. His eyes, wide and wet, finally blazed at her fiercely. His chest heaved convulsively. For an instant they stood apart, then—I barely saw how it happened—Catherine sprang forward and he caught her, locking her in an embrace so fierce I thought she'd never come out alive. In fact, she seemed to lose consciousness immediately. He threw himself into the nearest chair, and when I rushed over to check if she'd fainted, he snarled at me like a mad dog, foaming at the mouth, clutching her with savage possessiveness. I didn't feel like I was in the presence of anything human. He seemed beyond understanding, though I tried to speak to him. So I backed away and kept silent, thoroughly bewildered.

Catherine stirred slightly, which relieved me. She raised her hand to clasp his neck, bringing her cheek to his as he held her. He covered her with frantic caresses, saying wildly:

"You're teaching me now how cruel you've been—cruel and false. WHY did you despise me? WHY did you betray your own heart, Cathy? I have no words of comfort. You deserve this. You've killed yourself. Yes, kiss me, cry, wring out my kisses and tears—they'll curse you, they'll damn you. You loved me—so what RIGHT did you have to leave me? What right—answer me—for that pathetic infatuation with Linton? Because misery, degradation, death, nothing that God or Satan could throw at us would have separated us. But YOU, of your own free will, you did it. I haven't broken your heart—YOU broke it, and in breaking it, you broke mine. So much the worse for me that I'm strong. Do I want to live? What kind of life will it be when you—oh, God! Would YOU like to live with your soul in the grave?"

"Leave me alone. Leave me alone," Catherine sobbed. "If I've done wrong, I'm dying for it. That's enough! You left me too, but I won't blame you! I forgive you. Forgive me!"

"It's hard to forgive when I look at those eyes and feel those wasted hands," he answered. "Kiss me again, and don't let me see your eyes! I forgive what you've done to me. I love MY murderer—but YOURS? How can I?"

They fell silent, faces pressed together, washed by each other's tears. I assume they were both crying—even Heathcliff could weep on an occasion like this.

I grew increasingly anxious as the afternoon slipped away. The servant I'd sent out had returned, and I could see by the western sun that people were gathering outside Gimmerton chapel.

"Service is over," I announced. "My master will be here in half an hour."

Heathcliff groaned a curse and pulled Catherine closer. She didn't move.

Soon I saw servants coming up the road toward the kitchen wing. Mr. Linton wasn't far behind—he opened the gate himself and strolled up slowly, probably enjoying the lovely afternoon that felt soft as summer.

"He's here now," I said urgently. "For heaven's sake, hurry

down! You won't meet anyone on the front stairs. Be quick and hide in the trees until he's inside."

"I have to go, Cathy," Heathcliff said, trying to free himself from her arms. "But if I live, I'll see you again before you sleep. I won't go more than five yards from your window."

"You can't go!" she answered, holding him as tightly as her strength allowed. "You WON'T, I tell you."

"For one hour," he begged.

"Not for one minute," she replied.

"I HAVE to—Linton will be up here any second," he insisted, alarmed.

He would have stood and pried her fingers loose, but she clung fast, gasping, her face set with mad determination.

"No!" she shrieked. "Oh, don't, don't go. It's the last time! Edgar won't hurt us. Heathcliff, I'll die! I'll die!"

"Damn the fool! There he is," Heathcliff cried, sinking back into his seat. "Hush, my darling! Hush, hush, Catherine! I'll stay. If he shot me now, I'd die with a blessing on my lips."

And there they were, locked together again. I heard my master climbing the stairs—cold sweat ran down my forehead. I was horrified.

"Are you going to listen to her ravings?" I said desperately. "She doesn't know what she's saying. Will you destroy her because she can't help herself? Get up! You could leave right now. This is the most evil thing you've ever done. We're all ruined—master, mistress, and servant."

I wrung my hands and cried out. Mr. Linton quickened his pace at the noise. In the midst of my panic, I was relieved to see Catherine's arms fall limp and her head drop.

"She's fainted or dead," I thought. "So much the better.

Far better she should die than linger as a burden and source of misery to everyone."

Edgar rushed to his uninvited guest, white with shock and rage. I don't know what he intended to do, but Heathcliff stopped him instantly by placing Catherine's lifeless-looking form in his arms.

"Look at her!" he said. "Unless you're a monster, help her first—then you can deal with me!"

He walked into the parlor and sat down. Mr. Linton called for me, and with great difficulty, using every method we knew, we managed to revive her. But she was completely confused—sighing, moaning, recognizing no one. Edgar, in his anxiety for her, forgot about her hated friend. I didn't. At the first opportunity, I begged Heathcliff to leave, insisting Catherine was better and he'd hear from me in the morning about how she spent the night.

"I won't refuse to leave the house," he answered, "but I'll stay in the garden. And Nelly, remember your promise tomorrow. I'll be under those larch trees. Remember—or I'll visit again whether Linton's here or not."

He glanced quickly through the half-open door, confirmed what I'd said was true, and freed the house from his wretched presence.

16

CATHERINE'S DAUGHTER CAME SCREAMING INTO THE WORLD AT midnight—too early, too small. Two hours later, her mother was dead. She never regained consciousness, never knew Heathcliff had left, never saw Edgar again.

I won't dwell on Edgar's grief—it's too painful, and its depth showed in everything that came after. What made it worse, at least to me, was that he had no male heir. As I looked at that fragile newborn, I silently cursed old Mr. Linton for leaving his estate to his own daughter instead of to his son's children. It seemed so unfair.

Poor little thing—nobody wanted her at first. During those first hours, she could have slipped away and no one would have cared. We made up for it later, of course, but she came into the world as alone as she'll probably leave it.

The next morning dawned bright and cheerful outside. Soft light filtered through the blinds of that silent room, bathing the bed and its occupants in a gentle, golden glow. Edgar had his head on the pillow, eyes closed. His young, handsome face looked almost as lifeless as Catherine's beside him—but his showed the exhaustion of unbearable grief, while hers showed perfect peace. Her forehead was smooth, her eyes closed, her lips curved in the hint of a smile. No angel in heaven could have looked more beautiful.

Standing there, I felt the infinite calm that surrounded her. I'd never felt more at peace than while gazing at that image of divine rest. Her words from the night before echoed in my mind: "Incomparably beyond and above us all!" Whether still on earth or already in heaven, her spirit was with God.

Maybe I'm strange, but death doesn't frighten me when I'm alone with it. There's a peace there that life never has—absolute, unbreakable. I see the promise of what comes after, where love and joy have no limits. That's when I noticed how selfish even Edgar's love was, the way he resented Catherine's release from suffering. True, after the wild, restless life she'd led, you might wonder if she deserved peace. But looking at her face, so tranquil now, you couldn't doubt her soul had found rest.

Do you think such people can be happy in the afterlife, sir? I'd give anything to know.

I didn't answer Mrs. Dean's question—it seemed inappropriate. She continued:

Looking back at Catherine Linton's life, I'm afraid we can't assume she is. But that's between her and her Maker.

Edgar seemed asleep, so just after sunrise I slipped out for some fresh air. The servants thought I needed to shake off my exhaustion from the long night, but really, I had to find Mr. Heathcliff. If he'd stayed by those larch trees all night, he wouldn't know what had happened—unless he'd seen the messenger racing to Gimmerton, or noticed the lights and activity at the Grange. Part of me hoped to find him, part of me dreaded it. I had to tell him the terrible news, but I didn't know how.

He was there, a little deeper in the park, leaning against an old ash tree. His hat was off, his hair soaked with dew from the budding branches that dripped steadily around him. He'd been standing there so long that a pair of birds had been building their nest just three feet away, treating him like part of the tree. They flew off when I approached.

He looked up. "She's dead!" he said. "I didn't wait for you to tell me. Put your handkerchief away—don't cry in front of me. Damn you all! She doesn't want your tears!"

I was crying as much for him as for her—sometimes we pity those who can't feel pity for themselves or anyone else. When I first saw his face, I could tell he already knew. For a foolish moment, seeing his lips move and his eyes downcast, I thought his heart might have softened, that he might be praying.

"Yes, she's dead," I confirmed, fighting back my sobs. "Gone to heaven, I hope, where we can all join her if we change our evil ways."

"Did SHE change her ways?" Heathcliff asked with a bitter attempt at mockery. "Did she die like a saint? Come on, tell me what really happened. How did—"

He tried to say her name but couldn't. His mouth clamped shut as he fought some internal battle, his eyes blazing defiantly at me, rejecting any sympathy.

"How did she die?" he finally managed, clearly needing something to lean against despite his determination to appear strong. After the struggle, he was trembling down to his fingertips.

Looking at him shaking, I realized he had the same heart as any man—he just couldn't bear to show it. His pride couldn't fool God. He was asking to be tortured until he broke.

"Peacefully as a lamb," I said aloud. "She sighed once, stretched like a child waking up, then drifted back to sleep. Five minutes later, I felt one faint pulse at her heart, then nothing."

"And—did she mention me?" he asked, hesitating as if afraid the answer would bring details he couldn't bear.

"She never regained consciousness after you left," I said. "She died with a sweet smile, her last thoughts wandering back to happier days. Her life ended in a gentle dream—may she wake just as peacefully in the next world."

"May she wake in TORMENT!" he exploded with terrifying violence, stamping his foot and groaning with uncontrollable rage. "She's a liar to the end! Where is she? Not there—not in heaven—not gone—WHERE? Oh, if she's in hell, then that's where I need to be! You said you didn't care about my suffering! And I pray one prayer—I'll repeat it until my tongue turns to stone—Catherine Earnshaw, may you not rest as long as I live! You said I killed you—haunt me, then! The murdered DO haunt their murderers. I know ghosts walk the earth. Be with me always—take any form—drive me mad! Just DON'T leave me in this abyss where I can't find you! Oh God! I can't bear it! I CANNOT live without my life! I CANNOT live without my soul!"

He wanted her in torment if that meant she still existed somewhere he could reach her. Peace meant nothing to him if it meant separation from her.

He slammed his head against the tree trunk, then looked up and howled—not like a man, but like a wild animal being tortured to death. I saw blood on the bark, on his hands and forehead. This wasn't the first time—he'd probably been doing this all night. It didn't stir my pity; it horrified me. Still, I couldn't just leave him.

But the moment he noticed me watching, he roared at me to go, and I obeyed. He was beyond any comfort I could offer.

CATHERINE'S FUNERAL was set for Friday. Until then, her open coffin lay in the drawing room, covered with flowers and scented leaves. Edgar spent every hour there, never sleeping, standing guard. And—though no one else knew—Heathcliff spent his nights outside, just as sleepless.

I didn't speak to him, but I knew he was trying to find a way inside. On Tuesday, after dark, when Edgar had finally collapsed from exhaustion and gone to rest, I opened one of the windows. I was moved by Heathcliff's persistence to give him a chance to say goodbye to what remained of his idol.

He took that chance, slipping in so carefully and quietly that he made no sound. I wouldn't have known he'd been there at all, except I noticed the cloth around her face had been disturbed, and on the floor lay a curl of light hair tied with silver thread. It had been taken from a locket around Catherine's neck. Heathcliff had opened it, thrown out the original lock of hair, and replaced it with his own black hair. I twisted both locks together and put them back.

We invited Earnshaw to his sister's funeral, of course. He didn't even send an excuse—just didn't come. So apart from Edgar, the mourners were all tenants and servants. Nobody thought to invite Isabella.

The villagers were surprised by where Catherine was buried. Not in the chapel under the ornate Linton monument, and not with her own family outside. Instead, they dug her grave on a green slope in the corner of the church-yard where the wall is so low that heather and bilberry plants spill over from the moor, and peat moss nearly covers everything. Her husband lies there now too. They each have a simple headstone and a plain gray stone at their feet to mark the graves.

17

THAT FRIDAY WAS THE LAST BEAUTIFUL DAY WE'D SEE FOR A month. By evening, everything changed—the wind swung from south to northeast, bringing rain, then sleet, then snow. The next morning, you'd never guess we'd had three weeks of summer. The primroses and crocuses were buried under winter drifts, the larks had gone silent, and the young leaves on the trees were blackened with frost. What a miserable, cold, depressing morning it was.

My master kept to his room. I took over the empty parlor and turned it into a nursery, where I sat rocking Catherine's crying baby on my knee. I watched the snow pile up against the uncurtained window when suddenly the door burst open—someone rushed in, breathless and laughing.

For a moment, my anger overtook my shock. I thought it was one of the maids and snapped, "Stop it! How dare you act so carelessly here? What would Mr. Linton say if he heard you?"

"Excuse me!" said a familiar voice. "But I know Edgar's in bed, and I can't help myself."

The speaker stumbled toward the fire, panting and clutching her side.

"I've run all the way from Wuthering Heights!" she gasped after catching her breath. "Except for the parts where I flew. I can't count how many times I fell. God, I ache everywhere! Don't panic—I'll explain everything as soon as I can. But first, please go tell someone to ready the carriage for Gimmerton, and have a servant pack some of my clothes."

It was Isabella Heathcliff. She certainly didn't look like she should be laughing. Her hair hung loose around her shoulders, dripping with melted snow. She wore a girlish dress that suited her age more than her married status—low-cut with short sleeves, nothing on her head or neck. The thin silk clung to her wet body, and she had only flimsy slippers on her feet. A deep cut below one ear would have been bleeding heavily if not for the cold. Her face was white, scratched, and bruised, and she could barely stand from exhaustion. Once I really looked at her, my initial shock turned to genuine alarm.

"My dear Isabella," I cried, "I'm not doing anything or listening to anything until you get out of those wet clothes and into something dry. And you're definitely not going to Gimmerton tonight—there's no point ordering the carriage."

"I absolutely am," she insisted. "Walking or riding, I don't care. Though I have no problem changing into something decent. And—oh, look how the blood runs down my neck now! The fire makes it sting."

She wouldn't let me touch her until I'd given orders to prepare the carriage and sent a maid to pack her things. Only then did she let me bandage her wound and help her change.

"Now, Ellen," she said once she was settled in an armchair by the fire with a cup of tea, "sit across from me and put poor Catherine's baby somewhere else—I can't stand looking at it. Don't think I don't care about Catherine just because I came in laughing like that. I've cried too, harder than anyone else has reason to. We never made peace, remember, and I'll never forgive myself. But I wasn't about to waste sympathy on him—that monster! God, give me the poker! This is the last thing of his I have."

She pulled the gold ring from her finger and threw it on the floor. "I'll smash it!" She struck at it with childish spite. "Then I'll burn it!" She kicked it into the coals. "There! He can buy another if he ever gets me back. He might come looking for me just to torment Edgar. I don't dare stay and give him that idea. Besides, Edgar hasn't been kind to me either, has he? I won't go begging for his help or bring him more trouble. I only came here because I had to. If I'd known he was out, I would've just stopped in the kitchen to wash up and warm myself, gotten what I needed from you, and disappeared somewhere out of reach of that—that demon!"

She paused, pressing her hand to her ribs as if in pain.

"God, he was furious! If he'd caught me..." She shuddered. "It's a shame Earnshaw isn't strong enough to fight him properly. I wouldn't have run until I'd seen Hindley beat him to a pulp—if only he could!"

"Slow down, Isabella!" I interrupted. "You'll mess up the bandage and start bleeding again. Drink your tea and catch your breath. And stop laughing—it's completely wrong in this house, especially in your condition!"

"True enough," she admitted. "Listen to that baby! It never stops crying. Get it away from me for an hour—I can't stay much longer anyway."

I rang for a servant to take the child, then asked what had driven her to escape Wuthering Heights in such a state and where she planned to go, since she wouldn't stay with us.

"I should stay," she said. "I want to—to help Edgar and take care of the baby, and because the Grange is my rightful home. But I'm telling you, Heathcliff wouldn't let me! Do you think he could stand seeing me happy and comfortable? He'd poison any peace we might find."

Her voice grew harder. "At least now I have the satisfaction of knowing he absolutely despises me—so much that my presence genuinely torments him. When I walk into a room, his face automatically twists with hatred. Part of it's because he knows I have every reason to hate him back, and part is just his natural revulsion. It's strong enough that I'm sure he won't chase me across England if I manage to escape properly. So I need to get far away."

She touched her bruised face gingerly. "I've gotten over wanting him to kill me—now I'd rather he killed himself! He's completely destroyed my love for him, so at least I'm free of that. I still remember loving him, and I can barely imagine I might still love him if—no, no! Even if he'd adored me, his evil nature would have shown itself eventually."

She shook her head violently. "Catherine must have had seriously twisted judgment to love him so much, knowing exactly what he was. Monster! I wish he could be wiped from existence and from my memory!"

"Stop! He's still a human being," I said. "Try to be more forgiving—there are worse men than him!"

"He's not human," she shot back, "and he doesn't deserve my forgiveness. I gave him my heart, and he crushed it to death and threw it back at me. People feel with their hearts, Ellen—and since he destroyed mine, I have no ability to feel for him anymore. I wouldn't care if he suffered until his dying day and cried tears of blood for Catherine! No, I absolutely wouldn't!"

Isabella started crying then, but quickly wiped her eyes and continued. "You asked what finally made me run? I had to escape because I'd pushed him past his usual calculated cruelty into actual murderous rage."

She took a shaky breath. "You know, pulling someone's nerves out with hot pincers takes more self-control than just bashing their head in. I'd worked him up until he forgot all about his precious self-control and turned violent. I actually enjoyed making him that angry—it gave me such a thrill that my survival instinct finally kicked in and I broke free. If he ever gets his hands on me again, he's welcome to take his revenge."

She gulped her tea before continuing. "Yesterday, you know, Mr. Earnshaw should have been at the funeral. He stayed somewhat sober for it—didn't go to bed drunk at six and wake up drunk at noon. So he got up in a suicidal mood, dressed for church but ready for anything. Instead of going, he sat by the fire downing gin or brandy by the glassful."

Her hands trembled as she set down her cup. "Heathcliff—I hate even saying his name!—has been like a ghost in the house since last Sunday. I don't know if angels or devils have been feeding him, but he hasn't eaten with us in nearly a week. He comes home at dawn and locks himself in his room, as if anyone wanted his company! He stays up there praying like some religious fanatic, except the 'god' he prays to is just dust and ashes in a coffin."

She laughed bitterly. "And when he does pray to the actual God, he keeps confusing Him with his own evil father! After these lovely prayers—which go on until he's hoarse and choking—he leaves again, always straight to the Grange. I'm surprised Edgar didn't call the police!"

She paused to catch her breath. "For me, as sad as I was about Catherine, this break from his degrading presence felt like a holiday. I felt strong enough to endure Joseph's endless sermons without crying, and I could move around the house without creeping like a frightened thief."

A harsh laugh escaped her. "You wouldn't think Joseph could make me cry, but he and Hareton are horrible company. I'd actually rather sit with drunk Hindley and his awful rambling than with 'the young master' and that nasty old man! When Heathcliff's home, I'm forced to hide in the kitchen with them or starve in the cold, empty rooms. This week, with him gone, I set up my own little spot by the fire, and Mr. Earnshaw left me alone. He's quieter now if no one bothers him—more depressed and sullen, less violently drunk. Joseph swears the Lord has saved his soul, but I don't see any signs of improvement. Not my problem anyway."

She shifted in her chair, wincing. "Last night I sat in my corner reading until almost midnight. It felt too depressing to go upstairs with the wild snow outside and my thoughts stuck on the graveyard and Catherine's fresh grave. I could barely look at my book—that sad scene kept taking over my mind."

Her voice dropped. "Hindley sat across from me with his head in his hands, probably thinking about the same thing. He'd stopped drinking before getting completely wasted and hadn't moved or spoken for hours. The only sounds were the moaning wind rattling the windows, the coals crackling, and the click of my candle trimmer. Hareton and Joseph were probably fast asleep. It was so terribly sad—

while I read, I kept sighing, feeling like all joy had disappeared from the world forever."

She gripped the arms of her chair. "The miserable silence finally broke when we heard the kitchen door. Heathcliff had come back from his watch early, probably because of the storm. That door was locked, so we heard him coming around to try the other entrance. I stood up, unable to hide my feelings, which made my companion look away from the door and stare at me instead."

"'I'll keep him out for five minutes,' Hindley said. 'You don't mind?'

"'Keep him out all night for all I care,' I answered. 'Do it! Lock it and bolt it.'

"Earnshaw secured the door before Heathcliff reached it, then pulled his chair around to my side of the table. He leaned over, searching my eyes for the same burning hatred that blazed in his. He looked and felt like a murderer. He didn't quite find what he wanted, but he saw enough encouragement to continue.

"'You and I,' he said, 'both have scores to settle with that man out there. If neither of us is a coward, we could work together to pay him back. Are you as weak as your brother? Will you just keep taking it without ever fighting back?'

"'I'm tired of taking it,' I replied, 'and I'd love revenge that wouldn't backfire on me. But treachery and violence are double-edged swords—they hurt the person using them worse than the enemy.'

"'Treachery and violence are exactly what he deserves!' cried Hindley. 'Mrs. Heathcliff, I won't ask you to do anything—just sit still and stay quiet. Tell me honestly—wouldn't you enjoy watching him die? He'll be your death if you don't get him first, and he'll definitely be mine. Damn him to hell! Listen to him knocking like he already owns the place! Promise to keep quiet, and before that clock strikes one—you'll be free!'

"He pulled out the weapons I described in my letter and moved to blow out the candle. I grabbed it away and seized his arm.

"'I won't keep quiet!' I said. 'You can't touch him. Leave the door locked and calm down!'

"'No! I've made up my mind and by God I'll do it!' the desperate man cried. 'I'll save you whether you want it or not, and give Hareton justice! Don't worry about protecting me—Catherine's gone. Nobody would miss me or be ashamed if I cut my throat right now. It's time to end this!'

"I might as well have wrestled a bear or argued with a madman. My only option was to run to the window and warn Heathcliff.

"'You'd better find somewhere else to stay tonight!' I called out, almost triumphantly. 'Mr. Earnshaw plans to shoot you if you try to come in!'

"'You'd better open the door, you—' he answered with some choice words I won't repeat.

"'I'm not getting involved,' I said. 'Come in and get shot if you want. I've done my duty.'

"I shut the window and returned to the fire, not bothering to pretend I cared about the danger he faced. Earnshaw cursed at me furiously, saying I still loved that villain and calling me every name he could think of."

She pressed her hands to her temples. "And secretly—without any guilt—I thought what a blessing it would be if Heathcliff put Hindley out of his misery, and what a blessing for me if Hindley sent Heathcliff to hell where he belongs!"

Isabella's voice grew faster, more frantic. "As I sat thinking these things, Heathcliff smashed through the window behind me with one blow, his dark face glaring through murderously. The bars were too close together for his shoulders to fit, and I smiled, feeling safe. Snow covered his hair and clothes, and his sharp teeth—bared by cold and rage—gleamed in the darkness like a cannibal's.

"'Isabella, let me in or you'll regret it!' he snarled—or 'girned' as Joseph says.

"'I can't commit murder,' I replied. 'Mr. Hindley's waiting with a knife and loaded pistol.'

"'Let me in through the kitchen door,' he said.

"'Hindley will get there before me,' I answered. 'And what kind of love can't handle a little snow? We had peace all summer while the moon shone, but the moment winter comes back, you run for shelter! Heathcliff, if I were you, I'd go lie on her grave and die like a faithful dog. The world's surely not worth living in now, is it? You made it very clear that Catherine was your whole reason for living—I can't imagine how you plan to survive without her.'"

She clutched at her dress. "'He's there, is he?' Hindley exclaimed, rushing to the window. 'If I can get my arm through, I can shoot him!'

"I'm afraid you'll think I'm truly evil, Ellen, but you don't know everything, so don't judge me. I wouldn't have helped hurt even Heathcliff for anything. Yes, I wished he were dead—I had to—but I was terrified and horrified by what my taunting had caused when he threw himself at Earnshaw's weapon and ripped it from his hands."

Her words tumbled out faster. "The gun went off, and the knife's blade snapped back into Hindley's wrist. Heathcliff yanked it out by force, slicing through flesh as it came, then shoved it, dripping with blood, into his pocket. He grabbed a stone, smashed out the window frame between the bars, and jumped inside."

She shuddered. "Hindley had collapsed unconscious

from pain and blood loss—it must have hit an artery or major vein. Heathcliff kicked and stomped on him, smashing his head against the stone floor repeatedly while holding me back with one hand to keep me from calling Joseph. It took superhuman self-control for him not to kill Hindley completely. Finally, out of breath, he stopped and dragged the seemingly lifeless body to the bench. There he ripped off Earnshaw's sleeve and roughly bandaged the wound, spitting and cursing through the whole process as viciously as he'd kicked him before."

Isabella paused to steady herself. "Once free, I immediately ran for Joseph. When the old servant finally understood my frantic story, he rushed downstairs, gasping, taking the steps two at a time.

"'What's happening? What's going on now?'

"'What's happening,' Heathcliff thundered, 'is that your master's insane. If he lasts another month, I'll have him committed. And how the hell did you lock me out, you toothless old dog? Don't stand there muttering. Come on, I'm not nursing him. Clean up this blood and watch that candle—the floor's soaked in brandy!'

"'So you've murdered him?' Joseph cried, throwing up his hands in horror. 'I've never seen anything like this! May the Lord—'

"Heathcliff shoved him to his knees right in the blood and threw him a towel. But instead of cleaning, Joseph clasped his hands and started praying in such ridiculous language that I actually laughed. I was beyond shock at that point—as reckless as a criminal at the gallows."

She rubbed her eyes. "'Oh, I forgot about you,' the tyrant said to me. 'You can help clean. Get down there. Conspiring with him against me, were you, snake? This work suits you!'

"He shook me until my teeth rattled and threw me down

beside Joseph, who kept praying steadily before standing up and declaring he'd go straight to the Grange. Mr. Linton was a magistrate, and even if he had fifty dead wives, he'd investigate this.

"He was so determined that Heathcliff made me tell exactly what had happened, standing over me, radiating malice, as I reluctantly answered his questions. It took forever to convince Joseph that Heathcliff hadn't started it, especially with my forced answers. But then Earnshaw groaned, proving he was alive. Joseph quickly gave him some liquor, which brought him around. Heathcliff, knowing Hindley wouldn't remember what happened while unconscious, claimed he was just drunk and said he'd overlook his terrible behavior this time, but suggested he go to bed."

She exhaled shakily. "To my relief, after this 'helpful' advice, he left. Hindley collapsed by the fireplace, and I escaped to my room, amazed I'd gotten away so easily."

Isabella took another sip of tea, her hands still trembling. "This morning, when I came down around eleven-thirty, Mr. Earnshaw sat by the fire, deathly ill. His evil genius, almost as pale and ghastly, leaned against the chimney. Neither wanted to eat, so after the food got cold, I ate alone. Nothing stopped me from eating heartily—I actually felt satisfied and superior as I looked at my silent companions, comfortable with my clear conscience. After finishing, I dared to go near the fire, walking around Earnshaw's chair to kneel in the corner beside him."

Her voice turned venomous. "Heathcliff didn't look at me, and I studied his face as confidently as if it were made of stone. His forehead, which I once thought so handsome and now think so demonic, was shadowed by a dark cloud. His serpent eyes were nearly dead from lack of sleep and maybe crying—his lashes were wet. His lips had lost their cruel sneer, sealed in unspeakable sadness."

She paused, then continued with bitter satisfaction. "If it had been anyone else, I would have hidden my face from such grief. But with him, I was glad. And as low as it is to kick someone when they're down, I couldn't miss this chance to strike back—his weakness was the only time I could enjoy getting revenge."

"Shame on you, Isabella!" I interrupted. "Have you never read the Bible? If God punishes your enemies, that should be enough. It's both petty and presumptuous to add your own torture to His!"

"Generally I'd agree, Ellen," she continued. "But what misery could fall on Heathcliff that would satisfy me unless I caused it? I'd rather he suffered less if I could be the one making him suffer and he KNEW it was me. Oh, I owe him so much. I could only forgive him on one condition—if I could return every bit of pain he's given me, an eye for an eye, a tooth for a tooth, bringing him down to my level. Since he hurt me first, he should beg forgiveness first. Then—maybe then, Ellen, I might show some mercy. But it's impossible for me to get proper revenge, so I can't forgive him."

She straightened in her chair. "Hindley asked for water, so I brought him a glass and asked how he felt.

"'Not as bad as I'd like,' he replied. 'But except for my arm, every inch of me feels like I've been fighting demons!'

"'No wonder,' I said. 'Catherine used to brag that she protected you from physical harm—she meant certain people wouldn't hurt you because they'd upset her. Good thing the dead don't really rise from their graves, or she would have seen something horrible last night! Aren't you bruised and cut all over your chest and shoulders?'

"'I don't know,' he answered. 'What do you mean? Did he attack me while I was down?'

"'He stomped on you, kicked you, and smashed you against the ground,' I whispered. 'He wanted to tear you apart with his teeth—because he's only half human, the rest is demon.'"

Isabella's eyes gleamed with malice. "Mr. Earnshaw looked up at our mutual enemy, who was so lost in his agony he seemed unaware of anything around him. The longer he stood there, the clearer his dark thoughts showed on his face.

"'Oh, if God would just give me the strength to strangle him before I die, I'd go to hell happy,' Hindley groaned, trying to get up but falling back in despair, too weak to fight.

"'Well, he's already murdered one of you,' I said loudly. 'Everyone at the Grange knows your sister would still be alive if not for Mr. Heathcliff. Really, it's better to be hated by him than loved. When I remember how happy we were—how happy Catherine was before he came—I could curse the day.'

"Heathcliff probably noticed the truth in my words more than who said them. I saw I'd gotten his attention—tears were falling into the ashes, and his breathing came in suffocating gasps. I stared right at him and laughed mockingly. The windows to hell in his eyes flashed at me for a moment, but the demon behind them was so dimmed and drowned that I wasn't afraid to mock him again.

"'Get up and get out of my sight,' the grieving man said, barely audible.

"'Pardon me,' I replied, 'but I loved Catherine too, and her brother needs care, which I'll provide for her sake. Now that she's dead, I see her in Hindley—Hindley has exactly her eyes, if you hadn't tried to gouge them out and made them black and red, and her—'

"'Get up, you pathetic idiot, before I stomp you to death!' he cried, moving toward me, which made me ready to run."

She was speaking so fast now, reliving the terror. "'But then,' I continued, preparing to flee, 'if poor Catherine had trusted you and taken the ridiculous, degrading title of Mrs. Heathcliff, she would have ended up just like me! She wouldn't have tolerated your abominable behavior quietly —her hatred and disgust would have shown.'

"The bench and Earnshaw were between us, so instead of trying to reach me, he grabbed a dinner knife from the table and threw it at my head. It hit below my ear, cutting off my words. But I pulled it out, ran to the door, and shouted one more insult that I hope cut deeper than his knife."

Isabella touched the bandage at her ear. "The last I saw was him rushing at me furiously before Hindley grabbed him, and they both fell fighting on the floor. I ran through the kitchen, telling Joseph to help his master. I knocked over Hareton, who was hanging puppies from a chair in the doorway, and feeling like a soul escaped from purgatory, I bounded, leaped, and flew down the steep road. Then I cut straight across the moor, rolling over banks and wading through marshes, racing toward the beacon light of the Grange."

She slumped back in her chair, exhausted from the telling. "I'd rather be condemned to hell forever than spend one more night under the roof of Wuthering Heights!"

Isabella stopped and drank her tea. Then she stood, asking me to bring her bonnet and the shawl I'd fetched. Ignoring my pleas to stay another hour, she climbed on a chair, kissed the portraits of Edgar and Catherine, gave me a similar kiss, and went down to the carriage with Fanny, who was wild with joy at finding her mistress again. She drove away, never to return to this neighborhood. Later, when things calmed down, she and my master kept up a regular correspondence. I believe she settled in the south, near London, where she had a son a few months after her escape. She named him Linton and reported from the start that he was a sickly, irritable child.

MR. HEATHCLIFF RAN into me in the village one day and asked where Isabella lived. I refused to tell him. He said it didn't really matter, but she'd better not come near her brother—if she tried, he'd keep her himself if necessary. Though I wouldn't give him any information, he found out through other servants both where she lived and that she had a child. Still, he didn't bother her—probably because he couldn't stand her. He often asked me about the baby, and when he heard its name was Linton, he smiled grimly and said, "They want me to hate it too, do they?"

"I don't think they want you to know anything about it," I answered.

"But I'll have it when I want it," he said. "They can count on that!"

Fortunately, Isabella died before he could make good on that threat—about thirteen years after Catherine's death, when young Linton was twelve or so.

The day after Isabella's dramatic visit, I couldn't talk to my master—he avoided conversation and wasn't fit to discuss anything. When I finally got him to listen, I could tell he was relieved his sister had left her husband. He hated Heathcliff with an intensity that seemed impossible for someone so gentle. His hatred ran so deep that he wouldn't go anywhere he might see or hear about Heathcliff. Between grief and this aversion, he became a complete hermit. He gave up his position as magistrate, stopped going to church, avoided the village entirely, and lived in total isolation within his park and grounds. His only outings were solitary walks on the moors and visits to Catherine's grave, usually in the evening or early morning when no one else was around.

But he was too good a man to stay miserable forever. He didn't pray for Catherine's soul to haunt him. Time brought acceptance and a melancholy that was somehow sweeter than ordinary happiness. He remembered her with deep, tender love and hopeful faith that she'd gone to a better world.

And he had earthly comfort too. For a few days after Catherine died, he seemed to ignore the tiny baby she'd left behind. But that coldness melted like April snow. Before the little thing could say a word or take a step, she ruled his heart completely. He named her Catherine but never called her that—probably because Heathcliff always had. To him, she was always Cathy. The name kept her separate from her mother while still connecting them. His love for her came more from her being Catherine's daughter than from being his own.

I used to compare him to Hindley Earnshaw and puzzle over why they'd handled similar situations so differently. Both had been loving husbands, both adored their children. I couldn't understand why they hadn't taken the same path, for better or worse. But thinking about it, Hindley—who seemed to have the stronger mind—proved himself the weaker man. When disaster struck, he abandoned his post like a captain fleeing a sinking ship, while his crew fell into chaos, leaving no hope for their doomed vessel. Linton, on the other hand, showed the true courage of a faithful soul. He trusted God, and God comforted him. One chose hope, the other despair—and they each got what they chose.

But you don't want to hear me moralizing, Mr. Lockwood. You can judge these things as well as I can—or at least you'll think you can, which amounts to the same thing.

Earnshaw's end came as you might expect, following close after his sister's—barely six months between them. We never got a clear account of his final days at the Grange. I only learned about it when I went to help with the funeral arrangements. Dr. Kenneth came to tell my master the news.

"Well, Nelly," he said, riding into the yard one morning so early I immediately knew something was wrong. "It's our turn for mourning clothes again. Who do you think has left us now?"

"Who?" I asked anxiously.

"Guess!" he said, dismounting and hanging his bridle on the door hook. "And get your handkerchief ready—you'll need it."

"Not Mr. Heathcliff, surely?" I exclaimed.

"What, would you cry for him?" the doctor said. "No, Heathcliff's tough as nails and looking healthier than ever. I just saw him. He's been gaining weight since he lost his 'better half.'"

"Who is it then, Dr. Kenneth?" I repeated impatiently.

"Hindley Earnshaw! Your old friend Hindley," he replied, "and my wicked old drinking companion—though he's been too wild for me lately. There, I knew you'd cry! But cheer up—he died exactly as you'd expect, completely drunk. Poor boy! I'm sorry too. Can't help missing an old friend, even if he had the worst habits imaginable and played plenty of dirty tricks on me. He was barely twenty-seven, same age as you. Who'd have thought you were born the same year?"

This hit me harder than Mrs. Linton's death. Old memories flooded back, and I sat on the porch crying like I'd lost family. I asked Dr. Kenneth to find someone else to tell the master—I couldn't do it. But I kept wondering: had Hindley ever had a fair chance? The thought wouldn't leave me alone, so I finally asked permission to go to Wuthering Heights and help with the burial.

Mr. Linton really didn't want to let me go, but I argued that Hindley had no one, that my old master and foster-brother deserved my help as much as anyone. Plus, I reminded him that little Hareton was Catherine's nephew, and with no closer family, Edgar should act as his guardian and find out about the property and estate matters.

He wasn't up to dealing with such things then, but he told me to talk to his lawyer and eventually let me go. The lawyer had also represented Earnshaw. When I went to the village and asked him to come with me, he shook his head and said we should leave Heathcliff alone. If the truth came out, he said, Hareton would be found to have nothing.

"His father died in debt," he explained. "The whole property is mortgaged. The boy's only chance is if he can somehow make the creditor—Heathcliff—feel sorry enough for him to be lenient."

When I reached the Heights, I explained I'd come to make sure everything was done properly. Joseph, who looked genuinely distressed, was glad to see me. Mr. Heathcliff said he didn't see why I was needed, but I could stay and arrange the funeral if I wanted.

"By rights," he said, "that fool's body should be buried at a crossroads without any ceremony. I left him alone for ten minutes yesterday afternoon, and in that time he locked both doors against me and spent the night drinking himself to death on purpose! We broke in this morning because we heard him snorting like a horse. There he was, sprawled over the bench—you couldn't have woken him if you'd tried to skin him alive. I sent for Kenneth, but by the time he arrived, the beast had turned into a corpse—dead, cold, and stiff. So you can see there was no point making a fuss about it!"

Joseph confirmed this but muttered, "I'd rather he'd gone for the doctor himself! I would've taken better care of the master—and he wasn't dead when I left, not at all!"

I insisted on a respectable funeral. Mr. Heathcliff said I could have my way, but reminded me the money was coming from his pocket. He maintained a hard, careless attitude that showed neither joy nor sorrow—if anything, he seemed grimly satisfied at completing a difficult job successfully. I did notice something like triumph in his expression once—just as they were carrying the coffin out. He pretended to be a mourner, and before following with Hareton, he lifted the poor child onto the table and said with particular relish, "Now, my bonny boy, you are MINE! And we'll see if one tree won't grow as crooked as another with the same wind twisting it!"

The innocent child was pleased by this attention, playing with Heathcliff's whiskers and stroking his cheek. But I understood exactly what he meant and said sharply, "That boy is coming back with me to Thrushcross Grange, sir. There's nothing in the world less yours than he is!"

"Does Linton say so?" he demanded.

"Of course—he ordered me to take him," I replied.

"Well," said the scoundrel, "we won't argue about it now. But I fancy trying my hand at raising a child. So tell your master that if he tries to remove this one, I'll have to replace him with my own. I won't let Hareton go without a fight, but I'll definitely make sure to get the other one! Make sure you tell him that."

This threat was enough to tie our hands. I repeated it when I got back, and Edgar Linton, who hadn't been very interested at first, gave up any idea of interfering. I don't think he could have done anything anyway, even if he'd wanted to.

The guest had now become master of Wuthering Heights. He had firm possession and proved to the lawyer—who proved it to Mr. Linton—that Earnshaw had mortgaged every inch of land he owned to fund his gambling addiction, and Heathcliff was the one who held all those mortgages. That's how Hareton, who should have been the most important gentleman in the neighborhood, ended up completely dependent on his father's worst enemy. He lives in his own house as a servant, working without wages, unable to claim his rights because he has no friends and doesn't even know he's been wronged.

18

THE TWELVE YEARS AFTER THAT DARK PERIOD, MRS. DEAN continued, were the happiest of my life. My biggest worries came from our little lady's minor illnesses—the usual childhood troubles that every child faces, rich or poor. Otherwise, after those first six months, she shot up like a young tree. By the time the heather bloomed for the second time over Mrs. Linton's grave, she could walk and talk in her own sweet way.

She was the most enchanting thing to ever bring sunshine into that lonely house—truly beautiful, with the Earnshaws' striking dark eyes but the Lintons' fair skin, delicate features, and golden curls. Her spirit was lively but not wild, balanced by a heart that loved almost too deeply. That capacity for fierce attachment reminded me of her mother, though they weren't really alike. Cathy could be gentle as a dove, with a soft voice and thoughtful expression. Her anger never exploded; her love never burned out of control. It ran deep and tender instead.

Still, I have to admit she had her flaws. She could be cheeky, and she had that stubborn streak all spoiled children develop, whether they're sweet-natured or not. If a servant upset her, it was always, "I'll tell Papa!" And if he so much as looked at her disapprovingly, you'd think her heart was breaking. I don't think he ever said a harsh word to her in his life. He took complete charge of her education and made it into a game. Lucky for him, her curiosity and quick mind made her an eager student. She learned fast and made him proud.

Until she turned thirteen, she'd never once left the park grounds alone. Mr. Linton would occasionally take her a mile or so beyond, but rarely, and he wouldn't trust anyone else with her. Gimmerton was just a meaningless name to her. The chapel was the only building she'd ever entered besides her own home. Wuthering Heights and Mr. Heathcliff didn't exist in her world—she lived in complete isolation, and seemed perfectly happy with it.

Sometimes, though, looking out from her nursery window at the countryside, she'd say, "Ellen, how long before I can walk to the top of those hills? What's on the other side—is it the sea?"

"No, Miss Cathy," I'd answer. "Just more hills like these."

"And what are those golden rocks like when you stand under them?" she asked once.

She was especially fascinated by the steep drop of Penistone Crags, particularly when the sunset hit them and made the peaks glow while everything else fell into shadow. I explained they were just bare rocks with barely enough dirt in the cracks to feed a scraggly tree.

"Why do they stay bright so long after it gets dark here?" she wanted to know.

"Because they're much higher than us," I told her. "You couldn't climb them—too high and steep. In winter, the frost hits there before it reaches us. I've found snow in that dark hollow on the northeast side even in the middle of summer!"

"Oh, you've been up there!" she cried, delighted. "Then I can go too when I'm older. Has Papa been, Ellen?"

"Your father would tell you they're not worth the trouble, Miss," I said quickly. "The moors where you walk with him are much prettier. And Thrushcross Park is the finest place in the world."

"But I know the park, and I don't know those," she murmured. "I'd love to see everything from the top of that highest peak. My pony Minny will take me someday."

One of the maids mentioned something about the Fairy Cave, and that completely captured her imagination. She pestered Mr. Linton about it until he promised she could go when she was older. But Miss Catherine counted her age in months, constantly asking, "Am I old enough for Penistone Crags now?" The road there passed right by Wuthering Heights, and Edgar couldn't bear to go near it, so she always got the same answer: "Not yet, love. Not yet."

MRS. HEATHCLIFF—ISABELLA—LIVED about twelve years after leaving her husband. Her family had delicate constitutions. She and Edgar both lacked the robust health you usually find in these parts. I'm not sure exactly what killed her—some kind of fever, I think. The same thing that got them both eventually—slow to start but incurable, burning through them quickly at the end.

She wrote to tell Edgar she'd been sick for four months and probably wouldn't recover. She begged him to come if he could—she had things to settle and wanted to say goodbye and hand over young Linton safely. She hoped

Edgar would keep the boy. She'd convinced herself that Heathcliff had no interest in the burden of raising or educating him.

My master didn't hesitate. As much as he hated leaving home normally, he rushed to answer this call. He left Catherine in my care with strict orders—repeated several times—that she absolutely must not leave the park, even with me. He never imagined she'd go alone.

He was gone three weeks. The first day or two, my charge sat quietly in a corner of the library, too sad to read or play. That didn't last. She soon grew restless and irritable. I was too busy and honestly too old to run around entertaining her, so I came up with a solution. I'd send her exploring around the grounds—sometimes walking, sometimes on her pony—and when she came back, I'd be her patient audience for all her real and imaginary adventures.

It was high summer, and she loved these solo expeditions so much that she often stayed out from breakfast until tea. Then she'd spend the evenings telling me fantastic stories. I wasn't worried about her going too far—the gates were usually locked, and I figured she wouldn't dare go beyond them even if they were open.

Unfortunately, I was wrong.

One morning at eight o'clock, Catherine announced she was an Arabian merchant crossing the desert with her caravan. She needed provisions for herself and her beasts—a horse and three camels, played by our old hound and two pointers. I packed a basket full of treats and tied it to her saddle. She mounted her pony, bright as a fairy under her wide-brimmed hat and gauze veil against the July sun, and trotted off laughing, ignoring my warnings to stay close and come back early.

The naughty girl never showed up for tea. The old

hound came back—he liked his comfort too much for long adventures. But no sign of Cathy, the pony, or the pointers. I sent people searching in every direction, then went looking myself.

A workman was fixing a fence around the plantation at the edge of our property. I asked if he'd seen our young lady.

"Saw her this morning," he said. "Had me cut her a hazel switch. Then she jumped her pony over the hedge where it's lowest and galloped off."

My heart sank. She must have headed for Penistone Crags. "What's going to happen to her?" I cried, squeezing through the gap he was repairing and heading for the main road. I walked as fast as I could, mile after mile, until I could see the Heights in the distance. But no Catherine anywhere. The Crags were about a mile and a half past Heathcliff's place, which was four miles from the Grange. I started to panic that night would fall before I could reach them. What if she'd fallen climbing the rocks? What if she was hurt or worse?

My anxiety was torture. But as I hurried past the farmhouse, I felt a wave of relief—there was Charlie, the fiercest pointer, lying under a window with a swollen head and bleeding ear. I opened the gate and ran to the door, pounding frantically.

A woman I knew answered—she used to live in Gimmerton and had worked there since Mr. Earnshaw died.

"Ah," she said, "you've come looking for your little mistress! Don't worry, she's safe inside. Good thing it's not the master here."

"He's not home?" I panted, breathless from rushing and fear.

"No, no. Him and Joseph are both out. Won't be back for an hour or more. Come in and rest."

I went in and found my lost lamb sitting by the fire, rocking in a little chair that had been her mother's as a child. Her hat hung on the wall, and she looked completely at home, laughing and chattering away in high spirits to Hareton—now a strong young man of eighteen—who stared at her with amazement and confusion, barely understanding the stream of remarks and questions she kept firing at him.

"Well, Miss!" I said, hiding my relief behind an angry face. "This is your last adventure until your father returns. I'll never trust you outside again, you naughty, naughty girl!"

"Oh, Ellen!" she cried cheerfully, jumping up and running to me. "I'll have such a story to tell tonight! So you found me! Have you ever been here before?"

"Put your hat on and come home right now," I said. "I'm terribly upset with you, Miss Cathy. You've done something very wrong! Don't pout and cry—that won't make up for all the trouble you've caused, making me search the whole countryside. Your father specifically told me to keep you safe, and you sneak off like this! You're a sneaky little fox, and no one will trust you again."

"What did I do?" she sobbed, immediately deflated. "Papa didn't tell me anything. He won't scold me, Ellen—he's never mean like you!"

"Come on," I said. "Let me tie your hat ribbon. And stop being so dramatic. For shame! Thirteen years old and acting like such a baby!"

She pushed the hat off her head and backed toward the chimney, out of my reach.

"No," said the servant, "don't be hard on the pretty girl, Mrs. Dean. We made her stop—she wanted to ride on, worried you'd be upset. Hareton offered to go with her, and I thought he should. It's a rough road over those hills."

Hareton stood there during this discussion, hands in his pockets, too awkward to speak, though he clearly didn't appreciate my intrusion.

"How long do I have to wait?" I continued, ignoring the woman. "It'll be dark in ten minutes. Where's the pony, Miss Cathy? And where's Phoenix? I'm leaving unless you hurry up, so make your choice."

"The pony's in the yard," she replied, "and Phoenix is locked in there. He's been bitten—so has Charlie. I was going to tell you all about it, but you're in such a bad mood, you don't deserve to hear."

I picked up her hat and tried to put it on her, but seeing the servants take her side, she started dancing around the room. When I chased her, she darted like a mouse over, under, and behind the furniture, making me look ridiculous. Hareton and the woman laughed, and she joined in, getting even more cheeky until I snapped, "Well, Miss Cathy, if you knew whose house this is, you'd be eager to leave."

"It's YOUR father's, isn't it?" she said, turning to Hareton.

"No," he replied, looking down and blushing hard.

He couldn't meet her eyes—those dark Earnshaw eyes that were mirror images of his own.

"Whose then—your master's?" she asked.

He turned even redder, but with a different emotion, muttered a curse, and looked away.

"Who is his master?" the persistent girl asked me. "He talked about 'our house' and 'our folk.' I thought he was the owner's son. And he never called me 'Miss'—shouldn't he, if he's a servant?"

Hareton's face darkened like a storm cloud at this childish remark. I shook my head at her silently and finally managed to get her ready to leave.

"Now, get my horse," she said, addressing her unknown cousin like he was one of the stable boys at the Grange. "And you can come with me. I want to see where the goblin-hunter rises in the marsh, and hear about the fairies, as you call them. But hurry! What's the matter? Get my horse, I said."

"I'll see you damned before I'm YOUR servant!" the young man growled.

"You'll see me WHAT?" Catherine asked, shocked.

"Damned—you spoiled little witch!" he replied.

"There, Miss Cathy! Look at the company you're keeping," I interrupted. "Such language to use with a young lady! Please don't argue with him. Come, let's find Minny ourselves and leave."

"But Ellen," she cried, staring in amazement, "how dare he speak to me like that? Shouldn't he have to do what I say? You horrible creature, I'll tell Papa what you said—just you wait!"

Hareton didn't seem bothered by her threat, which made tears of indignation spring to her eyes. "You bring the pony," she demanded, turning to the woman, "and let my dog go right now!"

"Easy, Miss," the woman answered. "You won't lose anything by being polite. Though Mr. Hareton isn't the master's son, he's your cousin. And I wasn't hired to serve you."

"HE'S my cousin?" Cathy cried with a scornful laugh.

"Yes, indeed," the woman confirmed.

"Oh, Ellen! Don't let them say such things," she continued, deeply troubled. "Papa went to London to fetch my cousin. My cousin is a gentleman's son. That my—" She stopped and burst into tears, horrified at the very idea of being related to such a rough person.

"Hush, hush," I whispered. "People can have all sorts of cousins, Miss Cathy, without it meaning anything bad. You just don't have to spend time with them if they're unpleasant."

"He's not—he's not my cousin, Ellen!" she went on, fresh grief overwhelming her as she threw herself into my arms to escape the thought.

I was furious at her and the servant for revealing so much. No doubt the servant had mentioned young Linton's expected arrival, which would surely be reported to Mr. Heathcliff. And I knew Catherine's first thought when her father returned would be to ask about this claim that she was related to such rough people.

Hareton, recovering from being mistaken for a servant, seemed touched by her distress. After bringing the pony to the door, he tried to make peace by taking a cute terrier puppy from the kennel and offering it to her, his rough hand trembling slightly—a clumsy attempt at gentleness from someone who'd rarely received any himself. He told her to quiet down—he didn't mean any harm. She paused in her crying to look at him with fear and horror, then started sobbing again.

I almost laughed at her horror. He was actually well-built and athletic, good-looking and healthy, just dressed in work clothes suitable for farming and hunting rabbits on the moors. Still, I thought I could see in his face signs of better qualities than his father ever had. Good traits buried under neglect like flowers choked by weeds—but evidence of rich soil that could produce wonderful things under better circumstances.

Mr. Heathcliff, I believe, hadn't physically abused him—Hareton's fearless nature wouldn't have given him the satisfaction. He didn't have that timid quality that would have made tormenting him enjoyable in Heathcliff's eyes. Instead, he'd focused on turning him into a brute. Hareton was never taught to read or write, never corrected for bad behavior unless it annoyed his keeper, never guided toward good or warned against evil.

From what I heard, Joseph made things worse with his twisted favoritism, spoiling him as a boy because he was heir to the old family. Just as Joseph used to blame young Catherine Earnshaw and Heathcliff for driving old Mr. Earnshaw to drink with their "wicked ways," now he blamed all Hareton's faults on Heathcliff, the man who'd stolen his inheritance. If the boy cursed, Joseph wouldn't correct him no matter how badly he behaved. It seemed to satisfy Joseph to watch him go wrong—the boy was ruined, his soul damned, but Heathcliff would have to answer for it. God would demand Hareton's blood from Heathcliff's hands, and that thought gave Joseph immense comfort.

Joseph had given him pride in his name and heritage. He would have encouraged hatred between Hareton and Heathcliff if he'd dared, but his fear of Heathcliff was almost superstitious. So he kept his feelings to muttered complaints and private curses.

I don't claim to know exactly how they lived at Wuthering Heights in those days—I'm only repeating what I heard, since I rarely visited. The villagers said Mr. Heathcliff was stingy and a cruel landlord to his tenants. But inside, the house had regained its former comfort under the housekeeper's management. The wild parties from Hindley's time were over. The master was too dark-minded to want company, good or bad—and still is.

But I'm getting sidetracked. Miss Cathy rejected the peace offering of the puppy and demanded her own dogs, Charlie and Phoenix. They came limping over with their heads down, and we headed home, all of us in terrible moods.

I couldn't get my little lady to tell me how she'd spent her day, except that she'd headed for Penistone Crags as I'd guessed. She'd reached the farmhouse gate without incident when Hareton happened to come out with some dogs that attacked hers. There was quite a fight before the owners could separate them—that's how they met. Catherine told Hareton who she was and where she was going, and asked him to show her the way. She ended up charming him into going with her.

He showed her the Fairy Cave and twenty other strange places. But since I was in disgrace, she wouldn't describe any of the interesting things she'd seen. I gathered that she'd liked her guide until she hurt his feelings by treating him like a servant, and the housekeeper hurt hers by calling him her cousin. Then his rough language stuck in her heart—she who was always called "love" and "darling" and "queen" and "angel" by everyone at the Grange, to be cursed at by a stranger! She couldn't understand it.

It took work to get her to promise not to tell her father. I explained how he hated everyone at the Heights and how upset he'd be to know she'd been there. But mostly I emphasized that if she revealed I'd disobeyed his orders, he might be so angry he'd dismiss me. Cathy couldn't bear that thought. She gave her word and kept it, for my sake. After all, she was a sweet little girl.

19

A BLACK-EDGED LETTER ANNOUNCED WHEN MY MASTER WOULD return home. Isabella was dead. He wrote asking me to arrange mourning clothes for his daughter and prepare a room for his young nephew.

Catherine practically vibrated with excitement at the thought of her father coming back. She couldn't stop talking about all the wonderful things she imagined about her "real" cousin. When the evening of their arrival finally came, she'd been busy all day organizing her things. Now dressed in her new black dress—poor thing, her aunt's death didn't really mean much to her—she pestered me until I agreed to walk through the grounds with her to meet them.

"Linton is just six months younger than me," she chattered as we strolled over the mossy hills under the trees. "Won't it be wonderful to have him as a playmate! Aunt Isabella sent Papa a lock of his hair—it's lighter than mine, more golden, and just as fine. I've kept it safe in a little glass box. I've thought so many times about how nice it would be to meet him. Oh, I'm so happy! And Papa—dear, dear Papa! Come on, Ellen, let's run!"

She ran ahead and back again, over and over, while I walked steadily toward the gate. Finally she sat on the grassy bank beside the path, trying to wait patiently—but that was impossible. She couldn't sit still for a minute.

"What's taking them so long?" she burst out. "Oh, I see dust on the road—they're coming! No? When will they get here? Can't we go meet them—just half a mile, Ellen? Please say yes—just to those birch trees at the bend!"

I firmly refused. Finally her waiting ended—the carriage rolled into view. Miss Cathy shrieked and stretched out her arms the moment she saw her father's face in the window. He climbed out, almost as excited as she was, and for several minutes they had eyes only for each other.

While they hugged and talked, I peeked into the carriage to check on Linton. He was asleep in the corner, wrapped in a warm, fur-lined cloak as if it were winter. The boy looked like porcelain—translucent skin, bruised shadows under his eyes, as if the slightest touch might shatter him. He could have been mistaken for my master's younger brother, the resemblance was so strong. But there was a sickly irritability in his face that Edgar Linton never had. When Edgar saw me looking, he shook my hand and told me to close the door and let the boy rest—the journey had exhausted him. Cathy wanted to look, but her father told her to come along. They walked up through the park while I hurried ahead to prepare the servants.

"Now, darling," Mr. Linton said to his daughter as they paused at the front steps, "your cousin isn't as strong or cheerful as you are. Remember, he just lost his mother. Don't expect him to play and run around with you right away. And don't overwhelm him with talking—let him have some quiet tonight, all right?"

"Yes, yes, Papa," Catherine answered. "But I do want to see him, and he hasn't even looked out once!"

The carriage stopped, and the sleeping boy was lifted out by his uncle.

"This is your cousin Cathy, Linton," Edgar said, putting their small hands together. "She already likes you very much. Try not to upset her by crying tonight. Be cheerful now—the journey's over and you can rest and do whatever you like."

"Let me go to bed then," the boy answered, pulling away from Catherine's kiss and rubbing at his eyes to stop tears.

"Come on, there's a good boy," I whispered, leading him inside. "You'll make her cry too—look how worried she is about you!"

I'm not sure if it was actually worry, but Catherine put on a face as sad as his and went back to her father. All three went upstairs to the library where tea was waiting. I helped Linton out of his coat and hat and sat him in a chair by the table, but the moment he sat down, he started crying again. My master asked what was wrong.

"I can't sit on a chair," the boy sobbed.

"Go to the sofa then, and Ellen will bring you some tea," his uncle answered patiently.

I could tell the journey had been difficult with such a fussy, sickly child. Linton slowly dragged himself over and lay down. Cathy brought a footstool and her cup to sit beside him. At first she was quiet, but that couldn't last. She'd decided to make a pet of her little cousin, and she started stroking his hair, kissing his cheek, and offering him tea from her saucer like he was a baby. This actually pleased him—he wasn't much more than a baby himself. He dried his eyes and managed a weak smile.

"Oh, he'll do very well," the master said to me after watching them. "Very well, if we can keep him, Ellen. Having a child his own age around will give him new energy, and wanting to be stronger will make him stronger."

If we can keep him, I thought to myself, feeling a terrible doubt that we could. And then—how would that weakling survive at Wuthering Heights? That house would eat him alive. Between his father and Hareton, what kind of companions and teachers would they be?

Our doubts were answered even sooner than I expected. I'd just taken the children upstairs after tea and waited until Linton fell asleep—he wouldn't let me leave until then. I'd come back down and was lighting a bedroom candle for Mr. Edgar in the hall when a maid came from the kitchen to tell me that Joseph, Mr. Heathcliff's servant, was at the door asking to speak with the master.

"I'll find out what he wants first," I said, feeling very uneasy. "What a terrible time to bother people, right when they've come back from a long journey. I don't think the master can see him."

But Joseph had already walked through the kitchen while I was speaking and now stood in the hall. He was wearing his Sunday clothes with his sourest, most self-righteous expression. Holding his hat in one hand and his walking stick in the other, he wiped his shoes on the mat.

"Good evening, Joseph," I said coldly. "What brings you here tonight?"

"It's Master Linton I need to speak to," he answered, waving me aside dismissively.

"Mr. Linton is going to bed. Unless you have something

urgent to say, I'm sure he won't see you now," I said. "You'd better sit down and give me your message."

"Which room's his?" the fellow demanded, looking at all the closed doors.

I saw he was determined to bypass me, so I reluctantly went up to the library and announced the untimely visitor, suggesting he should be sent away until tomorrow. But Mr. Linton didn't have time to give me that authority—Joseph followed right behind me and pushed into the room. He planted himself on the far side of the table, both fists gripping the top of his walking stick, and announced in a loud voice, as if expecting an argument:

"Heathcliff sent me for his boy, and I'm not going back without him."

Edgar Linton was silent for a moment, his face overcome with sorrow. He would have pitied the child anyway, but remembering Isabella's hopes and fears for her son, her desperate wishes and how she'd entrusted the boy to his care, he was devastated at the thought of giving him up. He searched his mind for some way to avoid it. But there was no solution—showing any desire to keep Linton would only make Heathcliff more determined to take him. There was nothing to do but let him go. Still, he wasn't going to wake the child.

"Tell Mr. Heathcliff," he answered calmly, "that his son will come to Wuthering Heights tomorrow. He's in bed and too tired to travel tonight. You can also tell him that Linton's mother wanted him to stay in my care, and right now his health is very fragile."

"No!" Joseph said, thumping his stick on the floor and taking on an authoritative air. "No! That means nothing. Heathcliff don't care about the mother, or you neither. But he'll have his boy, and I'm taking him—so now you know!"

"You will not tonight!" Linton said firmly. "Go downstairs immediately and repeat to your master what I've said. Ellen, show him out. Go—"

And helping the angry old man along with a push, he got him out of the room and shut the door.

"Very well!" Joseph shouted as he slowly left. "Tomorrow he'll come himself—and then we'll see who gets thrown out!"

20

To prevent Joseph from making good on his threat, Mr. Linton ordered me to take the boy home early on Catherine's pony.

"Since we'll have no control over his future now," he said, "you absolutely can't tell my daughter where he's gone. She can't be around him anymore, and it's better if she doesn't know he's so close by—otherwise she'll be restless and want to visit the Heights. Just tell her his father sent for him suddenly and he had to leave."

Linton really didn't want to be dragged out of bed at five in the morning, and he was shocked when I told him we had more traveling to do. I tried to soften the blow by saying he was going to spend time with his father, Mr. Heathcliff, who was so eager to see him that he couldn't wait until Linton recovered from yesterday's journey.

"My father!" he cried, completely confused. "Mama never told me I had a father. Where does he live? I'd rather stay with Uncle."

"He lives just past those hills," I replied. "Not far at all—when you're feeling better, you could walk back here. And you should be happy to go home and meet him. You need to try to love him, like you loved your mother, and then he'll love you back."

"But why haven't I heard about him before?" Linton asked. "Why didn't Mama and he live together like normal people?"

"He had business that kept him in the north," I answered, "and your mother's health required her to live in the south."

"Why didn't Mama talk to me about him?" the child persisted. "She talked about Uncle all the time, and I learned to love him ages ago. How am I supposed to love Papa? I don't even know him."

"All children love their parents," I said. "Your mother probably thought you'd want to be with him if she mentioned him too often. Come on, let's hurry. An early morning ride is much better than another hour of sleep."

"Is SHE coming with us?" he demanded. "The girl I saw yesterday?"

"Not today."

"Is Uncle?"

"No, I'll be your companion."

Linton sank back into his pillow, lost in thought.

"I won't go without Uncle," he finally declared. "I don't even know where you're taking me."

I tried to convince him it was wrong to refuse to meet his father, but he stubbornly resisted getting dressed. I had to call Mr. Edgar to help coax him out of bed. We finally got the poor thing ready with several false promises that he'd be back soon, that Edgar and Cathy would visit, and other lies I made up along the way.

The fresh heather-scented air, bright sunshine, and Minny's gentle pace lifted his spirits after a while. He started asking questions about his new home with more interest.

"Is Wuthering Heights as nice as Thrushcross Grange?" he asked, turning for one last look at the valley, where mist was rising to form wispy clouds against the blue sky.

"It's not as hidden by trees," I replied, "and not quite as large, but you can see the countryside beautifully from every angle. The air is healthier for you—fresher and drier. The building might seem old and dark at first, but it's a respectable house—the second best in the neighborhood. You'll have wonderful walks on the moors. Hareton Earnshaw—Miss Cathy's other cousin, so yours too—will show you all the best spots. You can bring a book in good weather and make a green hollow your study. Sometimes your uncle might join you for walks—he often goes out on the hills."

"What's my father like?" he asked. "Is he young and handsome like Uncle?"

"He's as young," I said, "but he has black hair and eyes, and looks sterner. He's taller and bigger overall. He might not seem as gentle and kind at first—it's not his way. But be open and friendly with him, and naturally he'll love you more than any uncle could, because you're his own son."

"Black hair and eyes!" Linton mused. "I can't picture him. So I don't look like him?"

"Not much," I answered. Not at all, I thought, looking sadly at my companion's pale complexion, thin frame, and large, listless eyes—his mother's eyes, except they lacked her fiery spirit unless something upset him.

"How weird that he never came to see Mama and me," he murmured. "Has he ever seen me? If he has, I must have been a baby. I don't remember anything about him!"

"Master Linton," I said, "three hundred miles is a huge distance, and ten years feels very different to an adult than to you. Mr. Heathcliff probably planned to visit every summer but never found the right time. Now it's too late. Don't bother him with questions about it—it'll only upset him for no reason."

The boy stayed lost in his thoughts for the rest of the ride until we stopped at the farmhouse gate. I watched his face for his first impression. He studied the carved front, the small windows, the scraggly gooseberry bushes and crooked firs with serious concentration, then shook his head. He clearly didn't like the look of his new home, but he was smart enough not to complain yet—maybe it was better inside.

Before he got down, I went and opened the door. It was six-thirty. The family had just finished breakfast, and the servant was clearing the table. Joseph stood by his master's chair telling some story about a lame horse while Hareton was getting ready for the hayfield.

"Hello, Nelly!" Mr. Heathcliff said when he saw me. "I was afraid I'd have to come get my property myself. You've brought it? Let's see what we can make of it."

He stood and strode to the door, Hareton and Joseph following curiously. Poor Linton looked terrified as he scanned the three faces.

"Well now," Joseph said after studying him carefully, "he's swapped them on you, Master—this is his daughter!"

Heathcliff stared at his son until the boy was shaking with confusion, then let out a scornful laugh.

"God! What a beauty! What a lovely, charming thing!" he exclaimed. "Did they raise it on snails and sour milk, Nelly? Damn my soul, this is worse than I expected—and God knows I wasn't expecting much!"

I told the trembling, bewildered child to get down and come inside. He didn't fully understand what his father was saying or if it was even directed at him—he wasn't even sure this grim, sneering stranger WAS his father. He clung to me, increasingly frightened, and when Mr. Heathcliff sat down and ordered him to "come here," he hid his face against my shoulder and cried.

"Stop that!" Heathcliff said, reaching out and dragging him roughly between his knees, then holding his head up by the chin. "None of that nonsense! We're not going to hurt you, Linton—that IS your name? You're completely your mother's child! Where's my part in you, you whining little chicken?"

He pulled off the boy's cap and pushed back his thick blond curls, felt his thin arms and small fingers. During this inspection, Linton stopped crying and looked up at his examiner with huge blue eyes.

"Do you know me?" Heathcliff asked after confirming that every limb was equally weak and fragile.

"No," Linton said with vacant fear.

"You've heard of me, surely?"

"No."

"No? Shame on your mother for never teaching you about your father! You ARE my son, I'll tell you that. And your mother was a wicked bitch to leave you ignorant of what kind of father you had. Now don't flinch and blush! Though I'm glad to see you don't have completely white blood. Be a good boy and I'll take care of you. Nelly, if you're tired, sit down. If not, go home. I'm sure you'll report everything you see and hear to that cipher at the Grange, and this won't be settled while you're hanging around."

"Well," I replied, "I hope you'll be kind to the boy, Mr. Heathcliff, or you won't have him long. He's all the family you'll ever have—remember that."

"I'll be very kind to him, don't worry," he said, laughing. "But nobody else can be kind to him—I want all his affection for myself. And to start my kindness—Joseph, bring the boy some breakfast. Hareton, you worthless calf, get to work. Yes, Nell," he added after they left, "my son will inherit your place someday, and I don't want him dying before I'm sure he'll be my successor. Besides, he's MINE, and I want the triumph of seeing MY descendant become lord of their estates—my blood ruling over theirs, my child paying their children to work the land they once owned. That's the only reason I can stand the little wretch. I despise him personally and hate him for the memories he brings back. But that's enough reason—he's as safe with me as he'd be with your master. I've prepared a room upstairs, furnished nicely. I've hired a tutor to come three times a week from twenty miles away to teach him whatever he wants to learn. I've ordered Hareton to obey him. I've arranged everything to keep him superior, to maintain his gentleman status above his companions. I do regret he hardly deserves the trouble. If I could wish for anything, it would be to find him worthy of pride. Instead I'm stuck with this pathetic, whining creature!"

While he spoke, Joseph returned with a bowl of porridge and set it before Linton, who looked at the plain meal with disgust and said he couldn't eat it. I could see the old servant shared his master's contempt for the child, though he had to hide it since Heathcliff clearly wanted his staff to treat the boy with respect.

"Can't eat it?" Joseph repeated, peering into Linton's face and whispering so he wouldn't be overheard. "Master Hareton never ate anything else when he was little, and what was good enough for him is good enough for you!"

"I WON'T eat it!" Linton snapped. "Take it away."

Joseph grabbed the food indignantly and brought it to us.

"Something wrong with the food?" he asked, shoving the tray under Heathcliff's nose.

"What could be wrong with it?"

"Well!" Joseph answered, "this dainty boy says he can't eat it. But I suppose that's right! His mother was the same—we were almost too dirty to plant the grain for her bread."

"Don't mention his mother to me," the master said angrily. "Get him something he can eat, that's all. What does he usually have, Nelly?"

I suggested warm milk or tea, and the housekeeper was told to prepare some. Well, I thought, his father's selfishness might actually help him. He recognizes the boy's delicate health and knows he needs decent treatment. I'll comfort Mr. Edgar by telling him about this unexpected turn in Heathcliff's attitude.

Having no excuse to stay longer, I slipped out while Linton was nervously backing away from a friendly sheep-dog. But he was too alert to be fooled—as I closed the door, I heard him cry out, his voice cracking the way voices do when tears and terror fight for the same breath:

"Don't leave me! I won't stay here! I won't stay here!"

The latch lifted and fell—they wouldn't let him out. I mounted Minny and urged her to a trot, and so my brief guardianship ended.

21

CATHERINE WAS DEVASTATED THAT DAY. SHE'D WOKEN UP excited to spend time with her cousin, then completely fell apart when she found out he was gone. The crying and carrying on got so bad that Edgar himself had to calm her down, promising Linton would come back soon—though he added "if I can get him," and we all knew that wasn't happening.

The promise barely helped. Time did more to heal the wound. She kept asking when Linton would return, but by the time she actually saw him again, she'd forgotten what he even looked like.

Whenever I ran into Wuthering Heights' housekeeper on business in Gimmerton, I'd ask about the boy. He lived almost as isolated as Catherine, never seen by anyone. From what she told me, he stayed sickly and was a constant pain to deal with. Mr. Heathcliff seemed to hate him more every day, though he tried to hide it. He couldn't stand the sound of the boy's voice and could barely sit in the same room with him for more than a few minutes. They rarely talked. Linton did his lessons and spent evenings in what they called the parlor, or stayed in bed all day with endless coughs, colds, aches, and pains.

"Never seen such a coward," the woman added. "Or anyone so obsessed with their health. God forbid I leave a window cracked in the evening—'Oh, the night air is killing me!' Has to have a fire burning in the middle of summer. Joseph's pipe smoke is 'poison.' Always needs sweets and treats, milk, milk, forever milk—doesn't care that the rest of us are freezing and starving in winter. There he sits, wrapped in his fur cloak by the fire, sipping his toast-water or whatever slop he's got warming. When Hareton tries to be nice and keep him company—Hareton's not mean, just rough around the edges—it always ends with one cursing and the other crying. I swear the master would love to see Earnshaw beat him senseless if he wasn't his son. He'd throw him out if he knew half the babying that boy demands. But Heathcliff never goes near the parlor, and if Linton acts up anywhere else, he sends him straight upstairs."

From all this, I figured that being completely unloved had turned young Linton selfish and miserable—if he wasn't already. I lost interest in him, though I still felt sorry for the child and wished we'd kept him with us. Mr. Edgar wanted updates—he thought about the boy constantly and would've taken risks to see him. He once asked me to find out if Linton ever came to the village. The housekeeper said only twice, on horseback with his father, and both times he was "completely exhausted" for three or four days after. That housekeeper left about two years later. Her replacement, who I didn't know, still works there.

Life at the Grange continued peacefully until Cathy turned sixteen. We never celebrated her birthday—it was also the anniversary of her mother's death. Edgar always spent that day alone in the library, then walked to Gimmerton cemetery at dusk, often staying past midnight. So Catherine had to entertain herself.

This particular March twentieth was a gorgeous spring day. After her father went to his room, she came downstairs dressed to go out.

"I want to walk along the moor with you, Ellen. Papa said we could if we stay close and come back within an hour."

"Hurry up then!" she said. "I know exactly where I want to go—there's a spot where the grouse nest. I want to see if they've started yet."

"That must be pretty far up," I said. "They don't nest near the edge."

"It's not far. I've been there with Papa."

I grabbed my bonnet and went along, not thinking much of it. She bounded ahead like a puppy, racing back to me then darting off again. At first I enjoyed myself—listening to the larks singing, feeling the warm sun, watching my beautiful girl with her golden curls flying behind her, her cheeks pink as wild roses, her eyes bright with pure joy. She was an angel in those days. Such a shame she couldn't stay content.

"Where are these grouse, Miss Cathy?" I called after a while. "We should've found them by now. We're way past the park fence."

"Just a little further, Ellen," she kept saying. "Just over that hill, past that ridge—I'll flush out the birds any minute."

But there were so many hills and ridges that I finally got tired and said we had to turn back. I shouted after her—

she'd gotten way ahead—but she either didn't hear or didn't care. She kept going, and I had to follow.

She disappeared into a hollow, and when I caught sight of her again, she was two miles closer to Wuthering Heights than the Grange. I saw two people stop her, and I knew one was Heathcliff.

Cathy had been caught looking for grouse nests on his land—technically poaching.

"I haven't taken anything or even found anything," she said as I struggled to reach them, holding out her empty hands. "I wasn't going to take them. Papa told me there were lots up here, and I just wanted to see the eggs."

Heathcliff looked at me with a nasty smile that said he knew exactly who we were and enjoyed having us at a disadvantage. "And who's 'Papa'?" he asked.

"Mr. Linton of Thrushcross Grange," she answered. "I thought you'd recognize me, or you wouldn't talk to me like that."

"You think Papa is so highly respected?" he said sarcastically.

"And what are you?" Catherine asked, studying him curiously. Then she pointed to Hareton. "That man—I've seen him before. Is he your son?"

Hareton had grown bigger and stronger in two years but was still just as rough and awkward.

"Miss Cathy," I interrupted, "we've been out almost three hours already. We really need to go back."

"No, that's not my son," Heathcliff said, pushing me aside. "But I have one, and you've met him before. Since your nurse is in such a hurry, I think you'd both benefit from a rest. Just come around this patch of heather to my house. You'll actually get home faster, and I promise you'll be welcome."

I whispered urgently that she absolutely could not accept—it was completely out of the question.

"Why?" she asked out loud. "I'm tired of running and the ground's all dewy. I can't sit here. Let's go, Ellen. Besides, he says I've seen his son. I think he's wrong, but I bet I know where he lives—that farmhouse I found when I went to Penistone Crags. Right?"

"Exactly. Come on, Nelly, be quiet. She'll enjoy visiting us. Hareton, go ahead with the girl. You walk with me, Nelly."

"She's not going anywhere with you," I said, trying to pull my arm free from his grip. But she was already practically at the door, running around the corner at full speed. Hareton didn't even pretend to escort her—he slunk off down the road and disappeared.

"Mr. Heathcliff, this is wrong," I insisted. "You know you're up to no good. She'll see Linton, and everything will come out as soon as we get home. I'll get all the blame."

"I want her to see Linton," he answered. "He's been looking better lately—doesn't happen often. And we'll convince her to keep the visit secret. What's the harm?"

"The harm is that her father would hate me if he found out I let her in your house. I know you're up to something," I said.

"My plan is completely honest. I'll tell you everything," he said. "I want the two cousins to fall in love and get married. I'm being generous to your master—his daughter has no inheritance coming to her, and if she goes along with my plan, she'll be set up immediately as Linton's co-heir."

"If Linton dies—and his health is terrible—Catherine would inherit everything anyway," I pointed out.

"No, she wouldn't. There's nothing in the will that guarantees it. His property would come to me. But to avoid any disputes, I want them married, and I'm going to make it happen."

"And I'm making sure she never comes near your house again," I said as we reached the gate where Cathy was waiting.

Heathcliff told me to shut up and hurried ahead to open the door. Catherine kept looking at him like she couldn't quite figure him out, but now he smiled when he caught her eye and spoke gently to her. I was stupid enough to hope that remembering her mother might keep him from wanting to hurt her.

Linton stood by the fireplace. He'd been out walking—his cap was still on and he was calling for Joseph to bring dry shoes. He'd grown tall for almost sixteen, and looked better than I remembered—brighter eyes, better color—though it was just temporary improvement from fresh air and sunshine.

"Now, who's this?" Heathcliff asked Cathy. "Can you tell?"

"Your son?" she guessed, looking back and forth between them uncertainly.

"Yes, yes. But is this really the first time you've seen him since? Think! You have a short memory. Linton, don't you remember your cousin who you wanted so badly to meet?"

"What—Linton!" Cathy cried, lighting up with joy. "Is that little Linton? He's taller than me! Are you really Linton?"

The boy stepped forward to confirm it. She kissed him enthusiastically, and they stared at each other, amazed at how much they'd both changed. Catherine had reached her full height—she was perfectly proportioned, strong as steel, glowing with health and energy. Linton looked tired and fragile, painfully thin, but he had a certain grace that made him not entirely unappealing.

After showering her cousin with affection, Catherine went to Heathcliff, who was lurking by the door, pretending to look outside while actually watching everything inside.

"So you're my uncle!" she said, reaching up to kiss him. "I thought I liked you, even though you were mean at first. Why don't you visit us at the Grange with Linton? It's so strange—living this close all these years and never seeing us. Why?"

"I visited too often before you were born," he answered. "There—damn it! Save your kisses for Linton. They're wasted on me."

"Bad Ellen!" Catherine cried, turning on me with more kisses. "Wicked Ellen! Trying to stop me from coming in. But I'll take this walk every morning from now on. Can I, uncle? Sometimes I'll bring Papa. Won't you be happy to see us?"

"Of course," he replied with a barely hidden grimace, clearly dreading both potential visitors. "But wait," he continued, turning to her. "Now that I think about it, I should tell you—Mr. Linton has something against me. We had a terrible fight once, completely vicious. If you mention coming here, he'll forbid it completely. So you can't tell him, unless you don't care about seeing your cousin anymore. You can visit if you want, but you absolutely can't mention it."

"Why did you fight?" Catherine asked, deflated.

"He thought I wasn't good enough to marry his sister," Heathcliff answered. "He was upset that I got her. His pride was hurt, and he'll never forgive it."

"That's wrong!" she said. "Someday I'll tell him so. But

Linton and I aren't part of your fight. I won't come here then—he can come to the Grange."

"It's too far for me," her cousin whined. "Walking four miles would kill me. No, come here, Miss Catherine. Not every morning, but once or twice a week."

His father shot him a look of complete contempt.

"I'm wasting my time, Nelly," he muttered to me. "Miss Catherine—as the idiot calls her—will figure out what he's worth and dump him. Now if it had been Hareton! You know, twenty times a day I wish Hareton was mine, even degraded as he is. I would've loved that boy if he'd been anyone else's. But I think he's safe from her love. I'll set him against that pathetic creature, unless it gets its act together. We figure it'll barely make it to eighteen. God, look at the useless thing! So busy drying his feet he won't even look at her. Linton!"

"Yes, father?"

"Don't you have anything to show your cousin? Not even a rabbit hutch or bird's nest? Take her to the garden before you change your shoes, and show her your horse in the stable."

"Wouldn't you rather sit here?" Linton asked Cathy reluctantly.

"I don't know," she replied, looking longingly at the door, obviously wanting to be active.

He stayed put, huddling closer to the fire. Heathcliff got up and went through the kitchen to the yard, calling for Hareton. They both came back in. Hareton had been washing—his cheeks were glowing and his hair was wet.

"Oh, uncle," Cathy said, remembering what the housekeeper had told her. "That's not my cousin, is he?"

"Yes," he replied. "Your mother's nephew. Don't you like him?"

Catherine looked uncomfortable.

"Isn't he handsome?" he pressed.

The rude girl stood on tiptoes and whispered something in Heathcliff's ear. He laughed. Hareton's face darkened—I could see he was sensitive about being looked down on and vaguely aware of his inferior position. But Heathcliff covered for him.

"You'll be the favorite, Hareton! She says you're a—what was it? Well, something very flattering. Here, take her around the farm. And act like a gentleman, understand? No swearing. Don't stare when she's not looking, and hide your face when she is. When you speak, go slowly and keep your hands out of your pockets. Go on, entertain her as best you can."

He watched them walk past the window. Earnshaw kept his face completely turned away from Catherine, studying the familiar landscape like he'd never seen it before. Catherine snuck glances at him, clearly unimpressed, then focused on finding things to amuse herself, humming to fill the silence.

"I've shut him up," Heathcliff observed. "He won't say a single word! Nelly, you remember me at his age—actually, younger. Did I ever look that stupid, that 'gormless' as Joseph says?"

"Worse," I said. "Because you were sullen too."

"I enjoy him," he continued, thinking out loud. "He's exactly what I expected. If he were naturally stupid, it wouldn't be half as satisfying. But he's not stupid, and I understand exactly what he's feeling—I felt it all myself. I know what he's suffering right now, and it's just the beginning. He'll never escape his ignorance and coarseness. I've got him more trapped than his bastard father ever had me, and lower too, because he's actually proud of being a brute.

I've taught him to despise anything civilized as silly and weak. Don't you think Hindley would be proud of his son if he could see him? Almost as proud as I am of mine. But here's the difference—one is gold being used as paving stones, the other is tin polished to look like silver. Mine has nothing valuable about him, but I'll squeeze whatever I can from such poor material. Hareton had first-rate qualities, and they're all wasted—worse than wasted. I have nothing to regret; he has more to regret than anyone knows. And the best part? Hareton absolutely adores me! I've beaten Hindley there. If that dead villain could rise from his grave to curse me for wronging his son, he'd get to watch his son defend me—angry that his father would dare insult his only friend in the world!"

Heathcliff laughed wickedly at the thought. I said nothing—he wasn't expecting a response.

Meanwhile, Linton was getting restless, probably regretting that he'd given up Catherine's company just to avoid a little effort. His father noticed him glancing at the window and reaching for his cap.

"Get up, you lazy boy!" he said with fake enthusiasm. "Go after them! They're just by the beehives."

Linton dragged himself up and went outside. Through the open window, I heard Cathy asking Hareton about the inscription over the door. Hareton stared up and scratched his head like an idiot.

"It's some damn writing," he said. "I can't read it."

"Can't read it?" Catherine exclaimed. "I can read it—it's English. But I want to know why it's there."

Linton giggled—the first sign of amusement he'd shown.

"He doesn't know his letters," he told his cousin. "Can you believe such a complete dunce exists?"

"Is he all there?" Cathy asked seriously. "Or is he simple —not right? I've asked him questions twice and he looked so blank I don't think he understands me. I can barely understand him!"

Linton laughed again and looked at Hareton mockingly. Hareton definitely seemed confused at that moment.

"There's nothing wrong except laziness, right, Earnshaw?" Linton said. "My cousin thinks you're an idiot. This is what you get for scorning 'book-learning,' as you'd say. Have you noticed his horrible Yorkshire accent, Catherine?"

"Why the devil would I need that?" Hareton growled, more comfortable answering his daily tormentor. He was about to say more, but the two cousins burst out laughing. My silly girl was delighted she could turn his rough speech into entertainment.

"Where's the 'use of the devil' in that sentence?" Linton giggled. "Papa told you not to swear, and you can't open your mouth without cursing. Try to act like a gentleman for once!"

"If you weren't more of a girl than a boy, I'd knock you down right now, you pathetic stick!" Hareton shot back, retreating with his face burning from rage and humiliation. He knew he was being insulted but didn't know how to fight back properly.

Heathcliff had heard everything, just like I had. He smiled watching Hareton leave, then looked at the chattering pair in the doorway with pure disgust. Linton had come alive gossiping about Hareton's faults and telling stories about him, while Catherine laughed at his mean, spiteful comments without realizing how cruel they were. I started to dislike Linton more than pity him, and almost understood why his father thought so little of him.

We stayed until afternoon—I couldn't get Cathy to leave

earlier. Luckily, her father hadn't left his room and didn't know how long we'd been gone. Walking home, I wanted to explain what kind of people we'd just left, but she'd decided I was biased against them.

"Aha!" she said. "You're on Papa's side, Ellen. You're not fair—otherwise you wouldn't have lied to me for years about where Linton lived. I'm really angry, but I'm too happy to show it! But don't say anything bad about my uncle. He's my uncle, remember, and I'll scold Papa for fighting with him."

She went on like that until I gave up trying to change her mind. She didn't mention the visit that night since she didn't see her father. But the next day it all came out, much to my frustration—though I wasn't completely sorry. I thought he'd do a better job than me of warning her off. But he was too gentle in explaining why she should stay away from the Heights, and Catherine wanted solid reasons for any rule that limited what she wanted to do.

"Papa!" she said after their morning greetings. "Guess who I saw yesterday on the moors! Oh, Papa, you jumped! You haven't been honest with me, have you? I saw—but listen, I'll tell you how I found you out. And Ellen, who's been helping you, pretended to feel sorry for me when I kept hoping Linton would come back!"

She told him everything about her trip and what happened. My master gave me several reproachful looks but said nothing until she finished. Then he pulled her close and asked if she knew why he'd hidden that Linton lived nearby. Did she think it was to deny her harmless pleasure?

"It was because you don't like Mr. Heathcliff," she answered.

"So you think I care more about my feelings than yours, Cathy?" he said. "No, it wasn't because I dislike Mr. Heathcliff—it's because he dislikes me. He's an evil man who enjoys destroying people he hates if they give him any chance. I knew you couldn't be friends with your cousin without dealing with him, and I knew he'd hate you because of me. So for your own good—nothing else—I made sure you wouldn't see Linton again. I meant to explain when you were older. I'm sorry I waited."

"But Mr. Heathcliff was perfectly nice, Papa," Catherine said, not convinced at all. "He didn't mind us seeing each other. He said I could visit whenever I wanted—I just couldn't tell you because you'd fought with him and wouldn't forgive him for marrying Aunt Isabella. And you won't. YOU'RE the one being difficult. He's willing to let Linton and me be friends, and you're not."

Seeing she wouldn't believe him about Heathcliff's character, Edgar quickly told her about how he'd treated Isabella and stolen Wuthering Heights. He couldn't bear talking about it long—though he rarely mentioned it, he still felt the same horror and hatred for his old enemy since Catherine's mother died. "She might still be alive if not for him!" was his constant bitter thought. To him, Heathcliff was a murderer.

Miss Cathy—who'd never known real evil, only her own small acts of disobedience and temper that she always regretted immediately—was shocked to learn someone could hold onto revenge for years and carry out their plans without any remorse. This new view of human nature, which she'd never encountered in her sheltered life, impressed and horrified her so much that Edgar didn't need to say more.

"You'll understand later, darling, why I want you to avoid his house and family. Now go back to your usual activities and forget about them."

Catherine kissed her father and quietly did her lessons for two hours as usual. She spent the day with him in the grounds, and everything seemed normal. But that evening, when I went to help her undress, I found her crying on her knees beside the bed.

"Oh, stop it, silly child!" I said. "If you had real problems, you'd be ashamed to cry over this small disappointment. You've never had any real sorrow, Miss Catherine. Imagine if your father and I were dead and you were alone in the world—how would you feel then? Compare that to this situation and be grateful for the friends you have instead of wanting more."

"I'm not crying for myself, Ellen," she answered. "It's for him. He's expecting me tomorrow, and he'll be so disappointed. He'll wait for me, and I won't come!"

"Nonsense! Do you think he's thought about you as much as you have about him? He has Hareton for company. Not one person in a hundred would cry over losing a relative they'd only met twice. Linton will figure out what happened and forget about you."

"But can't I write a note explaining why I can't come?" she asked, standing up. "And send those books I promised? His books aren't as nice as mine, and he really wanted them when I told him how interesting they were. Can't I, Ellen?"

"Absolutely not!" I said firmly. "Then he'd write back, and it would never end. No, Miss Catherine, you have to cut off all contact. That's what your father expects, and I'll make sure it happens."

"But how can one little note—" she started, looking pleading.

"Quiet! We're not starting with your little notes. Get in bed."

She gave me such a nasty look that I wouldn't kiss her

goodnight at first. I tucked her in and shut her door, very annoyed. But halfway down the hall I felt bad and went back quietly. There was Miss standing at the table with blank paper and a pencil, which she quickly hid when she saw me.

"Nobody will deliver that, Catherine, even if you write it. And I'm putting out your candle now."

I snuffed out the flame, getting slapped and called a "cross thing!" for my trouble. I left again, and she locked her door in one of her worst moods.

The letter got finished and sent anyway, delivered by the milk delivery from the village—though I didn't find that out until later. Weeks passed, and Cathy's mood improved, though she developed a habit of hiding in corners by herself. If I came near while she was reading, she'd jump and bend over her book, obviously trying to hide it. I noticed loose papers sticking out from the pages. She also started coming down early in the morning and hanging around the kitchen like she was waiting for something. She had a small drawer in a library cabinet that she'd spend hours fussing with, always careful to take the key when she left.

One day while she was looking through this drawer, I noticed her toys and trinkets had been replaced with folded papers. My curiosity and suspicion kicked in. I decided to investigate her secret treasures. That night, after she and Edgar were safely upstairs, I found a key that fit the lock among my housekeeping keys. I emptied everything into my apron and took it to my room to examine in private.

I couldn't believe it, even though I'd suspected—they were love letters, written almost daily between them. Linton's early ones were awkward and short, but they gradually became long, gushing love letters—silly, as you'd expect from someone his age, but with bits that seemed borrowed from someone more experienced. Some were bizarre mixtures of passion and emptiness, starting with real feeling but ending in the fake, overblown style a schoolboy might use writing to an imaginary girlfriend. Whether Cathy liked them, I don't know—they looked like worthless garbage to me. After reading enough, I tied them in a handkerchief, put them aside, and relocked the empty drawer.

Following her new routine, she came down early the next morning and went to the kitchen. I watched her meet a certain delivery boy at the door. While the dairy maid filled his milk can, she slipped something into his jacket pocket and pulled something out. I went around through the garden and ambushed the messenger. He fought hard to protect his delivery, and we spilled milk everywhere, but I got the letter. After threatening him with serious consequences if he didn't hurry home, I stayed behind the wall to read Miss Cathy's loving note. It was simpler and more heartfelt than her cousin's—very sweet and very stupid. I shook my head and went back inside thinking.

Since it was raining, she couldn't wander the grounds. After her morning lessons, she went straight to her drawer for comfort. Her father sat reading at the table. I deliberately found some mending to do on the curtains, keeping my eyes on her the whole time.

No bird returning to find its nest robbed could have shown more complete despair than she did with her single "Oh!" and the way her happy face transformed. Mr. Linton looked up.

"What's wrong, love? Are you hurt?"

His tone told her he hadn't found her stash.

"No, Papa!" she gasped. "Ellen! Ellen! Come upstairs—I'm sick!"

I followed her out as commanded.

"Oh, Ellen! You took them," she said immediately, dropping to her knees once we were alone. "Please give them back, and I'll never do it again! Don't tell Papa. You haven't told Papa, have you? Say you haven't! I've been terribly bad, but I won't do it anymore!"

I told her sternly to stand up.

"Well, Miss Catherine, you've really gotten yourself into something, haven't you? You should be ashamed! What a pile of trash you've been studying in your free time—good enough to publish! What do you think your father will say when I show him? I haven't yet, but don't think I'll keep your ridiculous secrets. For shame! And you must have started this—he wouldn't have thought to begin writing, I'm sure."

"I didn't! I didn't!" Cathy sobbed, heartbroken. "I didn't even think about loving him until—"

"LOVING!" I said as mockingly as possible. "LOVING! Has anyone ever heard such nonsense? I might as well talk about loving the miller who comes once a year to buy grain. Pretty love indeed! You've seen Linton for maybe four hours total in your life! Now here's this baby nonsense. I'm taking it to the library, and we'll see what your father says about this LOVE."

She lunged for her precious letters, but I held them over my head. She begged frantically for me to burn them—do anything but show them to her father. Since I was more inclined to laugh than scold—it was all just girlish silliness—I finally gave in a little.

"If I agree to burn them, will you promise never to send or receive another letter, or book—I see you've been sending him books—or locks of hair, or rings, or toys?"

"We don't send toys," Catherine said, her pride overcoming her shame.

"Nothing at all then, my lady? Otherwise, here I go."

"I promise, Ellen!" she cried, grabbing my dress. "Oh, put them in the fire, please!"

But when I started to open up the fireplace with the poker, the sacrifice was too much for her. She begged me to save one or two.

"One or two, Ellen, to keep for Linton's sake!"

I untied the handkerchief and started dropping them in one by one, watching the flames curl up the chimney.

"I'll have one, you cruel thing!" she screamed, shoving her hand into the fire and pulling out some half-burned pieces, burning her fingers in the process.

"Fine—and I'll keep some to show your father!" I said, shaking the rest back into the bundle and heading for the door again.

She threw her blackened pieces into the flames and gestured for me to finish burning them. When it was done, I stirred up the ashes and buried them under fresh coals. She went to her room, silent and deeply wounded.

I went down to tell Edgar that his daughter's sickness had mostly passed but she should rest. She skipped dinner but appeared at tea, pale, red-eyed, and remarkably subdued. The next morning I answered the correspondence with a note: "Master Heathcliff is requested to send no more notes to Miss Linton, as she will not answer them."

22

Summer faded into early autumn. We were past the harvest season, but it came late that year—some of our fields still hadn't been cleared. Mr. Linton and Cathy often walked out to watch the farmworkers, and on the last evening of gathering grain, they stayed until dusk. The night turned cold and damp, and my master caught a terrible cold that settled deep in his lungs. It kept him trapped indoors for the entire winter.

Poor Cathy had been noticeably sadder since her secret correspondence ended. Her father insisted she read less and exercise more. Without his company, I tried to fill the gap as best I could—though I was a poor substitute. I could only spare two or three hours from my daily duties to walk with her, and we both knew my company wasn't what she wanted.

One October afternoon—or maybe early November—the sky was watery blue, half-hidden by dark clouds racing in from the west, promising heavy rain. The paths rustled with wet, dead leaves. I asked my young lady to skip her walk, certain we'd get caught in a downpour.

She refused. Reluctantly, I grabbed my cloak and umbrella to accompany her on a walk to the bottom of the park—the formal path she always chose when she was depressed. And she was always depressed when Mr. Edgar's health got worse. He never complained, but she and I could tell from his silence and the sadness in his face.

She walked slowly, no running or skipping now, even though the cold wind should have made her want to race. From the corner of my eye, I kept catching her wiping something from her cheek. I looked around for something to distract her.

On one side of the road, a high bank rose up with hazel trees and stunted oaks clinging to it, their roots half-exposed. The soil was too loose, and strong winds had blown some trees nearly horizontal. In summer, Miss Catherine loved to climb these trunks and sit in the branches, swinging twenty feet above the ground. I was proud of how agile and fearless she was, though I always scolded her when I caught her up there—gently enough that she knew she didn't really have to come down. From lunch until tea, she'd lie in her wind-rocked cradle, singing old nursery songs I'd taught her, or watching birds teach their babies to fly, or just dozing with her eyes closed, half-thinking, half-dreaming—happier than I can describe.

"Look, Miss!" I said, pointing to a spot under the roots of a twisted tree. "Winter's not here yet. There's a little flower up there—the last bluebell from all those that covered the hill in July. Will you climb up and pick it to show your father?"

Cathy stared at the lonely flower trembling in the dirt for a long moment. "No," she finally said. "I won't touch it. It looks so sad, doesn't it, Ellen?"

"Yes," I agreed. "About as withered and lifeless as you

look—your cheeks have no color at all. Come on, let's hold hands and run. You're so down today, I bet I could actually keep up with you."

"No," she repeated, and kept wandering along, pausing to look at moss, pale grass, or bright orange mushrooms among the brown leaves. Every few moments, she lifted her hand to wipe her face.

"Catherine, why are you crying, love?" I asked, putting my arm around her shoulders. "Don't cry just because Papa has a cold. Be grateful it's nothing worse."

She stopped holding back then—her breath came in gasping sobs.

"Oh, but it will be something worse," she said. "What will I do when Papa and you leave me all alone? I can't forget what you said, Ellen—I hear it all the time. How different life will be, how empty the world will be, when Papa and you are dead."

"You might die before either of us," I replied. "It's wrong to expect the worst. We probably have years and years ahead of us. Your father is young, and I'm strong and only forty-five. My mother lived to eighty, sharp as ever. Even if Mr. Linton only lives to sixty, that's more years than you've been alive, Miss. Isn't it foolish to grieve for something that might not happen for twenty years?"

"But Aunt Isabella was younger than Papa," she said, looking up with fragile hope.

"Aunt Isabella didn't have you and me to take care of her," I answered. "She wasn't as happy as your father—she didn't have as much to live for. All you need to do is take good care of him and keep him cheerful. Don't give him anything to worry about—remember that, Cathy! I won't lie to you—you could kill him if you were reckless and kept pining over Heathcliff's son, who'd be happy to see your father in his grave. If your father found out you were still grieving over that separation, it would destroy him."

"I don't care about anything except Papa's illness," she said. "Nothing else matters compared to him. And I'll never —never—oh, never do or say anything to upset him as long as I live. I love him more than myself, Ellen. I know because I pray every night that I'll outlive him—I'd rather be miserable myself than have him suffer. That proves I love him more than myself."

"Good words," I said. "But you need to prove it with actions too. After he's better, don't forget the promises you make when you're scared."

As we talked, we approached a door that opened onto the road. My young lady, brightening a bit, climbed up and sat on top of the wall, reaching over to pick rose hips that bloomed scarlet on the wild rose bushes hanging over the road. The lower berries were gone—only birds could reach the high ones, except from where Cathy sat. Stretching to reach them, her hat fell off. Since the door was locked, she decided to climb down to get it.

"Be careful," I warned, but she'd already disappeared over the wall. Getting back up proved much harder—the stones were smooth and well-fitted, and the rose bushes and blackberry vines gave no help for climbing. Like an idiot, I hadn't thought of that until I heard her laughing.

"Ellen! You'll have to get the key, or I'll have to run around to the porter's lodge. I can't climb back up from this side!"

"Stay there," I called. "I have my keys with me—maybe one will work."

Catherine entertained herself by dancing around while I tried every large key on my ring. None of them fit. I was about to tell her to wait while I ran home for the right key when I heard the sound of a horse approaching. Cathy stopped dancing.

"Who is that?" I whispered.

"Ellen, I wish you could open the door," she whispered back anxiously.

"Miss Linton!" called a deep voice—the rider's. "I'm glad to see you. Don't rush inside—I need to talk to you."

"I won't speak to you, Mr. Heathcliff," Catherine answered. "Papa says you're wicked and you hate both of us. Ellen says the same."

"That's beside the point," said Heathcliff—for it was him. "I don't hate my son, and it's about him we need to talk. Yes, you should blush. Two or three months ago, weren't you writing to Linton? Playing at being in love? You both deserved a beating for that! Especially you—you're older and should know better. I have your letters, and if you give me any attitude, I'll send them to your father. I suppose you got bored with your game and dropped it? Well, you dropped Linton into despair along with it. He was serious—genuinely in love. I swear he's dying for you, breaking his heart over your cruelty. Not metaphorically—actually dying. Hareton's been mocking him for six weeks, and I've tried everything to snap him out of it, but he gets worse every day. He'll be dead before summer unless you come back to him!"

"How can you lie like that to the poor child?" I called from inside the wall. "Keep riding! How can you make up such ridiculous stories? Miss Cathy, I'll break this lock with a stone—don't believe his lies. You know it's impossible to die of love for someone you barely know."

"I didn't realize we had an audience," the villain muttered. "Mrs. Dean, I like you, but not your two-faced behavior," he said louder. "How can YOU lie by claiming I hate the 'poor child'? Making up horror stories to keep her away from my door?"

He paused, letting his words sink in. "Catherine Linton —even your name makes me warm—my dear girl, I'll be away all week. Come see if I'm telling the truth. Do this: imagine your father in my position and Linton in yours." His voice softened dangerously. "How would you feel if your lover refused to comfort you when your own father begged him to? Don't make the same mistake out of stubbornness."

He looked directly at her. "I swear on my soul, he's dying. And only you can save him."

The lock finally gave way and I rushed out.

"I swear Linton is dying," Heathcliff repeated, staring hard at me. "Grief and disappointment are killing him. Nelly, if you won't let her come, you can check for yourself. But I won't be back until next week. I think even your master wouldn't object to her visiting her cousin."

"Come inside," I said, grabbing Cathy's arm and pulling her back through the door. She resisted, staring at Heathcliff's face with troubled eyes. His expression was too stern to reveal the lies beneath.

He brought his horse closer and leaned down. "Miss Catherine, I'll admit I have little patience with Linton, and Hareton and Joseph have even less. He's stuck with harsh people. He's desperate for kindness and love—a kind word from you would be the best medicine. Ignore Mrs. Dean's cruel warnings. Be generous and find a way to see him. He dreams about you day and night, convinced you hate him since you don't write or visit."

I shut the door and rolled a stone against it to help the broken lock hold. Opening my umbrella, I pulled my charge underneath as rain began driving through the moaning trees. We hurried home without discussing the encounter, but I could tell Catherine's heart was now doubly troubled. Her face looked so sad it barely seemed like hers—she clearly believed every word she'd heard.

The master had already gone to bed when we got back. Cathy crept to his room to check on him—he was asleep. She came back and asked me to sit with her in the library. We had tea together, then she lay on the rug and asked me not to talk because she was tired. I grabbed a book and pretended to read. As soon as she thought I was absorbed, she started crying silently again—apparently her new favorite activity.

I let her cry for a while, then tried to reason with her, mocking everything Heathcliff had said about his son, certain she'd agree with me. But I couldn't undo the damage his words had done—exactly as he'd planned.

"You might be right, Ellen," she said, "but I won't feel better until I know for sure. I need to tell Linton it's not my fault I haven't written, and prove I haven't changed."

What good would it do to argue with her naive trust? We went to bed angry with each other. But the next day found me riding alongside my stubborn young mistress's pony toward Wuthering Heights. I couldn't bear to see her so miserable—her pale face and heavy eyes. I gave in, hoping that seeing Linton would prove how much of his father's story was lies.

23

THE MORNING WAS MISERABLE—YESTERDAY'S RAIN HAD turned to sleet, and temporary streams rushed across our path, gurgling down from the hills. My feet were soaked through, and I was in exactly the right mood to make everything seem worse than it was.

We went into the farmhouse through the kitchen to check if Mr. Heathcliff was really gone—I didn't quite trust his word. Joseph sat alone in his own little paradise beside a roaring fire, a huge mug of ale on the table next to him, surrounded by chunks of toasted oatcake, his black pipe clenched between his teeth.

Catherine rushed to the fireplace to warm herself. I asked if the master was home. The old man took so long to answer that I thought he'd gone deaf and repeated it louder.

"No!" he snarled through his nose. "No! Get back where you came from!"

"Joseph!" a whining voice called from the next room, just as I spoke. "How many times do I have to call you? There's barely any fire left. Joseph! Come here right now!"

He puffed harder on his pipe and stared stubbornly at the fireplace, completely ignoring the summons. The housekeeper and Hareton were nowhere to be seen—one out on errands, the other probably working. We recognized Linton's voice and went in.

"Oh, I hope you die starving in an attic!" the boy said, mistaking us for his useless servant.

He stopped when he realized his mistake. Catherine flew to him.

"Is that you, Miss Linton?" he said, lifting his head from the armchair where he was sprawled. "No—don't kiss me. It makes me lose my breath. God! Papa said you'd visit," he continued after recovering from Catherine's embrace, while she stood looking guilty. "Would you shut the door, please? You left it open, and those—those horrible creatures won't bring coal for the fire. It's freezing!"

I stirred up the coals and fetched a bucket of them myself. The invalid complained about getting ashes on him, but he had a nasty cough and looked feverish, so I didn't snap at him.

"Well, Linton," Catherine murmured when his scowl relaxed. "Are you happy to see me? Can I help with anything?"

"Why didn't you come sooner?" he asked. "You should have visited instead of writing. Those long letters exhausted me. I'd much rather have talked to you. Now I can't stand talking or anything else. Where the hell is Zillah? Would you"—looking at me—"go check the kitchen?"

Since he hadn't thanked me for fetching the coal and I wasn't about to run around at his command, I said, "Nobody's out there except Joseph."

"I need something to drink," he whined, turning away.

"Zillah's always running off to Gimmerton since Papa left. It's miserable! And I have to come downstairs—they've decided to ignore me when I'm in my room."

"Does your father take care of you, Master Heathcliff?" I asked, seeing Catherine's friendly attempts were being rebuffed.

"Take care of me? He makes them pay a little more attention, at least," he cried. "Those bastards! You know what, Miss Linton? That brute Hareton laughs at me! I hate him! Actually, I hate all of them—they're disgusting."

Cathy started looking for water. She found a pitcher on the sideboard, filled a glass, and brought it over. He told her to add a spoonful of wine from a bottle on the table. After drinking a little, he seemed calmer and said she was very kind.

"And are you glad to see me?" she asked again, pleased to see the hint of a smile.

"Yes, I am. It's nice to hear a voice like yours," he replied. "But I've been angry because you wouldn't come. Papa swore it was my fault—he called me a pathetic, shuffling, worthless thing. He said you despised me, and if he were in my place, he'd already own the Grange instead of your father. But you don't despise me, do you, Miss—?"

"I wish you'd call me Catherine, or Cathy," my young lady interrupted. "Despise you? No! After Papa and Ellen, I love you more than anyone alive. Though I don't love Mr. Heathcliff, and I don't dare come when he's back. Will he be gone long?"

"Not really," Linton answered, "but he goes out on the moors a lot during hunting season. You could spend an hour or two with me while he's gone. Say you will! I don't think I'd be so irritable with you. You wouldn't provoke me, and you'd always help me, wouldn't you?"

"Yes," said Catherine, stroking his long, soft hair. "If I could just get Papa's permission, I'd spend half my time with you. Sweet Linton! I wish you were my brother."

"Then you'd love me as much as your father?" he said more cheerfully. "But Papa says you'd love me more than him and everyone else if you were my wife. So I'd rather have that."

"No, I could never love anyone more than Papa," she said seriously. "And people hate their wives sometimes, but not their sisters and brothers. If you were my brother, you'd live with us, and Papa would love you as much as he loves me."

Linton insisted people never hated their wives, but Cathy argued they did, and brought up his own father's hatred for her aunt as proof. I tried to stop her before she said too much, but failed. She blurted out everything she knew. Young Heathcliff, furious, claimed she was lying.

"Papa told me, and Papa doesn't lie," she answered sharply.

"MY papa thinks yours is worthless!" Linton cried. "He calls him a sneaking fool."

"Yours is evil," Catherine shot back. "And you're horrible for repeating what he says. He must be evil to make Aunt Isabella leave him like she did."

"She didn't leave him," the boy said. "Don't contradict me."

"She did!" my young lady cried.

"Well, I'll tell you something!" said Linton. "Your mother hated your father. So there."

"What?" Catherine gasped, too angry to continue.

"And she loved mine," he added.

"You little liar! I hate you!" she panted, her face flushing with rage.

"She did! She did!" Linton sang out, sinking back into

his chair and tilting his head back to enjoy watching her fury as she stood behind him.

"Stop it, Master Heathcliff!" I said. "That's just your father's story, I suppose."

"It's not! Shut up!" he answered. "She did, she did, Catherine! She did!"

Cathy, beside herself, shoved the chair hard, making him fall against the armrest. He immediately started coughing so violently it ended his triumph. The fit lasted so long that even I got scared. Catherine cried with all her might, horrified at what she'd done, though she didn't say a word. I held him until the coughing stopped. Then he pushed me away and hung his head in silence. Catherine stopped crying too, sat down across from him, and stared solemnly at the fire.

"How do you feel now, Master Heathcliff?" I asked after waiting ten minutes.

"I wish SHE felt like I do," he replied. "Spiteful, cruel thing! Hareton never hurts me—he's never hit me in his whole life. And I was feeling better today, and now—" His voice faded to a whimper.

"I didn't hit you!" Cathy muttered, biting her lip to keep from crying again.

He sighed and moaned like he was dying, keeping it up for fifteen minutes—obviously trying to upset Catherine, because whenever he heard her stifle a sob, he'd add more pain and drama to his voice.

"I'm sorry I hurt you, Linton," she finally said, unable to take it anymore. "But I couldn't have been hurt by that little push, and I had no idea you could be either. You're not that fragile, are you, Linton? Don't let me go home thinking I've really hurt you. Answer me! Say something."

"I can't speak to you," he murmured. "You've hurt me so badly I'll be awake all night choking with this cough. If you had it, you'd understand. But YOU'LL sleep comfortably while I'm in agony with no one near me. I wonder how you'd like spending those awful nights!" And he started wailing, completely pitying himself.

"Since you're used to having dreadful nights," I said, "it won't be Miss Catherine who ruins your sleep. You'd be the same if she'd never come. But she won't bother you again. Maybe you'll calm down when we leave."

"Do I have to go?" Catherine asked miserably, leaning over him. "Do you want me to go, Linton?"

"You can't undo what you've done," he replied irritably, shrinking away from her, "unless you make it worse by working me into a fever."

"So I should go?" she repeated.

"At least leave me alone," he said. "I can't stand your talking."

She lingered, ignoring my attempts to get her to leave. But since he wouldn't look up or speak, she finally moved toward the door, and I followed.

A scream brought us back. Linton had slid from his seat onto the hearth and was writhing around—pure dramatics from a spoiled brat determined to be as difficult as possible. I could see right through him and knew it would be stupid to play along. But not Catherine—she ran back terrified, knelt down, cried, soothed, and begged until he finally stopped from lack of breath, not from any guilt about upsetting her.

"I'll put him on the bench," I said, "and he can thrash around all he wants. We're not staying to watch. I hope you see now, Miss Cathy, that you're not helping him, and his bad health has nothing to do with caring about you. There—he's fine! Come on. Once he realizes nobody's around to watch his performance, he'll settle down."

She put a cushion under his head and offered him water. He refused the water and tossed around on the cushion like it was made of stone. She tried to adjust it.

"That won't work," he said. "It's not high enough."

Catherine brought another cushion to stack on top.

"That's too high," the little pest whined.

"How should I arrange it then?" she asked desperately.

He twisted himself toward her as she knelt by the bench, using her shoulder as a pillow.

"No, that's enough," I said. "You'll make do with the cushions, Master Heathcliff. Miss Catherine has wasted enough time on you. We can't stay another five minutes."

"Yes, yes we can!" Cathy replied. "He's being good and patient now. He's starting to think I'll feel worse than him tonight if I believe I've made him sicker. Then I won't dare come back. Tell me the truth, Linton—I can't visit if I've hurt you."

"You have to come back to make me better," he answered. "You should come because you hurt me—you know you did! I wasn't this sick when you arrived, was I?"

"But you made yourself sick by crying and getting worked up. I didn't do all of it," his cousin said. "Anyway, we'll be friends now. And you do want me here—you'd like to see me sometimes, really?"

"I told you I did," he replied impatiently. "Sit on the bench and let me rest my head on your knee. That's what Mama used to do, whole afternoons together. Sit still and don't talk. But you could sing if you know any songs, or recite one of those long ballads you promised to teach me. Or tell a story. I'd prefer a ballad though. Start."

Catherine recited the longest one she could remember. They both loved it. Linton wanted another, then another, despite my strong objections. They kept going until the clock struck twelve and we heard Hareton coming in from the courtyard for dinner.

"Will you come tomorrow, Catherine?" young Heathcliff asked, holding onto her dress as she reluctantly stood up.

"No," I answered, "or the next day either." But she must have whispered something different in his ear, because his face brightened.

"You're not going tomorrow, remember that, Miss!" I said once we were outside. "You're not even thinking about it, are you?"

She smiled.

"Oh, I'll be careful," I continued. "I'll get that lock fixed, and you won't have any other way out."

"I can climb over the wall," she said, laughing. "The Grange isn't a prison, Ellen, and you're not my jailer. Besides, I'm almost seventeen—I'm a woman. And I know Linton would get better quickly if I took care of him. I'm older than him, you know, and wiser—less childish, right? He'll soon do what I tell him with a little coaxing. He's sweet when he's good. I'd make such a pet of him if he were mine. We'd never fight once we got used to each other, would we? Don't you like him, Ellen?"

"Like him!" I exclaimed. "He's the worst-tempered, sickly brat that ever made it to his teens. Lucky for us, as Mr. Heathcliff guessed, he won't make it to twenty. I doubt he'll even see spring. No great loss to his family when he goes. And fortunate his father took him—the better he's treated, the more tedious and selfish he becomes. I'm glad you have no chance of marrying him, Miss Catherine."

My companion grew serious at this. Speaking so carelessly about his death hurt her feelings.

"He's younger than me," she said after a long pause. "He should live longer—he will—he must live as long as I do.

He's as strong now as when he first came north, I'm sure of it. It's just a cold, same as Papa has. You say Papa will get better, so why shouldn't he?"

"Well, well," I said, "we don't need to worry about it. But listen, Miss—and I mean this—if you try going to Wuthering Heights again, with or without me, I'll tell Mr. Linton. And unless he allows it, you can't see your cousin anymore."

"We're already seeing each other," Cathy muttered sullenly.

"Then it has to stop," I said.

"We'll see," was her reply, and she galloped off, leaving me to struggle behind.

We both got home before dinner. My master assumed we'd been walking in the park and didn't ask where we'd been. As soon as I got in, I hurried to change my soaked shoes and stockings. But sitting in that cold house had done its damage. The next morning I was bedridden, and for three weeks I couldn't work—something that had never happened before and, thankfully, never happened again.

My little mistress was an angel, coming to take care of me and keep me company. Being stuck in bed made me terribly depressed—it's torture for someone used to being active, though I had less reason to complain than most. The moment Catherine left Mr. Linton's room, she'd appear at my bedside. She split her day between us, never taking a minute for herself. She neglected her meals, her studies, and her play—she was the most devoted nurse imaginable. She must have had such a warm heart, loving her father as she did, to give so much to me.

I said she divided her days between us, but her father went to bed early, and I usually didn't need anything after six o'clock, so the evenings were hers. Poor thing! I never wondered what she did after tea. And though I often noticed fresh color in her cheeks and pink fingertips when she came to say goodnight, I stupidly assumed it was from sitting by the hot library fire instead of from cold rides across the moors.

24

After three weeks in bed, I could finally move around the house again. That first evening up, I asked Catherine to read to me—my eyes were still weak. We settled in the library after Edgar had gone to bed. She agreed, though I could tell she wasn't thrilled about it. Thinking she might not enjoy my choice of books, I told her to pick whatever she wanted.

She chose one of her favorites and read steadily for about an hour. Then the interruptions started.

"Ellen, aren't you tired? Shouldn't you lie down? You'll make yourself sick staying up this late."

"No, dear, I'm fine," I kept telling her.

When she saw I wasn't giving in, she tried a different approach—yawning, stretching, and finally announcing, "Ellen, I'm tired."

"Then stop reading and we'll talk."

That was worse. She fidgeted and sighed, checking her watch every few minutes until eight o'clock, when she finally escaped to her room, clearly exhausted. Her eyes were red from rubbing them, and she looked absolutely miserable. The next night she was even more restless, and on the third night after I'd gotten up, she complained of a headache and left me alone.

Her behavior struck me as odd. After sitting by myself for a while, I decided to check on her—maybe she'd feel better lying on the sofa instead of alone upstairs in the dark. But Catherine wasn't in her room, or anywhere downstairs. The servants hadn't seen her. I listened at Edgar's door—silence. Back in her room, I blew out my candle and sat by the window.

The moon lit up the snow-covered ground, and I thought maybe she'd gone for a walk in the garden to clear her head. I did spot someone creeping along the park fence, but it was one of the grooms, not Catherine. He stood watching the road for a while, then hurried off and returned leading Catherine's pony—with her walking beside it. The groom led the horse quietly across the grass to the stable while Catherine slipped in through the drawing room window and crept upstairs to where I waited.

She closed the door softly, kicked off her snowy shoes, untied her hat, and was about to remove her cloak when I stood up. She froze, letting out a small gasp.

"My dear Catherine," I began, remembering her recent kindness too well to scold her immediately, "where have you been riding at this hour? And why lie to me about it? Where were you? Tell me!"

"The bottom of the park," she stammered. "I didn't lie."

"And nowhere else?"

"No," she muttered.

"Oh, Catherine!" I said sadly. "You know you've done something wrong, or you wouldn't be lying to me now. That hurts me more than anything. I'd rather be sick for three more months than hear you tell me a deliberate lie."

She rushed forward and threw her arms around my neck, tears streaming down her face.

"Ellen, I'm so afraid of you being angry! Promise not to be angry, and I'll tell you everything. I hate keeping secrets from you."

We sat together in the window seat. I promised not to scold, whatever her secret was—though I'd already guessed it.

"I've been to Wuthering Heights, Ellen. I've gone every single day since you got sick, except for three times before and twice after you left your room. I've been paying Michael with books and pictures to get Minny ready each evening and put her back afterward—don't scold him either, please. I'd get there by six-thirty and usually stay until eight-thirty, then gallop home. I wasn't going for fun. Most of the time I was miserable. Maybe once a week I was actually happy.

"At first, I thought I'd have to convince you to let me keep my promise to Linton—I'd told him I'd visit again the day after we left him there. But since you stayed in bed the next day, I avoided that problem. While Michael was fixing the park door lock that afternoon, I got hold of the key and told him how my cousin was sick and wanted me to visit, but Papa would never allow it. Then I made a deal with him about the pony. He loves reading and he's planning to leave soon to get married, so he agreed to help if I'd lend him books from the library. But I gave him my own books instead, which he liked even better.

"The second time I went, Linton seemed much happier. Zillah—that's their housekeeper—had prepared a clean room with a good fire. She told us that since Joseph was at a prayer meeting and Hareton was out with his dogs—poaching pheasants from our woods, I found out later—we could do whatever we liked. She brought us warm wine and gingerbread and was surprisingly nice to us. Linton sat in the armchair and I took the little rocking chair by the fire, and we laughed and talked for hours. We had so much to say, planning what we'd do in summer. I won't bore you with the details—you'd think them silly.

"Once, though, we nearly fought. He described his perfect July day: lying on a heathery bank in the middle of the moors from morning to night, bees humming lazily in the flowers, larks singing high above, the blue sky and sun shining steady and clear. That was his idea of perfect happiness. Mine was swaying in a rustling green tree with the west wind blowing, bright white clouds racing overhead, and not just larks but thrushes, blackbirds, linnets, and cuckoos all singing at once. The moors visible in the distance, broken up by cool, shaded valleys, but nearby, great waves of tall grass rippling in the breeze, with woods and the sound of water, and the whole world awake and wild with joy. He wanted everything peaceful and still; I wanted everything to sparkle and dance. I said his heaven would be half-dead; he said mine would be drunk. I said I'd fall asleep in his; he said he couldn't breathe in mine. We were getting quite sharp with each other when we finally agreed to try both when the weather was right. Then we kissed and made up.

"After sitting for an hour, I looked around that big room with its bare floor and thought how fun it would be to play there if we moved the table. I asked Linton if we could call Zillah to play blind man's bluff with us—like you used to play with me, Ellen. He said there was no fun in that but agreed to play ball instead. We found two balls in a cupboard with a bunch of old toys, tops, hoops, and badminton sets. One ball was marked 'C' and the other 'H.' I wanted the C for Catherine, and the H could be for Heathcliff, his name, but the H was broken and stuffing came out. Linton didn't like that. I kept winning, and he got upset again, started coughing, and went back to his chair. But that night he cheered up quickly. He loved hearing me sing a few pretty songs—your songs, Ellen—and when I had to leave, he begged me to come back the next evening. I promised I would. Minny and I flew home like we had wings, and I dreamed about Wuthering Heights and my sweet cousin all night.

"The next day I was sad, partly because you were still sick and partly because I wished Papa knew about my visits and approved. But after tea, the moonlight was so beautiful that my mood lifted as I rode. I'll have another wonderful evening, I thought, and better yet, so will my dear Linton. I rode into their garden and was heading to the back when Hareton Earnshaw stopped me, grabbed my bridle, and told me to use the front entrance. He patted Minny's neck and called her a 'bonny beast,' looking like he wanted to talk. I just told him to leave my horse alone or she'd kick him.

"He answered in that rough accent of his, 'It wouldn't do much hurt if it did,' and looked at her legs with a grin. I almost wanted to let her try, but he moved to open the door. As he lifted the latch, he looked up at the inscription above and said, with this weird mix of awkwardness and pride, 'Miss Catherine! I can read that, now.'

"'Wonderful,' I said. 'Please, let's hear you—you ARE grown clever!'

"He spelled out slowly, syllable by syllable: 'Hareton Earnshaw.'

"'And the numbers?' I asked encouragingly, seeing him stuck.

"'I can't tell them yet,' he answered.

"'Oh, you dunce!' I laughed cruelly at his failure.

"The fool just stared at me with a grin twitching at his lips and a scowl darkening his eyes, as if he couldn't decide whether I was being playfully familiar or genuinely contemptuous. I settled his doubts by suddenly turning serious and telling him to go away—I'd come to see Linton, not him. He reddened—I could see it in the moonlight—dropped his hand from the latch, and slunk off, the picture of wounded pride. He probably thought he was as accomplished as Linton just because he could spell his own name, and was shocked that I didn't agree."

"Stop, Catherine, dear!" I interrupted. "I won't scold, but I don't like how you treated him. Hareton is your cousin just as much as Master Heathcliff is. You should have known better than to behave that way. It was admirable that he wanted to be as educated as Linton, and he probably wasn't just showing off. You'd already made him ashamed of his ignorance, I'm sure, and he was trying to improve himself to please you. Mocking his efforts was cruel. If you'd been raised in his circumstances, would you be any less rough? He was as quick and intelligent a child as you ever were. It hurts me to see him despised now just because Heathcliff has treated him so badly."

"Well, Ellen, you're not going to cry about it, are you?" she said, surprised by my intensity. "But wait—let me tell you if he learned his ABCs to please me, and if it was worth being civil to the brute. I went inside. Linton was lying on the settle and half sat up to greet me.

"'I'm ill tonight, Catherine, love,' he said. 'You'll have to do all the talking while I listen. Come sit by me. I knew you wouldn't break your word, and I'll make you promise to come again before you leave.'

"I could tell I shouldn't tease him since he was sick, so I spoke softly, asked no difficult questions, and tried not to irritate him at all. I'd brought some of my nicest books for him. He asked me to read a little, and I was about to start when Earnshaw burst through the door—he'd clearly been working himself into a rage. He charged straight at us, grabbed Linton by the arm, and yanked him off the seat.

"'Get to your own room!' he snarled, his voice almost choked with fury, his face swollen and red. 'Take her there if she comes to see you—you won't keep me out of this. Get out, both of you!'

"He swore at us and gave Linton no time to respond, practically throwing him toward the kitchen. He clenched his fist as I followed, looking like he wanted to knock me down. I was frightened and dropped one of my books. He kicked it after me and slammed the door on us. I heard a nasty, crackling laugh by the fire and turned to see that horrible Joseph standing there, rubbing his bony hands together and trembling with glee.

"'I knew he'd treat you right! He's a grand lad! He's got the right spirit in him! He knows—yes, he knows as well as I do who should be master here. Ha! He sent you packing proper!'

"'Where should we go?' I asked Linton, ignoring the old man's mockery.

"Linton was white and trembling. He didn't look pretty then, Ellen—oh no! He looked frightful. His thin face and large eyes were twisted into an expression of frantic, helpless fury. He grabbed the door handle and shook it—it was locked from inside.

"'If you don't let me in, I'll kill you! If you don't let me in,

I'll kill you!' he shrieked rather than said. 'Devil! Devil! I'll kill you—I'll kill you!'

"Joseph let out his croaking laugh again.

"'There, that's the father in him!' he cried. 'That's his father! We've always got something of both sides in us. Never mind, Hareton, lad—don't be afraid—he can't get at you!'

"I grabbed Linton's hands and tried to pull him away, but he shrieked so horribly that I didn't dare continue. Finally, his screams were cut off by a terrible coughing fit. Blood gushed from his mouth and he collapsed. I ran into the yard, sick with terror, calling for Zillah as loud as I could. She heard me from the shed where she was milking cows and hurried over, asking what was wrong. I couldn't catch my breath to explain. I dragged her inside to look for Linton. Earnshaw had come out to see what damage he'd caused and was carrying the poor boy upstairs. Zillah and I followed, but he stopped me at the top of the steps.

"'You can't come in. Go home.'

"I cried that he'd killed Linton and I would go in. Joseph locked the door and told me I'd do 'no such thing,' asking if I was 'going to be as mad as him.' I stood there crying until the housekeeper came back out. She said he'd be better soon but couldn't handle all that shrieking and noise. She took me and practically carried me out of the house.

"Ellen, I wanted to tear my hair out! I sobbed so hard I could barely see, and that brute you have such sympathy for stood there, occasionally telling me to 'hush' and denying it was his fault. Finally, when I threatened to tell Papa and have him thrown in prison and hanged, he started blubbering himself and ran off to hide his cowardly panic. But I still wasn't rid of him. When they finally made me leave and I'd gotten about a hundred yards away, he suddenly appeared from the shadows by the road and grabbed Minny's bridle.

"'Miss Catherine, I'm truly sorry,' he began, 'but it's rather too bad—'

"I struck him with my whip, thinking he might murder me. He let go, shouting one of his horrible curses, and I galloped home half out of my mind with fear.

"I didn't say goodnight to you that evening, and I didn't go to Wuthering Heights the next day. I desperately wanted to go, but I was strangely agitated—sometimes terrified that Linton was dead, sometimes shuddering at the thought of seeing Hareton again. On the third day, I found my courage—or at least, I couldn't stand the suspense any longer—and snuck off again. I went at five o'clock and walked, thinking I might be able to slip into the house and up to Linton's room without being noticed. But the dogs announced my arrival. Zillah met me and said 'the lad was mending nicely,' then showed me into a small, neat, carpeted room where—to my incredible relief—I found Linton lying on a little sofa, reading one of my books. But he wouldn't speak to me or even look at me for a whole hour, Ellen. He has such an awful temper. And what really shocked me was when he finally did speak, it was to lie and say that I had caused all the trouble and Hareton wasn't to blame! I couldn't respond without losing my temper, so I got up and left the room. He called after me weakly—'Catherine!'—but he hadn't expected me to actually leave. I didn't turn back, and the next day was the second day I stayed home, nearly determined never to visit him again. But it was so miserable going to bed and waking up without knowing anything about him that my resolution dissolved before it really formed. It had felt wrong to go before; now it felt wrong to stay away. When Michael came to ask if he should saddle Minny, I said yes, feeling like I was doing my duty as she carried me over the hills. I had to pass the front windows to reach the courtyard—there was no point trying to hide.

"'Young master is in the house,' Zillah said when she saw me heading for the parlor. I went in. Earnshaw was there too, but he left immediately. Linton sat in the big armchair, half asleep. I walked up to the fire and began seriously, partly meaning it:

"'Since you don't like me, Linton, and since you think I come here just to hurt you and pretend that I do every time—this is our last meeting. Let's say goodbye. Tell Mr. Heathcliff you don't want to see me anymore, and he shouldn't make up any more lies about it.'

"'Sit down and take your hat off, Catherine,' he answered. 'You're so much happier than I am, you ought to be better. Papa talks enough about my faults and shows enough contempt for me that it's natural I doubt myself. I often wonder if I'm not as worthless as he says. Then I feel so angry and bitter, I hate everyone! I am worthless, and bad-tempered, and mean-spirited, almost always. If you want, you can say goodbye—you'll be rid of an annoyance. Only, Catherine, do me this one justice: believe that if I could be as sweet and kind and good as you are, I would be—more willingly than being happy and healthy. And believe that your kindness has made me love you more deeply than if I deserved your love. Though I couldn't help showing you my nature, I regret it and repent it, and I'll regret and repent it until I die!'

"I felt he was telling the truth, and I had to forgive him. Even though we'd probably quarrel again the next moment, I'd have to forgive him again. We made up, but we both cried the whole time I stayed—not entirely from sorrow, though I was sorry Linton had such a twisted nature. He'll never let his friends be at peace, and he'll never be at peace himself! I've gone to his little parlor every visit since that night, because his father returned the day after.

"Maybe three times we've been as happy and hopeful as that first evening. The rest of my visits have been dreary and troubled—sometimes because of his selfishness and spite, sometimes because of his suffering. But I've learned to endure the first almost as patiently as the second. Mr. Heathcliff deliberately avoids me—I've hardly seen him at all. Last Sunday, though, I came earlier than usual and heard him abusing poor Linton cruelly for his behavior the night before. I don't know how he found out unless he was eavesdropping. Linton had certainly been provoking, but it was nobody's business but mine. I interrupted Heathcliff's lecture by walking in and telling him so. He burst out laughing and left, saying he was glad I saw it that way. Since then, I've told Linton to whisper his bitter comments. So now, Ellen, you've heard everything. I can't be kept from going to Wuthering Heights without making two people miserable. But if you just don't tell Papa, my visits won't disturb anyone's peace. You won't tell, will you? It would be heartless if you did."

"I'll decide by tomorrow, Miss Catherine," I replied. "It requires some thought, so I'll leave you to rest while I think it over."

I thought it over aloud—in her father's presence. I went straight from her room to his and told him the whole story, except for her conversations with her cousin and anything about Hareton. Mr. Linton was more alarmed and distressed than he let me see. In the morning, Catherine learned of my betrayal and also that her secret visits were over. She wept and pleaded against the ban, begging her father to have pity on Linton. All she got was a promise that Edgar would write to him and give him permission to visit the Grange when he pleased, but explaining that he must no longer expect to see Catherine at Wuthering Heights. Perhaps if Edgar had known his nephew's temperament and poor health, he wouldn't have offered even that small comfort."

25

"All this happened last winter, sir," said Mrs. Dean. "Barely a year ago. Last winter, I never imagined I'd be sitting here now, telling the whole story to a stranger! Though who knows how long you'll remain a stranger? You're too young to stay content living alone forever, and I can't imagine anyone meeting Catherine Linton without falling for her. You're smiling—but why do you light up whenever I mention her? Why did you ask me to hang her portrait above your fireplace? And why—"

"Stop right there!" I interrupted. "I might very well love her, but would she love me? I doubt it too much to risk my peace of mind. Besides, my home isn't here. I belong to the busy world, and I need to return to it. Please, continue. Did Catherine obey her father?"

"She did," the housekeeper went on. "Her love for him was still the strongest feeling in her heart. When he spoke to her, there was no anger—only the deep tenderness of someone about to leave their most precious treasure surrounded by danger, knowing that remembered words would be the only protection he could leave behind. A few days later, he said to me, 'I wish my nephew would write, Ellen, or visit. Tell me honestly—what do you think of him? Has he improved, or is there hope he'll become a better man?'

"'He's very delicate, sir,' I replied. 'I doubt he'll live to adulthood. But I can say this—he's nothing like his father. If Miss Catherine were unfortunate enough to marry him, she could manage him easily, unless she spoiled him completely. But master, you'll have plenty of time to know him better and see if he'd suit her. He won't come of age for more than four years.'"

Edgar sighed and walked to the window, gazing toward Gimmerton Church. The February afternoon was misty, but weak sunlight filtered through, just enough to make out the two fir trees in the yard and the scattered gravestones beyond.

"I've prayed often," he said, half to himself, "for what's coming. Now that it's near, I'm starting to shrink from it, to fear it. I thought remembering the day I walked down that valley as a bridegroom would be less sweet than knowing I'd soon—in months, maybe weeks—be carried up and laid in that lonely hollow. Ellen, I've been so happy with my little Cathy. Through winter nights and summer days, she was my living hope. But I've also been happy alone among those stones, under that old church—lying through long June evenings on the green mound of her mother's grave, wishing, yearning for the time I could lie beneath it.

"What can I do for Cathy? How can I leave her? I wouldn't care that Linton is Heathcliff's son. I wouldn't care if he took her from me, if he could comfort her after I'm gone. I wouldn't even care if Heathcliff got everything he wanted and stole my last blessing! But if Linton proves worthless—just a weak tool for his father—I can't abandon her to him. And yet, as hard as it is to dim her bright spirit, I have to keep making her sad while I live, so she'll be prepared for solitude when I die. My darling girl! I'd rather give her to God and see her buried before me."

"Give her to God as things are, sir," I answered. "And if we lose you—God forbid—I'll be her friend and guide to the end. Miss Catherine is a good girl. She won't deliberately do wrong, and people who do their duty are always rewarded eventually."

Spring arrived, but my master didn't truly recover, though he started walking the grounds again with his daughter. To her inexperienced eyes, this seemed like recovery—his cheeks were often flushed, his eyes bright. She felt certain he was getting better. On her seventeenth birthday, he didn't visit the churchyard. It was raining, and I mentioned, "You won't go out tonight, surely?"

"No," he answered, "I'll wait a little longer this year." He wrote again to Linton, expressing how much he wanted to see him. If the boy had been well enough to travel, I'm sure Heathcliff would have let him come. Instead, following instructions, Linton wrote back saying Mr. Heathcliff wouldn't allow him to visit the Grange. But he was delighted by his uncle's kindness and hoped they might meet during walks, and personally ask that he and his cousin not be kept apart so completely.

That part of his letter seemed genuine, probably his own words. Heathcliff knew the boy could plead convincingly for Catherine's company.

"I'm not asking for her to visit here," Linton wrote, "but am I never to see her, when my father forbids me to go to her home, and you forbid her to come to mine? Please, sometimes ride with her toward the Heights and let us exchange a few words with you there. We've done nothing to deserve this separation. You're not angry with me—you have no reason to dislike me, you've said so yourself. Dear uncle, send a kind note tomorrow and agree to meet anywhere you choose, except Thrushcross Grange. I believe if we met, you'd see my character isn't like my father's. He says I'm more your nephew than his son. Though I have faults that make me unworthy of Catherine, she's forgiven them, and for her sake, you should too. You ask about my health—it's better. But while I'm cut off from all hope, condemned to loneliness or the company of those who never have and never will like me, how can I be cheerful and well?"

Edgar felt sorry for the boy but couldn't grant his request, since he couldn't accompany Catherine himself. He said perhaps they might meet in summer. Meanwhile, he encouraged Linton to keep writing and promised to offer what advice and comfort he could by letter, knowing the boy's difficult position in his family. Linton agreed, and if left to himself, would probably have ruined everything by filling his letters with complaints and self-pity. But his father monitored every word, reviewing each letter my master sent. So instead of describing his personal suffering—the thoughts that consumed him—Linton focused on the cruelty of being kept from his friend and love, gently suggesting that Mr. Linton must arrange a meeting soon, or he'd think he was being deceived with empty promises.

Cathy was a powerful ally at home. Between them, they finally convinced my master to let them ride or walk together about once a week, with me as guardian, on the moors nearest the Grange. By June, he was still declining. Though he'd set aside part of his income yearly for my young lady's inheritance, he naturally wanted her to keep—or at least return to—her ancestral home. He thought her only chance was marriage to his heir. He had no idea the boy was failing almost as fast as himself. No one did, I think —no doctor visited the Heights, and none of us saw Master Heathcliff to report on his son's condition. I began to think my fears were wrong, that the boy must be improving, when he wrote about riding and walking on the moors with such apparent enthusiasm. I couldn't imagine a father treating a dying child as cruelly as I later learned Heathcliff had treated him, forcing this desperate eagerness—his efforts intensifying as death threatened to ruin his greedy, heartless plans.

26

Summer had already begun to fade when Edgar finally gave in to our pleas, and Catherine and I rode out to meet her cousin for the first time. It was a close, humid day—no sunshine, but the hazy sky too uncertain to threaten rain. We'd agreed to meet at the guide-stone by the crossroads. But when we arrived, a young shepherd boy was waiting with a message.

"Master Linton's just this side of the Heights," he said in his Yorkshire accent. "He'd be much obliged if you'd come a bit further."

"Then Master Linton has already broken his uncle's first rule," I observed. "We were told to stay on Grange land, and here we're being asked to leave it immediately."

"We'll just turn back when we reach him," Catherine said. "We'll keep our ride pointed toward home."

But when we found him—barely a quarter mile from his own door—he had no horse. We had to dismount and leave ours to graze. He was lying on the heath, waiting for us, and didn't get up until we were just yards away. When he finally stood, he walked so unsteadily and looked so pale that I burst out, "Master Heathcliff, you're not well enough for a walk this morning. You look terrible!"

Catherine stared at him with shock and distress. The joy on her lips transformed into alarm, and instead of celebrating their long-awaited reunion, she anxiously asked if he was worse than usual.

"No—better—better!" he gasped, trembling and gripping her hand as if he needed it to stay upright. His large blue eyes moved nervously over her face, the dark hollows around them turning his once-dreamy expression into something wild and desperate.

"But you've gotten worse," his cousin insisted. "Worse than when I saw you last. You're thinner, and—"

"I'm tired," he interrupted quickly. "It's too hot for walking. Let's rest here. In the mornings I often feel sick—Papa says I'm growing too fast."

Catherine sat down, clearly unsatisfied with his explanation, and he lowered himself beside her.

"This is almost like your paradise," she said, forcing cheerfulness into her voice. "Remember when we planned to spend two days in the places we each loved best? This is nearly yours, except for the clouds—but they're so soft and gentle, nicer than harsh sunshine. Next week, if you can manage it, we'll ride down to Grange Park and try mine."

Linton didn't seem to remember what she was talking about. He was obviously struggling to keep up any kind of conversation. His lack of interest in everything she mentioned, his inability to contribute anything to entertain her—it was all so obvious that she couldn't hide her disappointment. Something fundamental had changed about him. The bratty behavior that could be coaxed into sweetness had given way to lifeless apathy. HeHe was less like a child who whines for attention and more like someone genuinely sick, rejecting comfort and treating others' attempts at cheerfulness as insults.

I watched Catherine's face change as understanding dawned—each attempt at conversation seemed to pain him more than silence would have. Without ceremony, she suggested we should go.

Unexpectedly, this jerked Linton from his stupor into strange agitation. He shot a terrified glance toward the Heights and begged her to stay another half hour at least.

"But I think," Catherine said, "you'd be more comfortable at home than sitting here. I can see I'm not entertaining you today with my stories and chatter. You've grown beyond my silly diversions in these six months—or if I could entertain you, I'd gladly stay."

"Stay to rest yourself," he replied. "And Catherine, don't think or say that I'm very sick. It's just the humid weather making me sluggish. I walked quite a bit before you came—a lot for me, anyway. Tell Uncle I'm in decent health, will you?"

"I'll tell him you said so, Linton. I can't honestly say it myself," my young lady observed, puzzled by his insistence on what was obviously untrue.

"And come again next Thursday," he continued, avoiding her confused gaze. "And thank him for letting you come—give him my best thanks, Catherine. And—if you happen to meet my father and he asks about me, don't let him think I've been silent and stupid. Don't look sad and worried like you are now—he'll be angry."

"I don't care about his anger," Catherine exclaimed, thinking she'd be the target.

"But I do," said her cousin, shuddering. "Don't turn him against me, Catherine. He's very harsh."

"Is he cruel to you, Master Heathcliff?" I asked. "Has he gotten tired of spoiling you and turned hostile?"

Linton looked at me but didn't answer. After sitting beside him another ten minutes—during which his head drooped drowsily and he made only suppressed sounds of exhaustion or pain—Catherine started searching the heath for wild berries, anything to occupy herself. She shared what she found with me but didn't offer any to him, seeing that more attention would only irritate him.

"Has it been half an hour, Ellen?" she finally whispered to me. "I don't see why we should stay. He's asleep, and Papa will be expecting us."

"We can't leave him sleeping," I answered. "Wait until he wakes. Be patient. You were so eager to come, but your desire to see poor Linton has evaporated quickly!"

"Why did he want to see me?" Catherine returned. "Even in his worst moods before, I liked him better than this strange state he's in now. It's like this meeting is a chore he's been forced to complete—to keep his father from scolding him. But I'm not coming here to please Mr. Heathcliff, whatever reason he has for making Linton endure this. And while I'm glad he's supposedly healthier, I'm sorry he's so much less pleasant and affectionate."

"You think he's healthier?" I said.

"Yes," she answered, "because he always exaggerated his suffering before. He's not as well as he told me to tell Papa, but he's probably better."

"That's where we disagree, Miss Cathy," I remarked. "I'd guess he's much worse."

Linton suddenly jerked awake in confused terror, asking if someone had called his name.

"No," said Catherine. "Unless in your dreams. I can't

understand how you can fall asleep outdoors in the morning."

"I thought I heard my father," he gasped, looking up at the dark cliff above us. "You're sure nobody spoke?"

"Quite certain," his cousin replied. "Only Ellen and I were debating about your health. Are you really stronger, Linton, than when we parted last winter? If you are, I'm certain one thing isn't stronger—your feelings for me. Tell me—are you?"

Tears poured from Linton's eyes as he answered, "Yes, yes, I am!" Still haunted by the imaginary voice, his gaze searched frantically for its source.

Catherine stood. "We have to leave now," she said. "And I won't pretend I'm not terribly disappointed by our meeting —though I'll only tell you. And not because I fear Mr. Heathcliff."

"Quiet," Linton whispered urgently. "For God's sake, be quiet! He's coming." He clutched at Catherine's arm, trying to hold her back, but at this warning she quickly pulled free and whistled for Minny, who came at once.

"I'll be here next Thursday," she called, swinging into the saddle. "Goodbye. Quick, Ellen!"

And we left him there, barely aware we'd gone, completely absorbed in his dread of his father's approach.

Before we reached home, Catherine's irritation had softened into confused pity and regret, mixed with vague, troubling doubts about Linton's real situation—both his health and his circumstances. I shared her concerns, though I advised her to keep her worries close. A second visit would tell us more.

My master wanted a full report of our outing. His nephew's thanks were properly delivered, with Miss Cathy carefully skirting the troubling details. I kept my own answers vague, torn between what needed telling and what was better left unsaid.

27

A WEEK PASSED, AND EACH DAY BROUGHT DEVASTATING changes to Edgar Linton's condition. What months of illness had gradually worn away, hours now destroyed with brutal efficiency. Catherine tried to hide from the truth, but her sharp mind wouldn't let her deceive herself. She understood what was coming—the terrible possibility hardening into certainty with each passing day.

She couldn't bring herself to mention Thursday's planned visit to Linton. When the day came, I brought it up instead and got Edgar's permission for her to go outside. She'd been living in two rooms—the library where her father spent his few waking hours, and his bedroom. She resented every moment not spent at his side, leaning over his pillow or holding his hand. Watching and grief had left her pale and hollow-eyed, so her father eagerly sent her off, hoping the fresh air and company would do her good. He comforted himself with the thought that after his death, at least she wouldn't be completely alone.

I'd caught several hints that Edgar had fixed on an idea—since his nephew resembled him physically, surely Linton must share his character too. The boy's letters gave no real insight into his weak, selfish nature. And I, through misguided kindness, didn't correct Edgar's mistake. What good would it do to disturb his final days with truths he had no power to change?

We postponed our ride until afternoon—one of those golden August afternoons where the air itself seems alive, as if it could revive even the dying. Catherine's face mirrored the landscape around us—shadows and sunlight chasing each other across her features. But the shadows lingered longer, the brightness fled more quickly, and her heart blamed itself for even those brief moments of forgetting her sorrow.

We found Linton waiting at the same spot as before. Catherine dismounted and told me that since she planned to stay only briefly, I should hold her horse and stay mounted. But I refused—I wouldn't risk losing sight of her for a minute. So we climbed the moorland slope together.

Young Heathcliff greeted us with more energy than last time, though it wasn't happiness or excitement. It looked more like fear.

"You're late!" he said, his words coming short and strained. "Isn't your father very ill? I thought you wouldn't come."

"Why can't you just be honest?" Catherine burst out, skipping any greeting. "Why don't you just say you don't want me here? This is strange, Linton—twice now you've brought me here seemingly just to upset us both, and for no reason!"

Linton shivered and glanced at her, half-pleading, half-ashamed, but Catherine's patience had run out.

"My father IS very ill," she said. "Why am I being called away from his bedside? Why didn't you send word releasing me from my promise if you didn't want me to keep it? Tell me the truth! I have no patience for games right now—I can't indulge your moods anymore!"

"My moods?" he whispered. "What moods? For God's sake, Catherine, don't look at me like that! Despise me all you want—I'm worthless, a coward. I can't be scorned enough. But I'm too pathetic for your anger. Hate my father, and save your contempt for me."

"This is ridiculous!" Catherine snapped. "Foolish boy! Look at you trembling, as if I'd actually hurt you! You don't need to beg for contempt, Linton—anyone would give it freely. Get up! I'm going home. It's stupid to drag you from your house for—for what exactly? Let go of my dress! If I pitied you for crying and looking terrified, you should reject that pity. Ellen, tell him how disgraceful he's being. Stand up and stop degrading yourself—stop it!"

Linton had collapsed to the ground, his face twisted in agony, his whole body shaking with what seemed like pure terror.

"Oh!" he sobbed. "I can't bear this! Catherine, Catherine, I'm a traitor and I can't tell you why! But if you leave me, he'll kill me! Dear Catherine, my life is in your hands. You said you loved me—if you did, this wouldn't hurt you. You won't go, will you? Kind, sweet Catherine! Maybe you'll agree to it—and he'll let me die with you!"

Seeing his genuine anguish, Catherine bent to help him up. Her old tenderness overcame her frustration, and real alarm replaced her anger.

"Agree to what?" she asked. "To stay? Explain this strange talk and I will. You're contradicting yourself and confusing me! Be calm, be honest, and just tell me what's wrong. You wouldn't hurt me, Linton, would you? You wouldn't let someone harm me if you could prevent it? I'll believe you're a coward for yourself, but not that you'd betray your best friend."

"But my father threatened me," the boy gasped, wringing his thin hands. "And I'm terrified of him—terrified! I can't tell you!"

"Fine!" Catherine said with scornful pity. "Keep your secret—I'M not a coward. Save yourself. I'm not afraid!"

Her courage broke him completely. He wept uncontrollably, kissing her hands, but still couldn't force himself to speak. I was trying to figure out what this mystery was, determined that Catherine shouldn't suffer for his sake or anyone else's, when I heard movement in the heather. Looking up, I saw Heathcliff approaching, descending from the Heights.

He didn't even glance at the young people, though he was close enough to hear Linton's sobs. Instead, he greeted me with unusual warmth—so unusual I couldn't help doubting it.

"Good to see you so near my house, Nelly. How are things at the Grange? Tell me—the rumors say," he lowered his voice, "that Edgar Linton is dying. Surely they're exaggerating?"

"No, my master is dying," I replied. "It's true. It will be sad for us all, but a blessing for him."

"How long does he have?" he asked.

"I don't know."

"Because," he continued, watching the two young people frozen under his gaze—Linton too terrified to move, Catherine held in place by his terror—"because that boy there seems determined to die before me, and I'd appreciate it if his uncle would hurry up and go first! Well, well! Has the pup been playing this game long? I did teach him not to snivel. Is he usually this pathetic with Miss Linton?"

"Pathetic? He's genuinely distressed," I answered. "Looking at him, he should be in bed with a doctor, not out on the moors with his sweetheart."

"He will be, in a day or two," Heathcliff muttered. "But first—get up, Linton! Get up!" he shouted. "Don't grovel on the ground—up, now!"

Linton had collapsed again in helpless terror at his father's look. He tried several times to obey, but his strength failed him and he fell back with a moan. Heathcliff strode over and propped him against a bank of earth.

"Now," he said, his fury barely controlled, "I'm getting angry, and if you don't pull yourself together—damn you! Get up!"

"I will, Father," Linton panted. "Just let me alone or I'll faint. I've done what you wanted, I'm sure. Catherine will tell you I've been cheerful. Oh, stay with me, Catherine—give me your hand."

"Take mine," his father said. "Stand up. There—she'll help you. That's right, look at her. You'd think I was the devil himself, Miss Linton, the way he fears me. Would you be kind enough to walk home with him? He shudders if I touch him."

"Linton, dear," Catherine whispered, "I can't go to Wuthering Heights. Papa has forbidden it. He won't hurt you—why are you so afraid?"

"I can never go back to that house," he answered. "I'm NOT to go back without you!"

"Stop," his father commanded. "We'll respect Catherine's duty to her father. Nelly, take him in, and I'll follow your advice about the doctor immediately."

"Good idea," I replied. "But I must stay with my mistress. Your son is not my responsibility."

"You're very stubborn," said Heathcliff. "I know that. But

you'll force me to hurt the baby and make it scream before you'll help. Come then, my hero. Will you come back with me?"

He moved toward Linton as if to grab him. The boy shrank back, clinging to Catherine, begging her to come with him with such desperate terror that she couldn't refuse. I disapproved, but couldn't stop her—how could she refuse him? We had no idea what terrified him so completely, but he was helpless in its grip, and any added stress might drive him mad.

We reached the threshold. Catherine walked in, and I stood waiting, expecting her to settle Linton in a chair and come right back out. But Heathcliff pushed me forward, saying, "My house isn't contaminated, Nelly. I'm feeling hospitable today—sit down, and let me shut the door."

He shut and locked it. I jumped.

"You'll have tea before you go home," he added. "I'm alone today. Hareton's taken cattle to the Lees, and Zillah and Joseph are off enjoying themselves. Though I'm used to solitude, I'd rather have interesting company when I can get it. Miss Linton, sit by HIM. I'm giving you what I have—it's not much of a gift, but it's all I've got. It's Linton, I mean. How she stares! It's strange how savage I feel toward anything that fears me. If I lived where laws were more flexible and tastes less refined, I'd enjoy dissecting these two for an evening's entertainment."

He drew a sharp breath, struck the table, and swore to himself, "By hell, I hate them."

"I'm not afraid of you!" Catherine exclaimed, not hearing his last words. She stepped close, her dark eyes blazing with passion and determination. "Give me that key—I will have it!" she said. "I wouldn't eat or drink here if I were starving."

Heathcliff held the key he'd left on the table. He looked up, surprised by her boldness—or perhaps reminded by her voice and expression of someone she'd inherited them from. She grabbed for the key and almost pulled it from his loosened fingers, but the movement brought him back to himself. He snatched it back quickly.

"Now, Catherine Linton," he said, "stand back, or I'll knock you down—and that will upset Mrs. Dean."

Despite his warning, she grabbed his closed fist again, fighting to pry open his iron grip. When her nails made no impression, she bit down hard on his fingers. Heathcliff shot me a look that kept me from interfering. Catherine was too focused on his hand to notice his face. He suddenly opened his fingers and let go of the key—but the instant she grabbed it, he seized her with his freed hand, pulled her onto his knee, and slapped her hard across both sides of her head, again and again, each blow violent enough to knock her down if she hadn't been held in place.

At this brutal violence, I rushed at him furiously. "You villain!" I started to shout, "You villain!" A shove to my chest silenced me. I'm heavy-set and quickly winded—between that and my rage, I staggered back dizzy, feeling ready to suffocate or burst a blood vessel. The attack was over in two minutes. When he released Catherine, she pressed both hands to her temples, looking dazed, as if unsure whether her ears were still attached. She trembled violently, her whole body in shock, and leaned against the table, too stunned to process what had happened.

"I know how to discipline children, you see," the monster said grimly, bending to pick up the fallen key. "Go to Linton now, as I told you, and cry all you like. I'll be your father tomorrow—all the father you'll have in a few days—and you'll have plenty of that. You can take it; you're no weakling. You'll get a daily dose if I see that devil's temper in your eyes again!"

Cathy ran to me instead of Linton and knelt down, pressing her burning cheek to my lap, sobbing. Her cousin had shrunk into a corner of the bench, quiet as a mouse, probably relieved the beating had fallen on someone else. Heathcliff, seeing us all in shock, stood and quickly made tea himself. The cups were already laid out. He poured and handed me one.

"Calm your nerves," he said. "And help your naughty pet and mine. It's not poisoned, though I made it. I'm going to find your horses."

The moment he left, our first thought was to escape. We tried the kitchen door—locked from outside. We checked the windows—too narrow even for Catherine's small frame.

"Master Linton," I said, seeing we were truly trapped, "you know what your diabolical father is planning, and you'll tell us, or I'll box your ears like he did your cousin's."

"Yes, Linton, you must tell," said Catherine. "I came here for your sake. It would be wickedly ungrateful if you refuse."

"Give me some tea, I'm thirsty, then I'll tell you," he answered. "Mrs. Dean, go away. I don't like you hovering over me. Now, Catherine, you're crying into my cup. I won't drink that. Give me another."

Catherine pushed another cup to him and wiped her face. I was disgusted by the little wretch's composure now that he was no longer afraid for himself. His terror on the moor had vanished the moment we entered Wuthering Heights. I realized he'd been threatened with terrible punishment if he failed to lure us here—and having succeeded, he had no immediate fears.

"Papa wants us to be married," he continued after sipping his tea. "He knows your papa wouldn't let us marry now, and he's afraid I'll die if we wait. So we're to be married in the morning, and you'll stay here tonight. If you do as he wishes, you can go home tomorrow and take me with you."

"Take you with her, you pathetic wretch!" I exclaimed. "YOU marry? The man is mad! Or he thinks we're all fools. Do you imagine this beautiful young lady, this healthy, strong girl, will tie herself to a sickly little manipulator like you? Do you think anyone, let alone Miss Catherine Linton, would have you for a husband? You deserve a beating for bringing us here with your cowardly, whining tricks—and don't look so stupid! I've half a mind to shake you hard for your contemptible treachery and delusional arrogance."

I did shake him slightly, but it brought on his cough, and he resorted to his usual moaning and weeping. Catherine scolded me for it.

"Stay all night? No," she said, looking around slowly. "Ellen, I'll burn that door down to get out."

She would have started immediately, but Linton panicked again for his precious self. He grabbed her with his weak arms, sobbing, "Won't you have me and save me? Let me come to the Grange? Oh, darling Catherine! You can't leave me after all. You MUST obey my father—you MUST!"

"I must obey MY father," she replied, "and save him from this cruel worry. The whole night! What will he think? He'll be frantic already. I'll either break or burn my way out. Be quiet! You're in no danger—but if you try to stop me—Linton, I love Papa more than you!"

The mortal terror he felt of Heathcliff's anger gave the boy desperate eloquence. Catherine was nearly beside herself, insisting she must go home, trying to persuade him to overcome his selfishness—but he only clung tighter, weeping.

"Your horses have run off," he said. "And—now, Linton! Sniveling again? What has she done to you? Come, come—enough. Get to bed. In a month or two, my lad, you'll be able to pay her back for these tyrannies with interest. You're pining for pure love, aren't you? Nothing else in the world? And she shall have you! There, to bed! Zillah won't be here tonight; you'll have to undress yourself. Quiet! Stop that noise! Once you're in your room, I won't come near you. You needn't fear. By luck, you've managed well enough. I'll handle the rest."

He held the door open for his son, who slunk out like a beaten dog expecting another kick. The lock clicked shut again. Heathcliff approached the fire where Catherine and I stood silent. Catherine looked up and instinctively raised her hand to her cheek—being near him brought back the pain. Anyone else would have pitied her childish gesture, but he scowled and muttered, "Oh! You're not afraid of me? Your courage is well disguised—you seem damn afraid!"

"I AM afraid now," she replied, "because if I stay, Papa will be miserable. And how can I bear making him miserable when he—when he—Mr. Heathcliff, let me go home! I promise to marry Linton. Papa would approve, and I love him. Why force me to do what I'll do willingly?"

"Let him dare to force you," I cried. "There's law in this land, thank God! Even in this remote place. I'd report him if he were my own son—it's a felony!"

"Silence!" the brute said. "To hell with your noise! I don't want YOU to speak. Miss Linton, I shall thoroughly enjoy knowing your father will be miserable. I won't sleep for the satisfaction. You couldn't have found a better way to ensure you stay under my roof for the next twenty-four hours than telling me it would hurt him. As for your promise to marry

Linton, I'll make sure you keep it. You won't leave here until it's done."

"Send Ellen to let Papa know I'm safe!" Catherine cried, weeping bitterly. "Or marry me now. Poor Papa! Ellen, he'll think we're lost. What shall we do?"

"Not at all! He'll think you're tired of nursing him and ran off for some amusement," Heathcliff answered. "You can't deny you entered my house willingly, against his explicit orders. It's natural for someone your age to want entertainment, to grow weary of nursing a sick man—and that man only your father."

He paused, his eyes glinting with malice as Catherine's face went white.

"Catherine, his happiest days ended when yours began. He cursed you for being born, I'm sure—I did, at least."

She flinched as if struck again.

"It would be fitting if he cursed you as he died. I'd join him. I don't love you! How could I? Weep away. As far as I can see, that will be your main entertainment from now on, unless Linton makes up for other losses—and your protective father seems to think he might."

His voice dripped with mockery.

"His letters of advice and consolation amused me greatly. In his last one, he recommended I be careful with his jewel and kind to her. Careful and kind—how paternal. But Linton needs all his care and kindness for himself. Linton can play the little tyrant well. He'll happily torture any number of cats if their teeth and claws are removed. You'll be able to tell his uncle fine stories of his KINDNESS when you get home again, I assure you."

"You're right there!" I said. "Explain your son's character. Show how he's like you—then I hope Miss Cathy will think twice before taking the snake!"

"I don't mind discussing his charming qualities now," he answered, "because she must either accept him or remain a prisoner—and you with her—until your master dies. I can keep you both hidden here. Once she's married, everything she owns becomes his—including herself. If you doubt it, encourage her to break her word, and you'll see!"

"I won't break my word," said Catherine. "I'll marry him within the hour if I can go to Thrushcross Grange afterward. Mr. Heathcliff, you're a cruel man, but you're not a fiend. You won't destroy all my happiness from pure malice. If Papa thought I'd left him on purpose, and if he died before I returned, how could I bear to live? I've stopped crying, but I'm going to kneel here at your feet, and I won't get up, and I won't look away until you look back at me! No, don't turn away! LOOK! You'll see nothing to provoke you. I don't hate you. I'm not angry that you struck me. Have you never loved ANYBODY in all your life, uncle? NEVER? Oh, you must look once. I'm so wretched, you can't help being sorry for me."

She was searching desperately for any trace of the man her mother had loved—but found only hatred staring back.

"Keep your hands off me and move, or I'll kick you!" Heathcliff cried, shoving her away brutally. "I'd rather be hugged by a snake. How the devil can you dream of groveling to me? I DETEST you!"

He shrugged his shoulders—shuddered, really, as if his skin crawled with disgust—and pushed back his chair. I stood up and opened my mouth to unleash a torrent of abuse, but was silenced mid-sentence by his threat to lock me in a room alone if I uttered another syllable. It was getting dark. We heard voices at the garden gate. Our host hurried out instantly—he had his wits about him; we didn't.

There was talk for two or three minutes, then he returned alone.

"I thought it might be your cousin Hareton," I said to Catherine. "I wish he would come! Who knows, he might take our side?"

"It was three servants sent from the Grange to find you," said Heathcliff, overhearing me. "You should have opened a window and called out. But I'd swear that girl is glad you didn't. She's glad to be forced to stay, I'm certain."

Learning of the missed chance, we both broke down crying without restraint, and he let us wail until nine o'clock. Then he ordered us upstairs through the kitchen to Zillah's room. I whispered to Catherine to obey—perhaps we could escape through the window there, or into an attic and out through a skylight. But the window was narrow like those below, and the attic hatch was secured. We were as trapped as before.

Neither of us lay down. Catherine stationed herself by the window, watching anxiously for morning, answering my frequent pleas that she try to rest with only deep sighs. I sat in a chair, rocking back and forth, tormenting myself with thoughts of all my failures of duty, which seemed that night to be the source of all my employers' misfortunes. It wasn't true, I know that now, but in my imagination that dismal night, I felt more guilty than Heathcliff himself.

At seven o'clock he came and asked if Miss Linton had risen. She ran to the door immediately and answered, "Yes." "Here, then," he said, opening it and pulling her out. I rose to follow, but he locked the door again. I demanded my release.

"Be patient," he replied. "I'll send up your breakfast soon."

I pounded on the panels and rattled the latch angrily.

Catherine asked why I was still locked in. He answered that I must endure it another hour, and they left. I endured it two or three hours. Finally, I heard footsteps—not Heathcliff's.

"I've brought you something to eat," said a voice. "Open the door!"

Eagerly complying, I saw Hareton, carrying enough food for a full day.

"Take it," he added, shoving the tray into my hands.

"Stay one minute," I began.

"No," he said, and left, ignoring all my pleas to stay.

And there I remained locked in for the whole day, and the whole next night, and another, and another. Five nights and four days I was imprisoned, seeing nobody but Hareton once each morning. He was a model jailer—sullen, silent, and deaf to every appeal to his sense of justice or compassion.

28

On the fifth morning—or afternoon, really—different footsteps approached. Lighter, quicker steps, and this time the person actually came in. It was Zillah in her scarlet shawl, a black silk bonnet on her head, and a willow basket swinging from her arm.

"Lord! Mrs. Dean!" she cried. "Well! Everyone at Gimmerton's talking about you. We all thought you'd drowned in the Blackhorse marsh, and the young miss with you, till master told me you'd been found and he'd put you up here! What—did you get stuck on an island or something? How long were you in that hole? Did master rescue you? But you don't look too thin—you haven't been poorly, have you?"

"Your master is a true scoundrel!" I shot back. "But he'll answer for it. He didn't need to spread that lie—the truth will come out!"

"What do you mean?" Zillah asked. "It's not his story—that's what they're saying in the village, about you being lost in the marsh. When I came in, I said to Earnshaw, 'Eh, there's been strange happenings since I left, Mr. Hareton. Such a pity about that lovely young lady, and poor Nelly Dean.' He just stared. I thought he hadn't heard anything, so I told him the rumor. The master listened and just smiled to himself, then said, 'If they've been in the marsh, they're out now, Zillah. Nelly Dean is in your room right this minute. You can tell her to leave when you go up—here's the key. The bog-water got to her head and she would've run home half-mad, but I kept her here till she came to her senses. Tell her to go to the Grange right away, if she's able, and take a message from me—her young lady will follow in time for the squire's funeral.'"

"Mr. Edgar's not dead?" I gasped. "Oh, Zillah, Zillah!"

"No, no, sit down, my good mistress," she replied. "You're still sickly. He's not dead—Doctor Kenneth thinks he might last another day. I met him on the road and asked."

Instead of sitting, I grabbed my coat and rushed downstairs—the way was clear. When I entered the house, I looked around for someone to tell me about Catherine. The place was filled with sunshine, the door wide open, but no one seemed to be around. As I hesitated, wondering whether to leave immediately or go back to find my mistress, a slight cough drew my attention to the hearth. Linton lay on the settle, alone, sucking on a stick of candy and watching me with dull, indifferent eyes.

"Where is Miss Catherine?" I demanded sternly, hoping to frighten him into talking since I'd caught him alone. He kept sucking his candy like an innocent child.

"Is she gone?" I asked.

"No," he replied. "She's upstairs. She's not allowed to go—we won't let her."

"You won't let her, little idiot!" I exclaimed. "Take me to her room right now, or I'll make you regret it."

"Papa would make *you* regret it if you tried to get there," he answered. "He says I'm not to be soft with Catherine—she's my wife, and it's shameful that she wants to leave me. He says she hates me and wants me to die so she can have my money. But she won't get it, and she won't go home! She never will! She can cry and be sick as much as she likes!"

He closed his eyes as if he meant to fall asleep.

"Master Heathcliff," I said, "have you forgotten all Catherine's kindness to you last winter? When you swore you loved her? When she brought you books and sang to you, and came through wind and snow to see you? She cried if she missed even one evening because she knew you'd be disappointed. You felt then that she was a hundred times too good for you. And now you believe the lies your father tells, even though you know he despises you both. And you're taking his side against her. That's fine gratitude, isn't it?"

The corner of Linton's mouth drooped, and he took the candy from his lips.

"Did she come to Wuthering Heights because she hated you?" I continued. "Think for yourself! As for your money, she doesn't even know you'll have any. And you say she's sick, yet you leave her alone up there in a strange house! You, who know what it's like to be neglected! You could pity your own suffering, and she pitied it too, but you won't pity hers! Look—I'm crying, Master Heathcliff, an old woman, just a servant—and you, after pretending such love, after having every reason to worship her, you save all your tears for yourself and lie there perfectly comfortable. You're a heartless, selfish boy!"

"I can't stay with her," he answered irritably. "I won't stay by myself. She cries so much I can't stand it. And she won't stop, even when I threaten to call my father. I did call him once, and he threatened to strangle her if she didn't quiet down. But the second he left, she started again—moaning and grieving all night long. I screamed at her because I couldn't sleep."

"Is Mr. Heathcliff out?" I asked, realizing the wretched creature had no ability to sympathize with his cousin's mental torture.

"He's in the courtyard," he replied, "talking to Doctor Kenneth, who says uncle is dying, truly dying at last. I'm glad—I'll be master of the Grange after him. Catherine always called it her house. It's not hers! It's mine—papa says everything she has is mine. All her nice books are mine. She offered to give me them, and her pretty birds, and her pony Minny, if I would unlock our room and let her out. But I told her she had nothing to give—they were all, all mine. Then she cried and took a little picture from her neck and said I could have that—two pictures in a gold case, her mother on one side and uncle on the other, when they were young. That was yesterday. I said those were mine too and tried to take them from her. The spiteful thing wouldn't let me—she pushed me off and hurt me. I shrieked—that frightens her—she heard papa coming and broke the hinges, split the case, and gave me her mother's portrait. The other one she tried to hide, but papa asked what was happening and I explained. He took the one I had and ordered her to give me hers. She refused, and he—he struck her down and ripped it off the chain, then crushed it under his foot."

"And were you pleased to see her struck?" I asked, deliberately encouraging him to keep talking.

"I winced," he answered. "I wince when I see my father strike a dog or horse—he does it so hard. But I was glad at first—she deserved punishment for pushing me. But when papa left, she made me come to the window and showed me her cheek, cut on the inside against her teeth, her mouth filling with blood. Then she gathered up the pieces of the picture and went to sit with her face to the wall. She hasn't spoken to me since. Sometimes I think she can't speak because of the pain. I don't like thinking that, but she's naughty for crying all the time, and she looks so pale and wild—I'm afraid of her."

"And you can get the key if you choose?" I asked.

"Yes, when I'm upstairs," he answered, "but I can't walk up the stairs now."

"Which room is it?" I asked.

"Oh," he cried, "I won't tell YOU where it is. It's our secret. Nobody—not Hareton, not Zillah—is supposed to know. There! You've tired me out—go away, go away!" And he turned his face into his arm and shut his eyes again.

I decided it was best to leave without seeing Mr. Heathcliff and bring help for my young lady from the Grange. When I reached it, my fellow servants were astonished to see me, their joy intense. When they heard their little mistress was safe, two or three were about to rush up and tell Mr. Edgar, but I insisted on bringing him the news myself.

How changed I found him, even in those few days! He lay there, an image of sadness and resignation, waiting for death. He looked so young—though he was thirty-nine, you would have thought him ten years younger at least. He was thinking of Catherine, murmuring her name. I touched his hand and spoke.

"Catherine is coming, dear master!" I whispered. "She's alive and well, and will be here tonight, I hope."

I trembled at the first effects of this news—he half rose, looked eagerly around the room, then sank back in a faint.

As soon as he recovered, I told him about our forced visit and imprisonment at the Heights. I said Heathcliff forced me to go in, which wasn't quite true. I said as little as possible against Linton and didn't describe all his father's brutal behavior—I didn't want to add more bitterness to his already overflowing cup.

He understood that one of his enemy's purposes was to secure the personal property as well as the estate for his son —or rather, for himself. But why he didn't wait until after the death was a puzzle to my master, because he didn't know how close he and his nephew were to leaving this world together. Still, he felt his will should be changed. Instead of leaving Catherine's fortune in her own control, he determined to put it in the hands of trustees for her use during her lifetime, and for her children after, if she had any. That way, it couldn't fall to Mr. Heathcliff if Linton died.

After receiving his orders, I sent a man to fetch the attorney and four more armed men to demand my young lady from her jailer. Both parties were very late returning. The single servant came back first. He said Mr. Green, the lawyer, was out when he arrived and he'd had to wait two hours. Then Mr. Green told him he had business in the village but would be at Thrushcross Grange before morning.

The four men also returned empty-handed, saying Catherine was too ill to leave her room and Heathcliff wouldn't let them see her. I scolded those stupid fellows thoroughly for believing that story, which I wouldn't carry to my master. I resolved to take a whole group up to the Heights at daylight and storm the place unless they surrendered the prisoner quietly. Her father SHALL see her, I vowed, even if that devil gets killed on his own doorstep trying to stop it!

Fortunately, I was spared the journey and the trouble. I'd gone downstairs at three o'clock to fetch water and was passing through the hall with the jug when a sharp knock at the front door made me jump. "Oh! It's Green," I said to myself—"only Green," and I went on, intending to send someone else to answer it. But the knock repeated—not loud, but insistent. I put the jug on the banister and hurried to open it myself.

The harvest moon shone clear outside. It wasn't the attorney. My own sweet little mistress threw herself on my neck, sobbing, "Ellen, Ellen! Is papa alive?"

"Yes!" I cried. "Yes, my angel, he is. Thank God, you're safe with us again!"

She wanted to run straight up to Mr. Linton's room, breathless as she was, but I made her sit down on a chair. I gave her something to drink and washed her pale face, rubbing some color back into it with my apron. Then I said I must go first and tell him of her arrival, begging her to say she'd be happy with young Heathcliff. She stared at me, but quickly understanding why I counseled her to lie, she promised she wouldn't complain.

I couldn't bear to be present at their meeting. I stood outside the bedroom door for fifteen minutes and hardly dared approach the bed after that. All was quiet, though—Catherine's grief was as silent as her father's joy. She supported him calmly, at least in appearance, and he fixed his eyes on her face, eyes that seemed to grow wide with ecstasy.

He died blissfully, Mr. Lockwood—he died so peacefully. Kissing her cheek, he murmured, "I am going to her, and you, darling child, shall come to us!" and never stirred or spoke again, but kept that transported, radiant gaze until his pulse imperceptibly stopped and his soul departed. No one could have noticed the exact minute of his death—there was no struggle at all.

Whether Catherine had spent all her tears, or whether the grief was too heavy to let them flow, she sat there dry-eyed until the sun rose. She sat until noon and would have remained brooding over that deathbed, but I insisted she come away and rest. It was good that I succeeded in moving her, because at dinnertime the lawyer appeared, having stopped at Wuthering Heights to get his instructions on how to proceed. He had sold himself to Mr. Heathcliff—that was why he'd delayed obeying my master's summons. Fortunately, no thought of worldly affairs had crossed Edgar's mind to disturb him after his daughter's arrival.

Mr. Green took it upon himself to order everything and everyone around the place. He gave notice to all the servants except me. He would have gone so far as to insist that Edgar Linton shouldn't be buried beside his wife but in the chapel with his family. But the will prevented that, along with my loud protests against any violation of its directions. The funeral was hurried through. Catherine—Mrs. Linton Heathcliff now—was allowed to stay at the Grange until her father's corpse had left it.

She told me that her anguish had finally driven Linton to risk freeing her. She'd heard the men I sent arguing at the door and caught the gist of Heathcliff's answer. It drove her to desperation. Linton, who'd been carried up to the little parlor soon after I left, was terrified into fetching the key before his father came back upstairs. He had the cunning to unlock and relock the door without shutting it. When he should have gone to bed, he begged to sleep with Hareton, and for once his request was granted. Catherine stole out before dawn. She didn't dare try the doors for fear the dogs would raise an alarm. She visited the empty rooms and examined their windows. Luckily, finding her mother's room, she got out easily through its lattice and down to the ground by means of the fir tree close by. Her accomplice suffered for his part in the escape, despite his timid scheming.

29

THE EVENING AFTER THE FUNERAL, CATHERINE AND I SAT IN the library, lost in our grief—one of us mourning, the other despairing—and trying to imagine what dark future lay ahead.

We'd just agreed on the best we could hope for: that Catherine might stay at the Grange, at least while Linton lived, with him joining her here and me staying on as housekeeper. It seemed too much to hope for, but I clung to the possibility of keeping my home, my position, and most of all, my beloved young mistress. Then one of the dismissed servants—not yet gone—burst in.

"That devil Heathcliff is coming through the courtyard! Should I lock him out?"

Even if we'd been foolish enough to try, there wasn't time. He didn't bother knocking or announcing himself—he was master now and used that privilege to walk straight in without a word. The servant's voice led him to the library. He entered, waved the man out, and shut the door.

This was the same room where he'd been brought as a guest eighteen years ago. The same moon shone through the window; the same autumn landscape stretched beyond. We hadn't lit any candles yet, but the whole room was visible, even the portraits on the wall—the magnificent one of Mrs. Linton and the elegant one of her husband. Heathcliff walked to the fireplace. Time had barely touched him. He was the same man, his dark face perhaps a shade paler and more controlled, his body maybe ten or twenty pounds heavier, but nothing else had changed. Catherine had jumped up to run when she saw him.

"Stop!" He grabbed her arm. "No more running away. Where would you go? I've come to take you home, and I expect you'll be a dutiful daughter and not encourage my son in any more disobedience. I was at a loss for how to punish him when I found out his part in this scheme—he's so fragile that a touch would destroy him—but you'll see from his face that he's learned his lesson. I brought him downstairs two nights ago, sat him in a chair, and never laid a finger on him. For two hours we were alone in that room. Then I had Joseph carry him back up. Since then, just knowing I exist terrifies him like seeing a ghost. I think he imagines he sees me even when I'm not there. Hareton says he wakes screaming in the night, calling for you to protect him from me. Whether you care for your precious husband or not, you're coming—he's your problem now. I'm done with him."

"Why not let Catherine stay here?" I begged. "Send Master Linton to her instead. Since you hate them both, you wouldn't miss them. They can only make you miserable."

"I'm looking for someone to rent the Grange," he answered, "and I want my children close. Besides, that girl owes me. I'm not keeping her in luxury after Linton dies. Get ready now. Don't make me drag you out."

"I'll come," said Catherine. "Linton is all I have left to

love in the world. You've done everything you could to make him hate me and me hate him, but you can't make us hate each other. And I swear you won't hurt him while I'm there, and you won't frighten me!"

"Such brave words," Heathcliff replied. "But I don't care enough about you to hurt him. You'll get the full benefit of his suffering as long as it lasts. I won't need to make him hateful to you—his own sweet nature will do that. He's bitter as poison about your desertion and what came of it. Don't expect gratitude for this noble devotion. I heard him telling Zillah what he'd do if he were as strong as me. The desire is there, and his very weakness will make him clever about finding other ways to hurt you."

"I know he has a cruel nature," said Catherine. "He's your son. But I'm glad I have a better one, to forgive it. And I know he loves me, and for that I love him. Mr. Heathcliff, YOU have NOBODY to love you, and however miserable you make us, we'll always have the satisfaction of knowing your cruelty comes from your own greater misery. You ARE miserable, aren't you? Lonely like the devil, and envious like him? NOBODY loves you—NOBODY will cry when you die! I wouldn't be you!"

Catherine spoke with a kind of bleak triumph, as if she'd decided to embrace the spirit of her new family and find pleasure in her enemies' pain.

"You'll regret those words soon enough," her father-in-law said. "If you stand there another minute—get out, witch, and pack your things!"

She left with contempt. Once she was gone, I begged for Zillah's position at the Heights, offering to give her mine, but he wouldn't hear of it. He told me to be quiet, and then, for the first time, looked around the room and studied the pictures. After staring at Mrs. Linton's portrait, he said, "I'll take that home. Not because I need it, but—" He turned sharply to the fire and continued with what I can only call a smile, for lack of a better word.

"I'll tell you what I did yesterday! I bribed the gravedigger who was digging Linton's grave to clear the earth from her coffin lid, and I opened it. I thought about staying there with her. When I saw her face again—it's still hers!—he had to drag me away. He said the air would decay her if I left it open, so I loosened one side of the coffin and covered it back up—not Linton's side, damn him! I wish he'd been sealed in lead. And I've bribed the gravedigger to pull my side away when I'm buried there, and slide my coffin right next to hers. I'll have mine made so it opens on that side. By the time Edgar gets there, he won't know which is which!"

"You were very wicked, Mr. Heathcliff!" I exclaimed. "Weren't you ashamed to disturb the dead?"

"I disturbed nobody, Nelly," he replied. "And I finally found some peace. I'll rest easier now, and you'll have a better chance of keeping me underground when I get there. Disturbed her? No! She's haunted me, night and day, for eighteen years—every second, without mercy—until last night. Last night I was finally calm. I dreamed I was sleeping forever beside her, my heart stopped, my cheek frozen against hers."

"And if she'd been decayed to earth, or worse, what would you have dreamed then?" I asked.

"Of dissolving with her and being even happier!" he answered. "You think I'm afraid of that kind of change? I expected to see her transformed when I opened the lid, but I'm glad it won't start until I can share it. Besides, without seeing her unchanged face, this strange feeling would never have left me. It started strangely. You know I was wild after she died, praying from dawn to dawn for her spirit to return to me. I believe in ghosts—I'm convinced they can and do exist among us!

"The day she was buried, snow fell. That evening I went to the churchyard. The wind blew cold as winter, everything was desolate and empty. I wasn't worried that her fool of a husband would come up to the glen so late, and no one else had any reason to be there.

"Being alone, knowing only two yards of loose earth separated us, I said to myself, 'I'll have her in my arms again! If she's cold, I'll tell myself it's just this north wind chilling me. And if she's motionless, I'll tell myself she's only sleeping.'

"I grabbed a spade from the tool-house and started digging with all my strength, it scraped the coffin. I switched to using my hands. The wood began cracking around the screws. I was just about to reach my goal when I thought I heard a sigh from someone above, right at the edge of the grave, leaning down.

"'If I can just get this off,' I muttered, 'I don't care if they shovel the earth over both of us!' I wrenched at it even more desperately.

"Then another sigh, right at my ear. I could feel warm breath displacing the icy wind. I knew no living person was there, but as surely as you sense someone approaching in the dark even when you can't see them, I felt that Cathy was there. Not under me in the coffin, but on the earth beside me.

"Sudden relief flooded through me. I abandoned my agonized digging and turned away, instantly comforted. Unspeakably comforted. Her presence was with me. It stayed with me while I refilled the grave and led me home.

"You may laugh if you want, but I was certain I'd see her

there. I was sure she was with me, and I couldn't help talking to her.

"When I reached the Heights, I rushed to the door. It was locked, and I remember that cursed Earnshaw and my wife tried to stop me from entering. I remember pausing to kick the breath out of him, then hurrying upstairs to my room and hers. I looked around frantically. I felt her beside me. I could ALMOST see her, and yet I COULD NOT! I should have sweated blood from the anguish of my longing—from how desperately I begged for just one glimpse! But I got nothing. She tormented me the way she often did in life, like a devil!

"And since then, sometimes more and sometimes less, I've been tortured by it constantly! It's infernal! Keeping my nerves stretched so tight that if they weren't made of steel, they would've snapped to uselessness long ago like Linton's. When I sat in the house with Hareton, I felt that if I went outside I'd meet her. When I walked on the moors, I expected to meet her coming back. When I left home, I'd rush to return because she MUST be somewhere at the Heights, I was certain of it!

"And when I tried to sleep in her chamber, I was driven out. I couldn't lie there. The moment I closed my eyes, she was either outside the window, or sliding back the panels, or entering the room, or resting her head on the same pillow she used as a child. I had to open my eyes to check. So I opened and closed them a hundred times each night—always disappointed! It destroyed me! I groaned aloud so often that old Joseph probably thought my conscience was tormenting me from inside.

"Now, since I've actually seen her, I'm calmer—a little. It was a strange way of killing someone: not by inches, but by fractions of hairbreadths, tormenting me with the ghost of hope for eighteen years!"

Mr. Heathcliff paused and wiped his forehead, his hair clinging to it with sweat. His eyes were fixed on the red coals of the fire, his brows raised near the temples, softening the grim look of his face but giving him a peculiar troubled expression, a painful appearance of mental strain toward one consuming obsession. He was only half talking to me, and I stayed silent. I didn't like to hear him talk! After a moment, he went back to studying the picture, took it down, and leaned it against the sofa to see it better. While he was occupied, Catherine entered, announcing she was ready when her pony was saddled.

"Send that over tomorrow," Heathcliff told me. Then turning to her, he added, "You won't need your pony. It's a fine evening, and you'll need no ponies at Wuthering Heights. For any journeys you take, your own feet will do. Come along."

"Goodbye, Ellen!" my dear little mistress whispered.

When she kissed me, her lips felt like ice. "Come and see me, Ellen. Don't forget."

"You'll do no such thing, Mrs. Dean!" said her new father. "When I want to speak to you, I'll come here. I want none of your spying at my house!"

He motioned for her to go ahead of him, and casting back a look that broke my heart, she obeyed. I watched from the window as they walked down the garden. Heathcliff locked Catherine's arm under his. Though she clearly tried to pull away at first, with rapid strides he hurried her into the alley, where the trees hid them from view.

30

I've been to the Heights, but I haven't seen her since she left. When I went to ask about her, Joseph blocked the door and wouldn't let me in. He said Mrs. Linton was busy and the master was out. If it weren't for Zillah's gossip, I'd hardly know who was alive and who was dead up there. From the way she talks, I can tell Zillah thinks Catherine is stuck-up and doesn't like her. My young lady asked for help when she first arrived, but Mr. Heathcliff told Zillah to mind her own business and let his daughter-in-law take care of herself. Zillah, being narrow-minded and selfish, was happy to comply. Catherine reacted to this neglect like an annoyed child—she treated Zillah with contempt, turning the woman into an enemy as surely as if she'd done her real harm. About six weeks ago, just before you came, I ran into Zillah on the moor and had a long talk with her. This is what she told me:

"The first thing Mrs. Linton did when she arrived at the Heights," she said, "was run straight upstairs without even saying good evening to me or Joseph. She locked herself in Linton's room and stayed there till morning. Then, while the master and Earnshaw were at breakfast, she came into the house, trembling, and asked if we could send for the doctor —her cousin was very ill.

"'We know that!' Heathcliff answered. 'But his life isn't worth a penny, and I won't spend a penny on him.'

"'But I don't know what to do,' she said. 'If nobody helps me, he'll die!'

"'Get out of the room,' the master shouted. 'I don't want to hear another word about him! Nobody here cares what happens to him. If you do, then play nurse. If you don't, lock him up and leave him.'

"Then she started bothering me, but I told her I'd had enough trouble with that tiresome boy. We each had our jobs, and hers was to take care of Linton—Mr. Heathcliff had made that clear.

"How they managed together, I can't say. I imagine he cried and moaned constantly, day and night, and she barely slept—you could tell from her pale face and dark circles. Sometimes she'd wander into the kitchen looking lost, as if she wanted to beg for help, but I wasn't going to disobey the master. I never dare disobey him, Mrs. Dean, and it wasn't my place to get involved. Once or twice, after we'd gone to bed, I opened my door and saw her sitting on the stairs crying. I'd quickly shut myself in, afraid I might be tempted to help. I did pity her, but I didn't want to lose my job, you understand.

"Finally, one night she burst into my room and scared me half to death. 'Tell Mr. Heathcliff his son is dying,' she said. 'I'm certain of it this time. Get up right now and tell him.'

"She vanished as soon as she'd spoken. I lay there for fifteen minutes, listening and shaking. The house was silent.

"She's wrong, I told myself. He's gotten through it. No

need to disturb them. I started to drift back to sleep, but then came the sharp ring of the bell—the only bell we have, installed specially for Linton. The master called for me to see what was happening and tell them he wouldn't tolerate that noise again.

"I delivered Catherine's message. He cursed under his breath, then grabbed a candle and went to their room. I followed. Mrs. Heathcliff sat by the bedside, hands folded in her lap. Her father-in-law held the light to Linton's face, looked at him, touched him, then turned to her.

"'Now, Catherine,' he said, 'how do you feel?'

"She said nothing.

"'How do you feel, Catherine?' he repeated.

"'He's safe, and I'm free,' she answered. 'I should feel well—but,' she continued with a bitterness she couldn't hide, 'you left me to fight death alone for so long that all I can feel and see is death! I feel like death!'

"And she looked it too! I gave her some wine. Hareton and Joseph, wakened by the bell and footsteps, came in after hearing our voices. Joseph seemed almost glad the boy was gone. Hareton looked troubled, though he was more interested in staring at Catherine than thinking about Linton. But the master told him to go back to bed—we didn't need his help. He had Joseph move the body to his room and told me to return to mine. Mrs. Heathcliff stayed there alone.

"In the morning, he sent me to tell her to come down for breakfast. She'd undressed and looked ready to sleep, saying she was ill—which didn't surprise me. When I told Mr. Heathcliff, he said, 'Well, leave her be until after the funeral. Check on her now and then, bring her what she needs, and let me know when she seems better.'"

According to Zillah, Cathy stayed upstairs for two weeks.

Zillah visited her twice a day and would have been friendlier, but her attempts at kindness were proudly rejected.

Heathcliff went up once to show her Linton's will. The boy had left everything—his property and what had been hers—to his father. The poor creature had been threatened or manipulated into signing it during her week's absence, when her father died. As a minor, Linton couldn't legally control the land itself, but Mr. Heathcliff claimed and kept it all through his wife's rights and now his own. I suppose it's legal. Either way, Catherine, without money or friends, can't challenge him.

"Nobody except me ever went near her door," Zillah said, "and nobody asked about her. The first time she came downstairs was on a Sunday afternoon. When I brought up her dinner, she'd said she couldn't stand the cold any longer. I told her the master was going to Thrushcross Grange, and Earnshaw and I wouldn't stop her from coming down. As soon as she heard Heathcliff's horse leave, she appeared dressed in black, her blonde curls pulled back behind her ears, plain as a Quaker—she couldn't style them properly.

"Joseph and I usually go to chapel on Sundays." (The church has no minister now, Mrs. Dean explained, so they attend the Methodist or Baptist chapel at Gimmerton.) "Joseph had gone," she continued, "but I stayed home. Young people need supervision, and Hareton, despite his shyness, isn't exactly well-mannered. I told him his cousin would probably sit with us and that she was used to respecting the Sabbath, so he should put away his guns and projects while she was there. He blushed at the news and looked down at his hands and clothes. The gun oil and gunpowder disappeared in a minute. I could see he wanted to make himself presentable for her company. Laughing—since I'd never dare laugh when the master's around—I offered to help him and teased him about his embarrassment. He turned sullen and started swearing.

"Now, Mrs. Dean," Zillah went on, seeing I disapproved of her tone, "you probably think your young lady is too good for Mr. Hareton, and maybe you're right. But I'd love to knock her down a peg or two. What good will all her education and refinement do her now? She's as poor as you or me —poorer, probably."

Hareton let Zillah help him clean up, and she flattered him into a better mood. So when Catherine came down, he tried to be pleasant, according to the housekeeper.

"The mistress walked in," she said, "cold as ice and proud as a princess. I stood up and offered her my armchair. She dismissed my politeness completely. Earnshaw also stood and invited her to sit by the fire on the bench, saying she must be freezing.

"'I've been freezing for over a month,' she answered, emphasizing the words as scornfully as possible.

"She got herself a chair and placed it far from both of us. After warming up, she looked around and spotted some books on the dresser. She immediately stood and stretched to reach them, but they were too high. Her cousin watched her struggle for a while, then finally worked up the courage to help. She held out her skirt, and he filled it with whatever books he could reach.

"That was progress for the boy. She didn't thank him, but he seemed pleased she'd accepted his help. He even dared to stand behind her as she looked through them, pointing out interesting pictures in the old volumes. She kept jerking the pages away from his finger, but he didn't give up. He just stepped back a bit and watched her instead of the books. She kept reading, or looking for something to read. Gradually, his attention fixed completely on her thick, silky curls—he couldn't see her face, and she couldn't see him. Maybe half-asleep to what he was doing, drawn like a moth to flame, he finally went from staring to touching. He reached out and stroked one curl as gently as if it were a bird. She might as well have been stabbed—she spun around furiously.

"'Get away from me! How dare you touch me? Why are you standing there?' she cried, disgusted. 'I can't stand you! I'll go back upstairs if you come near me.'

"Mr. Hareton backed away, looking foolish. He sat down quietly on the bench while she spent another half hour with her books. Finally, Earnshaw came over and whispered to me:

"'Would you ask her to read to us, Zillah? I'm tired of doing nothing, and I'd like—I'd really like to hear her! Don't say I asked, though. Make it seem like your idea.'

"'Mr. Hareton would like you to read to us, ma'am,' I said immediately. 'He'd be very grateful—much obliged.'

"She frowned and looked up. 'Mr. Hareton, and all of you, need to understand that I reject your fake kindness! I despise you and want nothing to do with any of you! When I would have given my life for one kind word, even just to see one of your faces, you all stayed away. But I won't complain to you! I'm only down here because of the cold, not to entertain you or enjoy your company.'

"'What could I have done?' Earnshaw protested. 'How was I to blame?'

"'Oh, you're an exception,' Mrs. Heathcliff answered. 'I never expected anything from someone like you.'

"'But I offered more than once, and asked,' he said, getting angry at her rudeness. 'I asked Mr. Heathcliff to let me sit with you—'

"'Be quiet! I'll go outside, anywhere, rather than listen to your horrible voice!' my lady said.

"Hareton muttered she could go to hell for all he cared, grabbed his gun, and went back to his Sunday activities. After that, he talked freely enough, and she soon retreated to her solitude. But the frost had set in hard, and despite her pride, she was forced to endure our company more and more. However, I made sure not to waste any more kindness on her. Since then, I've been as cold as she is. Nobody here likes or loves her, and she doesn't deserve it. Say the slightest word to her, and she'll snap back without respect for anyone. She'll even snap at the master himself, practically daring him to hit her. And the more hurt she gets, the more vicious she becomes."

When I first heard Zillah's account, I decided to quit my position, rent a cottage, and have Catherine come live with me. But Mr. Heathcliff would never allow that, any more than he'd set up Hareton in his own house. I can see no solution right now unless she could remarry—and arranging that isn't my responsibility.

So ended Mrs. Dean's story. Despite the doctor's prediction, I'm recovering quickly. Though it's only the second week of January, I plan to go horseback riding in a day or two and ride over to Wuthering Heights. I'll inform my landlord that I'm spending the next six months in London, and if he wants, he can find another tenant for after October. I wouldn't spend another winter here for anything.

31

YESTERDAY WAS BRUTALLY COLD BUT DECEPTIVELY PEACEFUL. I went up to the Heights as planned—my housekeeper had begged me to take a note to young Mrs. Heathcliff, and I couldn't refuse. The good woman had no idea how awkward her request was.

The front door stood open, but the gate was locked, just like last time. I knocked and called for Earnshaw. He emerged from the garden beds, unlocked it, and let me in. The man is strikingly handsome for a farmhand, though I noticed this time how he seems determined to hide it—like he's ashamed of his own good looks.

I asked if Heathcliff was home. No, but he'd be back for dinner. It was eleven o'clock, and I announced I'd wait inside. Earnshaw immediately dropped his tools and followed me in—not as my host, but as a watchdog.

We entered together. Catherine was there, preparing vegetables for lunch. She looked more sullen and defeated than when I'd first met her. She barely glanced up, continuing her work with the same cold indifference as before. No acknowledgment of my greeting, nothing.

She's not as sweet as Mrs. Dean led me to believe, I thought. *Beautiful, yes—but hardly an angel.*

Earnshaw gruffly told her to take her work to the kitchen.

"Take it yourself," she said, shoving the vegetables away. She retreated to a stool by the window and began carving little animals from turnip peelings in her lap.

I walked over, pretending to admire the garden view, and carefully dropped Mrs. Dean's note onto her knee—trying to keep Hareton from noticing. But Catherine asked loudly, "What's this?" and flicked it away.

"A letter from your old friend, the housekeeper at the Grange," I answered, annoyed that she'd exposed my gesture and worried they'd think I'd written it myself.

She immediately wanted to grab it, but Hareton beat her to it. He stuffed it in his pocket, saying Heathcliff should see it first. Catherine turned her face away and quietly pulled out her handkerchief, dabbing at her eyes. Her cousin struggled with himself for a moment—fighting against his softer feelings—then yanked out the letter and threw it on the floor beside her, as roughly as he could manage.

Catherine snatched it up and read it hungrily. Then she asked me about everyone at the Grange, both the sane and the crazy, and gazed toward the hills, murmuring to herself:

"I'd love to be riding Minny down there! Or climbing up those hills! Oh, I'm so tired—I'm trapped, Hareton!" She leaned her head back against the windowsill with a half-yawn, half-sigh, and drifted into a distant sadness, not caring if we watched.

After sitting in silence for a while, I said, "Mrs. Heathcliff, you do realize I'm a friend of yours? Such a close friend that I find it strange you won't talk to me. My housekeeper never stops talking about you and praising you. She'll be crushed if I come back with no news—except that you got her letter and said nothing."

She seemed surprised. "Does Ellen like you?"

"Yes, very much," I said, hesitating.

"Tell her," she continued, "that I'd write back, but I have nothing to write with. Not even a book I could tear a page from."

"No books!" I exclaimed. "How do you survive here without them? If you don't mind me asking. Even with my huge library, I get terribly bored at the Grange. Without books, I'd go mad!"

"I used to read constantly when I had them," Catherine said. "But Heathcliff doesn't read, so he decided to destroy all my books. I haven't seen one in weeks. Once, I searched through Joseph's religious books—which made him furious. And once, Hareton, I found your secret stash—some Latin and Greek, some stories and poetry. All old friends of mine. I brought the last one here, and you hoarded them like a magpie hoards silver spoons—just for the thrill of stealing! They're no use to you. Or maybe you hid them out of spite—if you can't enjoy them, no one can. Did your jealousy inspire Heathcliff to rob me? Well, most of them are written in my brain and printed on my heart. You can't take those!"

Earnshaw turned crimson as his cousin exposed his secret book collection. He stammered out an angry denial.

"Mr. Hareton wants to improve himself," I said, coming to his defense. "He's not jealous—he admires your education. He'll be well-read in a few years."

"And meanwhile, he wants me to become an idiot," Catherine shot back. "Yes, I hear him trying to read and spell—what hilarious mistakes he makes! You should have heard him butchering 'Chevy Chase' yesterday. And then flipping through the dictionary for hard words, cursing because he couldn't understand the definitions!"

The young man clearly thought it was unfair to be mocked for his ignorance, then mocked again for trying to fix it. I agreed with him. Remembering Mrs. Dean's story about his first attempts at education, I said, "But Mrs. Heathcliff, we all started somewhere. We all stumbled when we began. If our teachers had mocked us instead of helping us, we'd still be stumbling."

"Oh," she replied, "I don't want to stop him from learning. But he has no right to steal what's mine and make it sound ridiculous with his terrible pronunciation! Those books, the prose and poetry, are sacred to me. I hate hearing them butchered in his mouth! And worst of all, he's deliberately chosen my favorite passages—the ones I love most—as if to hurt me on purpose."

Hareton's chest heaved silently. He was fighting down a crushing mix of humiliation and rage. I stood up and moved to the doorway, pretending to look outside to give him space. He followed my lead and left the room—but came back immediately with half a dozen books, which he threw into Catherine's lap.

"Take them! I never want to hear, read, or think about them again!"

"I don't want them now," she answered. "They'll always remind me of you, and I'll hate them."

She opened one that had obviously been read many times and read a passage in an exaggerated beginner's voice, her eyes glittering with malice. Then she laughed and tossed it aside. "Listen to this," she continued mockingly, starting to recite an old ballad the same way.

But he'd had enough. I heard—and didn't entirely disapprove of—the sound of his hand meeting her insolent mouth. The little brat had done everything she could to hurt her cousin's feelings, and since he wasn't educated enough to fight back with words, he'd evened the score the only way he knew how. Then he gathered up the books and threw them into the fire.

I could see on his face how much it killed him to sacrifice those books to his anger. As they burned, I imagined he was remembering all the pleasure they'd given him, all the future joy he'd hoped for. I could guess what had driven him to study in secret. He'd been content with hard work and simple pleasures until Catherine crossed his path. Her contempt shamed him; her approval became his hope. He'd tried to better himself for her, but it had only made things worse.

"Yes, that's all a brute like you could get from them!" Catherine cried, nursing her split lip and watching the fire with furious eyes.

"You'd better shut up now," he answered fiercely.

Too upset to say more, he rushed toward the door. I stepped aside to let him pass. But before he could leave, Heathcliff came up the path and grabbed his shoulder.

"What's going on, boy?"

"Nothing, nothing," Hareton said, breaking free to nurse his grief and anger alone.

Heathcliff watched him go and sighed.

"It'll be ironic if I sabotage myself," he muttered, not realizing I was behind him. "But when I look for his father in his face, I see HER more every day—Catherine's face, not his father's. How the devil does he look so much like her? I can barely stand to look at him."

He stared at the ground and walked inside, moody. There was a restless, anxious look in his face I'd never seen before. He looked thinner too. His daughter-in-law saw him through the window and immediately escaped to the kitchen, leaving me alone with him.

"Good to see you up and about, Mr. Lockwood," he said in response to my greeting. "Partly for selfish reasons—I couldn't easily replace you in this wasteland. I've been wondering what brought you here."

"Just a whim, I'm afraid," I answered. "And another whim is about to take me away. I'm leaving for London next week. I should warn you—I don't plan to keep Thrushcross Grange beyond the year I agreed to rent it. I don't think I'll be living there anymore."

"Oh, really? Tired of being cut off from the world?" he said. "But if you're here to weasel out of paying for a place you're not using, you've wasted your trip. I never let anyone off the hook for what they owe me."

"I'm not trying to weasel out of anything," I said, irritated. "If you want, I'll settle up with you right now." I pulled out my checkbook.

"No, no," he replied coolly. "You'll leave enough behind to cover your debts if you don't come back. I'm not in any rush. Sit down and have dinner with us. A guest who won't be coming back is usually welcome. Catherine! Bring the plates! Where are you?"

Catherine reappeared with knives and forks.

"You can eat with Joseph in the kitchen," Heathcliff muttered to her. "Stay there until he leaves."

She obeyed without hesitation—probably had no desire to stay anyway. Living among these bitter recluses, she probably couldn't recognize decent people when she met them.

With Heathcliff grim and brooding on one side, and Hareton completely silent on the other, it was a depressing meal. I left early. I would have gone out the back way to catch another glimpse of Catherine and annoy old Joseph, but Hareton was ordered to bring my horse, and Heathcliff himself walked me to the door. So much for that plan.

How suffocating life must be in that house! I thought as I rode away. *What a perfect fairy tale it would have been if Mrs. Heathcliff and I had fallen for each other, like her nurse wanted, and escaped together to the excitement of the city!*

32

September 1802

I was heading north to hunt on a friend's estate when I found myself just fifteen miles from Gimmerton. At a roadside inn, while the stable hand watered my horses, a cart loaded with fresh-cut oats rolled past.

"That's from Gimmerton," he remarked. "They're always weeks behind everyone else with their harvest."

"Gimmerton?" The name stirred something distant in my memory. "How far is it?"

"About fourteen miles over the hills. Rough road."

On impulse, I decided to visit Thrushcross Grange. It was barely noon—I could spend the night at my own property instead of an inn, settle things with my tenant, and save myself another trip to this remote corner of England. After three exhausting hours navigating terrible roads, we finally reached the village.

I left my servant there and continued alone into the valley. The gray church looked grayer than I remembered, the graveyard lonelier, with sheep grazing between the headstones. The September weather was perfect—almost too warm for riding, but ideal for admiring the dramatic landscape. These valleys, enclosed by hills and wild moorland, were desolate in winter but absolutely divine in summer.

I reached the Grange before sunset and knocked. No answer—though a thin blue thread of smoke from the kitchen chimney told me someone was home. I rode into the courtyard and found a girl about ten years old knitting under the porch while an old woman sat on the steps smoking a pipe.

"Is Mrs. Dean here?" I asked.

"Mrs. Dean? No sir, she's up at the Heights now."

"Are you the housekeeper then?"

"Yes, I keep the house."

"I'm Mr. Lockwood, the owner. Can you prepare a room for me? I need to stay the night."

"The master!" She jumped up in shock. "Lord, why didn't you send word? There's nothing ready—nothing fit for anyone!"

Her panic was so extreme I thought she might faint. I calmed her down, promising to take a walk while she prepared a bedroom and sitting room—nothing fancy, just clean sheets and a good fire. She seemed willing enough, though flustered, accidentally shoving the hearth brush into the grate instead of the poker. I left her to it and decided to walk up to Wuthering Heights.

"Everything alright up at the Heights?" I asked before leaving.

"Far as I know!" she called back, rushing off with a pan of hot coals.

I wanted to ask why Mrs. Dean had moved there, but she was too frantic to stop. So I set off, walking slowly as the sun set behind me and the moon rose ahead. By the time I could see Heathcliff's house, twilight had faded to darkness, but the brilliant moon lit every pebble on the path.

The gate was unlocked—an improvement from my last visit. Another surprise: the scent of flowers drifted from the fruit trees. Both doors and windows stood open, and despite the warm evening, a fire blazed in the hearth—typical for this coal-mining region. The house was so large that its inhabitants could easily escape the heat, and I could see they'd positioned themselves near a window. I stopped to watch and listen, driven by curiosity and, I'll admit, envy.

"Wrong AGAIN!" said a voice sweet as silver bells. "That's three times, you dunce! I'm not telling you again. Get it right or I'll pull your hair!"

"Contrary, then," answered a man's deep but gentle voice. "Now kiss me for getting it right."

"No, read it again perfectly first. Not a single mistake."

The man began reading. He was young, well-dressed, sitting at a table with a book. His handsome face glowed with pleasure, his eyes constantly wandering from the page to a small white hand on his shoulder, which slapped his cheek whenever its owner caught him looking. She stood behind him, her golden curls mixing with his brown hair as she leaned over to supervise his lesson. Her face—he was lucky he couldn't see it, or he'd never have concentrated. But I could see it perfectly, and I bit my lip in frustration at the chance I'd thrown away by leaving this place.

When he finished (not without errors), he claimed his reward: at least five kisses, enthusiastically returned. As they headed for the door, apparently planning an evening walk, I realized I'd better make myself scarce. Hareton Earnshaw would curse me to hell if he saw me lurking there. Feeling petty and mean, I slipped around to the kitchen.

The door was open there too. My old friend Nelly Dean

sat sewing and singing, though harsh Yorkshire cursing from inside kept interrupting her song.

"I'd rather hear swearing all day than listen to your unholy singing!" Joseph's voice grumbled from within. "It's a scandal! I can't open the Good Book without you singing Satan's songs! You're worthless, and she's no better, and that poor lad will be damned between you both! He's bewitched, I'm certain of it. Oh Lord, judge them, for there's no law or justice among our rulers!"

"We'd be burning at the stake if you had your way," Nelly retorted. "Now hush and read your Bible like a Christian. This is 'Fairy Annie's Wedding'—it's a dance tune!"

She was about to continue when I stepped forward. Recognizing me immediately, she jumped up.

"Mr. Lockwood! Bless me, why didn't you warn us? The Grange is all shut up!"

"I've arranged accommodation there for tonight. I leave tomorrow. But tell me, why are you here now?"

"Zillah left, and Mr. Heathcliff wanted me here after you went to London. But come in! Did you walk from Gimmerton?"

"From the Grange. While they're preparing my rooms, I need to settle business with your master."

"What business?" Nelly asked, leading me inside. "He's out and won't return soon."

"The rent."

"Oh! Then you'll need to speak with Mrs. Heathcliff—or rather, with me. She hasn't learned to manage business yet, so I handle everything."

I looked surprised.

"You haven't heard? Heathcliff is dead."

"Dead!" I exclaimed. "When?"

"Three months ago. Sit down, let me take your hat, and I'll tell you everything. Wait—have you eaten?"

"I've ordered supper at home. Just tell me what happened. You said the young people are out?"

"Yes, out walking until all hours, though I scold them for it. They don't listen to me anymore. At least have some ale—you look tired."

She fetched it before I could refuse, while Joseph muttered about the scandal of her having "followers" at her age and raiding the master's cellar. She ignored him, returning with a silver mug brimming with ale. After I'd praised it appropriately, she told me how Heathcliff had died—a "strange" death, as she put it.

MR. HEATHCLIFF SUMMONED me here two weeks after you left. "I came gladly, for Catherine's sake. But when I saw her, I was shocked at how much she'd changed. Heathcliff didn't explain why he'd changed his mind about me coming—just said he wanted me there and was tired of seeing Catherine. I was to keep her in the small parlor with me. He only wanted to see her once or twice a day.

"Catherine seemed happy with this at first. I brought books and things from the Grange to keep her entertained, and I thought we'd manage well enough. But that didn't last. She grew restless and irritable. Being confined to the garden as spring arrived frustrated her terribly. When I had to leave her to do housework, she complained of loneliness. She'd rather argue with Joseph in the kitchen than sit alone in peace.

"Their fights didn't bother me, but Hareton often came to the kitchen too when Heathcliff wanted the house to himself. At first, Catherine would leave when he arrived or quietly join me in whatever I was doing, never speaking to him. He was always silent and sullen. But after a while, she couldn't leave him alone. She'd talk at him constantly, mocking his stupidity and laziness, wondering aloud how he could bear such a life—just sitting by the fire all evening, half-asleep.

"'He's like a dog, isn't he, Ellen?' she said once. 'Or a cart horse? He works, eats, and sleeps. Nothing more. What a blank, dreary mind he must have! Do you ever dream, Hareton? What about? But you can't even speak to me!'

"He wouldn't open his mouth or look at her.

"'Maybe he's dreaming now,' she continued. 'He just twitched his shoulder like Juno does. Ask him, Ellen.'

"'Mr. Hareton will ask Heathcliff to send you upstairs if you don't behave!' I warned. He'd not only twitched but clenched his fist.

"'I know why Hareton never speaks when I'm here,' she announced another time. 'He's afraid I'll laugh at him. Ellen, did you know he tried to teach himself to read once? But when I laughed, he burned his books and gave up. Wasn't that foolish?'

"'Weren't you cruel?' I asked.

"'Maybe,' she admitted. 'But I didn't think he'd be so sensitive. Hareton, if I gave you a book now, would you take it?'

"She held out the one she'd been reading. He knocked it away and threatened to break her neck if she didn't stop.

"'Fine, I'll leave it here in the drawer,' she said, and went to bed.

"She asked me to watch if he touched it. He didn't go near it, which disappointed her. I could see she felt guilty for scaring him away from improving himself. So she tried a new approach: whenever I was ironing or doing other work in the kitchen, she'd read aloud from entertaining books. When Hareton was there, she'd stop at exciting parts and leave the book lying around. But he was stubborn as a mule. Instead of taking the bait, he'd go smoke with Joseph in bad weather. They'd sit like statues by the fire—Joseph too deaf to hear what he would've called her 'wicked nonsense,' Hareton trying his best to ignore it.

"Things changed when Hareton injured himself in early March. His gun exploded while he was out on the moors alone. He lost a lot of blood and was confined to the kitchen fireside while recovering. Catherine loved having him trapped there—it gave her more reason to hate her upstairs room and find excuses to be in the kitchen with me.

"On Easter Monday, Joseph went to Gimmerton fair with cattle. That afternoon, I was doing laundry while Hareton sat brooding by the fire. Catherine was drawing on the windowpanes, humming songs and shooting impatient glances at her cousin, who steadily smoked and stared at the grate. When I complained she was blocking my light, she moved to the hearth. I wasn't paying attention until I heard her say:

"'Hareton, I've realized something. I want—I'm glad—I'd like us to be proper cousins now, if you hadn't grown so cross and rough with me.'

"He didn't answer.

"'Hareton, Hareton, Hareton! Do you hear me?'

"'Get away from me!' he growled.

"'Let me take that pipe,' she said, carefully reaching for it. Before he could stop her, she'd grabbed it and thrown it in the fire. He swore and reached for another.

"'Stop! Listen to me first. I can't talk with smoke in my face.'

"'Go to hell and leave me alone!'

"'No, I won't. I don't know how to make you talk to me. You're determined not to understand. When I call you stupid, I don't mean it. I don't despise you. Come, Hareton, you're my cousin. Acknowledge me.'

"'I'll have nothing to do with you, your filthy pride, and your damned mocking tricks! I'll go to hell before I look at you again. Get out of here, now!'

"Catherine retreated to the window seat, chewing her lip, trying not to cry.

"'You should be friends with your cousin, Mr. Hareton,' I interrupted. 'She's sorry for being rude. It would do you good to have her as a companion.'

"'A companion!' he cried. 'When she hates me and thinks I'm not fit to wipe her shoes! I wouldn't seek her friendship if it made me a king.'

"'I don't hate you—you hate me!' Catherine burst out, tears flowing. 'You hate me as much as Heathcliff does, maybe more!'

"'You're a damned liar! Why did I defend you a hundred times then? When you sneered at me and—Go on, keep plaguing me, and I'll tell them you drove me out of the kitchen!'

"'I didn't know you defended me,' she said, wiping her eyes. 'I was miserable and angry at everyone. But now I thank you and beg you to forgive me. What else can I do?'

"She came back to the hearth and frankly offered her hand. He scowled like a thundercloud, keeping his fists clenched and his eyes on the ground. Catherine must have realized it was stubborn pride, not dislike, that made him act this way. After hesitating, she leaned down and kissed his cheek gently. The little schemer thought I hadn't seen, and returned to the window trying to look innocent. I shook my head at her, and she blushed.

"'Well, what should I have done, Ellen? He wouldn't shake hands or look at me. I had to show him somehow that I like him—that I want to be friends.'

"Whether the kiss convinced him, I can't say. He kept his face hidden for several minutes, and when he finally looked up, he didn't know where to direct his eyes.

"Catherine wrapped a beautiful book in white paper, tied it with ribbon, and addressed it to 'Mr. Hareton Earnshaw.' She asked me to deliver it.

"'Tell him if he accepts it, I'll teach him to read it properly. If he refuses, I'll go upstairs and never bother him again.'

"I delivered the message while she watched anxiously. Hareton wouldn't take it, so I set it on his knee. He didn't push it away. Catherine waited until she heard him unwrapping it, then quietly sat beside him. He trembled, his face flushed—all his roughness and surliness melted away. He couldn't speak when she looked at him questioningly.

"'Say you forgive me, Hareton. Please. Just that one little word would make me so happy.'

"He mumbled something I couldn't hear.

"'And you'll be my friend?'

"'No, you'll be ashamed of me every day. The more you know me, the more ashamed you'll be. I couldn't bear it.'

"'So you won't be my friend?' she said, smiling sweetly and moving closer.

"I couldn't hear what followed, but when I looked again, they were both bent over the book together, faces glowing. The peace treaty was clearly signed by both parties—enemies had become allies.

"They stayed absorbed in the illustrated book until Joseph returned. The poor old man was absolutely horrified to find Catherine sitting next to Hareton with her hand on his shoulder. His favorite's tolerance of her closeness shocked him too deeply for comment. He just sighed enormously, spread his big Bible on the table, and covered it with dirty banknotes from the day's business. Finally, he summoned Hareton.

"'Take these to the master, lad, and stay there. I'm going to my room. This place isn't proper or decent for us anymore—we need to get out and find somewhere else.'

"'Come, Catherine,' I said. 'We should go too. I'm done with the ironing.'

"'It's not even eight o'clock!' she protested.

"'Hareton, I'll leave this book on the mantelpiece and bring more tomorrow.'

"'Any books you leave, I'll throw in the house,' Joseph threatened, 'and good luck finding them again! You can please yourself!'

"Catherine warned that his library would pay for hers. Smiling at Hareton, she went singing upstairs—lighter of heart than I'd ever seen her in that house, except perhaps when she first visited Linton.

Their friendship grew quickly after that, though it had its ups and downs. Hareton couldn't be civilized overnight, and Catherine was no patient saint. But they both wanted the same thing—one longing to love and respect, the other longing to be loved and respected. Eventually, they found their way.

You see, Mr. Lockwood, it was easy enough to win Mrs. Heathcliff's heart. I'm glad you didn't try, though. My greatest wish is to see those two married. I'll be the happiest woman in England on their wedding day!"

33

The next day, with Earnshaw still unable to follow his usual work and therefore keeping to the house, I realized I couldn't keep Catherine beside me anymore. She slipped downstairs before I did and out to the garden, where she'd spotted her cousin doing some light work. When I went to call them for breakfast, I found she'd convinced him to clear a huge patch of ground—ripping out currant and gooseberry bushes—and they were planning to transplant flowers from the Grange.

I was horrified at what they'd destroyed in just half an hour. Those blackcurrant trees were Joseph's pride and joy, and she'd chosen to plant her flowers right where they'd stood.

"There! The master will hear about this the second it's discovered," I said. "And what excuse will you give for destroying the garden? We'll have hell to pay—mark my words! Mr. Hareton, what were you thinking, making that mess just because she asked?"

"I forgot they were Joseph's," Hareton answered, looking confused. "But I'll tell him I did it."

We always ate our meals with Mr. Heathcliff. I served as mistress of the house—making tea and carving meat—so I had to be at the table. Catherine usually sat by me, but today she moved closer to Hareton. I could see she'd be just as reckless with her friendship as she'd been with her hostility.

"Mind you don't talk to your cousin too much," I whispered as we entered the room. "It'll anger Mr. Heathcliff, and he'll punish you both."

"I won't," she answered.

A minute later, she'd sidled up to him and was sticking primroses in his porridge.

He didn't dare speak to her there—could barely look at her—but she kept teasing until he nearly laughed twice. I frowned, and she glanced at the master, whose mind was clearly elsewhere, his dark expression proving it. She turned serious for a moment, studying him intently. Then she went back to her games until Hareton let out a stifled laugh.

Mr. Heathcliff's head snapped up. His eyes swept our faces. Catherine met his gaze with her usual mix of nervousness and defiance—a look he despised.

"Good thing you're out of my reach," he said. "What demon possesses you to stare at me with those hellish eyes? Look down! Don't remind me you exist. I thought I'd broken you of laughing."

"It was me," Hareton muttered.

"What did you say?"

Hareton stared at his plate and didn't repeat himself. Mr. Heathcliff watched him a moment, then returned silently to his breakfast and his brooding. We'd nearly finished, and the two young people had wisely moved apart, so I thought we'd escaped trouble—until Joseph appeared in the doorway. His trembling lip and furious eyes told me he'd discovered the destroyed bushes. He must have seen Catherine and Hareton near them earlier, because while his jaw worked like a cow chewing cud, making his words hard to understand, he burst out:

"I want my wages, and I'm leaving! I'd planned to die where I've served sixty years. Thought I'd move my books up to the attic, all my things, and they could have the kitchen to themselves—for peace and quiet. It was hard giving up my own hearth, but I thought I could bear it! But now she's destroyed my garden, and by God, master, I cannot stand it! You may bend to her if you will—I'm not used to it, and an old man doesn't soon get used to new burdens. I'd rather earn my bread with a hammer on the road!"

"Shut up, idiot!" Heathcliff interrupted. "What's your complaint? I won't interfere between you and Nelly. She can throw you in the coal cellar for all I care."

"It's not Nelly!" Joseph answered. "I wouldn't leave for Nelly—nasty thing that she is. Thank God! She can't steal anyone's soul! She was never pretty enough to turn men's heads. It's that shameless witch who's bewitched our lad with her bold eyes and forward ways—until—No! It breaks my heart! He's forgotten everything I've done for him, and gone and torn up a whole row of the finest currant trees in the garden!"

Here he broke down completely, overcome by the injuries and Earnshaw's ingratitude.

"Is the fool drunk?" asked Mr. Heathcliff. "Hareton, is he complaining about you?"

"I pulled up two or three bushes," the young man replied, "but I'm going to replant them."

"And why did you pull them up?"

Catherine spoke up boldly. "We wanted to plant flowers there. I'm the only one to blame—I asked him to do it."

"And who the devil gave you permission to touch anything?" her father-in-law demanded, clearly surprised. "And who ordered you to obey her?" he added, turning to Hareton.

Hareton was speechless. His cousin replied, "You shouldn't grudge me a few yards of earth to decorate when you've taken all my land!"

"Your land, you insolent slut! You never had any."

"And my money," she continued, glaring back at him while biting into a crust of bread left from breakfast.

"Silence! Get out!"

"And Hareton's land, and his money," the reckless girl went on. "Hareton and I are friends now, and I'll tell him everything about you!"

The master froze for a moment. He went pale and stood up, staring at her with pure hatred.

"If you strike me, Hareton will strike you," she said. "So you might as well sit down."

"If Hareton doesn't throw you out, I'll beat him to hell," Heathcliff thundered. "Damnable witch! You dare turn him against me? Get her out of here! Do you hear? Drag her to the kitchen! I'll kill her, Ellen Dean, if you let her near me again!"

Hareton tried quietly to persuade her to leave.

"Drag her away!" Heathcliff shouted. "Why are you still talking?" He moved to enforce his command himself.

"He won't obey you anymore, wicked man," said Catherine. "And soon he'll hate you as much as I do."

"Hush! Hush!" the young man said reproachfully. "I won't hear you speak to him like that. Stop."

"But you won't let him strike me?"

"Come, then," he whispered urgently.

Too late—Heathcliff had grabbed her.

"Now you go!" he said to Earnshaw. "Accursed witch! This time she's provoked me beyond endurance. I'll make her regret it forever!"

His hand twisted in her hair. Hareton tried to free her, begging him not to hurt her just this once. Heathcliff's black eyes blazed—he looked ready to tear Catherine apart. I was about to risk intervening when suddenly his fingers loosened. He shifted his grip from her hair to her arm and stared intensely at her face. Then he covered his eyes with his hand, took a moment to compose himself, and turned back to Catherine with forced calm.

"You must learn not to provoke me, or I really will murder you one day. Go with Mrs. Dean and stay with her. Save your insolence for her ears. As for Hareton Earnshaw, if I catch him listening to you, I'll throw him out to beg for his bread. Your love will make him an outcast and a beggar. Nelly, take her. All of you—leave me!"

I led my young lady out; she was too relieved to resist. Hareton followed, and Mr. Heathcliff had the room to himself until dinner. I'd advised Catherine to eat upstairs, but as soon as he noticed her empty chair, he sent me to fetch her. He didn't speak to any of us, barely ate, and left immediately after, saying he wouldn't return until evening.

The two new friends took over the house in his absence. I heard Hareton sharply stop his cousin when she tried to tell him about his father's treatment by Heathcliff. He said he wouldn't hear a word against him—devil or not, he'd stand by him. He'd rather she insulted him like she used to than attack Mr. Heathcliff. Catherine was getting angry, but he silenced her by asking how she'd like him speaking ill of her father. Then she understood that Earnshaw had taken the master's honor as his own, bound by ties stronger than reason—chains forged by habit that would be cruel to break. She showed her good heart after that, avoiding all complaints about Heathcliff. She confessed to me her regret at trying to turn them against each other. I don't think she's breathed a word against her oppressor in Hareton's presence since.

Once this small dispute ended, they were friends again, busy as ever with their lessons. I came to sit with them after finishing my work, and felt so peaceful watching them that I lost track of time. They both seemed like my children—I'd long been proud of one, and now I was sure the other would bring equal satisfaction. His honest, warm, intelligent nature rapidly shook off the ignorance and degradation of his upbringing. Catherine's genuine praise spurred him on. His brightening mind transformed his features, adding spirit and nobility to his appearance. I could hardly believe this was the same person I'd found with my little lady at Wuthering Heights after her trip to the Crags.

While I watched them work, dusk fell, and with it came the master. He entered unexpectedly through the front door and saw all three of us before we noticed him. Well, I thought, there was never a more pleasant or harmless sight—it would be shameful to scold them. The red firelight glowed on their two beautiful heads, showing faces animated with the eager interest of children. Though he was twenty-three and she eighteen, both had so much to discover and learn that neither showed the weariness of disillusioned adulthood.

They looked up together to meet Mr. Heathcliff's gaze. Perhaps you've never noticed that their eyes are identical—and they're Catherine Earnshaw's eyes. The present Catherine has no other resemblance to her mother except a broad forehead and a certain arch of the nostril that makes her seem haughty whether she means to or not. With Hareton, the resemblance goes deeper. It's always striking, but particularly so then, because his senses were alert and his mind fully engaged.

I suppose this resemblance disarmed Mr. Heathcliff. He walked to the hearth clearly agitated, but it faded as he looked at the young man—or rather, changed its nature. The emotion was still there. He took the book from Hareton's hand, glanced at the open page, then returned it without comment, merely gesturing for Catherine to leave. Her companion followed shortly after, and I was about to go too, but he told me to stay.

"It's a poor ending, isn't it?" he said after brooding on what he'd witnessed. "An absurd conclusion to my violent efforts? I prepare to demolish both houses, train myself to work like Hercules, and when everything's ready, I find the will to lift a single slate has vanished. My old enemies haven't beaten me—now would be the perfect time for revenge on their children. I could do it. No one could stop me. But what's the point? I don't care about striking. I can't be bothered to raise my hand. That sounds like I've been laboring all this time just to show how magnanimous I am. Far from it—I've lost the ability to enjoy their destruction, and I'm too tired to destroy for nothing.

"Nelly, there's a strange change coming. I'm in its shadow now. I take so little interest in daily life that I barely remember to eat and drink. Those two who just left are the only things that still seem real to me, and seeing them causes me agony. I won't speak about her, don't want to think about her, but I desperately wish she were invisible—her presence brings only maddening sensations. He affects me differently. If I could do it without seeming insane, I'd never look at him again."

He attempted a bitter smile. "You probably think I'm losing my mind. But I'll try to explain—though you mustn't repeat this. My mind has been locked inside itself so long, it's tempting to finally let someone in.

"Five minutes ago, Hareton seemed like my youth personified, not a human being. His shocking resemblance to Catherine connects him to her, but that's the least of it—what isn't connected to her for me? I can't look at this floor without seeing her features in the stones. In every cloud, every tree—I'm surrounded by her image. Every face mocks me with resemblance. The entire world is a memorial that she existed and I've lost her. Hareton's face was the ghost of my immortal love, my wild attempts to claim what was mine, my degradation, my pride, my happiness, my anguish—

"But it's madness to tell you this. I only wanted you to understand why his company brings no relief. It worsens my constant torment. That's why I don't care how he and his cousin carry on together. I can't pay attention to anything anymore."

"But what do you mean by a change, Mr. Heathcliff?" I asked, alarmed by his manner. He wasn't losing his mind or dying, as far as I could tell. He was strong and healthy, and his reason was sound on every point except this. From childhood, he'd loved dwelling on dark things and strange fancies. He might have had a fixation about his lost idol, but otherwise his wits were intact.

"I won't know until it comes," he said. "I'm only half-aware of it now."

"You don't feel ill?"

"No, Nelly."

"Then you're not afraid of death?"

"Afraid? No!" he replied. "I have no fear, no premonition, no hope of death. Why should I? With my strong constitution and moderate living, I should probably stay alive until there's barely a black hair on my head. And yet I can't continue like this! I have to remind myself to breathe—almost remind my heart to beat. It's like bending back a stiff spring. I force myself to do the smallest act not driven by one thought. I force myself to notice anything, living or dead, not connected to one universal idea. I have a single wish, and my whole being yearns for it. They've yearned so long and so constantly that I'm convinced it will happen—soon—because it's consumed my existence. I'm swallowed by anticipating its fulfillment. My confession hasn't relieved me, but it might explain my otherwise inexplicable moods. God! It's been a long fight. I wish it were over."

He began pacing, muttering terrible things, until I believed, as Joseph did, that conscience had turned his heart into an earthly hell. I wondered how it would end. Though he rarely showed this tormented state, I knew it was his constant condition. No one would have guessed from his general behavior. You wouldn't have known when you saw him, Mr. Lockwood. He appeared the same as always—only fonder of solitude and perhaps even more silent in company.

34

For several days after that evening, Mr. Heathcliff avoided us at mealtimes. He couldn't bring himself to formally ban Hareton and Cathy from the table—that would mean surrendering completely to his feelings, and he'd rather just stay away. He seemed to survive on one meal a day, if that.

One night, after everyone had gone to bed, I heard him go downstairs and out the front door. He didn't come back, and in the morning he was still gone. It was April then—the weather was sweet and warm, the grass brilliant green from spring showers and sunshine, and the two dwarf apple trees by the southern wall were in full bloom. After breakfast, Catherine insisted I bring my sewing outside to sit under the fir trees at the end of the house. She coaxed Hareton, who'd fully recovered from his accident, into working on her little garden—we'd moved it to that corner after Joseph complained about its original location.

I was enjoying the spring air and the soft blue sky when Catherine, who'd run down to the gate to dig up some primrose roots for a border, came back only half-loaded with plants. "Mr. Heathcliff is coming," she announced, looking puzzled. "And he spoke to me."

"What did he say?" Hareton asked.

"He told me to get out of his way," she answered. "But he looked so different from usual that I stopped and stared at him."

"Different how?"

"Almost bright and cheerful. No—*almost* nothing—he looked excited, wild, and *glad*!"

"So he enjoys his midnight wandering," I said, trying to sound casual. But I was as surprised as she was and desperate to know if she was right. Seeing Heathcliff look glad would be extraordinary. I made an excuse to go inside.

Heathcliff stood at the open door. He was pale and trembling, but his eyes held a strange, joyful glitter that transformed his whole face.

"Will you have some breakfast?" I asked. "You must be hungry after walking around all night." I wanted to find out where he'd been, but didn't want to ask directly.

"No, I'm not hungry," he said, turning his head away with contempt, as if he knew I was fishing for information about his sudden good mood.

I was bewildered and wondered if I should say something.

"I don't think it's right to wander around instead of sleeping," I ventured. "It's not healthy, especially in this damp weather. You'll catch cold or fever—something's clearly wrong with you already!"

"Nothing I can't bear," he replied. "In fact, I bear it with the greatest pleasure. Just leave me alone—go inside and don't bother me."

I obeyed, but noticed as I passed that he was breathing as hard as a cat.

We're going to have a medical crisis, I thought. *What has he been doing?*

At noon he sat down to dinner with us, and I handed him a heaped plate as if he meant to make up for his fasting.

"I don't have a cold or fever, Nelly," he said, referring to my morning lecture. "And I'm ready to do justice to your cooking."

He picked up his knife and fork to eat, then suddenly seemed to lose all interest. He set them down, stared eagerly toward the window, then got up and went outside. We watched him pace the garden while we finished eating. Earnshaw said he'd go ask why he wouldn't eat—he thought we'd offended him somehow.

"Well, is he coming?" Catherine asked when her cousin returned.

"No," he answered. "But he's not angry. He seemed strangely pleased, actually. I just annoyed him by talking to him, and he told me to come back to you all—said he couldn't understand why I'd want anyone's company."

I kept his plate warm by the fire. After an hour or two, when the room was empty, he came back in—no calmer than before. That same unnatural joy showed beneath his black brows, the same deathly pallor, his teeth occasionally visible in a kind of smile. His body wasn't shivering from cold or weakness, but vibrating like a taut string—thrilling rather than trembling.

I have to ask what's going on, I thought. "Have you heard good news, Mr. Heathcliff? You look remarkably animated."

"Where would good news come from for me?" he said. "I'm animated with hunger, but apparently I can't eat."

"Your dinner's right here. Why won't you eat it?"

"I don't want it now," he said quickly. "I'll wait until supper. And Nelly, once and for all—warn Hareton and everyone else to stay away from me. I want to be left alone."

"Is there a new reason for this exile?" I asked. "Tell me why you're acting so strange. Where were you last night? I'm not just being nosy—"

"You are absolutely being nosy," he interrupted with a laugh. "But I'll answer. Last night I was on the threshold of hell. Today, I'm within sight of my heaven. I can see it—barely three feet away! Now go! You won't see or hear anything frightening if you stop prying."

After cleaning up, I left, more confused than ever.

He stayed in the house that afternoon, and no one disturbed him. At eight o'clock, though he hadn't asked, I thought I should bring him a candle and supper. He was leaning against an open window, but not looking out—his face turned toward the dark room. The fire had died to ashes; the room was filled with damp evening air, so quiet I could hear the stream down in Gimmerton, its water gurgling over stones. I made a noise of frustration seeing the dead fire and started closing windows. When I reached his, I asked, "Should I close this?" trying to get his attention since he hadn't moved.

The candlelight hit his face. Oh, Mr. Lockwood, I can't describe the shock I got from that glimpse! Those deep black eyes! That smile and ghostly paleness! He looked like a goblin, not Mr. Heathcliff. In my terror, I tilted the candle toward the wall and plunged us into darkness.

"Yes, close it," he said in his normal voice. "How clumsy! Why did you hold the candle sideways? Hurry and get another one."

I rushed out, frightened, and told Joseph, "The master wants you to bring him a light and restart the fire." I didn't dare go back myself.

Joseph took some coals in a shovel but came back immediately with the supper tray, explaining that Mr. Heathcliff was going to bed and didn't want anything until morning. We heard him go upstairs, but not to his usual room—he went to the one with the paneled bed. Its window, as I've mentioned, is wide enough for anyone to climb through. I suspected he was planning another midnight excursion that he didn't want us to know about.

Is he a ghoul or a vampire? I wondered. I'd read about such demons. Then I told myself how absurd it was to be horrified—I'd cared for him since infancy, watched him grow up, been with him almost his whole life. *But where did he come from, this dark little thing that a good man took in, only to be destroyed?* whispered Superstition as I dozed off. Half-dreaming, I wore myself out imagining possible origins for him, replaying his life with dark variations, finally picturing his death and funeral. All I remember is being frustrated about writing his gravestone inscription. Since he had no surname and we didn't know his age, we had to settle for just "Heathcliff." That came true—we did. If you visit the churchyard, you'll see only that name and his death date on his headstone.

Dawn brought back my common sense. I went to the garden as soon as it was light to check for footprints under his window. There were none. *He stayed home*, I thought. *He'll be fine today.*

I made breakfast as usual but told Hareton and Catherine to eat before the master came down, since he'd sleep late. They chose to eat outside under the trees, so I set up a small table for them.

When I came back in, Mr. Heathcliff was downstairs talking to Joseph about farm business. He gave clear, detailed instructions but spoke rapidly, constantly turning his head aside, with that same excited expression—even more intense than before. When Joseph left, Heathcliff sat in his usual place. I put coffee in front of him. He pulled it closer, rested his arms on the table, and stared at the opposite wall—or so I thought. He studied one particular spot with such glittering, restless intensity that he stopped breathing for half a minute at a time.

"Come on," I said, pushing bread toward his hand. "Eat and drink while it's hot. It's been waiting an hour."

He didn't notice me, but he smiled. I'd rather have seen him grinding his teeth.

"Mr. Heathcliff! Master!" I cried. "For God's sake, don't stare like you're seeing ghosts."

"For God's sake, don't shout," he replied. "Turn around —are we alone?"

"Of course we are."

Still, I found myself obeying, as if I wasn't quite sure. He swept his hand across the table, clearing a space among the breakfast things, and leaned forward to look more comfortably.

Then I realized he wasn't looking at the wall. When I watched him carefully, he seemed to be looking at something two yards away. Whatever it was, it gave him both exquisite pleasure and pain—at least that's what his anguished yet enraptured expression suggested. The object wasn't stationary either—his eyes followed it tirelessly, never looking away even when speaking to me.

I kept reminding him he hadn't eaten in days. If he tried to comply with my pleas, if he reached for bread, his fingers would clench before touching it and remain frozen on the table, forgetting their purpose.

I sat there patiently, trying to break through his obsessive focus, until he got irritated and stood up. "Why won't you let me eat in my own time?" he demanded. "Next time, don't wait—just leave the food and go."

With that, he left the house, walked slowly down the garden path, and disappeared through the gate.

The hours dragged by anxiously. Another evening came. I stayed up late, and when I finally went to bed, I couldn't sleep. He returned after midnight but instead of going to bed, shut himself in the room below. I listened, tossed and turned, then finally got dressed and went downstairs. It was too maddening to lie there with a hundred worried thoughts.

I could hear Heathcliff's restless pacing and frequent groans. He was muttering broken words—the only one I caught was "Catherine," mixed with wild endearments or cries of suffering, spoken as if she were right there with him, low and urgent, torn from his soul. I didn't have the courage to walk in, but I wanted to distract him, so I made noise with the kitchen fire, stirring up the coals. It brought him out sooner than expected. He opened the door immediately.

"Nelly, come here—is it morning? Bring your light."

"It's four o'clock," I answered. "You need a candle to go upstairs—you could have lit one from this fire."

"No, I don't want to go upstairs," he said. "Come in and start a fire for me. Do whatever needs doing in the room."

"I need to get the coals hot first," I said, fetching a chair and the bellows.

He paced back and forth meanwhile, almost frantic, his heavy sighs coming so fast he could barely breathe normally between them.

"When daylight comes, I'll send for Green," he said. "I need to handle some legal matters while I can still think clearly and act calmly. I haven't written my will yet, and I can't decide how to leave my property. I wish I could wipe it from the face of the earth."

"Don't talk like that, Mr. Heathcliff," I interrupted. "Wait on your will—you'll live to regret your many cruelties yet! I never expected your nerves to fail like this, but they clearly have, and it's entirely your own fault. The way you've spent these last three days would destroy a titan. Please, eat something and rest. Just look in a mirror—you'll see how desperately you need both. Your cheeks are hollow, your eyes bloodshot, like someone starving and going blind from lack of sleep."

"It's not my fault I can't eat or rest," he replied. "I assure you, it's not deliberate. I'll do both as soon as I can. But you might as well tell a drowning man to rest when he's within arm's reach of shore! I have to reach it first, then I'll rest. Well, forget Mr. Green. As for repenting my injustices—I've done no injustice and repent nothing. I'm too happy, yet not happy enough. My soul's bliss is killing my body but can't satisfy itself."

"Happy, master?" I cried. "Strange happiness! If you'd let me speak without getting angry, I might give you advice that would make you happier."

"What? Tell me."

"You know, Mr. Heathcliff, that from age thirteen you've lived a selfish, unchristian life. You probably haven't touched a Bible in all that time. You must have forgotten what's in it, and you may not have time to look now. Wouldn't it help to send for someone—any minister, denomination doesn't matter—to explain it and show you how far you've strayed from its teachings, and how unfit you'll be for heaven unless you change before you die?"

"I'm grateful rather than angry, Nelly," he said, "because you've reminded me how I want to be buried. Take me to the churchyard in the evening. You and Hareton can come if you like. And make absolutely sure the sexton follows my instructions about the two coffins! No minister needed, no words over me. I tell you, I've nearly reached MY heaven—I don't care about anyone else's."

"And if you keep up this stubborn fasting and die from it, and they refuse to bury you in consecrated ground?" I said, shocked by his godless indifference. "How would you like that?"

"They won't refuse," he replied. "If they do, you'll have to move me secretly. And if you fail, you'll learn firsthand that the dead aren't gone!"

As soon as he heard the family stirring, he retreated to his den, and I breathed easier. But that afternoon, while Joseph and Hareton were working, he came back to the kitchen with a wild look and told me to come sit in the house—he wanted company. I refused, telling him plainly that his strange talk and behavior frightened me. I had neither the nerve nor the will to be alone with him.

"You think I'm a fiend," he said with his grim laugh, "something too horrible to live under a decent roof." Then turning to Catherine, who was there and shrank behind me as he approached, he added half-mockingly, "Will YOU come, dear? I won't hurt you. No! To you I've made myself worse than the devil. Well, there is ONE who won't shrink from my company! By God, she's relentless. Oh, damn it! It's unbearably too much for flesh and blood—even mine."

He didn't seek anyone's company after that. At dusk, he went to his room. All night and into the morning, we heard him groaning and muttering to himself. Hareton wanted to go in, but I told him to fetch Mr. Kenneth instead. When the doctor arrived and I tried to open the door, it was locked.

Heathcliff told us to go to hell—he was better and wanted to be left alone. So the doctor left.

The next evening was very wet—it poured until dawn. During my morning walk around the house, I noticed the master's window wide open, rain driving straight in. *He can't be in bed,* I thought. *Those sheets would be soaked. He must be up or out. But I'll stop tiptoeing around—I'll go look.*

I got in with another key and ran to push open the panels—the room was empty. But when I looked closer, Mr. Heathcliff was there, lying on his back. His eyes met mine so fierce and keen that I jumped. Then he seemed to smile. I couldn't believe he was dead, but his face and throat were washed with rain, the bedclothes dripping, and he was perfectly still. The window, banging back and forth, had scraped one hand resting on the sill. No blood came from the broken skin, and when I touched it, I knew for certain—he was dead and cold.

I fastened the window, combed his long black hair from his forehead, tried to close his eyes—to extinguish that terrible, lifelike look of triumph before anyone else saw it. They wouldn't shut; they seemed to mock my attempts. His parted lips and sharp white teeth sneered too. Overcome with cowardice again, I called for Joseph. Joseph shuffled over and made noise but absolutely refused to touch him.

"The devil's carried off his soul," he cried, "and he can have the carcass too, for all I care! Lord! What a wicked one he looks, grinning at death!" The old sinner grinned mockingly himself. I thought he might dance around the bed, but suddenly he composed himself, fell to his knees, raised his hands, and gave thanks that the rightful master and ancient bloodline were restored.

I was stunned by this awful event, my memory inevitably returning to earlier times with oppressive sadness. But poor Hareton, the most wronged of all, was the only one who truly grieved. He sat by the body all night, weeping bitterly. He held its hand and kissed that sarcastic, savage face that everyone else shrank from. He mourned with the powerful grief that springs naturally from a generous heart, even one tough as tempered steel.

Mr. Kenneth was puzzled about what killed him. I didn't mention that he hadn't eaten for four days—it might have caused trouble. Besides, I'm convinced he didn't starve himself on purpose; it was the result of his strange illness, not the cause.

We buried him exactly as he wished, scandalizing the whole neighborhood. Earnshaw and I, the sexton, and six men to carry the coffin—that was everyone who attended. The six men left after lowering it into the grave; we stayed to see it covered. Hareton, face streaming with tears, dug up green sods and laid them over the brown earth himself. Now it's as smooth and green as the graves beside it—and I hope its occupant sleeps as soundly. But the country people, if you ask them, would swear on the Bible that he WALKS. Some claim to have met him near the church, on the moor, even in this house. Idle tales, you'll say, and so say I. Yet that old man by the kitchen fire insists he's seen two figures looking out of his bedroom window every rainy night since his death. And something odd happened to me about a month ago.

I was going to the Grange one evening—a dark evening, threatening thunder—and just at the turn of the Heights, I met a little boy with a sheep and two lambs. He was crying terribly, and I assumed the lambs were being difficult.

"What's wrong, little one?" I asked.

"There's Heathcliff and a woman over there, under the cliff," he sobbed, "and I can't get past them."

I saw nothing, but neither the sheep nor the boy would continue, so I told him to take the lower road. He probably imagined phantoms from thinking about the nonsense he'd heard from his parents and friends while crossing the moors alone. Still, I don't like being out in the dark now, and I don't like being left alone in this grim house. I can't help it—I'll be glad when they leave and move to the Grange.

"They're going to the Grange, then?" I asked.

"Yes," answered Mrs. Dean, "as soon as they're married, on New Year's Day."

"And who will live here then?"

"Joseph will take care of the house, maybe with a boy to keep him company. They'll live in the kitchen, and the rest will be shut up."

"For any ghosts who want to live there?" I observed.

"No, Mr. Lockwood," said Nelly, shaking her head. "I believe the dead are at peace, but it's not right to speak of them lightly."

Just then the garden gate swung closed—the walkers were returning.

"THEY fear nothing," I muttered, watching them approach through the window. "Together, they'd face Satan and all his legions."

As they stepped onto the doorstep and paused to look at the moon—or more accurately, at each other in its light—I felt compelled to escape again. Pressing payment into Mrs. Dean's hand and ignoring her protests about my rudeness, I vanished through the kitchen as they opened the front door. I would have confirmed Joseph's opinion about his fellow servant's improper behavior if he hadn't fortunately recognized me as respectable by the sweet ring of gold at his feet.

My walk home was extended by a detour toward the church. Even in seven months, I could see decay had progressed—many windows showed black gaps without glass, and slates hung crooked from the roof, ready to be torn off by autumn storms.

I found the three headstones on the slope next to the moor: the middle one gray and half-buried in heath; Edgar Linton's harmonized with turf and moss creeping up its base; Heathcliff's still bare.

I lingered there under that gentle sky, watched moths flutter among the heath and harebells, listened to the soft wind breathing through the grass, and wondered how anyone could imagine unquiet sleep for those resting in that quiet earth.

THANK YOU!

You made it through! Congratulations on surviving Heathcliff, the moors, and approximately seventeen terrible decisions by every character involved.

But seriously, thank you for taking a chance on this edition. I know "modernized classic" can sound suspicious, and trusting a translator with a book this iconic is a big ask. The fact that you gave it a shot means everything.

If you're sitting there thinking "what the hell did I just read" or "I can't believe Catherine did that" or "Heathcliff is absolutely unhinged"...good. That's exactly the right response to *Wuthering Heights.*

And if you want to share any of those feelings with other readers (or let them know whether this edition actually worked for you), I'd be so grateful. Reviews on Amazon, Goodreads, or wherever you talk about books help people like you find out this approach exists. They also help me keep making more of these so readers can experience the classics without the language getting in the way.

Even "this book was bananas and I have feelings" counts as a review.

Thanks so much for reading.

ABOUT THE TRANSLATOR

Avery Frost holds an MA in English and graduate certificate in Professional Editing (focused on textual theory and scholarly editing) from a Big Ten university, plus a BA in European History (where they spent entirely too much time arguing that old books shouldn't feel like homework).

After watching countless readers abandon classics halfway through, they decided these stories deserve to be enjoyed, not endured. When not translating dead authors for the living, they're probably explaining to horrified academics why 'readable' isn't a dirty word. Making sure you won't abandon Wuthering Heights on page 47 is their first crime against literature, with many more planned.

You can connect with Avery on Instagram or subscribe to their Substack for updates and announcements about upcoming editions.

instagram.com/averyfrostbooks

averyfrostbooks.substack.com

ABOUT EMILY BRONTË

Emily Brontë (1818–1848) lived most of her life in the parsonage at Haworth, a remote village on the Yorkshire moors. She was intensely private, rarely leaving home, and preferred the company of her siblings and her dogs to society.

She published *Wuthering Heights* in 1847 under the pen name Ellis Bell, a necessary disguise in an era that didn't take women writers seriously. The novel was her only published work of fiction, and critics initially hated it. They called it too dark, too violent, too strange.

They missed the point entirely.

Emily died of tuberculosis at thirty, just a year after *Wuthering Heights* was published. She never knew her book would become one of the most influential novels in English literature, or that readers 175 years later would still be captivated by the dark, unflinching story she had the courage to tell.

THE READABLE CLASSICS SERIES

More books are on the way...

Made in United States
North Haven, CT
06 February 2026

88250713R00232